A KINGDOM DISCOVERED

THE VAZULA CHRONICLES BOOK TWO

DEBOROH GRACE WHITE

LUMINANT PUBLICATIONS

A KINGDOM DISCOVERED

By Deborah Grace White

For my brother James,
who discovers new worlds no one else has found,
and sees things no one else can see.

KYONA
GREAT RIVER
LOCH ARINE
VALORIA
BASAL HEADLANDS
WYVERN ISLANDS
VAZUCA
BRYFORD
BERKLEY MANOR
TRIPLE KINGDOMS
KELP FARMS
TILSSTED
SKULSSTED
HEMSSTED
CENTER OF CULTURE
OYSTER FARMS
E
S

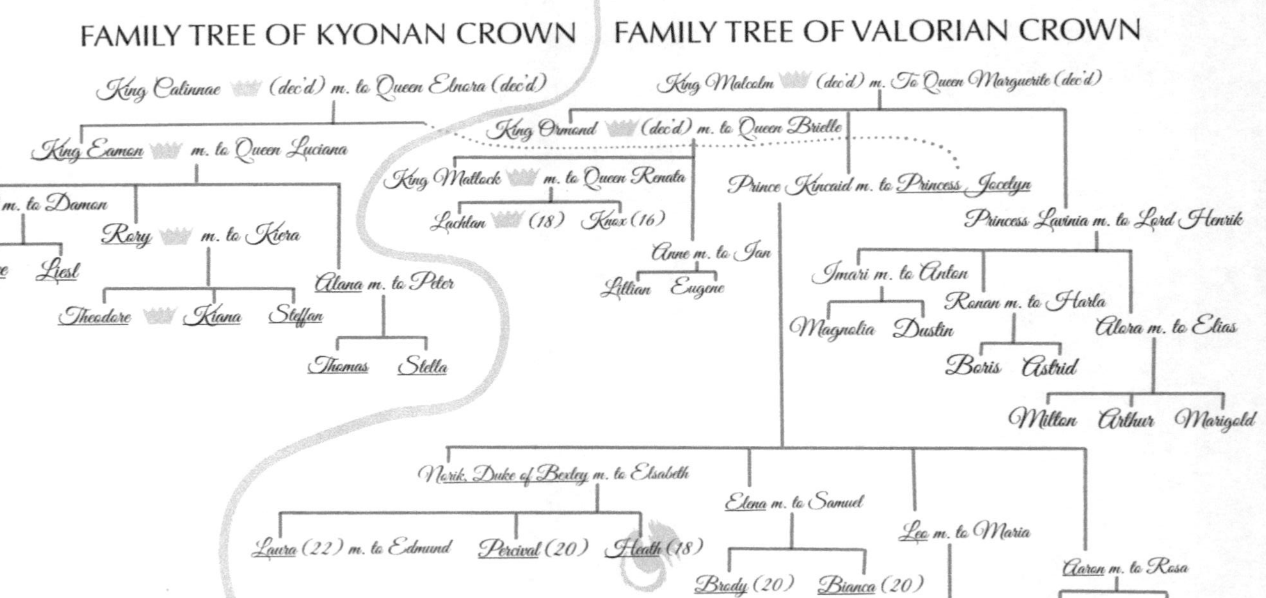

FAMILY TREE OF KYONAN CROWN   FAMILY TREE OF VALORIAN CROWN
King Calinnae (dec'd) m. to Queen Elnora (dec'd)
King Malcolm (dec'd) m. To Queen Marguerite (dec'd)
King Eamon m. to Queen Luciana
King Ormond (dec'd) m. to Queen Brielle
King Matlock m. to Queen Renata
Prince Kincaid m. to Princess Jocelyn
Violet m. to Damon
Rory m. to Kiera
Lachlan (18)   Knox (16)
Princess Lavinia m. to Lord Henrik
Renee   Liesl
Anne m. to Ian
Lillian   Eugene
Imari m. to Anton
Magnolia   Dustin
Ronan m. to Harla
Atora m. to Elias
Theodore   Kiana   Steffan
Alana m. to Peter
Boris   Astrid
Thomas   Stella
Milton   Arthur   Marigold
Norik, Duke of Bexley m. to Elsabeth
Elena m. to Samuel
Leo m. to Maria
Laura (22) m. to Edmund   Percival (20)   Heath (18)
Brody (20)   Bianca (20)
Aaron m. to Rosa
Max (16)   Alex (14)
Jasmine (18)   Leonora (16)   Lucas (15)
= in the direct line of succession
Underline = born to power-wielding line
(Brackets) = age at start of A Kingdom Submerged

CHAPTER ONE

Thwack.

Heath could feel rather than hear the dull thud of the arrow sinking into the branch, his eyes confirming he had hit his mark a moment before his arm felt the sudden tug on the rope wrapped around it.

"Whoa!" His companion's laughter was barely audible over the roar of the water. "That's a big one!"

Heath couldn't even hear the clatter of his bow landing at his feet on the wooden bridge, as he dropped it in order to grip the rope with both hands. He grunted in reply to the other young man's words as he strained against the furious tug on the line.

"Seriously, Lord Heath," his companion tried again, struggling with his own rope. "I think it's too big."

"Feel free to concede if you want," Heath shouted. He continued to haul on the rope, attempting to pull the enormous branch up out of the torrent and onto the bridge.

The other man made no more protest, turning his attention to his own branch. When Heath spared him a glance, he saw that his rival had almost managed to get his trophy clear of the water. The branch, much smaller than Heath's chosen target, had been hauled back from its passage under the bridge, and was pulled upright by the rope which stretched from an arrow buried into it, all the way up to the young man standing on the bridge.

Heath's own branch was out of sight by now, pulled under the bridge by the relentless current, toward the roaring waterfall on the other side. Heath kept his back to the waterfall, all his focus on tugging the rope hand over hand as he attempted to pull the branch against the current. It crawled inch by inch back up the river to his side of the bridge.

All at once, his companion stumbled backward with a cry, falling hard against the wooden railing of the bridge, his unanchored rope in his hand. Heath gave a grim smile. As with his own previous two attempts, the other man's arrow had come loose from the branch, unable to withstand the intensity of the pull created by the battering water. It was the reason Heath had chosen such a large branch this time. His arrow was buried so deeply in the wood, it would be difficult to dislodge.

He made a guttural sound deep in his throat as he hauled on the rope, his hands burning from the tension. He felt the branch inch back against the current, and he braced his legs on the bottom rung of the bridge's railing, ignoring the burn in his still-healing leg as he did so.

The other man made no immediate attempt to find a new branch to shoot an arrow into. He sat for a moment on the bridge, looking a little winded from his sudden fall. If he was honest, Heath thought his opponent had done well to get his branch so close to clearing the water. He was an archer, like Heath, and an excellent one. He had been the victor in the previous year's archery tournament, when Heath—along with all the other power-wielders—had sat out of the competition in order to appease the crown.

Of course, no one had been appeased when Heath was accidentally witnessed achieving the tournament's final impossible feat. On the contrary, he had put everyone's backs up, including the winner. Perhaps it was why the man had been so ready to accept this stupid challenge when Heath suggested it.

But like many archers, both of them were wiry rather than bulky, and being able to accurately shoot an arrow into a branch was different entirely from being able to haul that branch bodily out of a raging river. Percival would be able to do it in a heartbeat, of course, but Heath had made a point of not telling his brother what he was up to.

He pushed Percival from his thoughts, keeping his eyes and his focus firmly on the rope in his hands. Distraction seemed to be the only way to force everything else to the edge of his mind, at least temporarily.

"HEATH! WHAT IN THE BLAZES ARE YOU DOING?"

His brother's raised voice sounded faintly above the roar of the falls. A moment later his familiar form appeared in Heath's peripheral vision, as if summoned by his thoughts.

Heath's focus slipped for a moment, his eyes flicking to Percival. His brother looked equal parts bemused and angry. Heath ignored the question, turning back to his branch, its tip just starting to emerge from under the bridge.

But Heath's attention had been pulled from his simple physical task, and it was hard to recapture the detachment. A splash of water from the raging river hit his face, and he seized up. His limbs locked in place as his mind was tugged ruthlessly back to the feeling of driving rain against his skin as someone dragged him desperately up a beach, his senses alight with pain. He stared in panic into the plunging, churning water below the bridge, sure for a moment that he could see a shimmering purple tail amidst the spray.

A face swam before his eyes, warm brown skin, bright, inquisitive brown eyes, tangled dark hair. She wasn't in the water, but above the surface, the green fronds of a palm tree waving lazily behind her against a clear blue sky. Her expression was determined, almost triumphant, no trace of the defeat and pain that had marred her features as she lay dying.

Heath gasped at this crystal-clear image of Merletta's face, his arms losing all strength to keep pulling. The branch, released from its reluctant upward progress, sprang free of his control and surrendered gladly to the insistent pull of the current.

Heath's limbs were still locked in place, and his hands seemed frozen in their grip on the rope. Instead of letting go, he was tugged suddenly and violently forward. He was aware of two startled shouts, but his mind was too blank to register his own danger until he felt an iron grip close around both of his legs. He cried out involuntarily as pain lanced through his injured leg, but the sensation was enough to bring him out of his stupor. He realized all at once that he was dangling over the edge, his torso already past the railing, and his brother's speed in grabbing his legs the only thing keeping him from pitching all the way over into the furiously writhing river below.

Control returned, and he let go of the rope, falling back on top of Percival with a thump that shook the whole bridge. He scrambled upright, his heart racing at the realization of how close he had come to death. He was facing the other way now, with an excellent view of the place, a very short distance downstream, where the river plunged over the edge of the massive waterfall. If he had fallen in, there was no way he could have avoided being swept down the falls, and no way he would have survived that experience.

"Sorry," he gasped, as Percival pushed himself to his feet. "And, you know, thanks."

"What is wrong with you?" Percival roared, not in the least softened by the apology. "Are you *trying* to get yourself killed?"

"Calm down," Heath muttered, although he knew his brother wouldn't be able to hear. He turned to his original companion. "I guess it's a draw," he shouted, shrugging.

The man didn't respond, his face pale as he leaned on the railing for support. With a sudden flash of certainty, Heath realized that the other archer was wondering what would have become of him if a noble—one from a power-wielding family, and one against whom he arguably had a grudge—had plunged over the edge of the falls to his death while in his sole company. Heath felt a twinge of guilt at the reminder of how little he had thought about the impact on others of his own foolish behavior. He pushed the thought aside. He didn't want to be responsible for anyone else.

"Come on," he shouted to Percival.

His brother was still glaring at him, but he made no protest as Heath strode toward the end of the bridge, his attempt at casual unconcern somewhat marred by his limp. The other two followed him, no one attempting further speech until they had their feet on solid ground again. Heath saw that Percival had tied his own horse next to the two he and his companion had left grazing. Ahead, he could see the city of Bryford rising up, all gray stone and waving pennants. Heath felt no enthusiasm about returning to the capital, and his new responsibilities.

A sudden gust of wind caught at Heath's clothes as he mounted his horse, the movement awkward due to his injuries. He looked up, and a brief rush of excitement coursed through him before he remembered. The feeling subsided instantly, replaced by the dull ache that always sat uncomfortably in his chest now. He was annoyed with himself for the reaction, however involuntary it had been. The trouble was that no matter how angry he still felt with the dragon, after nineteen years of friendship, he couldn't just erase the sense of beckoning adventure he always felt at Reka's approach.

Not that Reka was here now, of course. The sudden breeze was just that, and not the unnatural wind that had so often heralded the dragon's arrival.

No, he hadn't seen Reka in more than three weeks, and he didn't want to. His last memory of the dragon was of being carried in his talons, zooming at an impossible speed over storm-tossed waves, the dragon ignoring his pleas to turn around, to help the mermaid whose life was slowly draining from her on the beach of an abandoned, forgotten island...

Heath dragged his thoughts away from the image of Merletta's unmoving form with an effort. It was much less painful to focus on his anger toward Reka. He stared moodily ahead as he urged his horse forward. Over the last few weeks, he had raged aloud at Reka many times—trusting in the dragon's farsight to allow him to witness the tirades from afar—but he was done with such foolish outbursts.

The past was done. There was nothing more to say.

It seemed his friend felt the same way. Reka must know from the use of his farsight that Heath had mostly recovered from his wounds, but the dragon had shown no sign of reappearing, had made no attempt to communicate with Heath.

So much the better, Heath thought petulantly, glancing back at the dancing spray of the waterfall. He had no desire to talk to Reka.

But his friend's absence gnawed at him, as corrosive as his guilt over Merletta's fate. Much as he didn't want to admit it, it felt wrong to be at odds with Reka.

He winced as he shifted in the saddle, a dull pain radiating from his side as well as his leg. Hopefully he hadn't reopened either spear wound, or the castle physician would have his hide. The gashes from the coral had all but disappeared, but the injuries caused by the merguards' weapons would take much longer to completely heal. He wasn't really supposed to be going for unsanctioned rides—which was almost certainly why Percival had come after him—let alone attempting pointless and foolhardy feats of strength. He shuddered to think what either his father or the physician would say if they heard about the stunt.

But there wasn't too much risk of that. Heath doubted the other archer would want to advertise the incident. And as much as Perce might rage at him, he wouldn't rat him out. He never had before. And he would be an absolute toad to start now, considering all the countless times Heath had covered for him.

"Have you gone mad, Heath?"

Percival's voice snapped Heath from his thoughts, alerting him to the fact that his brother had pulled his horse alongside Heath's. The other man trailed behind, still looking shaken, and showing no inclination to eavesdrop on their conversation.

"Relax," said Heath mulishly. "It was just a friendly competition. We were shooting arrows with ropes attached into branches. The first one to haul one up onto the bridge wins."

"What's the point of that?" Percival stormed.

Heath shrugged. "Does there need to be a point?"

Percival glared at him from under lowered brows. "If we were talking about me, then no. I don't need you to tell me I've done stupider things for the sake of competition. But this is you, Heath. You're smarter than this."

Heath just shrugged again. "Apparently not."

"Heath." Percival's voice had changed, and Heath met his brother's eyes in spite of himself. "Do you realize that you almost just died?"

"You distracted me."

"I distra—" Percival's eyes bulged, and for a moment he seemed incapable of speech. "Are you really trying to blame me for—"

"No, of course not," Heath cut in quickly. "I'm sorry, I

shouldn't have said that. It's my own fault. I just...I know I was being dumb, all right? Can we just forget about it?"

Percival was silent for a long moment, his gaze uncomfortably searching. Heath kept his eyes ahead, wishing the path wasn't wide enough for them to ride side by side.

"Heath, you've got to tell me what happened."

"I can't," said Heath, his voice strangled. "I told you...I promised someone. I can't explain."

"Well, if not me, then someone," Percival argued. "Honestly, I still can't believe you managed to get away without properly answering Father's questions. I think his heart almost failed when that dragon of yours carried you into the courtyard of the manor, bleeding everywhere, and looking more than half dead. And," he added reflectively, "I think Mother's heart actually did fail."

Heath sighed, trying to ignore the guilt that gnawed at him over his parents' ongoing concern. "Father may be able to magically detect deception, but even he can't force me to speak."

"Well, I almost wish he could," Percival said frankly. "Whatever it is, it's eating you up inside. You're not yourself, and I'm worried." He reached out an elbow to nudge Heath, attempting a light-hearted tone. "I mean, if I'm the one telling you to be more careful, something must be seriously wrong."

Heath gave a half-hearted smile, and Percival's expression became serious again.

"You're still not fully recovered. You'll make Father regret letting you come to Bryford so soon. You're supposed to be exerting your influence to keep all the power-wielders in line, not risking your life on stupid pranks."

Heath snorted. "As if I have any influence with any of you." He gave his brother a look. "I think you know I wasn't bursting with eagerness to take on an official role as the king's liaison with the power-wielders. I just wanted to get away from Mother and Father's fussing." He dropped his voice to a mutter. "If I'd known the whole blasted family would follow me here like a bunch of flapping hens, I wouldn't have bothered."

"I heard that," said Percival dryly. "And I don't appreciate being called a flapping hen."

A smile broke through Heath's moodiness in spite of himself. It was certainly not an image he would normally associate with the great Lord Percival, heir of the influential Duke of Bexley, skilled fighter, gifted with power in the form of the strength of five men.

But the flash of mirth was immediately drowned by guilt. What right did he have to be laughing with Percival, when Merletta was lying dead on Vazula, killed because of him?

The two brothers rode in silence, and within minutes, the walls of Bryford rose up before them. Heath was in considerable pain now, the time in the saddle doing nothing to help his re-agitated wounds. And he was weary, with a weariness that went beyond the physical, an exhaustion of the mind that no amount of sleep seemed to lessen. The half-buried, more sensible part of him regretted his idiotic prank. But at the same time, he knew that the next time he found his own thoughts unbearable, he would be tempted to do something just as stupid in an attempt to drive them away.

They rode through the gates, Percival nodding to the guards on duty. Heath shot them a dark look, sure that they had been the ones to tell his brother where to find him. Although he supposed he should be grateful to them, given Percival's timely intervention.

The horses' hooves clattered over the cobblestones, and the hot afternoon sun beat down on Heath's back. The mood of the city was increasingly festive as they moved toward the castle, and the wealthy district surrounding it. The Summer Solstice Festival had happened a couple of weeks before—Heath had been bedridden with his injuries, and not at all sorry to miss it. But there were always lots of noble families in the capital over summer, and there were plenty of galas and parties still happening.

One of the worst parts of his new position was that he seemed to be expected to attend every social event put on by any member of King Matlock's court. Being forced to take part in endless celebrations while struggling inwardly with guilt and despair was a kind of torture Heath had never endured before.

He glanced up out of habit as the castle loomed into view, his eyes drawn to the stone basin jutting out above the main entrance. The Flame of Friendship was a symbol of the peace between the human kingdom of Valoria, and the dragon colony located on Wyvern Islands, off the eastern coast. As always, flickering orange flame was visible inside the basin. But the tinge of purple to the fire made him narrow his eyes. Those were Reka's flames.

He sighed, lowering his eyes to the castle itself. When he was recovered enough to remember the position he had accepted right before Reka whisked him away to Vazula on that terrible day, he had been surprised—and not altogether pleased—to discover that the king's offer was still open. He'd thought that his hasty disappearance with the dragon would probably disqualify him from holding any official position. He had almost hoped the king would adopt Heath's own view, that at nineteen he was too young for a formal court role.

But whether because the magical beasts were so revered, or because his friendship with Rekavidur was so well known, he had not even been chastised for leaving with the young dragon. And it seemed that King Matlock fully expected him to assume the position he had accepted, as soon as he was completely recovered.

"Lord Heath! There you are."

Heath had just dismounted in the castle's courtyard when the greeting drew his attention.

"Your Highness," he said quickly, when he saw the crown prince descending the castle's steps. "Am I needed? My apologies."

"Oh, sure, you apologize to *him* for almost killing yourself, but not to your own brother," muttered Percival.

Heath elbowed him in the side as surreptitiously as possible. He recognized the humor in his brother's voice, but someone else might not. And it wasn't a good time for anyone to think Percival was complaining about deference being shown to the royal family. Heath might be feeling reckless lately, but that didn't mean he wanted to see his brother get himself into trouble.

"No need to apologize," said Prince Lachlan lightly. "You couldn't have known you'd be missed. But as it happens, we've just received a messenger from Kyona."

"Oh?" Heath asked vaguely, surprised by the mention of the neighboring kingdom. He couldn't imagine why anyone would want his opinion on such a matter.

"The messenger came with an invitation from King Eamon."

"An invitation for King Matlock?" Heath asked, still confused as to why he would be needed to help prepare a royal delegation for a visit to Kyona.

"No," said Prince Lachlan, watching him closely. "For you."

CHAPTER TWO

Merletta balled her fists in determination, her eyes on her target. She took a step toward the crumbling structure, pleased that her legs weren't shaking nearly as strongly this time.

Her legs!

She still couldn't get used to the idea of it, let alone the reality. It had been weeks, and she was still expecting to wake at any moment from this bizarre and exhilarating dream.

She took another step and another, a smile growing as she didn't even wobble. She passed the structure, wincing slightly as she stepped from the soft sand to the sharp rocks. Heath's boots dangled over one arm, ready in case her feet became too sore. She was determined to make it all the way to the lagoon this time. But she would prefer not to use the boots if she could help it. They didn't fit right, and as long as her feet could handle the surface, she walked more steadily without the coverings.

At first she had been concerned, after finding the boots on the beach, that they didn't sit well on her new feet. She was worried that her feet were stunted, too small for the legs which now sprouted impossibly from her body. But on reflection, she figured it was probably like how fins varied in size from mermaid to mermaid. She would just have to trust that her feet were proportionate to the rest of her.

She had feet!

She kept being pulled up by the thought, hardly able to process it even after all this time. She made it over the rocks, letting out a breath of relief as her feet found the relatively soft surface that marked the start of the jungle. She glanced down at her legs, admiring the smooth brown of her skin for the hundredth time. She wobbled slightly as a result of her loss of focus, and as always, had to fight the urge to use her fins to restore her balance. It was the strangest feeling, and she couldn't decide what was more unnerving...the fact that half of her body was missing, or the fact that she had an entire new portion of body to use.

Or the fact that on one level, it all felt impossibly natural. Like she was supposed to be this way.

She shook off the thought. Wrestling with the implications of her new legs was too overwhelming. She wanted to master the mechanics of it first.

And there was no doubt she was making progress. She moved much more slowly than she'd seen Heath walk, but she made it to the lagoon without falling once. She smiled as she dipped one foot into the water, almost overbalancing as she tried to stay upright on the other. She was hot now, and tired, and she had achieved her goal. Allowing herself to relax, she pushed off the rocks with shaky feet, landing in the water of the lagoon with a not-very-graceful splash.

The moment she was fully submerged, she felt the change happen. Without looking to check, she flicked her tail, propelling herself toward the center of the lagoon. She pulled in a mouthful of water, her muscles relaxing as the hot, parched feeling at the back of her throat disappeared. She wondered if humans ever felt that way, or if it was just a feature of being a mermaid out of water.

She remembered Heath commenting sometimes that it was hot. A stab of bittersweet emotion passed through her at the thought of her only human acquaintance. It had been almost four weeks since that stormy day, but the horror of watching the life fade from his eyes as she dragged him out of the water was still fresh. The rain had long since washed it away, but sometimes, alone on her island under a setting sun, she thought she could still see his blood staining the sand.

She felt a surge of anger at Ileana's malice, the fiery emotion sitting more comfortably in her roiling stomach. It made her feel less helpless, although she knew it wasn't logical. There was nothing she could do to make Ileana pay for attacking Heath, or for spurring the other guards on to do the same.

A spear to the side. A spear to the leg.

Merletta let herself float upward, her throat opening to allow her to breathe air as she lay on her back on the surface of the water.

Were such injuries survivable for a human? She had no idea. She was fairly certain he'd been alive when Reka had lifted him from the beach, but had that still been true by the time he'd reached his own kingdom?

No, a despairing voice whispered inside her head. *Because if he was alive, he'd be here.*

Maybe not, she argued with herself. It was equally possible that he had survived, but had recognized that returning to her was too dangerous, given the merpeople's evident hostility.

She sighed, swimming back toward the edge of the lagoon with sure strokes. She would just have to choose to believe that was the case. As much as it ached, she would much rather believe he had decided not to continue their friendship under such circumstances than that he had died from his wounds.

Whatever the case, there was nothing to be gained from giving in to her despair or her guilt. The dragon had certainly seemed to think it was worth carrying Heath away with all speed. Surely that meant he had hope for Heath's recovery.

All right, she told herself. *That's enough of a break.* Instructor Agner might not be here to train her in this new skill, but that didn't mean she couldn't push herself hard. She placed her hands on the rocks, pulling herself up until her tail was only half in the water. She took a deep breath before continuing, still nervous despite having done this so many times now. The memory of the prickling heat of the first time she'd dried out, and the terror that had accompanied what she had thought was her death, created an almost physical resistance to getting out of the water. She no longer had to fight the instinct with everything in her, but it still made her pause.

She pushed her hesitation aside, pulling herself up and twisting her tail around in a motion that had become practiced. At once, a prickling heat passed over her body, no longer anywhere near as painful as it had been that first time. At most, she would have called it a discomfort.

Instantly, her tail split into two, smooth skin appearing in place of purple scales. Her fins disappeared altogether, as did the scales on the lower half of her legs. But the top half of her legs remained covered, as always. Like a sea snake shedding its skin, the scales forming the upper half of her tail remained intact, sitting around her hips. They were no longer attached to her body—she could pull them loose if she so desired. But if she left them in place, they formed a short covering of sorts.

It was nothing like any covering she'd ever seen Heath wear, but she liked it. The purple-green sheen of it was comfortingly familiar, like her tail wasn't missing, just hidden inside her human form.

She stooped, almost falling onto the rocks as she picked up

Heath's discarded boots. For a moment she just stared at them, another rush of emotion sweeping over her. She was both glad and regretful that he'd left them behind. It was foolish, of course —boots were hardly a sentimental item. But the painful memories they evoked were worth having a physical reminder of him. It made him feel more real, like surely he must be alive somewhere.

She wished for the hundredth time that he was there. She had so many new questions to ask, since the dramatic change in her...circumstances. She began the slow and measured walk back to the beach, breathing a sigh of relief when her spear came back into view, buried point down in the sand. It made her feel vulnerable to be without her weapon, but she wasn't yet coordinated enough to carry it while upright.

She sat next to it on the sand, looping her arms around her knees in the way she'd seen Heath do many times. The water lapped at her feet, like a familiar friend. The waves weren't venturing far enough up the shore to trigger the change from legs to tail. With weeks of experimenting, she was pretty familiar with the limits now.

Her stomach gave a rumble, and she turned her eyes to the ocean. She'd need to submerge herself soon, to find some food. She'd barely eaten all day. She thought wistfully of the times Heath had brought her food from his world to try. Her eyes glazed over as she lost herself in memory. She had accepted the fact that she would probably never see Heath again, but it was hard to just move forward and put him from her mind without knowing whether he had survived. The uncertainty ate at her, no matter how she tried not to dwell on it.

Her vision was suddenly filled with the silent pleading in his blue eyes when he'd told her to leave him, to stop risking her own life in her attempt to save him.

I don't want you to die, he'd said. How desperately she wished she could tell him that she hadn't died. Quite the reverse.

Her cheek tingled, and she raised a hand to touch the place where his fingers had rested. Sometimes she could swear she still felt the pressure of his hand.

She knew she was being foolishly sentimental, but she couldn't help it. For someone who'd been orphaned as an infant, and raised in the harsh environment of a charity home, such a gentle gesture was unprecedented. Given her upbringing, and the year she'd spent fighting for a place in the Center of Culture surrounded mainly by merpeople who didn't want her there, was it any wonder that the warmth in Heath's eyes as they rested on her had been intoxicating from the beginning?

And a hundred times more potent had been the moment when he'd come out of his deathlike stupor to brush her hair from her face and lay his hand on her cheek. The memory was almost too overwhelming to handle. She couldn't remember ever experiencing that kind of gentle touch before.

He was the first—and probably only—one to ever look at her like that. And she had most likely gotten him killed.

She shook her head, trying to physically flick off these thoughts. Neither daydreaming nor wallowing in guilt would help her survive, stranded and alone. If she intended to remain alone, that was.

She wiggled her toes deeper into the sand as her gaze drifted southwest, toward the underwater world of the triple kingdoms. Her tangled thoughts took on an edge of panic as she saw the sun beginning to set on another day. She was running out of time, and she still couldn't decide what to do.

No matter how good she was getting with her new legs, it was hard to imagine actually staying here on the island alone forever. But the thought of returning to the world of her own people was terrifying. Could she even return? Or would she be killed on sight?

It was the question she'd been asking herself for almost four weeks. At first, she hadn't even considered returning. On the contrary, she'd spent the first few days after her initial transformation hiding in the jungle, sure that someone would appear from the triple kingdoms to finish her off. After all, she'd been aware that someone from the Center wanted her dead, even before Ileana abandoned her to die on Vazula's beach.

But at that thought, her forehead creased in a frown. *Did Ileana abandon her to die?* Merletta had been sure when she locked eyes with Ileana, as she began to dry out, that her rival was satisfied that Merletta was about to die. But she hadn't died. Did that mean she'd misunderstood Ileana's expression? The older mermaid had made it to the end of her third year in the Center of Culture's four year training program before failing and dropping out to join the guards. Merletta knew for a fact that Ileana was privy to information which she, as a recent graduate of first year, didn't know. Not that Merletta could be blamed for her ignorance. She'd learned the hard way that the instructors not only withheld things from younger trainees, but actively taught them false information.

But how much did Ileana know? She had known that humans were real, no doubt about it. But she hadn't seemed to know about the location of Vazula, so close to the triple kingdoms, which were supposedly built far from any land.

Did she know the truth about drying out?

It was such a world-shattering discovery, that Merletta kept shying away from thinking about the implications of it. There was no way it was specific to her. That idea made no sense. The ability to change form must be universal to merpeople.

In fact, it explained the phenomenon of how her throat had always opened the moment her head broke the surface, allowing her to breathe water while below, and air while above. She'd never really questioned it before, but what would be the point of such an ability if mermaids were always mermaids, plain and simple? If they were restricted to just sticking their heads above water, they would surely have to just hold their breath while out of water, the way Heath held his while under it?

There were so many things like that, so many little details that kept coming to her, making her new reality seem almost obvious.

But it scared her to dwell on them. She'd discovered at a very young age that the carers at the charity home had no qualms about lying to the beneficiaries when it was convenient. The realization had been disillusioning at the time, but she had long since gotten over that discomfort.

Discovering that those in power at the Center also lied about basic aspects of the merpeople's existence—even to trainees— had been considerably more disconcerting.

But this final piece of the puzzle took her disillusionment to a whole new level. Her mind spun every time she tried to comprehend the width and complexity of the lie that kept most merpeople believing that drying out meant instant death, and that land was as deadly to mermaids as a stonefish's venom.

How many merpeople knew it was a lie? Did Ileana?

Did Sage?

Merletta sighed at the thought of the only other trainee she considered a friend. Sage had finished her second year, and begun her third before Merletta's first year test. What was she thinking now? What, if anything, had Ileana told the others about what happened on that horrible day?

Merletta's heart raced as she played with the idea of returning to the triple kingdoms. In one way, it was a simple thing. She knew the way like she knew her own fins. She could swim there in less than an hour. But in another way, it was the most terrifying choice she'd ever been faced with.

And if it was a mistake, it would almost certainly be the last she ever made.

But far from the first. She scowled to herself as she thought of her idiotic decision to lead the merguards to Vazula. If only she'd known Heath would be there.

She forced the thought down, focusing her mind back on the problem at hand. It was time to stop putting it off, and decide what in the ocean she was going to do. It would help if she had any idea what to make of the fact that no one had come looking for her. It might mean that everyone relevant thought she was dead. Or it might mean that no one was even aware of what happened. It wouldn't be the first time that Ileana had kept an incriminating discovery about Merletta to herself, for inscrutable reasons.

When she had left the triple kingdoms, it had been the day after her successful test. Trainees who passed were always afforded a month of holiday after their tests, before commencing the next year's study.

Merletta's seventeenth birthday was only two days away, which meant that her month was almost up. And if, for a moment, she optimistically assumed that she wouldn't be killed on arrival at the Center, there were still lots of people looking for her to fail. If she wanted to have any chance of continuing her studies, she needed to present herself on time to commence second year.

She looked around her at the beautiful paradise of Vazula. She had once wanted nothing more than to be free to explore its secrets. She had felt chafed at being restricted to the water. But now that she was up here, on the land, she realized her mistake.

It shouldn't be a surprise. Going from the slums of Tilssted to the opulence of the Center hadn't freed her from the necessity of proving that she deserved a chance. In the same way, switching from water to land hadn't freed her from the sense of being trapped, being held back. If she was afraid to return to the water, she was no better off than she'd been in the triple kingdoms. Worse, in fact, since her island sanctuary was smaller and more isolated than the underwater cities.

She gripped her spear as she stared into the sunset. Her mind was made up. She had never allowed herself to make decisions out of fear, and she wasn't going to start now.

She was going back.

CHAPTER THREE

Heath

"Not bad."

Heath grunted his assent, raising a hand to hide a yawn. He hadn't slept well the night before, plagued with his usual dreams about Merletta and the abandoned island kingdom.

But weariness aside, he had to agree with Percival's assessment. Kynton, Kyona's capital city, was an impressive sight. They had passed into the neighboring kingdom by way of the main highway that ran along the coast, south of the mountain range that separated Valoria and Kyona. Consequently, they had already been in Kyona for a few days as they traveled north again on their journey to Kynton.

It was a pleasant land, not unlike Valoria, but a little less rugged. The farmland had seemed almost endless—clearly it was a fertile kingdom.

"I'll be glad to sleep in a proper bed tonight," Percival said. "That inn last night wasn't anything to speak of, was it?"

"If they have a bed for you," muttered Heath.

Percival glowered at him. "If you mention one more time

that I wasn't invited," he started menacingly. "You're in no state to go wandering over the land alone."

Heath raised his hands in a gesture of surrender, thinking it best not to remind his brother that in the midst of their twenty-person delegation, he wouldn't exactly have been alone. He knew what Percival meant. And, generally speaking, he wouldn't have minded his brother's company. But these days, he so often just wanted to be alone.

Plus, he felt genuinely uneasy about the fact that Percival had inserted himself into the delegation. Unless Heath was mistaken, King Matlock hadn't been especially eager about the idea, and he had no idea how King Eamon would respond. But no one could exactly tell Percival he wasn't allowed to go, considering the primary purpose of Heath's trip was to visit their grandparents.

No one except their parents, of course, and they seemed to think it was desirable for Heath to be shadowed like a fragile child. He scowled.

He tried to overcome his surly mood as they spurred their horses down the slight incline, toward the stone towers of Kynton. Much as he often avoided the company of others lately, he was looking forward to seeing his grandparents. And he was both flattered and intrigued by the invitation his grandmother had apparently asked King Eamon to extend. The elderly princess had been born a princess of Kyona, before her marriage to a Valorian prince. She was therefore sister to the current Kyonan king. Even at their advanced age, she and Heath's grandfather continued their annual tradition of passing the summer as guests of King Eamon in Kynton. Heath's father had joined them when he was younger, and had visited once or twice as an adult. But neither Heath nor Percival had ever traveled to Kyona before.

If he'd been invited the year before, when he wasn't such a bear, he probably would have enjoyed the visit immensely.

The walls of the city loomed up before them, and Heath looked around with interest. They passed unchecked through the open gates, a nod between the guards on duty and those riding with the delegation confirming that they were expected. The road was crowded with various Kyonans going about their business, but the throngs parted for the mounted group, decked out in Valorian livery.

The road continued on the other side of the walls, clearly the city's main thoroughfare. Heath's general impression of Kynton was one of bright colors. Late summer flowers bloomed from window boxes, and cheerful fabrics swirled as locals hastened for a look at the visiting group. Even the expressions were bright, the general demeanor of the populace suggesting contentedness. Clearly Kyona's capital was thriving.

Thriving and curious.

Heath felt self-conscious under the eager gaze of those gathering to watch the delegation ride past. A group of people near his own age pushed their way to the front, not far ahead on the road. They jostled the rest of the crowd, their eyes scanning the group with purpose, and a trickle of uneasiness crept through Heath.

"Which one is the power-wielder?" a young woman called out audibly.

Heath drew in a breath. He hadn't expected to attract so much attention given that Kyona had power-wielders of its own, but perhaps that had been foolish. Across both kingdoms, and all three generations of power-wielders, there were still fewer than thirty of them.

He found his shoulders hunching with tension under the scrutiny, not sure what to expect. The general attitude toward magic in Valoria was fraught at best. He didn't know how suspicious Kyonans were regarding their own power-wielders, let alone foreign ones.

On the thought, he cast a look of concern toward his brother—Percival had never taken criticism of their innate magical power well.

Percival's attention had also been drawn to the group. He kept his gaze fixed on them, one eyebrow raised, as he spoke in good-humored mockery.

"Your fame has gone before you, Heath. Better wave to your admirers."

To Heath's embarrassment, Percival did so himself, sending a lazy wave to the group of young onlookers as the delegation drew level with them. Their focus centered on him immediately, and an excited murmuring spread through the crowd.

Heath shot his brother a long-suffering look. At least it seemed that Percival had been right to call them admirers. He could see no trace of the fear or suspicion he had been dreading. On the contrary, the girl who had called out gave a coquettish giggle as Percival grinned at her, and several people threw flowers onto the road. The news of their arrival clearly raced through the city as only gossip could, because the rest of their route was quickly lined with onlookers.

"Power-wielders!"

"There are two of them!"

"Welcome to Kynton!"

The cries leaped out at them from the crowd as they passed, the people's excitement palpable.

Heath blinked. He looked at Percival, and their eyes locked. Clearly his brother was just as taken aback by their reception as he was.

The main street curved to the east, and it wasn't long before the castle came into view. It was not dissimilar to the castle in Bryford, built for beauty as well as practicality. Bryford's castle had pennants of many colors flapping above it, but in Kynton, the pennants were all in the royal Kyonan blue, stitched around in gold. It was an imposing sight, if Heath was honest.

And there was no stone basin suspended above the castle, filled with dragon fire. In spite of the greater history between dragons and Kyona's royal family, they had no Flame of Friendship ceremony. The dragon colony located within Kyona's mountains remained more reclusive than that on Valoria's Wyvern Islands.

When they reached the castle itself, grooms hurried forward to relieve them all of their horses. Heath descended from his mount gratefully. His injured leg was aching painfully after so long in the saddle, and he was a little embarrassed to find himself limping as he ascended the steps into the building.

The broad entranceway was light and open, full of the bustle of servants and courtiers alike. Tapestries lined the walls, an enormous one of a descending dragon dominating the space. News of their arrival had obviously been sent ahead from the city gate, because a pleasant call of greeting drew Heath's attention to the landing above them. He directed his eyes to the large stone staircase that rose from the middle of the entranceway. The landing above it branched off into two short staircases on either side, leading up to the castle's second level. On that landing stood the familiar figures of Prince Kincaid and Princess Jocelyn, Heath's grandparents.

He and Percival both hurried forward, smiling in greeting. Their grandmother offered her hand to each of them in turn, and their grandfather smiled easily from behind her.

"Welcome to Kyona," the elderly princess said brightly.

"You're a very welcome sight," agreed their grandfather. There was a slightly amused lilt to his voice as his eyes passed from Heath to Percival. "Both of you."

Percival gave a rueful sigh. "If you're going to tell me I wasn't included in the invitation, Grandfather, there's no need. Heath hasn't stopped reminding me of it since we left Bryford. But my parents were concerned about Heath traveling so far while still recovering from his injuries."

"Of course we weren't going to say anything of the kind," said their grandmother calmly. "We're delighted to see you, Percival."

Heath frowned slightly. Her tone was warm enough, and her features were clear. So what was giving him that sense of lingering concern as her eyes rested on Percival? Before he could answer this question to his own satisfaction, she turned her gaze back to him.

"And I'm not surprised your parents are concerned, Heath." Her voice was serious now. "We were most alarmed ourselves when we heard of your injuries. I hope you haven't done yourself any harm by traveling so soon. Perhaps it was foolish of me to ask Eamon to invite you."

The rest of the delegation had followed the castle's steward off somewhere unknown, and as she spoke, Heath's grandmother gestured for them to ascend to the next level of the staircase.

"I did tell you to leave the boy be," her husband interjected, as he followed her. "But you were determined to see him." He sent a glance up and down Heath's form. "Your father's letter said you would make a full recovery, but she was still convinced you were in danger. I must say, I'm relieved to see you looking so well, in spite of junketing across kingdoms."

Heath thanked him appropriately, but he saw his grandmother pursing her lips. Her eyes lingered not on Heath's injured leg, but on his face, and she clearly didn't agree that he was looking well. Heath didn't blame her. He hardly recognized his own face in the mirror lately, it was so drawn and heavy-eyed.

"Mother and Father wouldn't have let me come if the physician didn't think I was up to it," he said lightly. He considered the matter. "And neither would King Matlock."

"I was trusting in that when I asked Eamon to invite you," his grandmother smiled. "And we heard about your new position as a liaison between the king and the power-wielders. It's a sign of great trust for King Matlock to give you such a responsibility at so young an age."

"My commiserations," said Heath's grandfather, and Percival gave a snort of laughter.

"He doesn't mean that," said their grandmother quickly, throwing a stern look at her husband as a servant bustled past.

"No, of course I don't," said the elderly prince easily. He gave Heath a more serious look than he usually wore. "But I do understand very well what a mixed blessing royal status can be."

"We can talk about all that later," said their grandmother, coming to a stop. She gestured to two doors set side by side in the stone corridor. "These suites have been prepared for you. King Eamon and Queen Lucy are looking forward to receiving you, but I thought you'd like a chance to settle in first."

Heath thanked her gratefully, and was about to slip into his allotted room when the princess's hand closed over his wrist with a surprisingly firm grip. "After that," she said, her gaze piercing, "I'll look forward to a little chat."

CHAPTER FOUR

Merletta gripped her spear in one trembling hand as the kelp forest loomed into view.

"I really hope this isn't a mistake," she muttered aloud.

There was only one way to find out, of course. She gave one wistful glance back in the direction of Vazula, pausing to watch a turtle coast lazily over a patch of coral behind her. Then she set her face forward, and swam between the towers of kelp.

She kept a wary eye on her surroundings, making absolutely sure that there was no sign of another guard patrol. No one was in sight, and she knew she needed to take her opportunity. She had already been hiding in a labyrinth of rock for half an hour, waiting for a gap. She'd made this journey countless times, and never before had she seen so many patrols. It was an ominous sign.

But none appeared as she darted across the open space, and she was soon concealed between the fronds of the uncultivated kelp forest. In no time at all, she reached the start of the outlying kelp farms, the northernmost part of the triple kingdoms. She paused at this boundary, brushing a long leaf out of her path and almost dislodging a starfish in the process. This was her last chance to turn back.

But she'd made her decision, and she wasn't one to change her mind easily. Drawing in a mouthful of cool, calming water, she propelled herself forward with a flick of her tail.

Casual voices indicated the presence of farm laborers, and Merletta changed course slightly, rising higher to avoid them. Normally she didn't worry too much about being seen by the workers—she'd never had any trouble from them before—but she thought it best to be extra cautious this time.

Dodging and weaving in this way, she crossed the whole kelp farm without encountering anyone. In her usual unobtrusive fashion, she slipped out from between the towers and entered the city of Tilssted, the poorest and least developed of the triple kingdoms.

Merletta was in her home current now, and she had no difficulty finding her way through the streets where she'd grown up. She gave her old neighborhood a decent berth, of course. It wasn't as though she had any desire to go near the charity home again. She briefly considered visiting the shellsmith tower where Letitia, her only real friend from the charity home, now lived and worked. But that could be dangerous for Tish. Better to first discover for absolute certain whether she had a target on her back.

So she hurried through the city without stopping. She attracted a bit of notice—her weapon and her armband both marked her as a trainee from the Center of Culture, a position of respect. But she didn't think anyone recognized her specifically. Certainly no one spoke to her.

The difference in her surroundings was marked when she crossed the boundary and entered the city of Skulssted. It was the wealthiest of the triple kingdoms, and it showed in the buildings, the decorations, even the attire of the merpeople going about their business. The very water tasted cleaner, although that didn't endear the place to Merletta.

Her experience of Skulssted wasn't especially positive. She glanced down a small side street, a memory flashing vividly through her mind of the time she had been attacked in just such a corner of Skulssted, when making her way from Tilssted back to the Center. It had been Center guards who'd done it, and she'd never found out exactly who they were or who had sent them.

Trying not to think about how likely she was to meet her end in just such an attack that very day, Merletta put on extra speed. The main entrance to the Center was located in Skulssted, not far away. She wanted to get this—whatever it would be—over with. She'd had enough of the tension.

The stone gateway had just appeared, the words *Center of Culture* etched into the lintel, and the pearl-encrusted bars standing open, when a delighted cry came from behind her.

"Merletta!"

She turned sharply, barely taking in the impression of a group of approaching merpeople before her gaze settled on an unpleasantly familiar figure. Merletta felt her eyes widen at the sight of Ileana, but it was nothing to the reaction of the young Center guard. Ileana went rigid, her mouth falling open in a soundless exclamation. Her pale skin went almost white, and her throat worked in a way that reminded Merletta of a fish out of water. For a frozen moment they simply stared at each other, then another cry drew Merletta's attention to the one who had actually called to her.

"You're back! I was starting to worry!"

Merletta summoned a weak smile as Sage hurried toward

her through the water. An open smile was on her face, and Merletta could read nothing in her eyes but genuine pleasure at seeing her friend again. Clearly Sage hadn't known that Merletta was supposedly dead.

Merletta's eyes flicked back to Ileana. Had Ileana thought Merletta was dead? Or did she know the incredible truth about drying out?

Sage had reached her now, and Merletta returned her friend's embrace. Her arms were shaking with the conflicting feelings of relief at being reunited with someone she trusted, and fear over how those in authority would receive her.

Her gaze slid over the rest of the group, noting a few familiar faces from the training program. It took her a moment to realize that it was strange for Ileana to be with the group, given she was no longer a trainee.

"Merletta! Welcome back."

The jovial voice of Agner, the instructor responsible for combat, and other more general physical training, cut across her confusion.

"Shame you're too late to join us on our patrol."

"Patrol?" Merletta repeated blankly, swimming forward slightly to shake his offered hand. He was also looking at her without surprise or discomfort. Could it be possible that no one knew what transpired between her and Ileana? But that couldn't be. Even if Ileana hadn't wanted to tell anyone, the two of them weren't the only witnesses. A small guard patrol had been part of the incident where Heath was speared.

"Yes, the trainees have just taken part in a patrol to one of the disputed areas," Agner said, still cheerful. "Good experience to see how the guards handle these situations. Not to worry, though. As a second year, you'll have plenty of chances to train with the guards." He grinned at her. "I was delighted to hear that you elected to continue with the program, Merletta. You'd be wasted as a scribe."

Merletta's mind was still whirling in confusion—she had no idea what he meant by disputed areas, apart from everything else—but her smile was a little more genuine this time. Agner was the only instructor who actually liked her, and wanted her to succeed. Of course he would be glad that she hadn't decided to stop with the qualification as a scribe that she had earned from passing first year. If she passed second year, she would qualify as a guard. Agner knew she intended to continue past second year, and eventually become a record holder, but that didn't stop him trying to convince her, from time to time, to change course and join the guards permanently.

"Come on," said Sage, slipping her arm into Merletta's and turning for the entrance to the Center of Culture. "We were just heading back for lunch. You can join us."

"Don't I have to...I don't know...check in or something?" Merletta asked cautiously, her eyes on Ileana as she allowed Sage to pull her through the Center's receiving hall. Some of the mermaid's coloring had started to come back, but her face was still a mask of shock.

"I don't think so," said Sage, surprised. "I never have after my breaks. You're due back in classes tomorrow, aren't you? As long as you're there then, I don't think you have to do anything else." She frowned. "You did speak to Instructor Ibsen before you left, didn't you? And told him that you were going to continue with second year?"

Merletta nodded, and Sage's expression cleared. "Then you'll be expected."

Again, Merletta's eyes flicked to Ileana. They had all passed through the receiving hall now, and were floating out over the drop off that lay between the building and the Center itself. The guard patrol, Ileana along with them, had broken off from the trainees and were swimming smartly toward the reef on the other side of the drop off. Merletta couldn't help but notice that Ileana was pulling ahead of the group. Where was she going? It would be telling to see who she went to with her discovery of Merletta's survival. But Merletta wasn't game to follow her. She had no desire to risk being alone with Ileana—who had twice tried to see her killed—until she felt herself to be in calmer water.

"All right, trainees," Agner said, addressing the group at large. "You're dismissed. I'll see you tomorrow morning, as discussed." He sent Merletta a wink. "I hope you haven't been too idle over your break, Merletta. We can't have you losing your fighting edge. You've got to be quick to survive around here."

Merletta stared at him. Was she imagining a certain intentness in his eyes, an extra layer of meaning behind those words?

Sage chuckled, clearly not noticing anything unusual. "As if you're in any danger of falling so far behind in training. Now that Emil has graduated, and Ileana is with the guards, only Oliver and I outrank you in the program." Her voice turned rueful. "And I at least am no threat to you when it comes to combat. It's barely worth your while to spar with me."

"Nonsense," said Agner, startling Merletta. She hadn't realized he was still listening. "Extra sparring with Sage is an excellent idea. You won't get far on your own."

Merletta made no answer as she met Agner's eyes. He held her gaze for an unblinking moment before turning and putting on a burst of speed to catch up with the other guards.

Merletta and Sage followed more slowly. They were halfway across the drop off now, and the Center rose up from the gloom ahead of them. It was a beautiful complex, really more like a city. Its buildings shot up from the ocean floor, tall, smooth, and even. They ascended in layers, one particularly tall spire marking the central point. A thick coral reef formed a living ring around the whole place, signaling the end of the drop off that separated the Center from the rest of the triple kingdoms.

Merletta checked her pace as they drew near, and Sage matched her. The others drifted past them. Oliver made straight for the Center, without so much as a glance at Merletta, but a young merman whom she didn't recognize cast a curious look back at her as he passed.

"I'm so glad you're back," Sage said warmly, once everyone was out of earshot. "I still can't believe you disappeared off for your break without even saying goodbye. I thought you said you were planning to spend your month off in the Center. At first I thought something had happened to you, but I figured that I would have heard if that was true. I was just being alarmist."

Merletta swallowed. Sage truly had no idea. Where did she even begin?

"Did you spend the break in Tilssted after all?" Sage pressed, when Merletta didn't speak. "With the friend you've told me about?"

Merletta came to a stop, turning to face Sage. She shook her head slowly.

Sage's forehead was creased now, and she stopped as well, hovering far above the ocean floor, which was dark but visible at the bottom of the drop off.

"I *was* just being alarmist, wasn't I?" she said. "When I thought something had happened to you? I really was nervous not hearing from you for a whole month. I thought at least you'd want to talk over these new developments. Everything's been in such an uproar at the Center—it's a crazy time to have been away."

"What new developments?" Merletta said quickly. "What did Ileana tell you?"

Sage blinked in astonishment. "Ileana? What do you mean?"

"No, you go first," Merletta insisted. "What did I miss?"

"But you must know," Sage said blankly. "Everyone must have heard, even in Tilssted."

"Assume I haven't," said Merletta grimly.

Sage's gentle face set in firm lines. "No, I'm not saying anything more until you give me a straight answer, Merletta. Where were you this last month? You didn't," her features showed a hint of fear, "you didn't leave the triple kingdoms, did you?"

Merletta didn't answer, but her silence clearly spoke volumes. Sage's eyes grew rounder, and she clutched at Merletta's arm.

"Merletta, you could have been killed! What were you thinking? It's not safe out there, now more than ever."

"It's not nearly as dangerous as they claim, Sage," Merletta said. "It never has been. But what do you mean by now more than ever?"

Sage looked deeply alarmed now. Before she could answer, a movement behind them caught both of their attention. Someone was swimming across the drop off, most likely a Center employee returning from some errand to Skulssted.

"Come on," muttered Merletta, and the two mermaids began to swim toward the complex.

"Should we go to the barracks?" Sage asked, her anxiety still clear in her voice. "Everyone will be at lunch, so we'll be able to talk properly. I don't mind skipping the meal."

But Merletta shook her head. Agner's words had been rolling over in her mind. She couldn't shake the feeling that he'd been trying to give her a warning. What had he said? *You won't get far on your own.* Merletta still had no idea how it was possible, but it seemed that the other trainees didn't know what had happened a month ago, when Ileana had caught Merletta in the act of fraternizing with a human, and had led a guard patrol to attack the two of them. Someone had hushed the whole thing up, for reasons Merletta didn't yet know.

One thing was for certain though—her reappearance couldn't be helpful to whatever plan was behind the deception. It was really a stroke of incredible luck that she'd run into the group of trainees before anyone higher up got wind of her return. They couldn't make her disappear now without questions being raised. And she had a feeling that she would be smart to press that advantage. She should try to be seen by as many others as she could. And she should avoid being alone until she knew what to expect.

"I think we should go to lunch," she said decisively. "We can talk later."

"All right," said Sage, not sounding entirely happy. "But I have classes this afternoon, and we won't be able to talk in the trainee barracks tonight. Ileana might not be part of our class anymore, but Lorraine will be there."

"Oh, that's right," said Merletta absently, as the two of them swam toward the dining hall. "I forgot about Lorraine."

They entered the dining hall a minute later, and Merletta's eyes were drawn to the mermaid in question. She was sitting next to Oliver, and beside his darker skin, her pale face looked particularly white. Or perhaps it was the contrast with the brown of her hair, or the strong purple of her tail. It wasn't surprising that Merletta had forgotten about the new trainee. Lorraine had only started her first year studies a few weeks before Merletta had sat her own first year test, and they'd had little to do with each other. Merletta had gotten the impression that Lorraine had been avoiding her, although she'd been far too distracted by her upcoming test to care.

"Who's that sitting across from her?" Merletta asked Sage, as they drifted across the room.

Sage followed her gaze. "Oh, that's Andre. He only started a week ago. I'll introduce you."

Merletta nodded, slipping into a seat at the round trainees' table that stood at one end of the dining hall. In spite of the new faces, it felt strangely empty. Merletta realized with a jolt that she and Sage made the rest of the group. With Emil graduated, and both Ileana and Jacobi having failed out of the program, there were only five of them.

"Andre, this is Merletta," Sage was saying. "She's just finished her break after her first year test, and she's back for second year."

"Of course," said Andre, holding out an eager hand. "I've heard all about you, and I'm glad to finally meet you."

Merletta shook his hand, a little taken aback by his manner. His skin, almost as dark as Merletta's, looked a little flushed, and she could see his crimson tail swishing slightly in excitement. Oliver, Sage's fellow third year, had a look of disdain on his face at the enthusiastic display, but he said nothing. Lorraine, Merletta noticed, was watching the interaction with a guarded look.

"You've heard all about me?" Merletta repeated, carefully. "What do you mean?"

Andre gave a small laugh. "You're the first trainee from Tilssted in generations," he said lightly. "Surely you must realize that you're sort of...well, famous I guess."

Merletta blinked. "I am?"

He nodded wisely, shoving a handful of octopus tentacles into his mouth. "Did they mob you in Tilssted, over your break? They must be very excited to have a representative in the Center for a change."

Oliver cleared his throat, and Andre threw him a glance. He seemed to realize his exuberance was causing some irritation, because his tone dropped a little.

"Anyway, it's good to meet you."

The meal passed quickly, Merletta feeling like she was in a dream. When she left Vazula that morning, she'd considered it highly likely that she'd seen her last sunrise. The slim hope of it being possible for her to continue her studies had propelled her to take the risk of returning, but she hadn't really imagined she could just swim back in and keep going as if nothing had happened.

And why should she do that? Something *had* happened, something that changed everything. The Center might want to cover up what she'd discovered, but that didn't mean she had to help them along. She had the power to expose their secrets if she just told everyone what she'd seen.

But did she have that power? She hesitated, glancing around the bustling dining hall. What would actually happen if she rose from her seat and announced her activities to the room at large? How many of these Center employees already knew—and were helping to conceal—at least some of what she'd discovered? And even if they didn't, would they believe her? If they did believe her, she would surely be punished for her part in what happened. That might be worth it to expose the truth, but only if it would actually achieve that. She had no desire to sacrifice herself pointlessly.

She frowned as she thought it over. Playing along for now would decrease her credibility if she wanted to speak up later, but it would surely increase her chances of survival. She needed to find out what exactly Ileana had told people. And she needed to find those guards, the ones who'd seen her with Heath. Her frown turned into a scowl. The ones who'd attacked him.

"Are you all right?" Sage's soft voice brought Merletta back to her surroundings. The other trainees were finishing up, clearly ready to return to their classes.

"I'm fine," said Merletta quickly.

"I wish we could talk now," Sage said uncertainly, her eyes on Merletta's face, "but you know what Instructor Wivell is like about punctuality."

"I thought you were with Agner today," Merletta said.

"No, we train with Agner the last two days before rest day, remember?" Sage said. "We just took the morning off from Wivell's class to join that patrol."

Merletta had lost track of what day of the week it was, but she didn't say so. Sage was already looking at her with enough concern.

"Well, I'll join you," she said decisively.

"What, in class?" Sage looked dumbfounded. "But you literally just arrived back! You're not expected in class until tomorrow."

"What am I going to do all by myself?" shrugged Merletta. "Much better to get back into it."

Sage looked worried. She glanced around her. Oliver and Lorraine were gone, but Andre was hovering just out of earshot, clearly waiting hopefully for them to join him. Sage lowered her voice.

"Merletta, what aren't you telling me?"

A shot of pain lanced through Merletta at the concern in her friend's eyes. Sage deserved much more trust than Merletta had given her the year before.

"So much, Sage," she whispered, her control fleeing her for a moment. "I don't even know where to start."

A look of determination crossed Sage's features. "Forget Wivell. Let's talk now."

Merletta shook her head. "It's safer for me—" she grimaced, "—for both of us, if we're with the group. At least for now."

Sage looked more alarmed than ever, but she didn't argue, just grasped Merletta's wrist with one unyielding hand. "As long as you promise you'll tell me what's going on later."

Merletta nodded, a lump in her throat. Just the thought of telling Sage—of telling anyone—where she'd really been the previous month made her feel like a great weight had been lifted from her shoulders. But would it just put Sage in as much danger as she was in?

The question was impossible to answer without more information. The two of them hurried to the doorway, joined by a smiling Andre. Merletta noticed that his eager gaze encompassed Sage as much as her. Clearly he wanted to be part of their little group, although she couldn't imagine why.

They were trailing well behind the others by now, and they had to swim quickly to make it to Wivell's teaching room on time. As it was, he had already entered when they surged through the doorway.

The middle-aged merman checked slightly at the sight of Merletta, cocking one eyebrow. She met his eyes for a breathless moment, wondering what he would say. But after that initial reaction, he reverted to his usual unimpassioned manner.

"Merletta. You have returned. I wasn't expecting you today."

Or at all? Merletta wondered.

But if that was the case, he was concealing it well. His reaction was certainly nothing like the horror Ileana had displayed at sight of her. He wasn't exactly showing warmth, but then he never had. The detachment with which he proceeded to teach was absolutely normal for the chief instructor. The presence of a slum-dweller from Tilssted in his elite program was an inconvenience, but not one that he took personally, the way Instructor Ibsen seemed to do.

A shudder went over Merletta at the thought of the third instructor. He had always hated her, and she wouldn't have been at all surprised to discover that Ileana was taking her orders from him.

Instructor Wivell taught literacy, and Merletta allowed her

mind to wander a little as he went into detail, for the benefit of the two first year trainees, about the role of the scribes. Merletta didn't want to think about their work in copying out records day in and day out in a constant battle against the water. She would only get frustrated at the futility of the exercise, given that records above water could last for generation upon generation.

She spent the time scanning the class instead. Oliver was continuing to ignore her, as she would expect, and Lorraine was watching Instructor Wivell with the carefully uncommunicative expression that seemed to be habitual for her. But Andre's eyes kept flicking from the instructor to Sage and Merletta, and when he caught her eye, he gave her a quick smile. She returned it guardedly, still bemused by his manner toward her.

"Now, since you'll all be training with Instructor Agner for the next two days, with rest day following, you won't be with Instructor Ibsen again until next week. He has asked me to set you a practical task on his behalf, in preparation for your next class with him. It will require you to leave the Center. He wishes you to attend a marketplace in any of the three cities, and observe, without identifying yourself as a trainee."

"What are we looking for?" Oliver asked, frowning.

"You are to consider what non-physical dangers the aggression of humans poses to the merpeople population," Instructor Wivell answered calmly. "The question will be the focus of your first lesson next week."

Merletta made a strangled noise and half-rose from her seat, the movement involuntary. Every eye in the room turned to her, and she struggled to get hold of herself. She didn't want to give too much away to the wrong person. But she had to know what he was talking about.

"Did you say humans?" she said hollowly.

Instructor Wivell's eyebrow was once again raised. "I realize that you have been on your break, Merletta," he said, with a touch of impatience. "But you can hardly have remained ignorant of the dramatic discovery that has so altered our society in recent weeks. Not even the most backward corner of Tilssted could have failed to hear of it."

Merletta went still, aware that she was in dangerous waters. What could she possibly say that wouldn't reveal that she hadn't been in the triple kingdoms at all during her break?

"I just…" she swallowed, "I just didn't realize that discussion of humans would be included in our curriculum now."

"Naturally such a momentous event in our history could hardly fail to be discussed as part of the program," said Instructor Wivell reprovingly. "Our third years," his eyes lingered on Sage and Oliver, "would have been covering the matter regardless. But given recent events, all trainees will be part of those classes." His gaze traveled across the whole group. "The interaction of our own kind with humans—who, you must remember, most merpeople have until recently believed to be a myth—is history happening before our eyes. You should expect the matter to be a substantial feature of your history classes for some time to come."

Merletta looked at Sage, stunned. Her friend was watching her with the same concern she'd shown at lunch. Sage would have the answers. Merletta would avoid drawing any more attention to herself in front of the rest of the group and wait until she and Sage could be alone.

Instructor Wivell was still talking, but Merletta was too distracted now to take in a word. What was it he'd said? Something about the aggression of humans? A memory flashed before Merletta's eyes—Heath, floating just off Vazula, arms raised in a gesture of clear surrender, moments before the guards had thrown their spears and spilled his blood into the water. A stab of mingled pain and anger passed over her.

Aggression of humans?

Merletta's thoughts were grim as she pushed the image away with an effort and returned to the present. It was history in the making, all right. But it wasn't happening before their eyes. It was being written, and far away from the public eye. Written—or rather re-written—by the Center itself.

CHAPTER FIVE

Heath was pleased to find, after an hour of rest, that he was no longer limping as he made his way back into the corridor. Percival was already waiting for him, fidgeting impatiently. But after a glance at his brother's face, he didn't comment on Heath's slowness. They made their way together back to the landing at the top of the entranceway's broad staircase, as they'd been instructed. Heath looked around him with a flicker of interest.

The castle at Kynton was pleasant. His suite had been tastefully furnished and decorated, with windows looking out on an appealing garden. Windows also appeared quite frequently in the corridor, making the space lighter than the castle at Bryford, and a long rug softened the stones under their feet.

"I wonder what King Eamon is like," Percival mused, as they walked. "Do you think we'll be able to sense his power?"

"Yes," said Heath simply. "We can sense everyone else's magic, can't we?"

"I suppose it will feel like Grandmother's, since he's her twin," said Percival, a slight bounce in his step. "Sort of overwhelming and all-encompassing."

Heath chuckled. "Hers does feel that way, doesn't it? It's interesting how their power is less specific than ours. I suppose since they were the first two to have magic, it's not surprising that it's sort of been refined by the third generation."

"And King Eamon's magic is a general power of stability," said Percival thoughtfully. "They say that when he speaks, everyone is instilled with confidence." He threw a glance at Heath. "Even you have to agree that's an eminently desirable power for a monarch to have."

"I never said it would be bad for a monarch to have power," Heath pointed out. "Just that it's dangerous to talk about it as desirable when we're in Valoria, where the ruling branch of the royal family doesn't have magic." He gave Percival a meaningful look. "And where the ones with power happen to be our branch of the family."

Percival rolled his eyes. "Stop looking at me like I'm trying to overthrow the monarchy, Heath. All I said was that King Eamon's power must be handy."

Heath didn't answer. They had turned a corner as Percival spoke, and a young man of about Percival's age came into sight. He was dressed in the rich garments of a courtier, and he smiled warmly at the sight of them.

"Lord Percival, Lord Heath?" he asked, and they nodded. "Welcome to Kynton. Great Aunt Jocelyn sent me to fetch you. I'm Theodore, and I'm delighted you've come."

"Thank you, Your Highness," Heath said, trying to hide his surprise. He had a basic understanding of the family tree of the Kyonan royals, and he recognized Theodore's name—he was the eldest son of Crown Prince Rory. It was strange to hear this young man, whom he'd never met, calling Heath's grandmother "Great Aunt Jocelyn". And even stranger to think of her sending Kyona's future king on an errand.

"None of that," Prince Theodore said, waving a hand as he

led them toward the banquet hall. "No need for titles between cousins. We're all so pleased you've come." He threw a measuring glance at Percival. "Try not to annihilate my little brother, though."

There was a gleam of humor in his eyes as he spoke, but Percival still looked as taken aback by the request as Heath felt.

"What do you mean? Of course I won't—"

"I should have explained," laughed Theodore. "Steffan's gift is similar to yours. When he heard that the superhumanly strong, Valorian power-wielder had come as well, he became instantly determined to beat you in a fight." He shook his head indulgently. "He's only fifteen, you see. He hasn't yet grown out of his intoxication at being the strongest boy in the room, as you no doubt did years ago."

"Yes," Heath said with a straight face. "Years ago."

Percival managed to elbow him in the ribs without attracting Theodore's attention, and Heath felt his first flicker of real amusement in a long time. They had reached a carved wooden doorway, and the guards on either side bowed as Prince Theodore passed through it.

"Just a small group tonight," he said cheerfully. "Grandmother and Grandfather wanted to welcome you appropriately, but didn't want to overwhelm you with a state dinner the moment you'd arrived."

"We appreciate it," said Heath sincerely. But when he cast his eyes around the room, he saw that Prince Theodore shared the misconception of most royalty about what could be considered a "small group" of people. It probably came from never being able to go anywhere alone, and it was one of the many things Heath didn't envy his royal cousins.

The room wasn't enormous—it was clearly a smaller banquet hall—but it certainly seemed full of people. Heath and Percival were led to the slightly elevated chairs at the center of a long dining table where King Eamon and Queen Luciana were already seated. They greeted the pair graciously, and Heath cast a curious glance over Kyona's king when he straightened from his bow.

King Eamon was a generation older than Valoria's king, but he held his age well. His back was still straight, and his gaze was shrewd. Age had worn away any striking resemblance between him and his twin, but something about him still reminded Heath of his grandmother. Perhaps it was the magic. Identifying the presence of power was such a familiar part of Heath's senses, he couldn't separate it from the observations of his eyes, or his ears. But when he really tried to focus on King Eamon's magic, he thought he could find the thread weaving its way back and forth between the siblings, as though they were two sides of the same coin.

Princess Jocelyn sat beside her twin brother. She'd been leaning slightly forward to speak to Kyona's elderly queen on the king's other side, but at Heath and Percival's approach, she turned her attention to them, beaming as they were received by the king and queen. It was clear that she was delighted to have two of her grandchildren visiting her native land and meeting her brother.

King Eamon's smile was genuine, and if he resented Percival attaching himself to the invitation, he gave no sign of it. Queen Luciana, beside him, still bore the signs of the beauty for which she had been famous in her youth. Her warm brown skin wasn't as lined as her husband's, and although her hair was completely silver, it was still thick and long. Her eyes were kind as they rested on Heath, and he found his spirits lifting. It was nice to be greeted with such warmth. His own monarchs had never been unkind, but there was always caution, always careful formality when Valoria's royals interacted with the power-wielding branch of their family. Every interaction was loaded.

Not so here.

"Come," Prince Theodore said cheerfully, once the king had dismissed them. "My parents want to receive you as well, but then you'll be free to sit with the others our age."

He dutifully introduced them to Prince Rory, the middle-aged heir to Kyona's king, and his wife. The crown prince was several years younger than Heath's own father, and asked pleasantly after his cousin, whom he had met on more than one occasion. Heath and Percival returned polite, if not entirely truthful, answers. Heath wasn't about to say that his father had been grim and anxious since Heath's mysterious near-death injuries, and he could only be grateful that Percival showed similar restraint.

The long table formed three sides of a square, with the king and queen in the middle of the central expanse. Formalities over, Prince Theodore conducted his second cousins to one of the side wings, where they were greeted by a lively bunch of others their age. The prince introduced them to his own younger sister and brother, and Heath suppressed a laugh at the open way in which young Prince Steffan was sizing Percival up. Three of Prince Theodore's cousins were also there, all power-wielders, given their descent from King Eamon. But there were also a number of young people from the court, who could have no claim to magic, but nevertheless welcomed the Valorian brothers with flattering enthusiasm.

"Sit next to me, Lord Heath," invited one of them. Prince Theodore had introduced him as Lord Vincent. "I'd love to hear more about Bryford. My mother has cousins there, and I've always wanted to go, but never yet managed it."

"We would be glad to welcome you," smiled Heath, warming to the cheerful young man.

"So, Lord Heath," the Kyonan mused. "The younger son of the Duke of Bexley, right? Prince Kincaid and Princess Jocelyn's eldest son?"

Heath nodded, a little surprised.

"And, if memory serves, your power is something to do with eyesight, isn't it?" Lord Vincent turned his gaze on Percival, chatting happily with Prince Theodore nearby. "And your brother, of course, is the one with the strength of five men. That's an easy one to remember."

Heath realized his mouth was hanging open, and he shut it hastily. "How do you know what my power is?" he asked.

"Oh, we know your family tree well," Lord Vincent said, seeming surprised by Heath's reaction. "I mean, plenty of people don't remember quite where everyone fits. But those of us who are interested in studying magic are naturally aware of all the power-wielders in the Valorian line of the Dragonfriends, and your abilities." He grinned. "We were all very excited when His Majesty invited you to visit, so imagine our delight to meet two of you instead of one!"

Heath just stared, too astonished to respond. The idea that he would be well known in Kyona had never occurred to him. And his father's position as the cousin of King Matlock had nothing whatsoever to do with his apparent fame. It was his relationship to the Kyonan throne, and its legacy of power, that these people were interested in. Lord Vincent had referred to Heath's family, not as a branch of the royal family of Valoria, but of the House of Dragonfriend, the name given to Kyona's royal house since the time of the previous king, father to both King Eamon and Princess Jocelyn.

Some strange mixture of gratification and alarm stirred within Heath. It was nice to feel so accepted, so welcome. But it also felt ominous, somehow, to hear a Kyonan claim the Valorian power-wielders as belonging to Kyona's royal family instead of Valoria's.

Still, it was flattering to know the Kyonans counted him as a magic user. It had always been a matter of some debate whether he even had magic. His eyesight was unusually good, but he'd never been convinced that counted, not when compared to some of the more impressive—and more obviously unnatural—abilities of his siblings and cousins. The questionable status of his magic was, he suspected, what had led King Matlock to appoint him as liaison between the crown and the power-wielders, since he almost had a foot in each camp.

Judging by the attitude of Lord Vincent, a thoroughly non-magical member of King Eamon's court, the Kyonan crown had no need for a liaison between power-wielders and everyone else. Heath took note of the mood as the king rose to address the assembled group before the meal began, and throughout the evening. The respect for King Eamon was palpable. And it wasn't just the dutiful homage owed to a monarch. Clearly, he was beloved. Heath realized that, although he hadn't articulated it to himself, on some level he had expected that a throne filled by such an elderly king wouldn't project the strength portrayed by someone King Matlock's age. But he had been mistaken.

"A tribute!"

Heath turned, looking for the source of the call. A young nobleman, sitting not far from Prince Theodore—so probably someone of high rank—was looking beseechingly toward the royals.

"A tribute! A tribute for our guests!"

The cry was soon taken up by multiple others, and with a smile, King Eamon gestured his assent. The young people turned inward, muttering eagerly amongst themselves. Heath watched with interest.

Some agreement seemed to be reached, because the nobleman who had first called out stood, and swept an elegant bow to a dark-haired girl whom Heath recognized as Prince Theodore's sister. She was younger than him, perhaps seventeen.

"Princess Kiana," the nobleman said. "Would you honor us, Your Highness?"

She flushed slightly, but a dimple appeared as she inclined her head, not quite deeply enough to hide her smile.

"The honor," she said in a musical voice, "would be mine."

She rose, lifting her hands before her, palms down. Heath could feel Lord Vincent's excitement beside him, but he didn't take his fascinated eyes off Princess Kiana. She closed her eyes for a moment, her face twisted in concentration. Then she opened them, and swept her hands down, inward, and back up, as though scooping something. To Heath's amazement, water rose from pitchers all along the tables, soaring through the air to meet in one floating, spherical mass in the center of the room. Princess Kiana twisted her fingers in a complicated pattern, and before Heath's incredulous eyes, the water formed itself into a delicate flower, many times bigger than its real counterpart.

"A dianmon," Princess Kiana said, naming the elusive white flower that was Kyona's emblem. Heath knew that the bloom grew only in the mountain range at the eastern edge of Kyona, where a colony of powerful dragons had been concealed for hundreds of years.

"Found in the mountains that march along our border with your kingdom," the princess continued. She dipped her head respectfully to Heath and Percival, and to some other key members of their delegation, seated on the other wing of the table. "A symbol and reminder of the friendship between our fair lands."

She flicked her hands outward again, and the water separated into multiple streams, flowing through the air and returning to their pitchers, with not a drop spilled, as far as Heath could see. Heath sat mutely as the young princess turned to her grandfather, sweeping him a graceful curtsy.

"In your service, and for your honor, Your Majesty," she said, her look of concentration gone in favor of another sweet smile. King Eamon returned it with one of his own, raising his hands in dignified applause. The action unlocked the rest of the room, and cheers arose on all sides as Princess Kiana once again took her seat.

"Her power is controlling water," Lord Vincent said, unnecessarily. "She's a favorite for such entertainment. Her finesse is improving greatly."

"I've never seen a power quite like that," Heath replied, his eyes still riveted on Princess Kiana. "I have a cousin who has abilities with things that grow, but that...that was incredible."

Lord Vincent squinted in an effort of memory. "Lord Brody, is that? Son of Prince Kincaid and Princess Jocelyn's second child?"

Heath nodded, still not used to the fact that his family was so well known here.

"You may not have anyone who has power with water," Lord Vincent continued brightly, "but it's interesting, isn't it, how your generation of power-wielders tend to have more physical abilities, like strength, or sight, or moving matter? Compared to the previous generation, where it was often a more intangible skill, like your father's ability to detect deception. The same general pattern is true of our power-wielders, although not without exception." He shook his head. "Magic is simply fascinating."

Heath didn't respond. In all honesty, he was too stunned to think of anything to say. It wasn't just Princess Kiana's impressive display. It was the strangeness of seeing such a display welcomed, even celebrated, as a routine part of the evening's entertainment in King Eamon's court. More than half the people in the room carried no magic, but no one looked uncomfortable, no one suspicious. Except perhaps some of the other members of the Valorian delegation, Heath thought with a grimace.

Kyona was certainly a different kind of land.

Heath's eyes slid to his grandparents, their attention back on King Eamon and Queen Luciana now that the tribute was finished. Princess Jocelyn looked so at ease in the kingdom of her birth, and even Prince Kincaid appeared as relaxed as he did in Bryford. The sight rattled Heath further. He'd always known, of course, about his grandparents' yearly visits to Kynton. But he hadn't quite grasped how substantial a place they had in the community here, how familiar they must be to all the Kyonans. It was almost like having a second life, a second identity. He measured them both for a moment, as Lord Vincent chatted to the neighbor on his other side.

Prince Kincaid laughed at something his brother-in-law said, then cast his eyes over the room. His gaze locked with Heath, and he gave his grandson a reassuring smile. It was impossible to put words to it, but something passed between them in that moment. However much the elderly prince was at home in King Eamon's court, he was Valorian, down to his very bones. Just as Heath was.

Heartened, Heath examined his grandmother. Her posture held none of the tension he had often seen in the last year or two, as she tried, along with the rest of the power-wielders, to walk a delicate line in King Matlock's court. But while there was fondness in her demeanor toward her first home, perhaps even a sentiment of nostalgia, there was no regret, no conflict. She was Valorian now, too. She had embraced her new home decades ago, and she remained loyal to that decision.

Heath felt his shoulders relax in wordless relief. There was no danger there. He couldn't have said how he could see these truths about the state of his grandparents' hearts. He just could. And he had not the smallest doubt about the accuracy of his observations. He'd often been good at reading people, but this was a much stronger certainty. The skill was developing, apparently.

But his relief was short-lived, his reassuring thoughts interrupted by a catch of conversation from the noble girl currently listening with rapt attention to Percival.

"So you actually lifted the whole carriage off? You saved that boy's life!"

Heath's heart sank to the bottom of his stomach as his brother disclaimed credit with a lightheartedness that clearly did nothing to reduce the lady's admiration. Percival's features were as open and cheerful as ever, but to Heath, the light in Percival's eyes was almost feverish.

He barely held in a groan as all his unease returned. Not for the world would he have knowingly exposed Percival to this perplexing, intoxicating, unsettling environment. His mind swirled with unformed but potent fears about what might come of it. But there was nothing he could do now. Percival was here, and no unusual powers of observation were necessary to make it clear that he was already a big hit.

Heath felt a surge of determination. He hadn't invited his brother, hadn't really wanted him to come. But it was still because of him that Percival was in Kyona, and he therefore had some responsibility to make sure no harm came of the visit. Percival would have repudiated the very thought, but in some things, he needed his little brother to help protect him. And that was just what Heath would do.

He was so caught up in his thoughts that it didn't hit him until he was sinking into his bed several hours later. With a stab that was half guilt, half relief, he realized that for a whole evening, he'd forgotten all about Merletta's fate.

CHAPTER SIX

Heath sat up suddenly, a strangled cry escaping him. His mind raced frantically, trying to place his surroundings. The dim light of dawn was creeping over the room, and it took him a moment to recognize it as his suite in Kynton.

He pressed his palms to his eyes, one half of his mind trying to recapture the dream, the other half telling him he should try to forget. So much for a whole evening with no thought of Merletta's fate.

The morning air didn't carry much chill—Kyonan summers were even warmer than Valorian ones—but a shiver ran over him nevertheless. This dream had been especially vivid. At least in emotion. The details had actually been hazier than many other such dreams. Merletta had been surrounded by a murkiness that made it hard to discern physical details. But the sense of her situation had been crystal clear.

Vulnerable. Exposed. Surrounded by danger on all sides.

He let out a low moan. She was dead. Whatever danger she'd faced, it was over now. Surely his guilt over her death was enough. Why did he also have to be tormented by his mind's attempt to conjure up the risks she'd faced while she was alive? That was his best guess at what was happening, but even that didn't make a whole lot of sense.

He pushed himself out of bed, dressing quickly and wondering how best to distract himself during the morning. He had a couple of state meetings in the afternoon—a nod to his official role in King Matlock's court—but that was many hours away. He had to find something to fill the time, or his dream would continue to haunt him.

As it happened, the matter was decided for him. Early as it was, when he made his way from his sleeping chamber into his suite's small but comfortably appointed receiving room, he found not only a servant stoking a small fire, but a note left in a prominent place on a table.

Heath

I hope you slept well. I would be delighted to receive you for tea before you get swept into whatever frolics the young people are sure to have planned for you today.

I am an early riser. Like you, I believe.

Heath didn't know whether to laugh or grimace. There was no signature, but it wasn't necessary. He knew his grandmother's handwriting. He pocketed the note without delay. Clearly she wanted him to call on her first thing.

The servant directed him toward the right wing of the castle, and with additional instructions from others he passed on the way, he found himself in front of her door before the sun had fully cleared the forest that lay to the east of Kynton.

Heath paused in the corridor and drew a deep breath, surprised by his own nerves. He had always felt very relaxed with his grandmother. It was a strange experience to feel apprehensive about an invitation to have tea with her.

But although she hadn't written it in so many words, her summons had been clear. This was no friendly chat over pastries. He'd managed to stand his ground and refuse to tell his parents the details of what had happened to him a little more than a month ago. But he knew instinctively that he would have no such success with his grandmother. He was going to end up telling her everything, he was sure of it.

The thought was equal parts relieving and unnerving.

Enough brooding, he told himself. He raised his fist and knocked firmly on the door.

"Enter!"

The cheerful voice helped calm his tumultuous emotions. Of course she wasn't going to interrogate him. She had a gentle heart that never failed to set him at ease.

"Good morning, Grandmother," he said, smiling as he entered the chamber.

She was seated at a writing desk by the window, but she had turned in her chair to watch him enter.

"Heath." The smile dimmed slightly on her face, and her eyes searched his features shrewdly. "Are you hungry?" She gestured to the tray set on a nearby table, steam still rising from the teapot, and scones arranged on a plate alongside.

Heath glanced at the food. "Not really," he admitted. He felt slightly ill, not uncommon after waking from an unsettling dream.

"Hm." His grandmother was still watching him thoughtfully. "I think what you need is fresh air." She stood, and Heath moved forward quickly to offer her his arm. "Thank you," she said warmly, leaning on him slightly as they made their way out of the room. She led him along the quiet corridor, empty except for the servants. "I've been looking forward to a proper talk," she said calmly. "We can talk just as well walking as sitting still, can't we?"

"Better, probably," Heath agreed easily.

"Let me take you to my favorite spot for early morning strolls," the elderly princess said. "When I was young, I often wished to escape from the court to clear my head. I found not many of my father's nobles were early risers. I think that's why I got into the habit."

"It's strange to picture you here, in your childhood," Heath mused. "Valoria has always been your home in my memory."

She smiled. "It has been my home much longer than Kyona was. But Kyona is my past nevertheless, and I'm delighted to share it with you." She gave him a serious look. "The legacy of our power comes from Kyona, Heath, and I think it might help you embrace yours if you see that."

He was silent for a moment, noting the troubled look that crossed his grandmother's face as she spoke. She was leading him up a staircase he hadn't traveled before, and he could see the sun starting to peek through windows up ahead.

"You're worried about Percival embracing his power *too* much, though, aren't you?" he asked.

She gave him a startled look, not immediately speaking. They waited for a servant to pass, then stepped through a doorway onto the battlements that ran along the southern side of the building. The elderly princess nodded to a guard, and continued until they were out of the man's earshot. Then she let go of Heath's arm, resting a hand on the stone in front of her and looking out. Heath followed her gaze.

"It's a beautiful vista," he said quietly. "I can see why you liked to come here."

The city of Kynton stretched out before them, and beyond it was a vast expanse of green fields, golden wheat, and dotted villages. The dense Forest of Rune lay to his left, and somewhere, way beyond view, was the sea. For a moment he could see it, sunlight shimmering off the water, gulls calling harshly, spray leaping up as the waves crashed against submerged rocks.

He shook his head. A mere fancy. The sea was many leagues to the south, beyond even his sight.

"How did you know I was worried about Percival?" his grandmother asked abruptly. "Did you just guess because you're worried as well?"

Heath didn't meet her eyes, his gaze still on the far distance. "No," he said slowly. "I mean, I am worried as well. I can already see how taken Percival is with the culture around magic here. And I don't think it will do him any good to see the contrast." He sighed. "Of course, it doesn't take much to imagine you might share that concern. I'm guessing you were quite intentional in not inviting him to visit just now, and that you have good reasons. But sensing your concern was different. It wasn't a guess. When you frowned, I knew."

There was something difficult to read in his companion's would-be light voice. "You were reading my mind?"

"No, of course not," he said quickly. "It wasn't like that at all. Nothing that detailed or specific. I could just...see your concern for him." He shook his head helplessly. "I don't know how else to explain it."

He glanced over at last, and saw his grandmother watching him intently. He gave a reluctant smile.

"Sometimes I do seem to see things other people don't. I think...I think it might be part of my power."

"Bravo, Heath," she said, a smile breaking across her own face. "I think that might be the first time I've ever heard you actually admit that you have magic." Her gaze turned thoughtful. "The ability to see things other people don't," she mused. "It tallies with your excellent eyesight, doesn't it?"

"I suppose so," acknowledged Heath.

"Well, I'm glad to see that the culture here is helping you open your mind, at least," his grandmother said, with a touch of humor.

"Is that why you invited me to visit?" Heath asked suddenly. "To encourage me to embrace our Kyonan heritage, and my magic?"

She let out a sigh. "Not exactly. I thought that you, like my younger self, might feel in need of some...space. I was deeply concerned to hear that you wouldn't tell your parents how you acquired your life-threatening injuries."

Heath fidgeted, and she continued in her calm way.

"I don't mean to chastise you. But it's not in your nature to be mutinous, or secretive for the sake of it. I knew you must have a reason for your silence, and to be frank, I have been extremely apprehensive about what that reason might be."

"It certainly wasn't out of a desire to cause anyone grief," said Heath quickly.

She smiled. "Knowing you as I do, it is quite unnecessary to tell me that."

Heath averted his face, unable to bear the warmth in her eyes. "I'm not as wonderful as you seem to think, Grandmother," he said heavily. "I've made a lot of stupid decisions. It's because of me that..."

He broke off, unable to go on. His mind was overwhelmed with an image of Merletta, tail swishing as she moved through deep water, eyes alert and determined as they'd always been. A purely imagined scene, as he'd never actually witnessed her swimming while fully submerged.

"Tell me, Heath." The words were gentle, but it was an order.

"I can't," he choked out. "I promised someone that I wouldn't tell anyone about—"

"Do you trust me, Heath?" his grandmother interrupted.

"Of course I do," he said, frustrated. "But I trust my parents as well. The story I have to tell involves information that...that can't be taken back once it's been exposed. My father would be honor-bound to tell King Matlock what I know, and I swore to... someone, that I wouldn't reveal—"

"I am a princess of two kingdoms, Heath," his grandmother said, once again cutting him off. Her voice was more serious than he'd ever heard it. "A power-wielder born into a world where such a being was utterly unprecedented. I understand more about divided loyalties than you might think. And I'm asking you to trust me when I tell you that—where the safety of our kingdom is not at stake—my loyalty to you as my grandson is greater even than my loyalty to the crown of either Valoria or Kyona. You said that you have a story to tell. I can see that you're bursting to do so. You can trust me."

For a long moment, their gazes were locked, Heath feeling almost mesmerized. Then his senses as a power-wielder suddenly latched on to something. Her magic, while emanating from her in the constant flow that was common to all power-wielders, wasn't reaching out, wasn't wrapping around him. She had a potent ability to effect change—she could change his mind without even using words if she chose to. But she wasn't. She was simply asking him, person to person, to trust her. And he found that he did.

Without warning, the story poured out of him. He told her how a chance reference in an old captain's log had sent him and Reka searching for Vazula. How they'd found it, surrounded by a magical barrier that an ordinary human wouldn't be able to pass through, like the ones around the dragon colonies. He told her about his first sighting of Merletta, and how he'd gone back hoping to find her again. When he revealed the incredible truth he'd discovered on their second meeting—that she wasn't human at all, but a mermaid, something in his listener's eyes made him stop.

"What?" he asked, unsettled.

"I didn't speak," his grandmother said, her voice not sounding quite natural.

"I know you didn't, but I saw something," Heath pressed, his eyes narrowing slightly. "Some...reaction."

She gave a weak smile. "Did you expect me to have no reaction to the information that there are real mermaids living in the depths of the ocean?"

Heath shook his head. "It wasn't just astonishment. Why are you alarmed? Why are you afraid?"

She drew a shaky breath. "To be perfectly frank with you, Heath, I'm not sure if I should answer that. Please, finish your story first. You said Rekavidur was with you when you discovered that this Merletta is a mermaid?"

Heath nodded, his throat feeling strangely tight at hearing Merletta's name on someone else's lips. It made her feel more real, less a figment of his imagination.

"Of course. He was always with me when I went to Vazula. How else would I get there?"

He hurried on, telling her about the months where he and Merletta had met on the island every week, and the months where he'd been prevented from meeting her, first because he was detained in Bryford, then because Rekavidur stopped responding to his call. He couldn't help but notice that his grandmother seemed particularly interested in the dragon's behavior, but he didn't ask her about her reaction again. He'd reached the part that was hardest to say but that he most desperately needed to get out.

Haltingly, he told his grandmother what had happened a month before, when he'd finally returned to Vazula to find Merletta under attack by a group of her own kind. How he'd attempted to intervene, only to be attacked himself. How she'd sacrificed herself to pull him to the relative safety of the shore, drying herself out in the process. How Reka had refused to go back, to give her the minute it would have taken to return her to the water and save her life.

There was a long silence after he finished, and he found he couldn't look his companion in the eye. He felt depleted, empty. But a certain lightness came with the sensation as well.

"I'm sorry, Heath," his grandmother said at last. "You lost Merletta, and your closest friend in one blow." She laid a hand on his arm. "Although I trust Rekavidur isn't lost to you forever."

Heath shrugged one shoulder, unable to find words.

His grandmother looked thoughtful. "And the rest of this mermaid kingdom is still out there, undetected."

"Precisely," said Heath. "And even if Merletta is gone, my promise to her still stands, not to reveal the existence of her kind. They think humans are a myth, but they consider dragons to be their natural enemies."

His grandmother gave him a sharp look. "Merletta told you that?"

He nodded.

"Did she say why?"

Heath hesitated, taken aback by her tone. "Apparently they're taught that dragons are aggressive, and will kill mermaids on sight. The first time Merletta saw Reka, she almost dried herself out in her panic. She assumed he was about to eat her or something."

The elderly princess drew an audible breath. "And you say Reka began acting strangely, but he never told you why?"

Heath nodded again, his eyes narrowing. "You know why, don't you?"

"I have a pretty good guess," she said dryly. She made a clucking noise in her throat. "Poor Rekavidur. What a dilemma he must have found himself in."

"Poor Rekavidur?" Heath echoed, outraged. "He's not the one who deserves your sympathy!"

There was sadness in the older woman's eyes as she turned to him. "Don't be quick to judge others' troubles, Heath. You don't know what it is to have to hide things from those you care about."

"So what's he hiding?" Heath demanded.

She shook her head slowly. "I can't answer that question," she said. "I'm only guessing. You need to speak to him."

"I don't think so," said Heath flatly.

His grandmother didn't answer, just fixed him with a calm but penetrating look that made him squirm on the inside. He turned away from her, looking out over the city again.

"I wonder if he regrets it," he said softly. "Leaving her to die. I wonder if he ever dreams about it like I do."

"You dream about it?" pressed his companion.

Heath gave a curt nod, still not looking at her. "Almost every night. Sometimes even during the day...it's as if I lose focus on what's happening, and I can see her, as clearly as if I was back on Vazula."

"Describe these visions to me," said his grandmother.

Heath glanced over at her, surprised by her intent expression. "I don't know if I'd call them visions. It's just my imagination, I suppose. Just flashes, but vivid in detail." He described the dream he'd had the night before, comparing it to the clearer images he'd often seen in his mind before that.

"And you're sure they're not memories?" clarified his grandmother. "Not things you actually witnessed during your time with her?"

"I'm sure," said Heath. There was no need to say it aloud, but he remembered every moment he'd spent with Merletta. He knew his dreams weren't memories.

"Hm." Princess Jocelyn was thoughtful. "And you didn't actually see her die. For all you know, she may have made it back to the water."

Heath's eyes widened. "I don't think so, Grandmother. You didn't see her. She wasn't going anywhere."

His grandmother met his eye, looking almost amused. "What do you think your visions are, then? They don't sound like normal dreams to me."

"You mean..." Heath's mind spun as he grasped her meaning. "You mean you think it's part of my power somehow?"

"You said it yourself," his grandmother pointed out. "You often see things other people don't."

"You think she's alive?" Heath's voice came out as a whisper. "And I'm somehow seeing her, as she actually is, right now?"

His grandmother shrugged. "I think it's possible. I don't want to give you false hope, but I don't think you should rule it out. And I think the question will haunt you for the rest of your life unless you go and find out one way or another."

Heath didn't know what to say. That explanation for his recurring dreams had honestly never occurred to him. He didn't know if he dared to really consider it.

"You're in love with this girl, aren't you?"

The question pulled Heath out of his thoughts with a vengeance. He turned startled eyes on his grandmother, feeling blood rush into his face then drain out of it in quick succession.

"Of course not," he said, a little too quickly. "I hardly know her."

His grandmother raised an eyebrow. "Perhaps I spoke too strongly. I should have said you're very drawn to her."

"Not...not in the way you mean," said Heath, still speaking too quickly. "How could I be? She's not, I mean she wasn't...you know. Human."

The older woman looked like she was trying not to smile, but she forbore to tease him. "It wouldn't be wrong, Heath. To be attracted to her. She sounds a lot more human than I would have expected of a mythical creature."

Heath jumped gratefully at the opportunity to change the direction of the conversation. "That's what Reka said. He couldn't seem to get it into his head that she wasn't human."

"Is that so?" His grandmother's expression was once again thoughtful.

"Are you really not going to tell me what you know, or at least what you've guessed, about what's going on with Reka?"

She sighed. "I'm not trying to be frustrating, Heath. But it's like you said...some information can't be taken back once it's exposed. If I told you what's in my mind, it might cause all kinds of problems for you. You might very well wish you didn't hold that knowledge."

"That sounds extremely evasive," said Heath, unimpressed.

She smiled. "I know it does. But I need to think some things through. I'm going on memories from decades before you were born. I'm not at all sure of my guesses."

"You're as cryptic as Reka," Heath grumbled. "You obviously spent too much time around your dragon friend."

His grandmother laughed lightly. "I don't think I've spent half as much time with Elddreki as you have with Rekavidur." Her expression turned serious. "I meant what I said, Heath. I don't believe for a moment that Rekavidur's friendship is lost to you forever. You would be very foolish to let that happen. I haven't forgotten, if you have, that he publicly named you as a dragonfriend at the Winter Solstice Festival last year. Do you understand how rare a thing that is? Especially for a human who doesn't even wear a crown? Don't throw it away because you need someone other than yourself to blame for what happened to Merletta."

Heath was silent. There was a streak of rebellious defense

still inside him, but he was feeling more and more chastised as his grandmother continued.

"For what it's worth," she said gently, "I don't think either you or Rekavidur is really to blame for whatever did or didn't befall this Merletta. It sounds to me like she made her own choices, and would probably stand by them, regardless of the outcome."

Heath felt a curious mixture of pain and amusement. His grandmother was undoubtedly right.

"Mermaids don't stand," he pointed out.

Another low chuckle greeted his words. "Well, she'd probably float by them, then." She stepped away from the battlements. "I'd best return to the castle. But you take your time up here. It's a good place to think."

Without another word, she moved away, her steps graceful. Heath turned his attention back to the vista before him. The conversation had certainly given him a lot to think about. Was it possible that Merletta was alive?

It took very little thought to convince him that his grandmother was right about one thing. He would never be fully at peace until he confirmed it one way or the other.

It seemed it was time to communicate with Reka again after all.

CHAPTER SEVEN

Merletta

By the time they finished dinner on her first night back in the Center, Merletta could see that Sage was as on edge as she was. It had probably been cruel to tell her friend she had big news so long before they actually had the opportunity to talk. But she was still nervous about putting Sage at risk, not just with her information, but by pulling her off somewhere away from crowds.

But that was ridiculous, she told herself firmly. Sage wasn't just a trainee, she was a legacy applicant—her mother was a record holder as well. People would notice if someone attacked her. She wasn't as vulnerable as Merletta.

The thought stirred something in Merletta's mind, but she didn't have leisure to pursue it. The dining hall was beginning to empty, and Sage was looking at her meaningfully. She gave a tight nod, and they rose into the water together. Andre, the new trainee, showed signs of wanting to hover, so they headed for the girls' barracks, where no reason would need to be given for why he couldn't follow them.

But of course they couldn't really speak freely in their sleeping quarters. Lorraine shared their room, and she was drifting along not far ahead of them. When she was satisfied that Andre had gone elsewhere, Sage tugged on Merletta's arm, tilting her head toward the darkening streets.

They swam through the gloom, and Merletta quickly realized that Sage was leading her to a nearby coral garden. She did a quick circuit of the area, satisfying herself that no one else was there, before settling on a stone bench next to her friend.

"No one's likely to interrupt us here after dark," Sage said quietly. "This is more of a daytime garden."

She was right. They were enfolded in darkness, the only light coming from jellyfish lanterns set at the entrances to the garden. It was no great barrier to their mermaid eyes, but it created a sense of privacy. In the distance, Merletta could see the ubiquitous plankton lanterns casting their soft glow around the quietening streets, but the garden itself was fading away into a purplish black. It hadn't been cultivated for night enjoyment, like some of the gardens had. There were no bioluminescent species of coral to attract night wanderers to sit or swim between the orderly rows.

"Where were you during your break?" Sage asked, without preface.

"I was outside the triple kingdoms," said Merletta. "I was... on land."

For a long moment, Sage simply stared at her. "On...land?" she whispered. "Merletta, were you...were you part of this?"

"Part of what?" Merletta asked sharply. "What did they tell you happened?"

"I don't know who you mean by *they*," Sage said simply. "But after you left on your break, a guard patrol came back from outside the barrier with an incredible story. They said they saw a human. Apparently they went a lot further than they were supposed to, and they found...land."

"And?" Merletta pressed. "Is that all they said happened?"

Sage raised an eyebrow. "All? The discovery that there's land so close to the triple kingdoms is dramatic enough. I always thought we were far from any land."

"So did I," said Merletta dryly. "Until about a year ago, when I was exploring a short way outside the barrier, and I found land."

"A year ago?" Sage repeated, startled. "Why were you outside the barrier? And why didn't you tell me?"

"I barely knew you a year ago," Merletta said, her voice softer. "And even once I got to know you...well, it's complicated. What else did the guards say?"

Sage shrugged. "Well, it's not as though I've spoken to them myself. But you can imagine the chaos created by that information. Everyone was terrified—we all thought we were safe, far away from land and its predators."

"That's what we'd been told," said Merletta grimly.

"Yes." Even in the low light, Merletta could see how serious Sage's expression had become. "And with good reason. I can understand why the authorities wouldn't have wanted to advertise the proximity of land. It's not as though we can move the whole triple kingdoms, is it? It's like Instructor Ibsen said at our last lesson." She shook her head. "But of course, you weren't there. He told us—and much as he can be infuriating, I can see he's right—that by far the safest way is to simply keep everyone inside the barrier, where we're protected."

"Protected from what?" Merletta asked, exasperated. It was disheartening to see how easily even Sage, who was smart and well-informed, was buying the lies.

"From the humans," Sage responded matter-of-factly. "The one the guards saw attacked them, and they barely escaped with their lives."

Merletta made a noise of disbelief. "*He* attacked *them*?" She drew in a deep swirl of water, trying to calm her emotions as the memory of Heath's blood in the water danced across her vision. She had been right when she guessed that history was being re-written to suit the convenience of whoever was behind the various deceptions.

"You're telling me," she tried again, "that one unarmed human sent a whole group of trained guards fleeing for home? Don't you think that sounds absurd? Surely no one is believing that. Surely the guards are too embarrassed to stick to that story."

Sage was giving her a strange look. "The guards are dead, Merletta."

Merletta started, her eyes flying to Sage's face. "Dead? What do you mean?"

"None of them lasted long after they returned to the triple kingdoms," Sage explained sadly. "So some of the details are still a little hazy. There's no one who can tell us exactly what weapons the human used."

"They're claiming that he killed the guards?" Merletta demanded, outraged. Her heart was pounding at this ominous information. She'd been furious with the patrol at the time, but they were only doing what they'd been trained to do. She didn't actually think they deserved to die. What had happened to them?

"You mean the human?" Sage asked. "Of course not. And who is this *they* you're complaining about?"

"If I knew the answer to that..." Merletta muttered. She shook her head, blood still pounding in her ears. "How did the guards die, then?"

Sage pushed out a slow stream of water. "Land sickness got them all in the end."

"What in the depths is land sickness?"

"I'm not surprised you haven't heard of it," said Sage simply. "I hadn't either, before this. When I pressed him, Emil admitted he had, so I suppose they learn about it in fourth year, like we were apparently always going to learn about humans in third year. Anyway, it turns out that land sickness is one of the reasons we've been told all our lives of the importance of staying below water."

"I know exactly why we've been told that," Merletta said bitterly. "And it has nothing to do with any land sickness."

"All right, enough cryptic hints," said Sage, sounding a little irritable at Merletta's constant contradictions. "Tell me what you've been up to."

Merletta hesitated. "I'm scared to tell you," she admitted.

Sage's expression softened at once. She laid a hand over Merletta's. "You can trust me."

Merletta shook her head. "I'm not scared of you, Sage. I'm scared *for* you. I don't know what's going to happen. It was a huge risk even coming back here."

"What do you mean?" Sage demanded. "You were always coming back. Weren't you?"

Merletta closed her eyes. "I almost didn't. But I've never been one to swim from my problems, so here I am. Putting my head in the shark's mouth."

Sage was looking irritated again. "I said—"

"Enough cryptic hints," Merletta finished for her, the ghost of a smile appearing. It dropped immediately. "Sage...would you lie for me?"

Sage looked extremely taken aback, and didn't answer straight away. "I'm not sure I'm comfortable with that question," she admitted at last. "Why would you want me to lie for you? And to whom?"

"What if my life genuinely depended on it?" Merletta asked soberly.

Sage's eyes widened. "Merletta, what have you gotten involved in?"

"You haven't answered my question," Merletta reminded her calmly.

Sage's face remained troubled, but her quiet voice didn't waver. "Yes, Merletta, to save your life, I would lie."

Merletta felt tears prickle behind her eyes. Loyalty was something she hadn't experienced much in her life. It was a further reminder that she'd undervalued Sage's friendship when she neglected to tell her the truth months ago.

"Thanks, Sage," she said softly. She gave a crooked smile. "And for what it's worth, your hesitation relieves me almost as much as your agreement." She closed her eyes, taking a steadying pull of water, then opening them again. "Do you remember how someone sent Center guards to kill me last year? And we never found out who was behind it?"

Sage nodded, her expression tense.

"Well, I don't think it was just because I'm from Tilssted. The truth is I know things I'm not supposed to, and I'm pretty sure that's why I was targeted."

"That sounds...dramatic." Sage's eyebrow was raised eloquently.

"I know it does," sighed Merletta. "And I'd love to think I was wrong. Believe me, I'd prefer to think it's just prejudice against Tilssted. I don't know if they've found out what I know, or if they just suspect..."

She trailed off, her eyes fixed on Sage's serious face. Could she really do this to her friend? If she brought Sage into her secrets, would the other mermaid ever really be safe again?

"Sage," she said earnestly, "I honestly don't think you want to know everything I know. But I think you should at least know as much as Ileana does."

"What does Ileana have to do with it?" Sage demanded.

Merletta's brows lowered, anger passing over her as she remembered Ileana's heartlessness when she'd pursued, spear in hand, as Merletta dragged an injured Heath through the water. But spiteful as Ileana could be, there had been more than that behind her attack. Her words rang again in Merletta's ears.

This isn't just about you. I know my duty.

"Ileana was there," Merletta said quietly, in belated answer to Sage's question. "She was the one who followed me when I left, the day after my test. I was going to the island, like I always did on rest days."

Sage stared. "I thought you went back to Tilssted on rest days, to visit your friend."

"I know you did," said Merletta guiltily. "But it wasn't true. I discovered land not long after I joined the program, and I went there every week. That's where I met Heath." She swallowed nervously, casting a glance around to make absolutely sure no one was nearby. "A human."

Sage's mouth dropped open, but she didn't speak. She was clearly unable to find words.

"Humans aren't aggressive, Sage," Merletta hurried on. "Or at least, this one isn't. He's just like we are. He's not a threat to us, and he certainly didn't attack those guards. Ileana followed me, and she called a patrol when she saw me leave the barrier. I led them to the land—I wanted them to see that we'd been lied to. But I didn't know Heath would be there. He was—" For a moment she struggled with herself, before pushing on. "He was offering nothing but peace. They speared him. Ileana first, then the guards."

Sage's eyes were wide. "What happened to him?" she whispered.

"I don't know," Merletta answered dully. "He had…" she hesitated, then decided that Sage wasn't ready yet to find out about the role of a dragon in this story, "a friend with him. His friend took him and left, to go back to their home, far away to the west. I don't know if he survived."

"I'm sorry," Sage said gently, and unexpectedly. "I can see that you care about him." She hesitated. "Is he...is he really just like us?"

Merletta nodded vigorously. "Honestly, Sage, if you couldn't see his legs, you'd think he was a merman. He even spoke our language."

Sage frowned. "How is that possible?"

"It's not possible," Merletta said grimly. "Not if everything we've been told about our history is true. I have no idea if *anything* we've been told is true."

"Let's not get carried away with the tide," said Sage. She ran a hand over her braid, in a slightly anxious gesture.

Merletta watched her silently, recognizing in her friend's eyes the same feeling she had wrestled with when she first discovered the Center's lies. It was like being adrift on the currents, with no foundation, and no idea who or what to trust. Her heart went out to the other mermaid, and she knew that Sage wasn't ready for the full extent of Merletta's discoveries. The information that she could, if she chose, ascend onto land and shed her tail in favor of legs, would be too much right now.

One stroke at a time.

"I was sure, even before what happened after my test, that the instructors, Emil, even Ileana, knew that humans are real," Merletta said quietly. "And yet, I distinctly remember Ibsen telling us that there are no intelligent creatures on land other than dragons. He lied to us, Sage, even to his own trainees."

Sage looked troubled. "Well, I suppose it depends on your definition of 'intelligent', doesn't it?"

Merletta gave her a look. "Sage, Heath speaks our language. He's not a sea turtle."

Sage was biting her lip. "I understand why they kept the proximity of land quiet from the general populace," she said. "They must have had reasons for not telling us about humans straight away. And they were never going to keep it from us forever. You heard Instructor Wivell say it. It's covered in third year."

"Not everyone makes it to third year," Merletta pointed out. "Not to mention the rest of the population of the triple kingdoms, who never study in the program. By acknowledging that it's covered in third year, they're actually admitting to their deception. Frankly, I was surprised Wivell said as much, but I suppose he felt it was preferable to letting us think he didn't know something so substantial."

Sage was silent, again looking deeply troubled.

"Don't you see, Sage?" Merletta went on earnestly. "If they're the ones who get to decide what should and shouldn't be hidden from everyone else, then how can we ever be sure they're telling us the truth? Who's to keep them accountable?"

"They're just trying to protect us," argued Sage.

Merletta was silent for a moment. "I wish I could believe that," she whispered. "But there's too much that doesn't add up."

"Why did you stay near the land all this time?" Sage asked suddenly.

Merletta made no attempt to fight the change in direction, understanding that her friend needed time to process it all. "Honestly, I wasn't sure if I could come back. I thought I might have been attacked on sight. The guards all saw me helping Heath to get out of the water. They knew I'd been fraternizing with a human. And Ileana definitely didn't intend for me to survive. She left me for dead on the land."

"Oh Merletta!" Sage's eyes were as round as pearls. "How did you survive? How did you avoid drying out?"

"A story for another day," Merletta said firmly.

"I still don't know what to think," Sage said distractedly. "I never heard so much as a rumor that Ileana was involved in the incident with the human. I thought it was just the regular guard patrol."

"Someone is covering for Ileana," said Merletta, her eyes narrowed thoughtfully. "Or she's covering for someone. Someone must be giving her instructions, telling her what story to spin. There's no way she's the mastermind behind this tale that's been spread about." She frowned. "I bet it's Ibsen."

"Just because he doesn't like you doesn't mean he's behind some conspiracy," said Sage reprovingly. "Besides, if someone was trying to cover up about the land, and the humans, why tell people any of it?"

"I imagine the guards had already spread the word about seeing a human," said Merletta simply. "Once a tale like that is out there...well, you can't put the ink back in the squid, can you? All they could do was spin it in a way they could control."

"And then the guards were all taken sick, so no one could get the full details," Sage said sadly.

"Yes, about this supposed sickness," Merletta pressed, a crease forming between her brows.

But before Sage could answer, the sound of voices carried to them through the dark water. They looked over and saw a trio of merpeople, drifting past in the direction of a nearby public dining house. The Center might technically be an official complex rather than a city, but it still had its own nightlife. Clearly some of the residents who didn't have the restrictions of trainees were starting to seek out entertainment.

"We can talk more tomorrow," Merletta said. She was nervous about someone seeing the two of them hidden away in the garden and guessing that she was telling Sage things neither of them were supposed to know.

It struck her, even as she followed Sage back onto the street, that her current state of anxiety was unsustainable. Incredibly, she had managed to return to the Center, and to her classes, without being attacked or even confronted. But if she was going to be looking over her shoulder, jumping at every change in current, she may as well have stayed on Vazula. She simply couldn't function that way.

The thought had barely flashed through her mind when she saw a shimmer of dull green in her peripheral vision.

She paused. She knew that tail.

Sage turned, noticing the check in Merletta's movement. "What is it?"

"I need to follow something up, before I turn in for the night," Merletta said with determination. "I'll catch up with you."

Sage hesitated. "I thought you were reluctant to be alone."

"I was being dramatic," Merletta said dismissively.

It wasn't dishonest. She undeniably had been dramatic, even if she had reason for her fears. The truth was that after a month of being isolated and friendless on the abandoned island, her nerves had been stretched to breaking point. But the familiarity of being back in the Center, not to mention hours spent in the company of a friend whom she trusted, had done a great deal to restore her usual courage.

Was her life in danger? Very possibly. But sticking to Sage like a barnacle on a whale wouldn't protect her. It would just put Sage in danger. Besides, even if she was right that Sage was too well-connected to be targeted, it wasn't a solution. Merletta was back to stay, if all went well. Sooner or later Ileana would manage to get her on her own, if that was her intention. Better to make it sooner, and keep Sage out of it if possible.

Sage cast her one last uncertain look, then swept past her, brow furrowed. Merletta could only imagine that her friend was glad of some space to think over the evening's startling disclosures.

Merletta gave an intentionally stealthy glance around, then

headed down a different street, moving away from the barracks. She pretended to be focused on her destination, but her senses were on the alert, and she picked up the sound of a tail swishing softly through the water behind her. She slowed her pace slightly, resisting the urge to pull out her spear. She had slid it through the strap of her ever-present satchel, and she could feel it pressed reassuringly against her back.

When she felt the slight shift of the water that heralded an approach, she swirled around, bringing her tail up defensively. Ileana paused only a couple feet away, her eyes narrowed. Merletta noted that the young guard didn't have her own spear out either. For a long moment they stared one another down, neither saying a word. Merletta was determined to give Ileana nothing, but as the silence stretched out, her anger grew, and her self-control fled.

"Didn't expect to see me, did you?" she said, her voice quiet but shaking with suppressed emotion.

Ileana looked like she was also trying to keep herself in hand. "I don't know how you got back to the water," she hissed. "But you should have thanked your lucky tides to be alive, and swum for it. You were a fool to come back here."

"Big words, Ileana," Merletta spat. "But where's the sting? Aren't you brave enough to attack me without a patrol of guards to back you up?"

Ileana made a scoffing noise. "You think you scare me?"

Something in her voice made Merletta pause. She remembered the look on Ileana's face when she'd first caught sight of Merletta earlier that day. She'd been shocked, most definitely. But more than that, she'd been horrified. Perhaps she had even been a little scared.

For a moment, Merletta's anger was subsumed by curiosity. She regarded Ileana thoughtfully in the dull glow of a distant plankton lantern. "You really thought I was going to dry out, didn't you?" she said. The words were addressed to Ileana, but she spoke almost to herself.

"My mistake for not sticking around to make sure," Ileana said. It was hard to see her expression in the darkness, but there was a definite sneer in her voice. "I'll give you credit for being stronger than I thought, to get off the land in time. I'm guessing your human friend didn't help you. He didn't have enough life left in him for that. Who knew they bled red too?"

Merletta started forward, her hand itching for her spear as her anger flared back to life. "He's worth twenty of you!"

Ileana didn't rise to the bait, just regarded her silently. "I wonder, are you a traitor? Or just a fool?"

Merletta narrowed her eyes. "Have you come to finish the job, then?"

Ileana's scowl was clear in her voice. "If I had my way..." she muttered.

Merletta shifted back slightly, locking that information away for later. Ileana wasn't just pursuing her own inclinations where Merletta was concerned. Someone else was most definitely directing her movements. Was she here at that person's behest right now? Or had she been unable to help herself from confronting her old rival?

Merletta's mind raced, trying to grasp all the implications. What if Ileana *was* here under orders, and would carry the tale of their encounter back to someone with more power? Panic briefly clouded Merletta's thoughts. She didn't have enough information—she hadn't yet had a chance to decide how she should play the situation.

One thing seemed clear, however. She'd learned a lot in the last year, and not just about the secret realities of land and humans. She'd learned something of how the Center operated, and she knew that open defiance wasn't going to get her far. At best it would lead to her being blocked from learning anything beyond the bare basics essential for trainees to know. At worst... but she wasn't going to dwell on the worst-case outcome.

"Is it you who's spread this story about Heath being the one who attacked the guards?" she asked abruptly, done with their silent face off.

"Heath?" The sneer was back in Ileana's voice. "The creature had a name?"

But Merletta was thinking strategically now, and she wasn't about to give in to emotions. She felt a flicker of unease at having unguardedly given Ileana Heath's name, but after all, what harm could it do? It wasn't like Ileana was going to pursue him to his land kingdom.

"Why doesn't anyone know that you were there?" she tried again.

"I wasn't there," said Ileana, with a definite note of smugness. "Ask anyone."

Merletta was silent for a moment, thinking this over. If it came down to her word against Ileana's, she had a pretty good idea who would be believed. And she had much more to lose than Ileana if the true extent of both of their involvement was revealed.

"It seems like I wasn't there either," said Merletta carefully. Her eyes narrowed. "Care to explain that?"

Ileana was silent, and Merletta could almost feel the tension flowing out of her, like its own miniature current.

"Is that why you sought me out?" Merletta asked with dry humor. "Are we making some kind of pact of silence?"

"As if I would ever form an agreement with you," spat Ileana. "You'll keep quiet if you know what's good for you. And if you don't..." Her grim expression made the deep water feel even colder than usual. "Well, so much the better, as far as I'm concerned."

And yet, she gave no sign of aggression, issued no concrete

threat. A memory flashed vividly through Merletta's mind, of the time Ileana and Jacobi had cornered her in the training yard. Merletta felt the phantom sensation of the shaft of Ileana's spear pressed against her throat. Whatever Agner had said, it hadn't been a loss of temper in a heated fight. It had been an unprovoked and deliberate attack, and the other mermaid had intended to kill Merletta, she was sure of it. Yet now—even though Ileana knew Merletta had broken some of the triple kingdoms' most sacred rules—all she did was glower darkly at her and utter weak threats. Something had definitely changed since then.

Interesting.

Her heart a little lighter, Merletta cocked her head to the side. It was a very dragon-like posture, if Ileana only knew it. Rekavidur did it all the time.

"Well," Merletta said, her tone light, although she chose her words carefully, "I think I do have a pretty good idea of what's good for me, actually."

Ileana's gaze searched her face, her own expression giving nothing away. After a tense moment, she turned, water swirling around her as she swam away without another word.

Merletta pushed out a long stream of water. Her thoughts and emotions were a veritable maelstrom. She had basically just told Ileana that she wasn't going to spread the true story of what had happened in the shallows near Vazula. She supposed her decision was made, then. She was going to play along, at least for now.

It didn't sit entirely comfortably. She had never liked deception, and she would much prefer to face someone like Ileana in a battle with spears than be tangled in a complex net of politics where her very life might be on the line.

Possibly most interesting of all, though, was Ileana's comments about Merletta getting back to the water. Merletta was almost certain that Ileana had been genuine. She may have already known about the existence of humans, but she truly didn't know that drying out meant changing to a human form. Merletta had the feeling she would be wise not to let anyone know that she held that information. It was far more dramatic a discovery than any of the rest of it. It was a good thing she hadn't blurted it out to Sage. A revelation like that shouldn't be made without careful thought, even to someone she trusted.

She had a great deal to think about, but on the whole, she swam back toward the trainees' barracks feeling like a weight had been lifted. She would still have to proceed very carefully, but she no longer felt like death might be lurking around every corner. If someone wanted to get rid of her before she had the chance to fully reinsert herself into the life of the Center, they couldn't have hoped for a better opportunity than the one she'd just given Ileana. And Ileana hadn't even tried to do her any harm. It seemed Merletta wasn't the only one who'd decided to play along.

Lorraine was already settled in her hammock for the night, but Sage was waiting for Merletta to arrive. Her face lightened at the sight of her friend—clearly something in Merletta's demeanor showed her relief.

The various exertions of the day were finally catching up with Merletta. It was almost unbelievable that she'd woken that morning on a bed of leaves in Vazula's jungle. She sank into her own hammock with an unexpected feeling of homecoming.

Her descent into sleep was interrupted by the sudden memory of the guard patrol who had seen her with Heath. Surely they couldn't really all be dead. She wished she'd confronted Ileana with their fate, and seen how the other mermaid responded.

But she'd been too distracted by other things to think of it. She felt a little guilty that she had prioritized her own problems over the lives of several merpeople. On the other hand, she'd only been back for one day, and she couldn't unravel everything all at once. For now, it was enough to know that she'd re-entered the program without anyone showing signs of wanting to get rid of her.

She closed her eyes, letting everything drift from her mind. Within minutes, she achieved what had seemed impossible a short time before—she sank into a deep and dreamless sleep.

CHAPTER EIGHT

Heath cast a glance behind, at the carriage trundling along at the center of the cavalcade. He winced slightly as it hit a rut in the road. Good thing they had almost arrived. Turning his gaze ahead, he saw that the familiar gray walls of Bryford had indeed come into view. They were home.

A heavy sigh from the rider beside him made him raise an eyebrow. "Something wrong?" he asked dryly.

Percival shot him a look. "Can you honestly tell me you're glad to be back?"

Heath thought about it for a moment. "Yes," he said, a little surprised by his own answer. "I am glad to be home."

The truth was that he'd ridden out of Valoria in the midst of a thick fog of his own making, and he was arriving home with a much clearer head. He cast a glance at Percival's disgruntled expression, and almost sighed himself. A clearer head, but new problems to wrestle.

"We already stayed an extra week in Kynton," Heath reminded him. "We were only supposed to be there a fortnight.

We even missed the annual tournament back home! How long did you want to linger over there?"

"Forever," muttered Percival, although he said it without conviction. He sighed again. "What would have been the point of coming back for the tournament when I'm not allowed to compete anymore? I'd much rather be training with Prince Theodore than watching from the stands while other people fight." He cast Heath a meaningful look. "It was just nice, you know? To be...welcome."

"Welcome?" Heath snorted. "You mean hero-worshiped."

Percival just grinned, and Heath found he was smiling a little himself. He had suspected that his brother's desire to extend the visit might have been related to the tournament taking place back in Bryford. Not that he'd objected. The tournament meant nothing to him, and remembering the tension that had cast a shadow over the previous year's tournament, he'd been inclined to think it might be best for both of them to miss it.

And he couldn't really blame his brother for enjoying the atmosphere of Kynton, where power-wielders were cheered by the common folk everywhere they went, and treated with respect and admiration within the court. Even Heath had been offered the chance to showcase his skills with a bow and arrow. He had politely declined. He'd never shared Percival's love of being the center of attention.

"I'm sure no one will mind that we stayed longer," Percival said comfortably. "Not when Prince Theodore invited us so particularly. Anyway, an extra week was well worth it to be able to escort Grandmother and Grandfather home ourselves."

Heath rolled his eyes. "They've been traveling to and from Kyona every summer for decades without our assistance, Perce. I think they could have managed." He glanced again at the carriage. "But yes, it is nice to travel back with them. Even if

Grandfather says that watching us ride while he's stuck in the carriage makes him feel old," he added with a chuckle.

Percival grinned. "Do you think he'll ever realize that he is old?"

"Probably not," Heath acknowledged.

Percival sent him a sideways glance. "I'm glad to see you more like yourself, anyway. I think Kyona was good for you."

Heath's smile dimmed. He wished he could say the same for Percival.

The city gate loomed ahead, and the guard stationed on top of the wall set up a cry which spread out into the city. Heath knew the call was for the prince and princess in the carriage, not for him and Percival. But it was still a strange feeling to have their arrival heralded in such a way. Heath didn't miss how Percival straightened in the saddle, or his thoughtful expression as he surveyed the crowd who gathered to watch the royal group pass.

There were no welcoming shouts like there had been when they'd rode into Kynton, but Heath saw that there were still plenty of eyes on the pair of them. Percival in particular was the focus of many admiring glances. The commoners of Bryford weren't as open about expressing it as their Kyonan counterparts, but they were clearly also dazzled by the existence of magic in their court. Percival had lost none of his popularity during his absence.

Thanks to the presence of their grandparents, Heath and Percival would never know whether they would have otherwise been greeted by King Matlock himself. But as it happened, both the king and his eldest son welcomed them upon their arrival at the castle. King Matlock was focused on his elderly aunt and uncle, but Prince Lachlan gravitated toward Heath as soon as the general greetings were complete.

"How was your time in Kynton?" Prince Lachlan asked. "I trust King Eamon and Queen Luciana are in good health?"

"They certainly are," said Heath, trying to make his smile reassuring. "We had a very pleasant visit, but I'm glad to be home."

Prince Lachlan's answering smile was almost warm for the reserved royal. "We are glad to see you safely returned to us. And I'm happy to hear that all is well in Kyona."

Heath wasn't sure if it was his power once again coming into effect, or just normal intuition, but he was sure he saw tension in Prince Lachlan's face as the prince's gaze flicked to Percival. It seemed his grandmother wasn't the only one who shared Heath's concern about Percival's exposure to the culture in Kynton. It was very possible that Lachlan, as crown prince, had much better information about the state of King Eamon's court than Heath had, prior to his visit. He may have known what his power-wielding second cousins would experience.

It was, of course, inevitable that the travelers would draw a comparison. Heath could almost feel Percival's despondence at the stilted conversation happening between his brother and their future king. It was so markedly different from the lively camaraderie he'd been sharing with Prince Theodore, who would one day rule Kyona.

"We must send a courier to inform your parents of your arrival," Prince Lachlan was saying. "They returned to their estate soon after your departure, but I understand that they intended to come back to Bryford as soon as you reached us."

"Perhaps we should meet them at Bexley Manor," said Heath quickly. It had been so many weeks since he'd been home, and if he was going to attempt to contact Reka about traveling to Vazula again, it would be ideal to already be at the coast.

Prince Lachlan hesitated. "I believe my father was hoping to meet with you in the next few days, Lord Heath."

"Of course," said Heath quickly, feeling foolish.

He was still getting used to the fact that he had an official role now. Naturally King Matlock would wish to hear a report of his time in Kynton. He would have to think carefully about how best to communicate what he had learned. Perhaps the king could be tactfully encouraged to celebrate his cousins' magic more.

"I was hoping to speak with you as well," Prince Lachlan continued. His eyes once again flicked to Percival, then back to Heath. "My father has given me responsibility to organize our first loyalty ceremony, and I would be grateful for your advice, as the crown's liaison to our power-wielding community."

Heath started, his eyes also flying to his brother. He'd momentarily forgotten about the ceremony. Percival would be twenty-one in a matter of months. On that day, he would be the first to undergo the king's new requirement on power-wielders —a public ceremony at which they would swear their loyalty to the crown, and their intention to use their magic for the good of the kingdom.

In itself, it shouldn't really be controversial. Heath and Percival—and all their power-wielding relations—were, and always had been, loyal to King Matlock. And Heath didn't think any of them would hesitate to use their power to help Valoria. But Heath knew that Percival considered the ceremony to be an insult, implying that they weren't loyal already.

And he had to admit he saw his brother's point. It didn't help that they were perfectly aware that the ceremony had only been instituted in response to pressure from those in the court who disapproved of the power-wielders, and wanted to place limits on the exercise of their magic. And it really didn't help that Percival—who was the most resentful of the restrictions, and whom the crown seemed most concerned about—would be the first to turn twenty-one and have a ceremony.

"Of course," Heath said carefully. "I would be glad to speak further about the ceremony."

Prince Lachlan nodded, giving him a swift smile. "Tomorrow, then?"

Heath agreed to it, his eyes still on his brother. Perhaps by tomorrow their parents would be in Bryford, and Heath wouldn't have to keep such a close eye on Percival. The Duke of Bexley had a way of looking at his sons when they were behaving childishly—with calm bemusement, as though he found their conduct utterly incomprehensible. Heath smiled to himself at the thought. Even the volatile Percival wasn't immune to that look, and Heath didn't think Percival would express his dissatisfaction over the ceremony in any outrageous way once their parents were in the capital.

In the meantime, Heath had a challenge of his own. It was still early in the afternoon, and he and Percival were quickly settled into the city residence their family occupied whenever in Bryford. Percival lost no time in going in search of some of his friends, and without actually confirming it, Heath allowed his brother to believe that he was going to rest, for the sake of his leg.

But as soon as Percival was out of sight, Heath made for the stables where his father kept a few horses for just such situations. The groom was well-trained to serve more exacting noblemen than Heath, and he asked no questions. Within minutes, Heath was riding out of the city, heading northeast, with no specific destination in mind.

Once he had left Bryford behind, he veered off the road onto a series of gently sloping hills. His horse thundered across the turf, glad of the chance for a canter. Heath winced a little—it had been a long few days in the saddle, after all—but he didn't slow the pace. He made for the highest point in the area, pulling the horse to a stop at last when he crested the grassy hill.

He drew a deep breath, trying not to think too hard about what he was going to do. His emotions were still a tangled mess where Rekavidur was concerned, but his grandmother's words had made enough of an impression on him that he knew something had to change.

"Rekavidur," he called, the volume more for his own benefit than Reka's. It wasn't as though his shout could reach the dragon colony on Wyvern Islands by normal means. If his friend's farsight was still trained on Heath, he would respond to his name. If not, then no volume would make a difference.

Heath waited, feeling nervous in a way he never had before when calling for Reka. There was no response, not that he expected one so quickly. Even if Reka was willing to come, it would take time for him to fly from his colony.

"Reka, can we talk?" Heath tried again, for good measure. He focused his thoughts on Reka, wondering if the dragon was really listening. Was he angry at Heath's prolonged coldness? Perhaps it was too late to mend their friendship.

An image of Reka flashed before Heath's eyes, and he stilled. It had been weeks since he'd seen that vast reptilian face, bearded temples, yellow scales tinged with purple, penetrating, orb-like eyes. Reka's head was cocked to one side, as though he was listening intently. In light of his grandmother's speculation about his visions of Merletta, Heath didn't immediately dismiss the picture as his imagination. Now he thought about it, it wasn't even the first time he'd seen Reka's face in his mind's eye, when engaging in a one-sided conversation across a distance like this. It hadn't occurred to him last time that it might be actual sight rather than just his fancy. He leaned forward in the saddle, trying to focus his mind on Reka's face. The image sharpened, and Heath got a sense of Rekavidur's surroundings. The dragon was perched on a rocky crag, gazing out to sea. Was Heath getting a glimpse of Wyvern Islands?

"Reka," Heath said again. "We *need* to talk. I miss you." He could see the lines of Reka's face shift slightly. It probably wouldn't be notable to the average human, but Heath knew Reka well, and he recognized the softening about the dragon's eyes. Reka missed him, too, and the thought sent a pang through Heath's heart. His grandmother was right. He'd been too harsh in his treatment of Reka, not even trying to understand the dragon's actions, seeking blindly for someone to blame.

"I don't like being estranged from you," Heath went on. Honesty compelled him to add, "And I need to get back to Vazula, Reka. I need to know for certain whether she's dead."

At mention of Merletta, the dragon's lids lowered so his eyes were half closed, and Heath's heart sank. Rekavidur was retreating into the cryptic inaccessibility favored by most dragons. What was it about Merletta that made Reka so intractable? He hadn't been like that when they'd first met the mermaid.

"I'll never have peace otherwise," Heath said pleadingly. "Can you understand that?"

In his mind's eye, he saw Reka let out a long breath, the tiniest wisp of smoke curling from his mouth. The dragon didn't speak aloud—he couldn't know that Heath was actually seeing him. But there was sadness in his eyes, and sympathy. Whatever his behavior suggested, his heart wasn't actually hard toward his human friend. Heath just had to figure out how to get Reka to confide in him. Surely they could then find a way to overcome whatever obstacle had arisen.

"If we just check, Reka," he pressed, "then at least we'll know for sure. I'm not asking you to go every week like before. Just to take me one more time."

Reka shook his head sharply, as if flicking off a fly. Then he dove abruptly from the rocks where he was perched, his wings snapping out as he fell, and catching the wind. For a hopeful moment Heath thought the dragon was on his way. But Reka's flight didn't accelerate into the impossibly swift flight of a dragon seeking to cover a substantial distance. He wheeled slowly—sadly, Heath thought—back up and over the top of the rocks, heading further into Wyvern Islands.

The image suddenly cut off, and Heath let out a long, slow breath. Rekavidur wasn't going to come, and he wasn't going to take Heath to Vazula. That much was clear.

With no reason to remain on the hilltop, Heath urged his mount gently down the slope, back toward Bryford. He was frustrated with his friend, but he found that his anger was much less potent than before. It had only needed Heath to stop being so self-absorbed for one conversation for him to see clearly that Reka was carrying a heavy burden of his own. What it was, Heath didn't know, but that it had something to do with Merletta seemed certain.

Still, no amount of sympathy for the dragon changed Heath's predicament. He was so caught up in trying to figure out his next move, that he had almost reached Bryford before the full import of the interaction hit him. He definitely hadn't been imagining Reka's reaction to his call. He'd witnessed it from afar, in something astonishingly similar to Reka's own farsight. Such a thing seemed impossible, but he didn't know how else to explain what he'd seen.

The question of how to convince Reka to take him to Vazula was still occupying his mind when he met with Prince Lachlan the following day. It was with difficulty that he pulled his thoughts to the question of the loyalty ceremony. Prince Lachlan spent the first half hour of their conversation talking about practical details, and Heath struggled to restrain his impatience. He knew why he was really there, and he wished the prince would come to the point.

"Of course," Prince Lachlan said at last, and something in

the tone of his voice alerted Heath to a change in topic, "the ceremony will be most effective if the subject fully comprehends the significance of the gesture."

"True," Heath agreed dryly. "In fact, I would think the ceremony could do more harm than good if the subject doesn't enter into the spirit of it."

Prince Lachlan looked relieved that Heath had not only grasped his true meaning, but articulated what it would be awkward for him to say.

"I have had my concerns," the prince admitted. "And I want to see this ceremony succeed." He held Heath's gaze. "I want to see this whole endeavor succeed. Integrating power-wielders into our society is essential to Valoria's future."

"I agree," Heath said seriously.

Prince Lachlan was silent for a moment. "My father is the king, Lord Heath. And as such he deserves—and has—my absolute loyalty." He drew a breath. "But it's more than that. He's a good man. And he's trying to do what's best for our kingdom, and our people. No one has navigated this particular challenge before." He met Heath's eye. "Not even the Kyonans. Their situation is quite different, you know."

Heath took a moment to respond, feeling a little stunned by this speech. He'd never heard Prince Lachlan speak so plainly before, and he recognized the sign of trust.

"It is different," he agreed at last. "King Eamon doesn't have nearly as complex a situation on his hands. And I have no hesitation in believing that King Matlock wants what's best for us all." He regarded Prince Lachlan seriously. "I believe that you and I want the same thing, Your Highness."

"So do I," said Prince Lachlan, sounding gratified. "Which is why I've specifically requested Father to assign me to work with you, not just on this ceremony, but in general. I hope we can make real progress." To Heath's amazement, he gave a smile that was almost self-conscious. "I may not have magic in my blood, but after all, I'm as much your second cousin as King Eamon's descendants."

"If not more," Heath said staunchly. "There's more to family than just blood, isn't there? And while I may have Kyonan heritage, I'm Valorian, you know."

Prince Lachlan smiled with real warmth. The relaxed gesture made him look his real age for once, which was the same as Heath's.

"And I realize that as the crown's liaison to the power-wielders, it's my role to be aware of any looming disasters," Heath went on. "If I think the ceremony will be just such a disaster, you'll know it before the information is too late to be of any use."

"Thank you," said Prince Lachlan, gathering up the papers he'd spread on the table before him. "That sets my mind at ease, I admit." He gave Heath a straight look. "Please don't be offended by my plain speaking. But I hope you realize what an asset your unusual situation is. As part of the power-wielding line, you have a natural understanding of their perspective. But as someone without, uh, an extravagant type of magic, you are also in a position to understand the emotions of those surrounded by people who have a power they cannot match."

Aloud, Heath said everything that was proper. But on the inside, his heart was sinking. He was flattered by Prince Lachlan's faith in him, and he'd just been celebrating the most open communication he'd ever had with a member of the royal family. Now he felt guilty, as though he was harboring a secret. A few short months ago, Heath had been unsure whether he had magic of any kind. And as little as he'd wanted the job, he'd agreed with Prince Lachlan, that his lack of power had made him the perfect candidate for the role King Matlock had given him.

But now, as soon as that view was actually expressed openly, he was just beginning to discover a power that was not only strong, but totally unique, as far as he knew. And one that seemed to have multiple aspects, each with potentially enormous ramifications. His superior physical eyesight might prove to be the very least of his abilities. The situation was becoming painfully complex.

"I know you wanted to return to your home," Prince Lachlan was continuing. "But I hope you won't mind delaying. You've been away some time in Kyona, and I know Father is eager to receive your report on your time there."

"Of course," said Heath.

"And I would also appreciate further assistance from you," the prince continued. "Some of the members of Father's court have matters they'd like to discuss with you. Then there's the ceremony itself. We need to make some decisions soon regarding who to invite. If, for example, anyone is to attend from Kyona, they will need plenty of notice." He hesitated. "There's also been some discussion regarding whether a representative from the dragons should be invited. Some feel that to omit them would be offensive, while others feel that to *invite* them would be offensive." He gave Heath a rueful look. "You can see why the matter needs some attention."

Heath nodded, trying to hide his lack of enthusiasm. The politics of who to invite to a formal function was exactly the sort of tedious task that had made him reluctant to take on the role.

"However," said Prince Lachlan quickly, perhaps sensing what Heath was politely not saying, "I have mentioned your desire for time at home to my Father. He has agreed to give you leave of absence for a few weeks, in a couple of months' time. That will allow you to return two weeks before the ceremony, which should leave time to finalize any details."

"Thank you," said Heath, thinking he'd better take what he could get, even if it was a while away.

His thoughts were full of the offered leave as he parted from Prince Lachlan. It didn't take him long to decide what he wanted to do with the time, and it wasn't to visit Bexley Manor. He wandered the castle's corridors absently, as a plan began to take shape in his mind. He had intended to try a little harder to convince Reka to take him back to Vazula, and there was nothing stopping him doing that as well. But he shouldn't count on it—who knew how long that might take, or if he'd ever succeed? Dragons were never in a hurry, and Reka was no exception.

He shook his head slowly as his feet took him past the very dining room where he, Percival, and three of their cousins had been informed by King Matlock about the loyalty ceremony.

This wasn't like the previous times, when he'd needed Reka to fly him to Vazula and back within a day. He had weeks of leave coming up, and that was long enough to take action on his own.

He gave a decisive nod. Dragonflight wasn't the only way to reach an island in the middle of the ocean. He was going back to Vazula, one way or another.

If he couldn't convince Reka by the time he was free to go, then he was going to sail there.

CHAPTER NINE

Merletta floated into the dining area with a feeling almost of excitement. It had been surreal to wake in her hammock in the trainees' barracks. She hadn't slept in water for a month, and the familiar weight of it felt cool and comforting. She also realized that she was ravenously hungry. She'd eaten the day before, but she'd been too apprehensive about her return to really appreciate the food.

She intended to rectify that at breakfast. She eyed the basins of oysters, the rings of squid, and the ever-present salted cod eagerly. The fact that it was a training day helped, of course. Bruises notwithstanding, she'd always felt more comfortable in Agner's classes than in either of the other instructors'.

"Ready to spar with me?" she asked Sage brightly, as they took their seats at the round trainees' table.

Sage groaned. "If I have to."

Merletta couldn't help chuckling. "Unless Agner has changed dramatically in the last month, I'm pretty sure you will have to."

"He hasn't," Sage confirmed gloomily.

"I hope I get the chance to spar with you," Andre piped in

eagerly. "Agner often names you as an excellent example of how far hard work and persistence can take you. Doesn't he, Lorraine?"

His fellow first year didn't look enthusiastic about being appealed to, but she responded readily enough. "Yes, he does. He says that you had no skill whatsoever in combat when you started."

"Does he just?" said Merletta ruefully, as Sage snorted on a laugh.

Andre frowned at Lorraine. "He says that you're now quite a good fighter, and have a great deal of potential."

A quiet scoff drew Merletta's attention to Oliver, and she raised a challenging eyebrow. The look he cast her was as disdainful as ever, but he made no comment.

"I can't match Oliver's skill, of course," said Merletta with frigid politeness. "But I hope he'll give me the chance to improve my skills by pitting my spear against his."

"Gladly," said Oliver, the curl of his lips belying his polite tone. Merletta noticed that Lorraine had seated herself beside Oliver, and her body was angled subtly in his direction, as opposed to Andre, who was leaning toward Sage and Merletta.

"Is Lorraine from Hemssted, by any chance?" Merletta asked Sage quietly, as the five of them rose from the table a short time later.

Sage nodded. "Like Oliver."

"And Andre is from Skulssted like you?" Merletta pressed.

Sage gave her a wry smile. "Noticed the allegiances, have you? Yes, you're right. We're supposed to all be members of the Center now, of course, but old loyalties are hard to shake."

"So it seems," mused Merletta.

The politics of the other cities fascinated her. Even after a year in the Center, she was still a stranger to the dynamics between the different groups. Growing up in Tilssted, she had always seen Skulssted and Hemssted as one privileged block. But she had discovered the year before that their disdain for Tilssted was possibly the only thing on which they consistently agreed. They had their own rivalries and cultures. Skulssted was overall the wealthier city, with its showy fashions. But Hemssted had a stronger cultural history, and seemed to be more connected with the Center of Culture. Its residents, such as Oliver and Ileana, would certainly argue that it had the most influence.

"Is there an imbalance in the number of record holders?" Merletta asked Sage curiously. "Are there more from Hemssted than from Skulssted, or vice versa?"

"I think there are a few more from Hemssted, but not by a huge margin," said Sage. "My mother is a record holder, as you know, and she's obviously from Skulssted. But I did hear that Emil is the first Skulssted record holder in a few years."

"How is Emil?" Merletta asked. "Do you see him much, now that he's graduated?" She'd never had the chance to thank him for the report he'd made to Ibsen, which had led to Jacobi being officially reprimanded for his part in a series of dangerous pranks against Merletta the year before. Not that she was at all sure she would thank him, even if given the chance. She had no idea if the reserved former trainee would appreciate her raising the matter openly. He'd certainly never mentioned his decision to her.

"He was well, last I saw him," Sage answered. "I've seen him a few times." Her voice was a little too casual, and she cast a sideways glance at Merletta as she added, "He asked about you every time, wondering whether I'd heard from you during your break."

"Did he?" Merletta asked vaguely. "I wonder why he'd be interested. It's not as though I've ever spent much time with him."

Sage made a noise in her throat, but didn't actually say anything. Perhaps it was because they'd reached the training yard, and Agner was greeting their little group with his usual enthusiasm.

"Ready to hit the current swimming, Merletta?" the instructor asked with a grin.

"Of course," she answered, twirling her spear meaningfully. She had worked very hard to win the right to train with and have permanent custody of her sharpened spear. She still got a thrill out of carrying it with her everywhere. "Always."

Agner chuckled. "Well, we'll do some warm-up exercises, then let's get you straight into a bout with Andre, to start us all off."

Merletta cast an uncertain glance at the new trainee, who was beaming at this announcement. She felt a little bad about being paired with him straight away. She knew better than to hold back in a bout—what would be the point of training if she didn't try her best?—but he was so fresh, and so eager to please. She was a year ahead of him in training, and it would feel mean to wallop him, even with the blunt training poles they would surely be using.

She felt differently ten minutes later, when she found herself shooting backward through the water, winded by a solid blow from Andre's pole.

She straightened, rubbing her stomach ruefully as he gave her a grin that was half-apologetic, half-elated. She was glad that he didn't insult her by apologizing aloud, however.

"My father's a guard in Skulssted," he said cheerfully, flicking his head so his dark hair swirled out of his eyes. "I've been training in combat for a few years already."

"I can tell," said Merletta with a smile. "I have some catching up to do."

Andre was still grinning happily, and Merletta found she

bore him no ill will for outclassing her. There was no malice in his eyes, just the joy of a good fight, and she could relate to that. They finished their bout—in which Merletta most definitely came off worst—then Agner assigned Andre to spar with Oliver.

Merletta's respect for the new first year rose as she watched him skillfully defending Oliver's attack. Oliver triumphed, unsurprisingly. As a third year, he was eighteen years old, and had been training with Agner for over two years now. In fact, he was only a couple of months away from his nineteenth birthday when, if he passed his third year test, he would begin his fourth and final year of training.

Andre took the loss gracefully, his good humor seeming unaffected by the bruise now blooming below his ribs. Merletta regarded him thoughtfully as he drifted back to Sage's side. She had assumed that he looked up to her and Sage because he was as yet unskilled, and wanted friendships with more advanced trainees to give him credibility. But that didn't seem to be the case, at least not in physical training.

That made his friendliness more impressive, and more welcome. But it also made it more confusing. What did he have to gain? Why was he going out of his way to befriend Merletta, instead of keeping his distance and watching to see which way the current flowed, as Lorraine was clearly doing? He'd said his father was a guard. A Skulssted guard, rather than a Center one, but still...Ileana was a guard, and someone had sent guards to kill Merletta the previous year. Could Andre be operating under someone's direction? Was it possible he had some ulterior motive?

Merletta shook the thought off, focusing on the fight taking place between Sage and Lorraine. Sage undersold herself as a fighter. She'd managed to pass the difficult—and mysterious— second year test, and could have become a Center guard if she hadn't wanted to continue to third year. She defeated the first year girl without great difficulty, and she even had a hint of enjoyment in her eyes when Agner directed Merletta to join her. Even Sage wasn't immune to the thrill of a good win.

The two girls were fairly evenly matched, Merletta having a greater aptitude, and Sage more experience. They circled each other slowly, spears at the ready. They were both advanced enough to be trusted not to hurt each other by accident, and they were fighting with their weapons upside down, blunt ends exposed.

Merletta lashed out first, and Sage blocked her quickly.

"Don't be hasty now," Agner coached, watching their bout intently. Usually he would have assigned the rest of the group to other activities by now, but everyone was observing the two mermaids. "Make sure you're in a strong position before you strike. You can't take back a false move."

Merletta fell back, glancing sharply at Agner. Sage took full advantage of her distraction to advance, her spear flashing out with the speed of a striking sea snake. Merletta barely managed to deflect it, rolling in the water and flipping her tail around so that she was on Sage's other side.

"Don't lose focus, Merletta," Agner said warningly. Merletta tried to tune him out, her eyes on Sage again. She propelled herself forward, twisting her spear around and jabbing sharply with the dull end. Sage's deflection was imperfect, and she let out a grunt as the wood grazed along her tail.

Despite Agner's words, Merletta struggled to maintain her usual focus throughout the bout. When they pulled up, several minutes later, she cast another glance at the instructor. It was unusual for him to coach so actively during a bout. He usually saved his comments until afterward. Perhaps Merletta was being fanciful, but once she'd had a suspicion of hidden meaning in his words, it was hard to shake the thought. If he was trying to say something about her situation more generally, he'd now warned her to maintain her fighting edge, to stick close to Sage rather than wandering around on her own, and not to hurry into any confrontation. Was it simply because this was precisely the course she'd decided to take that she was reading into his comments?

Once Agner had put the trainees through every combination, he sent the two third years to complete exercises with the guards, and set a junior guard to drilling Lorraine and Andre. Only Merletta was left, and he turned to her, rubbing his hands together. If he wanted to say something about her situation, this, surely, was his opportunity. But there was no hint on his face that he was thinking of anything beyond her training.

"Now, Merletta," he began, his eyes alight, "you're back for your second year. You know what the focus of this year's test is, of course?"

Merletta nodded. "Guard training."

"That's right. Of course, you will continue to study both history and literacy, but to pass second year, you must successfully complete the guard test. Then you will have achieved your highest ambition, and can discontinue the training program, and join my guards."

Merletta chuckled responsively. "Nice try, sir, but I intend to continue to third year."

Agner sighed. "You all do, but record holders have dull lives compared to guards, you know. Never mind that." His tone had turned brisk. "My point is I'll be working you harder this year. The test is extremely difficult, and it's my job to make sure you're equipped to succeed."

Merletta restrained the groan she wanted to release at the news that he'd be pushing her even harder than the year before. He hadn't exactly taken it easy on her. But then, that was how she'd made so much progress. She'd known nothing whatsoever about combat when she started the program.

"Instructor Ibsen told me that trainees have died undertaking the second year test," she said, trying to sound casual. "But I'm not sure if he was just trying to scare me off."

"No reason both things can't be true," said Agner lightly. "I don't know if he was trying to scare you off, but I do know that trainees have died in the past. The Center takes the physical abilities of their record holders seriously. If you join their ranks, you're expected to be able to defend yourself against attack, and to survive in the harshest of environments if necessary."

Merletta nodded. "I can do it. I know I can."

"That's the spirit," grinned Agner. "I know you can, too. But we have a lot of water to cover before you're ready. And not all of it can be completed within this training yard. You'll be undergoing training by some of my most experienced guards, on their patrols throughout the triple kingdoms, and even outside the barrier."

Merletta raised an eyebrow, and Agner paused.

"Do you have an issue with that?"

"Of course not," said Merletta, trying to keep an innocent expression on her face. "I'm ready to perform whatever tasks are necessary as part of the training."

"Good show," said Agner briskly. "Now, I'm not convinced you haven't lapsed during your time off. I think you should join our first years for some drills before you're ready to train with the older ones."

He nodded dismissal, and Merletta swam over to where Lorraine and Andre were lifting rocks from the ocean floor and carrying them up to drop into large basins suspended from the walls of the training yard.

Agner wasn't entirely wrong that she needed to catch up. It had only taken a couple of short bouts to show that her arms weren't quite as strong as they'd been a month ago. She'd been neglecting them, although she wasn't going to admit that to

Agner. After all, she thought dryly, she couldn't exactly explain that she'd been too busy focusing on building strength in her legs.

The two days of training passed in a painful, but not entirely unpleasant blur. Merletta had always enjoyed the release of physical training, and Agner's cheerful but unrelenting attitude always spurred her on to great results. It all felt so familiar, she could almost forget that everything had changed. It was like being back in first year, but better, because Ileana and Jacobi were no longer there to throw her dirty looks, and sabotage her when her back was turned.

Of course, Ileana wasn't far away. Merletta saw her on both days, training with the guards first thing in the morning. But neither approached the other, and to Merletta's relief, Ileana didn't hang around long, departing each morning with a guard patrol. Having decided that it was unsustainable to live her life wondering at every moment whether the spear was about to strike, Merletta tried to put Ileana from her mind. For the most part, she succeeded.

Other times, she lay awake in her hammock, looking at the place where Ileana had once slept, and wondering what the older girl was thinking, and whether she'd reported their conversation to anyone.

If so, Merletta would have given her most treasured possession to know who.

CHAPTER TEN

On rest day, Merletta was sorely tempted to travel to Vazula, as she'd always done on rest days the year before. There was no Heath to meet there now, of course. But she had training of her own to think about, beyond her classes. And she couldn't complete that training in the underwater world. She was itching to practice her walking, and make sure her legs still worked as they should.

But when Sage asked her brightly if she wanted to complete Ibsen's task together, Merletta concluded with reluctance that leaving the triple kingdoms was too risky. The extra patrols at the kelp forest now made sense, given the supposed incident of guards being attacked by a human outside the barrier. She could probably get past them without too much difficulty—in theory, at least, they were focused on keeping creatures out, not keeping merpeople in—but for all she knew, she was being watched. Better to wait until she had settled in a little more, and demonstrated to whoever might be paying attention that she wasn't planning to reveal anything she shouldn't.

So she joined Sage for breakfast, discussing where they would go to find a suitable marketplace where they could observe as instructed. They were just rising from their seats when Andre swam in, hurrying to join them.

"Were you leaving already?" he asked, seeming crestfallen. "I should have gotten up earlier."

"We're heading off on Ibsen's task," Sage explained, in her usual kind way.

Andre brightened immediately. "Can I join you?" he asked, swiping a large chunk of fish from the table. "I hadn't decided where to go yet."

Sage sent Merletta a slightly exasperated glance, and Merletta gave a half shrug. She would have preferred the time with Sage, but Andre's presence might have other benefits. Busy as she'd been, she hadn't entirely forgotten the missing guard patrol. She remembered Andre saying that his father was a guard. Perhaps he would have useful information.

"Of course you can," she said smoothly. She glanced at his arm. "But I think we should remove our armbands. Three trainees together will be too conspicuous. We can't make accurate observations if our presence changes what we're observing."

Andre tilted his head slightly to the side. "Good point," he said enthusiastically. "I hadn't thought of that."

He glanced down at Merletta's spear. She knew most trainees didn't carry their weapons with them to meals, but she didn't like to be without it.

"You'd better leave that too, then."

Merletta frowned, but Sage chuckled at her. "He's right, you know. If you don't want to be conspicuous, you can't go swimming around with a valuable driftwood spear."

Merletta's frown deepened, although it wasn't because she disagreed. It was just the fresh reminder of the lies they'd all been fed. Driftwood was only valuable because everyone thought wood was a rare substance originating from somewhere deep in the ocean. In actual fact, wood grew freely on land, and there was plenty of it. Heath had called the plants trees. Merletta had no doubt that land was the true origin of the driftwood she held in her hand.

In the end, they decided to go to Hemssted. The others wanted to go to Tilssted, since it was a novel experience for them, but Merletta wouldn't agree. She was concerned that Sage would want to meet Tish. The trouble was, if they went to Tish's shellsmith tower, it would be obvious to Andre that instead of spending her whole break with Tish, Merletta hadn't seen her friend in a month. She would have been happy to go to Skulssted, but that was uninteresting for the other two, which only left one city.

"So your father is a guard, Andre," Merletta said conversationally, as they drifted through Hemssted in search of a marketplace.

"That's right," said Andre cheerfully.

"Are you nervous about him doing boundary patrols?" Merletta asked delicately. "I heard the story about the guards who ran into trouble outside the boundary."

"Didn't we all?" said Andre heavily. He blew out a gush of water. "I wouldn't exactly say I'm worried. My father can look after himself, and he's not one to take foolish risks. But it's certainly been a shock for us all." He glanced over at her sadly. "A good friend of his was one of the guards on that patrol."

Merletta met his look, startled. Her heart beat uncomfortably quickly at the sorrow in his eyes. She almost said, *which one?* but stopped herself in time. "Tell me about this friend. What did he look like?"

The question was still a little strange, and Andre raised an eyebrow. "He was my father's age. They trained together. Dark hair, silvery-blue tail." He shrugged. "He was quite senior, it was his patrol. His name was August."

Merletta's heart sank. She could picture the merman in question, the one who'd seemed to be leading the patrol. He hadn't attacked her, had told the others there was no need to shed blood. She even remembered him saying, in disbelief, that Heath couldn't be a human, because humans were a myth. Whatever his story, he hadn't been part of the deception that had hidden humans from the general population.

"I'm sorry," she said, the words carrying a little too much emotion for an impersonal apology. "Are...are they really all dead? What happened to them? I still don't understand how..."

She trailed off, and Andre swished his tail slowly from side to side as he swam.

"I didn't even know about land sickness," he admitted, "and my father goes outside the barrier on patrols all the time. But then, why would I know? He might go past the barrier, but it's not like he swims around at the surface looking for land. No one has been anywhere near land in living memory, before this."

Merletta didn't miss the glance Sage threw at her, but she kept her eyes on Andre.

"You know how it's dangerous to spend too much time at the surface?" Andre continued, the question directed at Merletta.

She was silent for a moment. This was one of the most maddening lies, and she didn't want to even pretend to agree. "I've been told that, yes," she said at last, when Andre continued to watch her expectantly.

"Well, it's not just the risk of dragons, or of drying out, that makes it dangerous," Andre said. "The air up there isn't good for our brains, apparently. Especially near the land."

How convenient, thought Merletta. "Why especially near land?" she asked aloud.

Andre frowned. "Not sure, exactly. Something about the plants that grow on land emitting some kind of unhealthy substance into the air."

"Then how do the humans survive up there?" Merletta asked dryly.

Andre gave her another strange look. "I suppose it's not bad for them," he said. "Just for us. It seems the guards spent too long with their heads above water, near the land. The air got to them, and they all fell sick not long after they got back home."

"What kind of sick?" Merletta asked, eyes narrowed.

"It addles the mind," Andre said sadly. "They started behaving strangely, from what I heard. Saying and doing bizarre things. Then they became violently ill, quite suddenly, and died."

There was a horrible churning in Merletta's gut. She had never heard such a suspicious description in her life. Her fear was now becoming almost a certainty—that those poor guards had been killed because of what they'd seen. Because of what she had showed them. The horror of that thought made her vision spin for a moment, and she passed a hand across her eyes.

It was clear that Andre had no suspicions regarding the guards' deaths, however. His voice had dropped so low that Merletta had to lean close to hear him in the bustle of a Hemssted street.

"August was the first to go. Father never even got to say good-bye." He squared his shoulders. "But at least he knew what happened to him, and that it was quick in the end. Not like that poor thief who the human got."

"*Thief?*" Merletta repeated sharply.

Andre threw her a surprised look. "Didn't you hear that part? The guards were chasing a thief who got caught stealing from the kelp farms, and made a swim for it outside the barrier. That's how they ended up where they were. The thief got more punishment than she deserved, though. The human got her, and she never made it back."

Merletta's eyes were narrowed as they passed from Andre's face to Sage's. Her friend's mouth fell open as she put the pieces together, and Merletta shook her head grimly. So that was how her role in the incident had been spun, was it? And any inconsistencies were explained away as the garbled nonsense of someone dying from land sickness.

"That looks like one," Andre said suddenly, pointing to a bustling square up ahead. Merletta and Sage followed the direction of his finger, and saw what was unmistakably a market. Merletta pulled her thoughts in line with an effort. She'd been so engrossed in the conversation, she'd forgotten all about their task.

"What is it we're supposed to actually do?" Sage asked.

"Observe," Merletta reminded her.

"What's the point of that?" Andre asked.

Merletta almost rolled her eyes. "You can learn a lot from watching people," she said. "Often a lot more than you'll learn from talking to them openly. Judging by Wivell's instructions, I imagine that Ibsen wants us to hear what people are saying about the incident with Hea—the human."

If Andre noticed her slip up, he gave no sign of it. They cruised around the edge of the market together, looking for a good place to settle. Hemssted was a pleasant city, Merletta noted. Neither the attire of the merpeople, nor the decorations on the buildings, were as elaborate as they tended to be in Skulssted. But, in her private opinion, the whole effect was more tasteful. No one had live starfish adorning their hair, or lavish strings of pearls wrapped around their arms. Instead, she saw mermaids with single pearls glistening on their earlobes, and mermen with their long hair woven through conical shells.

Andre generously bought them all fresh mussels, and they settled by a large rock sculpture which formed the centerpiece of the market square. Merpeople floated past in a constant stream, their conversation leaping toward the trio in catches. It took very little time for Merletta to see why Ibsen had set them such a task. The incident with the patrol was clearly still the main topic of conversation, and it was exercising powerfully on the merpeople's fear. They had all been told, from earliest memory, that the surface was dangerous, and the land doubly so. Now, that vague fear had solidified and taken form right in their midst, and all the frightening bedtime stories were coming to life.

She heard people talking about moving to dwellings closer toward the Center and away from the barrier. She heard fears expressed regarding friends or family members who were guards and therefore had to complete patrols. She even heard one mermaid declaring to her companion that she wasn't going to visit the oyster farms anymore, because the towers, with their clumps of oysters, ascended almost to the surface.

Merletta was fairly sure she knew what kind of answer Ibsen was looking for.

Sure enough, when she sat in Ibsen's class the following morning, she heard Oliver deliver the desired reply with beautiful simplicity.

"Panic," he said calmly. "It's been weeks, and people are still terrified. There's nothing they can really do to protect themselves, other than staying inside the barrier. But that doesn't stop them from coming up with absurd ideas for how to keep themselves safe. Some of the ideas are dangerous in themselves. "They were happier—and in fact safer—when they knew nothing of the humans, or the proximity of land."

"Excellent point, Oliver," said Ibsen approvingly, just as if it wasn't his own point that he'd made them all spend their rest day confirming. "Who else?"

His eyes skated over Merletta—he never gave her the opportunity to make herself heard in class, if he could help it—and settled on Andre.

"Where did you observe?"

"A marketplace in Hemssted, Instructor," said Andre.

"And did your reflections tally with Oliver's?"

"They did," Andre confirmed, nodding. Ibsen was already looking past him, but Andre continued. "But I was surprised by something."

"What was that?" asked Ibsen, with far more tolerance than he'd ever shown Merletta's interjections.

"Well, people were talking like they were afraid," said Andre. "But they weren't actually acting differently. I mean, life is going on much like before, isn't it? No one's actually in such a panic that things are falling apart."

"It's reassuring to know that the population of Hemssted has faith in their leaders to protect them," said Ibsen, as if closing the topic.

"Maybe that was it," Andre mused. "Or maybe the average merperson is capable of more understanding than we think. Maybe they could be trusted to make safe choices if they were more adequately informed."

Merletta looked at Andre with increasing approval. She would have liked to applaud him, but she was still pursuing her strategy of playing along with those in charge, so she held her peace.

"You are young, Andre," said the instructor, with indulgent disdain. "You have a great deal to learn. If you really think no one's safety is at stake, I suggest you speak with the families of the guards who died because they strayed too close to land."

Andre's eager expression dimmed, and he subsided. Merletta's eyes were on Ibsen, her expression thoughtful. It wasn't surprising that Ibsen failed to take Andre's very reasonable comment seriously. It wasn't even surprising that he'd been so insensitive as to play on Andre's grief about the dead guards.

What was surprising was the mildness of Ibsen's reaction. She couldn't help but compare this treatment with what she had received as a first year. Ibsen had always been offended to the point of fury when she expressed a view that was contrary to the official position. Even Wivell, while much more detached in manner, had always been absolute in rejecting any suggestion she made. Could it really just be prejudice against Tilssted that caused these overreactions?

"I suppose you used your observation time in Tilssted, did you?"

Ibsen's question took Merletta by surprise. He hadn't even greeted her at the start of the class, as if he wasn't quite ready to admit the unpleasant reality that she'd returned from her break.

"No, I was in Hemssted as well," she said lightly.

"But you spent your break in Tilssted, I assume?"

Merletta hesitated for only the briefest moment. "Yes, sir. With a friend from the home where I grew up."

She couldn't help but remember her optimism when she'd first started at the Center, that she didn't need to lie to her instructors. She'd even thought she could keep her excursions outside the barrier a secret without lying, if she was just careful with her words. The thought made her sad. Tish had already thought her cynical back then, but that version of herself had been blissfully naive compared to how she felt now.

Ibsen's eyes narrowed slightly, but he said nothing as he turned away to continue the lesson. Merletta hoped fervently that he wouldn't follow up on her story. It wouldn't be difficult to discover that Tish was her only notable friend from the charity home, and she didn't like the idea of Tish being questioned about Merletta's activities.

She would have to visit her soon to warn her that she'd

claimed to have spent a month in her company. What story should she tell Tish for why she'd told everyone that? How much did she dare to confide in her friend, who was more vulnerable even than Merletta?

"Instructor Agner said that we'll be called on to accompany a patrol to Tilssted next time there's a boundary dispute." Lorraine's voice cut across Merletta's thoughts. "Do we really have to go there? I thought it wasn't safe."

Merletta raised an eyebrow at the first year girl, and even Ibsen seemed unimpressed by her attitude.

"If you wish to succeed in the program, Lorraine, you cannot always avoid danger. The majority of the boundary disputes are taking place in Tilssted, so naturally you will need to spend some time there."

Merletta's forehead was creased in confusion by the end of his speech. She opened her mouth to ask what boundary disputes he was talking about, but closed it again, hampered by her own deception. Having just claimed that she'd spent the last month in Tilssted, she would be foolish to admit that she had no idea what was happening in the city.

She would have to ask Sage later. But her heart had grown heavy. If there were disputes involving boundaries, she knew who would lose out. It was always the same—those who most needed the help were least able to assert their rights. Visiting Tish had just become a priority.

And so had something else. Ibsen's suggestion to Andre— although it had clearly not been sincere—had given her an idea. A horrible, stomach-clenching mix of guilt and anger swept over her every time she thought of the lost guard patrol. She couldn't just forget about their fate, or about her role in it. She didn't believe the story of land sickness for a moment, and she was determined to find out what had really happened to them.

Not only did she need the answers for her own sake, but their families deserved that much.

She didn't actually intend to approach the families, of course. But as her eyes rested on Andre, she thought she might have another way of beginning her investigations.

CHAPTER ELEVEN

In a surprisingly short time, Merletta found that she had settled into the familiar weekly rhythm of the training program. The first three days were a mix of literacy and history classes, depending on the instructors' availability, and the topics to be covered by the trainees across the three different years. Soon to be four years, assuming Oliver passed his upcoming test and progressed to fourth year. The last two days of the week were training with Agner and the guards.

Merletta's memory journey—her mental recreation of the familiar stretch of water between the kelp farms north of Tilssted and the island of Vazula, with facts she'd learned figuratively stored at familiar points along the way—was becoming steadily more crowded with information. She might need to consider including the more familiar parts of the island's jungle. She was pleased to find that the repetition exercises she'd done on her own on the island during her break had been sufficient to keep the bulk of her first year learning straight in her mind. Of course, it helped that she'd been able to literally walk some of the memory journey while recalling the information stored there.

The main difference to Merletta's schedule as compared with the year before was that she no longer left the triple kingdoms during every rest day. Before many weeks had passed, she was itching to get back to Vazula, and not just to practice again with her legs. In her month on the island, she'd grown accustomed to the feeling of air on her face, and even before she'd discovered Vazula, she'd always made regular trips to the surface. Now, with a few uninterrupted months in the deep ocean, she felt suffocated by the constant heaviness of the water. She longed for sunlight and warmth, and for the freedom to explore her discoveries away from suspicious eyes.

But those suspicious eyes were the very reason she hadn't yet ventured back to Vazula. There had been no sign of aggression from anyone, but she still knew she had to tread water carefully. Also, she'd almost forgotten how hard she had to work to keep up when two of her three instructors made very little effort to actually teach her. At least the year before she'd had a classmate in Jacobi, ensuring that the first year material was adequately covered. But now she was the only one studying her year, and the instructors gave her significantly less time than the first years or the third years. She spent many of her rest days in the public records room, or badgering the ever-patient Sage to fill in gaps left by the instructors' prejudiced teaching. She hadn't even managed to visit Tish yet.

Agner, of course, worked her at least as hard as the other trainees. She'd never actually calculated it, but it felt like he spent half the training time drilling her, leaving the first years to do exercises with new guard recruits, and the third years to undertake more advanced training with experienced patrols. She was often sore, but she was improving steadily, and thought she would soon have a chance of beating Andre. Oliver, sadly, was still out of her reach.

The debrief of Ibsen's marketplace assignment in her very

first week back didn't exactly get her excited for her second year of studies. But in one of Wivell's classes the following week, she received a pleasant surprise. When the instructor swam into the room in his usual unhurried fashion, a familiar pale-haired figure followed him in with a flash of vibrant green scales.

Merletta heard a small noise of surprise from Sage beside her, but she kept her gaze on Emil, sending him a hesitant smile. The former trainee—now a junior record holder—had always been a little aloof, but Merletta had reason to think that he'd been a friend to her in a background kind of way on more than one occasion.

Emil met her look, and though it would be too much to say he smiled, his expression was pleasant enough as he nodded in greeting. She saw his eyes pass to Sage. They lingered there a little longer than they had on Merletta, his expression just as inscrutable.

"I believe you all know Emil, one of our junior record holders," Wivell said.

Merletta glanced at the other students. Oliver had nodded in greeting, and Lorraine dipped her head respectfully as well. Andre, however, was almost bouncing in his seat with excitement at the presence of the latest Skulssted trainee to achieve record holder status. Merletta hid a smile. Clearly, she and Sage weren't the only ones Andre admired. His enthusiasm was endearing.

"Emil is here to work with Merletta," Wivell said, drawing her attention instantly back to him.

"Me?" she said, her eyes flying to Emil's in surprise. He inclined his head again.

"You are our only second year trainee," Wivell reminded her unnecessarily. "Although your testing this year will focus on guard training, there are other skills you will be expected to master. One of those is the shorthand used by our scribes and record holders."

Merletta straightened in her seat, brightening at the prospect of learning a new skill. She knew that space was a precious commodity in light of the perishable nature of underwater records, and it made sense that those who kept the records would have developed some form of shorthand.

"This training is usually undertaken by a junior record holder. Emil is, of course, proficient in the use of shorthand, and he volunteered to assist me."

Merletta looked at Emil's calm face with interest. He'd volunteered? That had been kind of him. He must have known she would be the only second year trainee. Her heart lifted. She would much rather study with Emil than with Instructor Wivell. Or with another record holder, like the one who often barked at her when she left anything out of place in the records room, or the one who'd administered her entrance tests with such reluctance.

The rest of the group soon had their different tasks, and Merletta waved to Sage as she drifted out of the room with Oliver, heading for the records room for advanced training in records maintenance. If they passed third year, they would qualify as educators, and would need to have a high level of skill with handling records. Merletta thought Sage looked regretful as she cast a glance over her shoulder. No doubt she would also have enjoyed a lesson with the familiar face of their old fellow trainee.

The two first years moved forward to listen to Wivell's continued explanation of the work of the scribes, and Emil gestured for Merletta to follow him to a small adjoining room. When they were alone, he pulled several blank writing leaves out of his satchel, along with two sharpened coral writing implements. The leaves were treated by the scribes with a solution that made them last longer than they otherwise would, although still not nearly as long as above-water records.

"The shorthand seems complicated at first," Emil started calmly, without preamble, "but it's quite straightforward once you understand it. You're a quick learner. I imagine you'll pick it up without difficulty."

"Thank you," said Merletta, a little taken aback by his casual praise. "It's good to see you again," she added. "I hope you're enjoying your role as a record holder?"

"It's illuminating," said Emil, and he didn't seem inclined to elaborate.

They dove straight into their topic, and Merletta was soon fully focused on her task. It took her by surprise, therefore, when Emil spoke abruptly, half an hour later.

"I'm glad to see you back from your break. When no one had heard from you, I was concerned you might not be coming back."

Merletta lowered her stick of coral, looking at him warily. Did he mean he was worried she was never coming back, as in, deceased? Or just that she was discontinuing the program? He was a record holder now, a member of the Center's elite, albeit a junior one. How much did he know? Was he aware that the guards' story wasn't entirely accurate? Could he know of her involvement?

"I considered not coming back," she said carefully. "But I think I knew deep down that was never an option for me. I don't swim from my problems."

"I'm glad," said Emil, with a nod. "Your talents would be wasted if you did so."

Merletta smiled. "It was thoughtful of you to think of me during my break," she said. "Sage told me you asked after me."

"She did?" Emil looked a little startled, and Merletta raised an eyebrow. He almost seemed discomposed, something she had never before witnessed.

"Yes," Merletta confirmed. "*Didn't* you ask her?"

"I did," said Emil after a moment's pause. "Our families live in the same part of Skulssted," he added, as if he needed an explanation. "It's not unusual for us to run into one another, even now I've graduated from the program."

"Well, it's nice to keep up with fellow trainees," Merletta said cheerfully. "Sage will be a record holder in a couple of years, after all. She's plenty capable."

"She is," Emil agreed. "And she'll be an asset to the record holders."

Merletta nodded absently, her attention already returning to the shorthand. It wasn't until Wivell floated in to check on their progress twenty minutes later that she realized she hadn't heard Emil's coral resume its scratching.

With Emil's coaching and Agner's training, Merletta thought she would have been enjoying second year more than first year —if it wasn't for two things. The first was that she was barred from Vazula, and missing Heath. She still held out hope of his survival, but she thought the chances of her ever finding out for certain grew less with every passing week.

Tired as she was from her training, she still lay awake many nights, her hammock drifting gently to and fro as she thought about the human, and remembered that stormy day. She tried not to dwell on the attack, remembering instead the many happier times they'd spent on Vazula. But even those memories made emotion rise within her. She would suddenly call to mind a common gesture of his, or the way his face would set in concentration when he was describing his far away home. It was the same look he got when he was focusing his keen eyes on something at a great distance. These mundane memories sent pangs through her that were so sharp she would squeeze one hand fiercely in the other to stop tears from coming.

And always, try as she might to avoid thinking about it, she would always come back to that awful day. The passing weeks hadn't made the memory any less vivid. She could still hear the waves lashing against the shore, still see the gaping wound in his side. Still feel the phantom pressure of his hand on her cheek, and hear his voice.

I don't want you to die.

She didn't think anyone had ever cared as much about what happened to her as Heath had in that moment. It was an exhilarating feeling, and for all she knew, she might never experience it again.

But her tangle of emotions regarding Heath was only one of the two things keeping her awake. Memories of that day always brought her back to the guard patrol, and the terrible fate she'd brought on them by directing them toward the island. That, more than anything, made her unable to forget that everything had changed since first year, and it was always with her. At least during the day, when she was busy, she could push Heath to the back of her mind. It was when she was alone in the darkness that he returned to haunt her.

The guards, on the other hand, seemed to be everywhere. Talk had died down a little, but she still heard the group mentioned in passing almost every day. At first she'd felt an acute surge of guilt every time she heard it. But now it had settled into an almost constant discomfort, almost like a slight nausea. She was sure it wouldn't fully go away until she discovered what had really happened to them.

In spite of the matter being constantly in her thoughts, it was a few weeks before Merletta found both the opportunity and the courage to pursue her idea with Andre. She'd become used to his presence, since he seemed to prefer the company of her and Sage over that of Oliver and Lorraine. But it was unusual for the two of them to be alone. So when she found herself in the records hall with him one afternoon, while Sage was undertaking training with the junior record holders, she seized her opportunity.

"Andre, I've been thinking about your father's friend. The one who died."

"August?" Andre said, his tone heavy. "Yeah, I think about him a lot, too."

"How's your father doing?" Merletta asked delicately.

Andre shrugged. "Life goes on. He doesn't say it, but I can tell he's still pretty distressed by it all."

"Do you think...do you think he would talk to me about it?"

Andre had been looking down at the writing leaf he was studying, but at her words his eyes flew to hers, startled. "My father? You want to talk to him about August?"

"Well...yes. But only if he'd be comfortable," Merletta added quickly.

"I don't think he'd mind," said Andre. He gave her a lopsided smile. "He'd probably be interested to meet you. He's curious about you. He said..." He trailed off, his tone becoming rueful. "Actually, maybe he wouldn't thank me for repeating it."

"It's all right," said Merletta, a smile on her own face. "I have skin as thick as a whale shark's by now."

"Well, it's just that he's done a lot of patrols around Tilssted," Andre said apologetically. "Especially around the outer rim of it, which is, you know..."

"The roughest part of the triple kingdoms," Merletta supplied. "Don't worry, I have no illusions about the neighborhood I grew up in."

Andre nodded. "So he's seen some pretty appalling conditions and, if I'm honest, some pretty appalling behavior. He said that he would never have believed that someone from that part of Tilssted could make it to the second year of the training program. He thinks you must be exceptional to have succeeded with such a disadvantage."

Merletta was silent for a moment, taking Andre's words in. It wasn't the first time she'd heard such a comment. It was an odd feeling, to have someone she'd never met, someone more senior, experienced, and influential than her, assessing her as exceptional. She'd been proud of herself when she made it into the program against all opposition, but she hadn't imagined how notable her achievement would be in the triple kingdoms more widely.

"Well," she said at last, "hopefully he doesn't just find me exceptionally rude after I bring up the topic of his dead friend."

She'd expected that Andre might organize for her to speak to his father on an upcoming rest day. It didn't occur to her that the middle-aged guard might approach her in front of the other trainees. She was therefore thrown when he swam up to her in the dining hall over lunch the following week.

"Trainee Merletta?" he asked, his tone crisp.

She rose from her seat, greeting him with what poise she could. She had no need to ask who he was. His resemblance to Andre was striking, down to the crimson tail.

"I understand from Andre that you wanted to know about August, and the other guards who died from land sickness." The guard's eyes flicked to his son, sitting next to Sage, then back to Merletta. "I had business in the Center this morning, so I thought I'd take the opportunity to come by."

Merletta swallowed, trying to keep the panic off her face. She could see Oliver watching her with narrowed eyes, and even Lorraine had let her impassive mask slip. Merletta hadn't asked Andre to keep her request quiet—that would surely have made him suspicious. But she hadn't banked on her inquiries becoming quite so public. The merman wasn't speaking especially loudly, but it was inevitable that at least the other trainees would hear everything.

"I, uh...yes, sir," she said. "I'm just trying to better understand the ailment. I'd never heard of it before."

"Neither had I," said Andre's father frankly. "And I've been a guard for over twenty years. It is extremely rare that any of us are exposed to it." He assessed her with his gaze. "Second year, aren't you? Preparing for the guard test shortly? Very understandable that you'd want more information about the risks."

"Can you tell me what the symptoms were?" Merletta asked quickly, not correcting his assumption about why she was interested. "And how long after their return from the surface the land sickness kicked in? We've learned about it in class, but it's not the same as an eye-witness account. I understand from Andre that you...that you saw your friend, while he was unwell."

The older merman nodded calmly, showing no sign of any pain he felt on discussing his friend's death. "I spoke with him in the early stages. He'd begun to experience delusions. Thought I was a shark at one point, and rushed at me with his spear. Well, he thought it was his spear, but fortunately for me it was actually just a strand of seaweed from his curtains." He shook his head. "One of my oldest friends, and he didn't recognize me."

"How long after he came back was this?" Merletta asked.

Andre's father considered. "A day, perhaps a day and a half."

Merletta couldn't help raising an eyebrow. "Surprisingly long delay, isn't it?"

The guard shrugged. "There are many substances that build up in the body over time. I suspect the ailment was already at work, but it took that long to build to such a dramatic level."

"And then he was violently ill?" Merletta asked.

"So I've been told," said Andre's father. "I didn't see him in that stage. I went to report his condition to my superior, and the next thing I heard he was gone. It was very sudden. I didn't even get to see his body, because there was some concern that the illness might be contagious. We held a funeral, of course, but without his body."

Merletta's mind churned, contemplating all the possible implications of this detail. Would it have been obvious from the bodies that the guards didn't die from an illness?

"How did you know he was dead, then?" she asked, forgetting to be sensitive in her distraction.

"August's superior told me," said Andre's father simply. "We all received official notice of their passing."

"Who's that?" Merletta asked.

The guard raised an eyebrow. "August's superior? August was an experienced patrol leader. He reported directly to Skulssted's head guard."

Merletta frowned to herself. Skulssted's head guard definitely sounded like a senior enough position that he might conceivably be trusted with secrets that Andre's father wouldn't have. But would he really sacrifice the lives of several of his own guards for those secrets? Either way, she would have to paddle very carefully if she decided to approach him for more information.

She thanked both Andre and his father, but her heart was heavy as the older merman swam away. She was uneasily aware of the other trainees' curiosity. Even Sage looked taken aback—Merletta hadn't told her about her conversation with Andre. She hadn't wanted to involve Sage in her investigations, for her friend's safety. She gave Sage an apologetic look that promised an explanation later, and returned to her breakfast.

But she was so abstracted she barely noticed what she ate. She wasn't any closer to knowing what had actually happened, but she at least knew that the story wasn't completely a lie. The guards really had experienced some kind of hallucination. She didn't doubt Andre's father's account, and he'd known August well enough to recognize that the other guard's behavior was delusional.

But she had very good reason to know that the hallucinations couldn't have been caused by proximity to land. And she'd never heard of such an ailment before. The question was, what caused it? And, assuming someone had been trying to get rid of the guards, how did they expose all of them to it, and no one else?

The matter occupied her thoughts for the rest of the meal. But not so much that she failed to feel Oliver's shrewd gaze boring into her.

CHAPTER TWELVE

"I'm going to regret coming with you, aren't I?" There was a rueful note in Bianca's voice as she gazed out at the ocean, her expression long-suffering.

"Of course not," Heath said innocently, turning to his cousin. "Why would you regret it?"

"Because you're definitely up to something," Brody's voice cut in.

Heath turned to see Bianca's twin strolling across the deck to them, his gait uneven as they rolled over the swells.

"I'm offended, Brody," said Heath cheerfully. "I don't know why you'd think that."

"Yes, you do," said Brody, unimpressed. "For one thing, if you weren't doing something you shouldn't be, you wouldn't have given Percival the slip."

Heath rolled his eyes, leaning on the railing as the wind caught at the sail ahead of him, sending the canvas billowing out, and propelling the ship eastward.

"I'm not answerable to Percival," he said. "Besides, there was nothing stopping him from coming to Bexley Manor with us. He prefers to be in Bryford, where the action is. You know that."

Brody gave him a look. "Something tells me he would have joined us if he'd known that you intended to charter a ship and sail into the sunrise instead of spending a week resting your injuries at the manor, like you claimed."

"I never said that," Heath cut in quickly.

"You allowed everyone to assume it, though," Bianca interjected. "You know you did."

Heath just grunted. "Percival wasn't exactly itching to come with me, Bianca. You're wrong if you think I made a show of hiding my plans. Percival stopped hovering over me a couple months ago, and he certainly didn't ask what I planned to do on my trip home."

Bianca frowned slightly. She had clearly also noticed Percival's descent from solicitous older brother into surly bear as the date of his loyalty ceremony drew closer. Percival hadn't done anything outrageous. He'd just complained a lot, and in all honesty, Heath had been counting down the days to his leave just to get a break from it.

Plus his grandmother had proven right. Heath would know no peace until he knew Merletta's fate for certain. In the weeks that had passed since their conversation in Kynton, the tension of the unanswered question had grown to such a fever pitch inside him, he could barely sit still for more than five minutes at a time.

"Forget Percival, then," Bianca said, drawing his attention back to her. "I'm sure your parents wouldn't have been so relaxed about staying behind in Bryford if they'd known you intended to set off on a mystery voyage."

"Probably not," Heath acknowledged. "But I am nineteen years old, you know. I don't actually need my parents' permission to travel where I please during my leave of absence from my duties." He saw that Bianca looked unconvinced, so he added, "It's been months, Bianca. My injuries are well and truly healed now, honestly. There's no need for anyone to be concerned about me."

She eyed him with a motherly air, although she was only two years older than him. "You do seem more yourself," she acknowledged. "And I'm glad of it. But we're straying from the point. You still owe us an explanation of what you're up to. Normally I wouldn't care what you choose to do with your free time, but I have a bad feeling that you embroiled us in some kind of mischief when you convinced us to join you at Bexley Manor."

"To be fair, I didn't actually invite Brody," Heath pointed out. "I only wanted you."

"True," said Bianca, with the hint of a laugh. "But my brother is as difficult to shake as yours."

"I could tell you were up to no good," said Brody airily. "I wasn't about to let Bianca go off on a dangerous quest without me."

"Which brings us back to the question of where we're going," Bianca pressed. "And why you wanted me to come."

Heath sighed. "It's a little hard to explain."

"My Lord?"

Heath turned to see the captain approaching.

"We've set the course due east, as requested. But as I warned you, the waters that way are impassable after about two days' sail."

"I understand," said Heath quickly. "We'll be there before then."

The captain gave him a long, hard look. "I'm not asking questions, My Lord. But I won't do anything that endangers my crew or my ship, not for anyone."

"Of course not," said Heath. "I'm not asking you to put your people in danger."

With a curt nod, the captain strode off across the deck, no sign of unsteadiness in his firm steps.

Heath turned back to his cousins to find Brody staring at him with a raised eyebrow. "How much did you have to pay to find a captain so willing to ask no questions? You spent your whole quarter's allowance on this, didn't you?"

Heath shrugged one shoulder. "It was worth it."

"So where are we going?" Bianca asked. "What's less than two days' sail east of here?"

"Actually," said Heath, with a sheepish glance over his shoulder to where the captain had disappeared below deck, "it's more like three days' sail away, under normal circumstances."

"But you just said—"

"We're not exactly normal, though, are we?" Heath hurried on.

Both of Brody's eyebrows were raised now. "Suddenly I understand why you wanted my sister and not me."

"No offense, Brody," smiled Heath. "But your skills with plants won't help us much out here, unless the ship gets tangled up in seaweed or something."

"Whereas my ability to manipulate wind will," said Bianca. She gave Heath a shrewd look. "So it's my magic you want, not me."

Heath shrugged again. "What's the difference, Bianca? Your magic is an inextricable part of you." He smiled hopefully. "Can you do it, do you think? Speed us up?"

"Probably," she said. "But you do realize, don't you, that reaching the same area in two days instead of three won't make the waters more passable when we get there?"

Heath gave her a look. "Yes, I do have a basic grasp of how ocean travel works."

"So what's the point of getting there faster?"

"Well," said Heath, casting a glance behind him to make

sure none of the crew were listening, "no one else knows this, but there's a reason the water is impassable. There's an island out there, and it's surrounded by a magical ring of protection, like the one around each of the dragon colonies."

Brody was frowning. "How do you know this?"

"Reka and I found it," Heath said. "He flew straight through the magical barrier without any issues, of course. He was the one who identified what it was. To me it just felt like a sort of ripple of power passing over my body."

"Well, in case you hadn't noticed, your dragon friend isn't with us now," Brody pointed out. "So how is the ship supposed to pass through this impassable barrier?"

"We have magic," said Heath simply. "From what my grandmother has told me, power-wielders can pass through the dragons' protections. I doubt the dragons intended that, but when the barriers were created, there weren't any humans with magic, were there?"

"But what about the crew?" protested Bianca. "Even if you're right about us, you don't have any idea whether the ship itself can actually get through, do you?"

"Well...no," Heath admitted. "But what's the harm?" he added hastily, at their expressions. "If we can't get through, we'll just have to turn around. We will have wasted a few days, but it's worth the risk. I have to at least try to get to that island."

"Why?" asked Bianca, looking concerned for his sanity. "Why is it so important?"

"And why don't you get Rekavidur to take you, if it's so urgent?" Brody added.

Heath didn't look at them, his eyes instead on the eastern horizon. "Reka and I aren't on the best of terms right now," he said quietly. "And I need to get to the island because last time I was there, someone was...injured, because of me. And I need to know if that person is alive."

There was a long silence. Heath could sense rather than see the twins exchanging glances, and he had no doubt they were wondering what they'd gotten themselves into.

"There are people living on this island?" Brody asked, his voice a little strange.

Heath still wasn't looking him in the eye. "Not exactly."

"Heath." There was a warning in Brody's voice. "*Should* we be making contact with whoever these people are? Are we endangering Valoria by seeking them out?"

"Of course not!" Heath looked up quickly, locking gazes with his cousin. "I swear, there's no risk to our kingdom. This is…a purely personal matter."

Brody was still frowning, but after exchanging another glance with Bianca, he let the matter drop.

"I've never tried to direct a ship before," Bianca said softly. "I don't know much about sailing. I might send us the wrong way, or break the mast or something."

"Just start small," Heath encouraged, "and build if it's working."

Despite her show of reluctance, Heath got the sense that Bianca was a little excited by the challenge. He'd watched his relatives struggling with the growing suspicion toward their powers, reining themselves in and being especially cautious about how they used them. It must be liberating to be able to unleash her magic, try to do something big and dramatic, somewhere far away from the judging eyes of the court.

At first Heath could hardly tell the difference. Bianca sent a gentle breeze curling around the sails, encouraging the ship eastward. He only knew she was doing it because he could sense her power, branching out from her and reaching into the air in invisible strands that formed an intricate, ever-moving pattern.

But she seemed to get a feel for it quickly, and her power was soon drawing more wind toward them, gathering behind and around the ship, sending it speeding across the surface of the water. Her enthusiasm outstripped her finesse for a moment, and the boat lurched alarmingly to starboard, causing Brody and Heath to clutch at the railing.

Brody had to grab Bianca to stop her tipping over. She wasn't paying attention to her physical surroundings—her concentration hadn't wavered from her task, and Heath could tell that all her focus was locked on the invisible tapestry of power that connected her to the currents of air all around them. It was fascinating watching her at work. He was so used to Percival's more constant, straightforward magic, and he'd rarely seen power exercised like this. It was similar in some ways to the display put on by Princess Kiana in Kynton, when she made her water sculpture.

But Bianca's efforts were on a larger scale, and more sustained. Once she had worked out a level of wind that was effective while still being safe, she didn't have to give all her concentration to maintaining it. She was able to join the others in exploring the deck, and chatting about Percival's upcoming loyalty ceremony, and Heath's experiences in Kyona. But her power was still in play, and after several hours, Brody interrupted their conversation abruptly to tell her to take a break.

Heath realized, guiltily, that Bianca looked exhausted. He hadn't been paying enough attention to her state. He hastily agreed that she should rest for a while. But after an hour, he once again felt her power snaking out from the deck, dispersing into the air.

"It's quite exciting," she admitted to him, when he asked if she was pushing herself too hard. "It's rare to have an opportunity to experiment like this, with no one paying attention to what I'm doing."

Heath glanced at the crew. They had certainly noticed the unusual and extremely advantageous wind. But they didn't seem to have connected it with the slim young woman leaning into the spray at the ship's prow.

"It's exhilarating, isn't it?" Bianca said. "Exercising your power freely? Giving it total release to be as strong as it can be?"

Heath was silent. He didn't know how to answer. His power wasn't like Bianca's, and he didn't know how to set it free. Not to mention, he wasn't entirely sure he wanted to acknowledge the new aspects of it that had begun to emerge. Not when doing so might jeopardize the progress he and Prince Lachlan were attempting to make.

For a moment he leaned into the concept of his enhanced sight. He closed his physical eyes, trying to focus with his power instead. Merletta popped instantly into his mind, and instead of trying to evade the thought, he embraced it, willing his imagination to dwell on the details. However, as in his dream back in Kynton, the image wasn't clear. It was murky, and he had an impression of great cold. He could see her face, its expression thoughtful, but it was like he was looking through grimy glass.

He sighed, opening his eyes and cutting off the vision. He didn't know what to make of it, but it wasn't exactly encouraging.

The captain spoke to them as the sun was setting, commenting on the favorable conditions, and alerting Heath to the fact that they were making much better progress than he'd anticipated.

"At this rate, we'll reach the limit of how far east I've ever sailed before tomorrow morning," he said gruffly. "Not sure what to expect then. The waters will be impassable by sunset tomorrow. You sure you know what you're looking for?"

Heath set his eyes toward the east, an image in his mind of an island, peaceful and beautiful, sparkling like a jewel in a vast ocean.

"Very sure," he said firmly.

CHAPTER THIRTEEN

Wivell's classes may have been unexpectedly enjoyable, but Ibsen's were frustratingly predictable. Merletta was glad when, during a lesson a couple months after she returned to the program, a distraction occurred to interrupt Ibsen's monologue. He had mostly moved on from discussion of the human incident, but today Ibsen had decided to revisit it. Merletta felt a twinge of unease, wondering if the return to the topic could be related to her inquiries of Andre's father. But she was probably being overly sensitive. Either way, listening to Ibsen's descriptions of the brutality of humans, who—according to him—were unintelligent brutes with a primitive instinct of aggression, was trying her resolution to keep her head down.

The lithe young guard who appeared in the doorway seemed to be a signal, because Ibsen broke off and raised a questioning eyebrow. The merman, whom Merletta didn't recognize, nodded, and said, "Tilssted. Outlying kelp farms."

Merletta straightened her back, her attention caught by the mention of her familiar old waters. What was happening in the outlying kelp farms?

"All right, trainees," Ibsen said, turning to them. All five trainees were in class together. Ibsen generally liked to gather them when lecturing about humans. "You have five minutes to return to your barracks and collect your weapons if necessary. Then we will join this guard patrol in attending a dispute currently underway in Tilssted."

Merletta heard a low groan from Lorraine, but she ignored her, exchanging a look with Sage instead. Her friend grimaced. She'd explained to Merletta already about the tension that had been rising in the last few months regarding boundaries. In a sense, it was nothing new. The overpopulation of the triple kingdoms had been a problem for as long as Merletta could remember. Since they weren't allowed to expand outside the barrier, the only way for the cities to grow was inward, and they'd already done so to the point that three once separate cities had formed one giant sprawling mass, in three segments. Given the prevailing teaching on the dangers of the open ocean, the wealthier merpeople had always elected to live closer to the Center. As the population grew, the poorest residents were constantly pushed further toward the outer ring of the triple kingdoms.

Nowhere was this problem more pronounced than in Tilssted, and no one felt it more than the poorest, most vulnerable of the city's residents. The charity home where Merletta had grown up was a prime example. It was situated near the boundary of Tilssted and the outlying kelp farms that formed its edge. This had suited her just fine, of course, making her unsanctioned excursions beyond the barrier easier. But it was the source of a great deal of anxiety for others, who viewed the ocean beyond their kingdoms with nothing but fear.

It was no surprise that tension over this issue had grown to fever pitch in recent weeks, given the revelations about the proximity—and supposed danger—of land and humans.

Most of the trainees left to fetch their spears, or—in the first years' case, blunt poles—but Merletta had hers with her as always. She floated near Ibsen and the guard, waiting silently for the others to return.

"You said it's the kelp farms?" Ibsen asked the guard.

The young merman nodded. "Yes sir."

"Casualties?"

The guard shook his head. "Not from what we've heard. There's a Tilssted guard squad on site, but the regent requested a patrol of Center guards, to oversee."

Ibsen nodded, and Merletta frowned. Tilssted's regent had never been overly popular—according to rumor, he spent most of his time in the other cities, trying to ingratiate himself with the more influential regents. But surely even he should know better than to call in Center guards to oversee a simple, non-violent boundary dispute. It would only set the residents even further against both the regent and the Center.

She made no comment, but her thoughts were troubled as the group swam quickly out of the Center, and through the streets of Skulssted. The squad of guards they had joined was a dozen strong, and even Merletta, with the protection of her role as a Center trainee, found their throng of spear-tips intimidating. She could only be grateful that there were no familiar faces among the group—Ileana wasn't part of this squad.

She was surprised, however, to see another former trainee catch up to them before they left Skulssted. From the inquiring look Ibsen bent upon Emil, he hadn't expected the junior record holder, either.

"I heard the trainees were observing a containment patrol, and I wondered if I could join, sir," Emil said calmly. "There were no such opportunities when I was a trainee."

Ibsen hesitated for only a moment before nodding. "Certainly. I applaud your desire to expand your education." But

Merletta thought his gaze was a little wary as it rested on the junior record holder.

She saw Emil glance over at her and Sage. He had fallen into place behind the guard patrol. Merletta inclined her head invitingly, and Emil checked his pace for a moment before propelling himself forward to join them.

"So you haven't been on one of these patrols before?" Sage asked, once he'd drawn alongside them.

Emil shook his head.

"Did you call this a containment patrol?" Merletta asked curiously.

"That's the term used within the Center's administration," Emil said. "These disputes are now regularly escalating to violence, so the need for such patrols has become increasingly common."

"So they call it a containment patrol because it's a dispute over boundaries?" Sage asked innocently.

There was a pause before Emil replied. "Presumably."

Merletta pursed her lips. She didn't presume any such thing.

They were still in Skulssted, skirting around a large, cultivated tower of coral that formed the focal point of a public square. Tiny fish of a vivid blue were darting in and out of sight through the coral. Merletta didn't recognize the area, but Emil obviously did.

He threw an enigmatic look at Sage as he said, "Look out for the blue rings."

The comment surprised a choke of laughter out of Sage, and she glanced at the coral tower.

"Derek is such a brat," she said, shaking her head.

She seemed to suddenly become aware of Merletta watching her in astonishment, because the brown of her cheeks became tinged with pink, and she hastened to explain.

"My cousin. He convinced me once that those little blue fish were blue rings, this type of poisonous—"

"Octopus," Merletta finished for her. "I've see—heard of them," she corrected herself hastily. She didn't want to admit in front of Emil that she'd encountered the deadly creatures while outside the barrier.

"I've never seen anyone flip their tail that fast," Emil commented. His expression was still so calm, it took Merletta a moment to realize he was teasing Sage.

"I'd forgotten all about that," Sage mused, glancing back at the coral tower. "That was years ago. Both our families live close to here," she added, for Merletta's benefit. "Sometimes there are public events in this square."

"Sounds nice," smiled Merletta.

She reflected that they would probably be passing through her own old neighborhood soon, and that she didn't think she'd be recounting any of her childhood anecdotes for her companions. But she refrained from saying so, not wanting to ruin the moment the other two seemed to be sharing. She cast a glance between them, swimming on either side of her, as they crossed out of Skulssted and into Tilssted. Emil seemed as unruffled as ever, but Sage's face was still a little pink.

The guard patrol pulled ahead as they passed through the steadily grimier streets. Ibsen signaled for his class to leave some distance between their group and the patrol, and Emil stayed alongside the trainees.

They had almost reached the outer boundary of the city when Merletta noticed Sage wrinkling her nose. She raised an inquiring eyebrow.

"Sorry," Sage apologized, looking a little ashamed. "The water just tastes...different."

Merletta laughed, not offended. "If by different you mean dirty, then yes. It's one of the things I like most about living in the Center. You get used to it, though. I honestly didn't realize how bad the water was in Tilssted until I left."

Sage didn't answer, and Merletta quickly changed the subject.

"We're in my old waters," she said, nodding her head to their right. "The charity home where I grew up is just down there. And Tish's shellsmith tower isn't much further." She lowered her voice, speaking mainly to herself. "I really must make time to visit her."

"That's the friend you spent your break with, isn't it?" Emil asked unexpectedly. "She'll be missing you, now you're back in the program full time."

Merletta threw him a startled look. Apparently her former classmate was more aware of her supposed movements than she'd suspected. Why was he so interested? Was he asking on his own behalf, or was he under orders, like Ileana? She found herself surprised by how much she wanted to trust him, but there was no way she was going to tell him where she'd really been over her break.

"Which one is the charity home?" Sage cut in quickly, changing the subject a little too obviously. "I didn't realize it was this close to the boundary."

Merletta saw Emil's eyes pass shrewdly between the two mermaids, and she could have sworn his posture stiffened as his gaze rested on Sage. She was sure he'd noticed that Merletta hadn't answered his question. Was he offended at the possibility that Sage was helping hide something from him? The other mermaid either didn't notice, or pretended not to.

"That tall building there," Merletta said, and it was her turn to wrinkle her nose as she pointed. "It's nothing much to see."

"Is it strange, coming back here?" Sage asked curiously.

Merletta cast a look around her, at the familiar streets which now seemed so removed from any part of her life. "Yes," she said. "It's very strange."

An angry shout from up ahead drew all their attention to the point where the guard patrol had entered the kelp farms. Most of the trainees hung back, looking apprehensive about swimming between the fronds, and Merletta realized that the first years, at least, had probably never left the cities. She, of course, knew no such hesitation. She had swum through the kelp farms—and indeed the uncultivated kelp forests beyond—more times than she could count.

She hurried forward, pushing the long leaves aside as she followed the sound of voices. The Center guards had formed a block behind a small patrol of Tilssted guards, recognizable by the bands tied around their crude stone weapons. Those guards looked frustrated more than anything, but the merman facing off against them was livid. His face was red as he shouted at three stocky mermen who were ranged alongside the guards, stone axes in their hands. Several farm laborers hovered further back, their eyes wide as their employer raged at his opponents.

"What gives you the right to come in here, and destroy my—"

"We told you," one of the mermen cut across him, his voice impatient. "We're under city orders to clear the site for the outer row."

"You're well past the outer row!" the angry one cried, pointing behind the guards, toward the crude dwellings situated closest to the start of the kelp. "You're in my farm!"

"Come now," said one of the Tilssted guards wearily. "You know there's been a new ordinance. They're adding another row of dwellings, and the water must be cleared for building to start next week."

"Not on my watch," retorted the farmer belligerently. "Take the space from someone else's farm."

"We are," said one of the mermen with the stone axes, in exasperation. "We're clearing space from all of the farms on the inner ring. I don't know what the big fuss is about. We only cleared a small section."

"It might be a small section to you!" shouted the farmer, with a wild gesture to an expanse of severed kelp to one side, "but that's *half* my farm you've taken! And no doubt the other half will go next year, when our precious regent decides to cave to the other cities and give away more of our space!"

One of the clearers shrugged. "That's not our problem. If you have a problem with your regent, take it up with him. We're just doing our job, and we don't answer to any Tilssted authority."

"Just what I would expect from Hemssted," the farmer said bitterly. "You care about no one but yourselves."

An angry noise beside her alerted Merletta to the fact that the rest of the trainees had now followed her into the kelp farm. Lorraine was glaring at the farmer in evident offense at his slight on her home city.

Merletta turned to Sage, who, along with Emil, was once again at her side.

"Who's in charge of the housing expansion projects?" she asked quietly.

Sage frowned. "I thought it was the Center."

Merletta shot a sharp look at Emil, and he nodded, reluctantly, she thought.

"How could they be so inept as to send Hemssted workers to clear farms owned by Tilssted farmers?"

Sage shrugged. "Maybe they wanted to spare the Tilssted workers from having to clear the farms of their friends and neighbors."

Merletta snorted. Somehow she doubted the decision was

motivated by any such consideration. More likely they were too self-absorbed to know or care about such details.

"Are you going to do anything to defend my property?" the farmer was demanding of the Tilssted guards.

They shifted uncomfortably, and the clearers turned on them too.

"Aren't you going to protect us from this madman? We're going about our lawful business!"

One of the Tilssted guards cleared his throat. "The decision's been made," he said to the farmer, sounding apologetic. "There's nothing to be gained by fighting."

"You're taking *their* side?" the farmer said, outraged.

The Tilssted guard looked helplessly to the Center guards. They had so far watched silently, but one of them now swam forward. "We won't tolerate violence," he said curtly. "If you interfere with these workers, you'll have to be detained."

"I'm supposed to just move aside and let my livelihood be taken away without compensation?" the farmer demanded.

"You heard what I said," the Center guard replied tonelessly.

Merletta started forward, the movement almost involuntary.

"Trainee!" Ibsen's hiss came from behind her. "We are here to observe only."

"But surely he'll be compensated," Merletta said, turning to him with wide eyes. She'd spoken more loudly than she intended, and everyone in the cleared area turned to look at her, their expressions ranging from surprise to fury. "Surely if his farm is being cleared to make way for new settlements, he'll be compensated."

There was a moment of silence, and Merletta felt her own anger begin to build. She appealed to the Center guard who had threatened to detain the farmer.

"*Isn't* he being compensated?"

The guard shrugged. "That's a matter for the regent of

Tilssted, who approved this space for inclusion in the new settlement."

Merletta's eyes flashed. They were really going to pretend this was an internal Tilssted issue? "Because there's no pressure on the regent from the other cities," she said sarcastically.

"We can't be held responsible for tension between the cities," the guard said dismissively.

Merletta narrowed her eyes, turning to the Hemssted workers. "You're keeping records though, aren't you?" she insisted. "Of how much space is cleared from whose farms, to allow for compensation later?"

"Records?" muttered one of the workers. "Isn't that your area? We're not from the Center."

Merletta's frown deepened, but before she could say another word, Ibsen's angry voice cut through the water.

"Trainee! That's enough!"

Merletta turned to face him, scowling as he swam toward her. She knew she was supposed to be keeping her head down, but this incident was nothing to do with humans, or land, or drying out. Was she really supposed to just float by and watch a Tilssted farmer get cheated out of his livelihood?

"But why should—"

"Merletta." The interruption came not from Ibsen, but from Emil. Merletta's eyes flew to his. His face was entirely devoid of expression, but his eyes seemed to communicate a warning. The thought reminded her of Agner's words during her first bout with Sage, and how she had wondered if he'd been trying to subtly warn her. What had he said?

Make sure you're in a strong position before you strike. You can't take back a false move.

Merletta closed her mouth, battling with her own frustration as she bit back angry words.

"Merletta?" This time her name was spoken by one of the

farm laborers. The mermaid was young, probably no more than five years older than Merletta, and Merletta was sure she'd never seen her before. The mermaid swam forward, a note of excitement in her voice. "You're the Center trainee who comes from a Tilssted charity home, aren't you?"

Merletta blinked at her in surprise, her mouth falling slightly open as the farmer spoke, his tone brightening.

"I've heard of you! So the rumor is true. Good for you! Nice to have some representation in the Center for a change." He cast a venomous look at the Center guard who had threatened him.

But everyone else seemed to have temporarily forgotten the dispute. The farm laborers had all come closer, their gazes eager as they looked at Merletta. Even the Tilssted guards were watching her with interest. She realized her mouth was still open, and closed it self-consciously.

"Trainees." Ibsen's bark brought her attention back to him, and she could see on his face that this was not the time to argue. The five of them drew close, and at a curt order, they swam back through the fronds and into Tilssted. The Center guards stayed behind, but Emil joined the trainees.

"As *most* of you are well aware," Ibsen spat, with an angry glance at Merletta, "the aim of these outings is to observe and learn, *not* to hamper the efforts of the guards by getting involved. Thanks to Merletta," he glowered at her again, "our presence has become a hindrance to resolving the conflict. It is therefore necessary for us to leave."

Oliver and Lorraine both threw dirty looks at Merletta. She didn't know what the first year mermaid had to complain about. She'd wanted to get out of Tilssted as quickly as possible, hadn't she? Andre didn't scowl at her, but he looked tense, his eyes wide as they rested on Ibsen.

The trainees began to swim back toward the Center, but

Ibsen called Merletta to a stop with a curt command. She floated stiffly, her eyes fixed warily on the instructor's face.

"What were you thinking?" Ibsen growled. "Perhaps you've forgotten that you are a *trainee*. You are not a guard, and you hold no position that would give you authority to intervene on behalf of the Center."

"I haven't forgotten, sir," Merletta said, trying to keep the resentful note out of her voice.

Her eyes flicked to Sage, moving slowly away behind the other trainees, glancing frequently back. She looked like she was debating whether to wait, but Merletta saw Emil mutter something, and the two of them kept moving. Merletta turned back to Ibsen, her gaze fixing on the observers behind him. A few of the farm laborers had drifted out of the fronds of kelp, and were watching the confrontation.

There was such excitement in their eyes as they rested on Merletta, it was all she could do not to squirm. She had decided not to push too hard until she was in a stronger position, but keeping to that decision had never been harder than right now. What was the point of making it into the program if she didn't use her voice to speak up for the vulnerable of Tilssted? She swallowed her discomfort with an effort.

"I didn't realize we were supposed to remain silent," she said, the words as close to an apology as she could bring herself to give.

Ibsen looked irritated at her distraction, but when he followed her gaze and saw their audience, he moderated his own tone.

"Well, now you do realize." His words were clipped. "And I expect you to remember it in future."

Without another word, he flicked his tail, gliding through the water toward his retreating trainees. Merletta floated for a moment, amazed at having apparently escaped consequence, then hurried after him.

"That was...eventful," she muttered to Sage, as she swam up alongside her.

Sage turned quickly, anxiety on her face. "What did Ibsen say? Are you in a lot of trouble?"

Merletta shook her head. "I don't think so. He just told me off, and swam away."

Emil raised an eyebrow, but didn't comment.

Sage also said nothing, but she gave Merletta a very speaking look. She may not know the full extent of what her friend was hiding, but she did know about Merletta's confrontation with Ileana, and she knew that Merletta had decided not to pull anyone's fins until she knew who was behind Ileana's menacing hints.

Merletta sighed. "I know, Sage, and I am trying! I've just never been good at keeping my head down."

Emil shot a sharp look between them, and Merletta fell silent. She probably shouldn't speak even as freely as that in front of him, but she couldn't bring herself to see him as an enemy. Even if he was a record holder now.

She shook her head to clear it of that thought as the trio swam silently through the streets of Tilssted. Since she was a small child, it had been her dearest ambition to become a record holder. When had she started thinking of them as enemies?

They soon caught up to the rest of the trainees, and Merletta noticed that Andre drifted slowly over until he was part of their group, leaving Oliver and Lorraine swimming behind Ibsen. Merletta was grateful for the silent display of support, and even more grateful that Andre made no comment on the incident at the kelp farm.

The rest of the day's classes with Ibsen were tense and

uncomfortable. Merletta wasn't sure why he hadn't chewed her out more thoroughly, but the restraint was obviously infuriating him. He barked like a territorial seal at anyone who asked a question, and soon the trainees all settled into silence, while he lectured them on the very uninteresting subject of the governance structures of the three cities.

Merletta let her attention wander. Ibsen could say what he liked about the regents having authority in their own cities. She knew that in Tilssted at least, the reality was that decisions were all controlled by a complicated and many-layered bureaucracy and that their regent was cowed by the other cities, and even more by the Center. Most of the time, his role was little more than ceremonial.

Her thoughts were on Tish. The shellsmith tower where her friend worked was quite close to the boundary. Was Tish being affected by all the disputes? How many in Tilssted were in danger of losing their livelihoods because of the expansion issue? Thoughts of Tilssted residents conjured the image of the farmer, and the laborers. Merletta's stomach flopped strangely as she remembered the way they'd looked at her, and how they'd seemed to know her name and her story. She glanced at Andre, watching Ibsen with rapt attention. He'd said she was famous, as the first trainee from Tilssted in generations. She hadn't for a moment believed it was true.

As always, Merletta had been looking forward to further training with Agner much more than the four solid days of classes which preceded it. But by the time she reached her training days, she was so edgy that she struggled to focus. She earned a rare rebuke from Agner for inattentiveness, and she could see that Sage was watching her with concern.

When the sun finally rose on rest day—albeit far, far above her—Merletta had made her decision. The strain of being cautious was taking a toll, and she couldn't afford to be so distracted in her training. Add to that her feelings of guilt and inadequacy over still having no idea what really happened to the guards, and she felt suffocated. She was desperate to get out of the triple kingdoms for a while.

To that end, she was up with the sun. She fully intended to practice with her legs again, and having decided that Sage wasn't ready for that revelation, she'd realized she needed to find a way to keep her friend from coming with her. The Sage of a year ago wouldn't have contemplated crossing the barrier of protection around the triple kingdoms, of course, but Merletta had a feeling that she would come this time if given the chance.

It seemed Merletta had been a bad influence on her law-abiding friend.

So she had told Sage that she was going for her long overdue visit to Tish, and that due to her friend's unreasonably long working hours, she would have to catch her before the day's work began. The bit about the working hours of apprentices was true, and since Merletta had no desire to lie to Sage, she intended to make the part about visiting Tish true as well. She'd been meaning to check in on her oldest friend, and rest day was probably as good an opportunity as she was going to get. Sage usually spent her rest days at home with her family, so she wouldn't know what time Merletta returned.

She swam through the quiet pathways of the Center, resisting the impulse to look over her shoulder every ten seconds. She wanted to know if she was being followed, of course, but it was more important not to look like she was hiding something.

The streets of Skulssted were still quiet, but by the time she reached Tilssted, the city was bustling with activity. There weren't many in this corner of the triple kingdoms who could indulge in idle mornings. She passed her old charity home with barely a glance, not in the mood to be nostalgic. Tish's shellsmith tower loomed out of the lightening water, and Merletta hurried toward it. As much as she wanted to see her friend, she was eager to get to Vazula before too much of her free day had elapsed.

Her passage into the building was barred by a thick-armed merman with a crude stone weapon. Merletta floated to a stop, looking him up and down. There hadn't been a guard last time she visited. She supposed it must be in response to the rising tensions of the area, and it was heartening to see that the shell-smith took the safety of his apprentices seriously.

The guard was looking her over as well, his eyes resting on her armband and her spear in turn, before flicking to her face.

"What brings you here?"

"I'm here to visit a friend," said Merletta, trying to sound confident. "Her name is Letitia."

The guard studied her in silence for a moment, then blurted out, "Are you the Center trainee from Tilssted?"

"I—yes," said Merletta blankly.

The merman drew to the side, gesturing for her to enter. His face had broken into a grin, and he added, "That'll show 'em."

Merletta entered the building, feeling dazed. She hurried up the levels toward Tish's story. Early as it was, she had expected to find her friend in her room. But when she reached Tish's floor, she saw that there was a whole group of mermaids working together at a long bench in the landing area. Tish was among them.

The pale-haired mermaid looked up as Merletta entered, and their eyes locked. Tish looked startled, and for a moment, Merletta thought her friend wasn't happy to see her. But Tish's features softened into a smile, and she rose from her seat.

It quickly became clear, however, that there wasn't going to be an opportunity for private speech. When the other apprentices realized they were looking at the Tilssted trainee, they all began speaking at once. Merletta felt overwhelmed under the onslaught of their questions and eager approval, sure she didn't live up to whatever they thought she was. One voice rang out clearly above the others.

"Letitia, you didn't tell us you're friends with our Tilssted trainee!"

Everyone turned to look at Tish, Merletta with them. A flush spread across Tish's cheeks, and she cast an apologetic glance at Merletta. Merletta felt a sinking feeling in her stomach that she couldn't fully explain. Once again, she had the sense that her childhood friend wasn't entirely pleased about her visit.

Tish didn't answer the accusation, just swimming forward to address Merletta personally, although they couldn't really avoid being overheard.

"It's good to see you, Merletta. It's been too long. I didn't realize you were coming today."

"I'm sorry," said Merletta, still feeling thrown. "I shouldn't have barged in without arranging it with you."

"Don't be silly," Tish said quickly. "You're always welcome."

Merletta searched her friend's eyes, wondering why the words didn't feel sincere. "I've chosen a bad moment, though. We can catch up another time."

She'd half expected Tish to deny it, to tell her to stay, but she didn't. Merletta somehow managed to say goodbye around the lump that had unaccountably risen in her throat. She waved in a friendly way to the rest of the group, and swam out of the building as quickly as dignity would allow.

She told herself she was being foolish. Tish was in the middle of something, fully ensconced in the life she had with her fellow apprentices, and it was natural for her to be rattled by the sudden appearance of someone from an entirely different sphere of her life. Merletta would be discomposed if Tish floated into one of her training sessions with Agner.

But she couldn't quite make herself forget the hesitation in Tish's eyes. Where did it come from? Tish was her oldest and truest friend. She'd never been reluctant to range herself alongside Merletta back when Merletta was a hotheaded orphan with no friends or status, and an unhelpful habit of scratching everyone's scales the wrong way. Why would she not want to own their friendship now that Merletta was a Center trainee, and apparently known and admired in Tilssted?

It was with a heavy heart that Merletta ducked into a nearby kelp farm. She didn't know what she would have said to Tish—she still wasn't entirely sure how much she should tell her—but it was still disappointing not to have the chance to say anything at all.

Her preoccupation wasn't so great that she forgot to be careful. She only emerged into the uncultivated kelp forest once she'd satisfied herself that she wasn't being followed, or even observed. As when she'd entered the triple kingdoms after her month on Vazula, she had to wait some time for a big enough break between guard patrols. At least she now understood the reason for the extra guards, given the rumors about humans.

But once she was clear, she disappeared into the gloom of the deep water in no time at all, flipping her tail as she headed for Vazula. It was liberating to finally be out of the triple kingdoms, and her spirits rose as she swam. It was impossible not to feel more cheerful when surrounded by open ocean on all sides. She directed herself upward, not quite breaking the surface, just enjoying the sparkle of the sunshine and the warmer water.

The route was familiar, and soon her heart surged with excitement as the ocean floor began to slant up to meet her. She emerged into the sunshine, feeling her throat open as her mouth filled with air instead of water.

There it was, Vazula. Gleaming like something from a

dream, too good to be real. It was the sight of freedom, and it beckoned to her.

She splashed her way into the shallows, surprising herself by the strength of her desire to regain her legs. Despite the time it had been since her last change, she flopped herself onto the sand without hesitation, welcoming the prickling sensation that told her the switch was beginning.

Within moments, she was sitting on the shore, gazing fondly down at two brown feet, already caked in wet sand. Using her spear for support, she pushed herself shakily to her feet and straightened her snakeskin-like purple covering.

She took one step toward the rocks, then another, smiling as her body remembered what to do. It seemed she hadn't lost any of her progress, and that was encouraging. One leg ached a little as she put her weight on it, and she paused to examine the smooth skin. A bruise was blooming on the upper part of her right leg, and she touched it with fascination. She distinctly remembered receiving that resounding blow from the blunt end of Oliver's spear the day before. Interesting that the injury to her tail had transferred to her human form.

But enough distractions. She set her face toward the edge of the jungle. Using her legs was just like her other training. If she wanted to get good at it, she would need constant practice.

CHAPTER FOURTEEN

Despite the captain's prediction that the waters would be impassable by the second sunset of their voyage, it wasn't yet midday on their second day when the three cousins were alerted to something unusual by sudden shouts from on deck. The waters had grown steadily rougher as they traveled east, and the constant lurching had begun to wear on them all. They'd been holed up in Heath's tiny cabin, the boys playing a game of chance while Bianca continued to manipulate the wind from afar. She looked weary, but she was cheerful, and certainly seemed to have gotten the hang of her task.

All three of them froze at the cry of alarm sounding from above them. They exchanged a look, then leaped to their feet in unison. Heath was in the front as they surged up onto the deck, and he had no need to ask anyone what had caused the shouting.

The water to the ship's starboard side was churning alarmingly, the roar growing louder by the second. He ran to the railing, followed by the twins, and his eyes widened in horror. Not far across the surface of the ocean, and drawing steadily closer, was a thundering, fast-flowing spiral of water. The noise was nearly deafening now, and huge white crests were being thrown into the air as tides collided.

"The maelstrom!" he gasped.

The phenomenon was so much larger than he'd realized from the air, and so much more terrifying. He couldn't even see the other side of it, and he could feel the way the current was drawing them inexorably in.

"You knew about this?" Brody's furious roar was almost drowned out by the sounds of gushing, churning water.

"I saw it when I flew over, with Reka," Heath yelled. "But we shouldn't be passing close to it like this. We're much too far south!"

He caught sight of the captain, standing grim-faced beside the helmsman. Heath hurried toward them, his feet slipping on the wet deck as the ship slanted terrifyingly down toward the giant whirlpool.

"I thought the wind was strong, and blowing due east!" he said, when he was within hailing distance.

The captain threw him an impatient look, his mind clearly on more important things. "Wind isn't the only factor in sailing, My Lord," he snapped. "The current is powerful here. I've never felt anything like it. We've ventured too far east!"

"No, we're almost there!" Heath protested, but the captain had turned away, barking orders to his crew.

Heath ran back to his cousins, barely keeping his footing. The crew ignored him as they raced across the deck. Several were climbing the riggings, letting down the sails on one side and tying them up on the other. Heath saw that the helmsman had two others helping him to turn the wheel to its furthest extent.

None of it was helping much. Mere minutes ago, they had

been sailing smoothly east, unaware of the maelstrom's proximity, and now the edge of it was barely a stone's throw away.

He reached Brody and Bianca, both of whom looked white with fear. "Blow us the other way!" he shouted, and Bianca shook her head.

"I'm trying!" Her whole body was indeed straining with effort. "It's not enough! I can almost feel the current—it's like the underwater version of what I'm doing in the air. It's too strong, and it's dragging us in!"

Heath could sense it, too, and it didn't feel entirely natural. Perhaps he had been wrong to assume that the barrier itself was the only thing that made this water impassable. He just hoped no one on this ship would pay for his mistake with their lives.

He cast his eyes frantically toward the maelstrom. He could see inside it, now, and it wasn't smooth water as he'd pictured. He could see rocks protruding from its sides, disappearing into depths not visible from his angle. If they got sucked in there, the ship would be smashed to pieces. He stared into the foam. Was that steam he could see rising? Or just spray?

A high-pitched whistling sound suddenly cut through the water's roar. Then, with an explosive blast, a spout of water shot up into the air, out of the side of the maelstrom. A second and then a third followed soon after. The upward spray ceased abruptly, and swirling, foamy water rushed in to fill the temporary gap.

Heath could feel an incredible amount of power coming out from Bianca now, and the wind blowing out from the maelstrom, attempting to push them back to safety, was ferocious. Still the current fought against it.

"What can we use?" he muttered to himself. "I need to see." He looked away from the maelstrom, searching for something, anything that would help them. He stared at the ocean, and suddenly found that he was no longer seeing its choppy surface.

He was seeing murky depths, rocky shelves and clumps of seaweed appearing through the gloom like a view out a filthy window.

"Seaweed!" he shouted aloud. He seized his cousin's arm. "There's seaweed down there, Brody! Can you use it?"

Brody grasped his meaning instantly. He screwed his eyes tightly shut, and reached out his hand as though lowering it into the water far below them. He turned it palm upward, fingers curled, then suddenly clenched his fist as if grasping something. He gave a violent tug upward, and long, slimy lengths of seaweed shot out of the water, reaching toward the ship. They wrapped around its edges, joined quickly by more, and still more.

Heath ignored the terrified cries of the sailors, watching eagerly as the seaweed locked itself all around the ship, slowing its sideways momentum. Strands of seaweed kept snapping under the pressure, but they were quickly replaced with more, and the ship slowly pulled to a stop, creaking under the strain.

To his credit, the captain wasted no time in terror over the impossible phenomenon. He barked out more orders, and the crew hastened to obey, sending the ship skimming forward, alongside the maelstrom rather than directly away from it. Heath felt Bianca modify her wind, molding it to the captain's direction.

Things began to calm down as they put a bit of distance between them and the maelstrom. Brody let the seaweed fall gradually as the waters calmed, and the thunder of the whirlpool faded away. Another high-pitched whistle sounded behind them, followed by a blast of steamy water, but it was quieter now.

Heath looked ahead, tension starting to drain from his shoulders, when he suddenly became aware of a massive, jagged tower of rock, pointing straight upward not far ahead, fully below the surface.

"Port!" he screamed, running at the captain once again. "Turn to port!"

The captain shook his head. "We'll fare better moving out of the current by degrees, My Lord, not trying to fight directly against it."

"Not the current!" Heath cried. "Submerged rocks!"

The captain stared at him, confusion etched on his brow.

"Port!" Heath shouted again, and something in his voice must have convinced the captain of the situation's urgency.

With a shouted order, the captain sent the ship lurching violently to the left, and Heath threw himself back toward the railing. The ship fell heavily into the trough of a wave, and Heath caught a glimpse of a lethal point of rock, emerging briefly from the water just to their right, before it was swallowed up again by the surging water.

"How did you know?"

The captain's voice close at his elbow made Heath turn quickly. He hadn't realized the man had followed him, but the captain had obviously seen the rock tower as well.

"I..." Heath trailed off, completely at a loss for what to say. How could he explain that he'd seen the rocks, just not with his physical eyes?

The captain's gaze passed from Heath's face to something over his shoulder, and Heath realized that Brody and Bianca had clustered behind him.

"You're power-wielders," the captain said abruptly. "All three of you." His eyes returned to Heath's face, and his expression was inscrutable. "I don't know whether to thank you for your part in saving the ship, or blame you for sending us into danger under false pretenses."

"I had no idea we'd fall afoul of the maelstrom," Heath said earnestly. "I didn't think we'd be anywhere near it."

The captain shook his head slowly. "That current was stronger than anything I've ever experienced. The maelstrom came up faster than I would have believed possible."

He looked back at the ship's stern, and Heath followed his gaze. The maelstrom was fading out of sight, its thunder already a dull roar. Heath could feel Bianca, even through her exhaustion, directing the wind to propel them eastward again. They were no longer being drawn into a rocky whirlpool, but the water was far from calm. The swells were alarmingly large, and the ship slapped at each one as it fell from the peaks. The day had been clear before all the chaos began, but the very air was darkening now, as if fog was descending.

"We'll have to turn back," the captain said. "I don't know what you were hoping to find out here, but we've reached the edge of the passable stretch of ocean."

"No!" Heath protested. "We're almost there!"

He turned his face toward the east, focusing with all his might on Vazula. It sprang instantly into his mind's eye, and he knew it wasn't a memory. It was Vazula as it currently looked, sparkling like a jewel under a midday sun. His physical eyes saw the gathering fog, but with his other sight, he could see that the island was close, almost within reach.

"I won't risk my crew," the captain said bluntly. "I don't know what force is at work here, but these waters aren't supposed to be traveled. There's a reason no one sails this way."

Heath felt frustration bubbling up within him. They were so close—he couldn't turn back now. What if his grandmother was right? What if Merletta was there, even now? He'd done his calculations when planning the trip, and he knew it was a rest day for the trainees in her program. He tried again to picture Vazula, and it appeared in his mind. But he was seeing it from the sky, as it looked to the dragon's eye. He couldn't see the detail he needed. He had to get closer.

"If I wasn't asking you to go further east," he said, turning suddenly back to the captain, "could you safely sail around in this general area for a few hours?"

The captain's brow was furrowed, but he considered the question. "Aye, I reckon we could," he acknowledged, although he cast a glance back in the direction of the maelstrom, which was no longer visible. "But what would be the use of that? What are you expecting to happen?"

"You never know," said Heath vaguely.

The captain regarded him shrewdly for a long moment, and Heath had the sense that he was remembering the promise of double payment upon return to Valoria.

"A few hours," he barked at last. "Then we sail west, back to Valoria."

"Thank you," Heath said gratefully.

He turned back to his cousins, who were both watching him warily.

"What are you planning, Heath?" Brody demanded.

Heath was already striding to the stairs, ready to gather some things from his cabin. "I think we're as close to the barrier as a boat full of non-power-wielders can get," he said briskly. "I'm going to take one of the rowboats and try to get through it on my own. I think I'll be able to pass when it's just me."

"You think?" Bianca echoed, her voice a little shrill. "Heath, that's a terrible idea. Have you seen the state of the sea out there?"

"Of course I have," said Heath impatiently. "But do you think I came this far to give up because of a few waves?"

"Heath, you're going to get yourself killed," said Brody firmly. "You may not care, but I for one have no desire to throw my life away."

But Brody's eyes flicked to his sister as he spoke, and Heath could tell he wasn't concerned only for himself. He didn't blame Brody for being anxious. Bianca looked incredibly pale, still exhausted from her prolonged efforts with the wind.

"I'm not asking either of you to come with me," Heath said quickly. They'd reached his cabin by now, and he slung his bow over his back. "I just need some help getting a rowboat into the water—I have a feeling the captain will put up a fight if I tell him my plan."

"I wonder why," said Brody dryly.

Heath ignored him. A minute later, he was back on the deck, trying to look inconspicuous as he moved toward one sturdy rowboat, hoisted above the edge of the ship. The other two trailed behind him, not looking excited, but apparently resigned to his determination.

With difficulty, the three of them began to operate the capstan, causing the rowboat to swing outward. It hadn't quite cleared the side of the ship when a cry went up, and a crew member raced toward them. Heath leaped into the boat, and Bianca, apparently more sympathetic to his mission than Brody, hastily worked the ropes. The boat was dangling fully above the water by the time a few of the sailors reached them.

Brody leaped into motion, loosing one of the ropes so that the rowboat tilted crazily.

"Try to convince the captain to wait for me!" Heath shouted, as he pulled out his bow. "Give me three hours, and if I don't come back, then..."

But he had nothing to suggest for what they should say or do if he disappeared into the ocean, so he gave up trying to yell across the wind and the sound of the water lashing against the ship. He loosed two arrows in quick succession, his eyes finding no difficulty in locking on the target of the main rope still connecting the rowboat to the ship. It frayed dangerously, and a third arrow detached it completely.

With a stomach-churning drop, the rowboat fell onto the choppy surface of the ocean. Heath returned his bow to his back and seized the oars. He wasn't sure if the captain would try to pursue him, or cut his losses and sail for home. Heath pulled at the oars, straining with the effort of fighting the waves. He could feel Bianca's power reaching out across the water between them, sending a helpful gust of wind that supplemented his uninspiring efforts.

Heath moved slowly but steadily east, the rowboat rising and falling dramatically with each swell. Water sloshed over the sides, and more than once the edge of the rowboat dipped dangerously close to the water's surface, but Heath felt no fear. Perhaps it was foolish, but he was convinced he could reach Vazula, convinced it was barely out of sight. And if he made it there, he didn't much care what the captain did. It would be awkward to be stranded, but Heath didn't think he was at risk of dying alone on Vazula. Despite their current estrangement, he was almost certain that if his life depended on it, Reka would come for him.

He was just reassuring himself of this conclusion when he felt a familiar ripple pass over him. The magic was potent, a thousand times more so than the power Bianca had been pouring into the wind for the last day and a half. Immediately, the swells began to lower, the ocean calming, and the fog-like gray dissipating.

Heath looked up eagerly, and sure enough, there it was.

Green trees, white sand, ruins of stone just peeking out from the jungle. His heart lurched with a bewildering mixture of emotions, and his arms stilled, letting the tide draw him toward it.

Vazula.

CHAPTER FIFTEEN

Heath's heart was in his throat as he rowed the boat clumsily toward the beach. He couldn't stop his eyes from scanning the sparkling sand, but at the same time he was terrified of what he might see. The waves had been unusually high on that stormy day, a few months ago. If, as he'd first thought, Merletta hadn't survived, the tide since then might not have reached far enough up the beach to reclaim her body into the ocean. What would she look like after all this time? He didn't want to think about it.

But the place where he finally pulled his boat ashore, panting with the effort, was definitely the same beach where the nightmare had unfolded, and there was no sign of Merletta's body. That was one relief, at least.

He looked back out to sea as he scrambled out onto the sand and pulled the boat out of reach of the waves. He could see no sign of the ship, although he knew it wasn't far away. Apparently he couldn't see through the magic barrier, so presumably they couldn't see him. He hoped Brody and Bianca would succeed in keeping the ship waiting.

Heath stepped back from the boat, glancing toward the

jungle, and the ruins poking out. His eyes were caught by something, and he stilled in place. Merletta's spear, standing point down in the sand, near the start of the rocks.

Did that mean she was here? He took a hasty step toward it, then stopped, thinking it over. He shouldn't get his hopes up. Perhaps it had been there this whole time, untouched. He had no recollection of what, if anything, Merletta had done with her weapon on that terrible day.

He began walking toward the spear, more slowly now. He'd almost reached it when he heard a rustling from the foliage ahead, and a form began to emerge from the jungle. Heath gasped, reaching instinctively for the bow still slung across his back. He'd never seen anyone but Merletta and Reka on Vazula, and the presence of someone else here now seemed ominous. Friend or foe? It was impossible to guess.

But he'd barely gotten hold of his bow when the person cleared the tree line and moved onto the rocks with careful steps. Heath's mouth fell open, and his bow dropped from his suddenly numb hand, barely making a sound as it hit the sand below him. Not all his wildest hopes or fears had prepared him for what he'd actually find on Vazula.

It was Merletta.

It was Merletta, and she was walking. Merletta had legs.

Heath opened his mouth to call out, but no sound would come. The intense emotions chasing through his mind seemed to have paralyzed him, and he could only stare as she made her slow way toward him, still oblivious to his presence. Even if he wasn't so completely floored, it would have been hard *not* to stare. She was so...complete. He wasn't talking to her torso, while she bobbed in the water. She was completely present, and he could see every inch of her.

He could also see a lot more skin than he'd ever seen on any other girl. That wasn't exactly new—although it had thrown him at first, he'd become used to the fact that Merletta wore only the large shells that were apparently the sole coverings used by mermaids. But now, instead of a tail, she had a very shapely pair of legs, and her skirt—which seemed to be made of scales—only went to about her knees.

Heath's eyes flew back to Merletta's face. Her hair was pulled back from her eyes in the braid she'd adopted since becoming a trainee, and her hands were balled into fists in her concentration. Her eyes were fixed firmly on her feet—*dragon's flame, she had feet!*—but he could still see her look of determination. It was such a familiar, such an utterly characteristic expression that his heart swelled painfully. He couldn't even begin to wrap his mind around the implications of what he was seeing, but one fact drowned out all other thoughts. She was alive! And not barely clinging to life, but from all appearances, thriving.

His words still wouldn't come, but his limbs suddenly unstuck, and he took a convulsive step forward. The movement at last brought him to Merletta's attention, and her head snapped up. The wary look that had sprung into her eyes vanished instantly, and she also froze on the spot.

"Heath," she whispered, her familiar voice carrying across the quiet beach. "You're alive. You're *here*."

She wobbled slightly in her shock, and when she tried to take a shaky step toward him, she teetered wildly. Heath closed the distance between them in a few strides, and she fell forward against him, gladly, he thought.

Without conscious thought, his arms closed around her, and she leaned into him, burying her face in his shirt as she took great, steadying breaths. Heath's mind was swimming, and it was hard to form any coherent thought—there really was an awful lot of skin.

He didn't try too hard to master the emotions swirling through him. He just focused on the sensation of resting his chin on the top of Merletta's head. It was something he'd never even imagined doing before, and he noted with an inconsequential thrill that he was taller than her in this form.

Merletta's breaths gradually began to slow, but she didn't immediately pull back, and Heath made no move to release her. His mind was still in a strange state, racing frantically in response to all the sensations washing over him, but sluggish and unresponsive when he tried to form sensible words.

"You're so warm," he said abruptly, one hand splaying across Merletta's mostly bare back. "Your skin was always so cold before, even in the sunshine."

Merletta pulled back at that, letting out a snort. She swayed unsteadily, and Heath gripped her arm until she seemed stable, then let his hand drop.

"My skin is warm now? That's the difference you're focusing on? I'm not sure if you've noticed, Heath, but *I have legs*." She stretched one out to prove her point, wobbling slightly, but waving Heath's offered hand away. Clearly she'd been practicing, and wanted to show off her skills.

Heath laughed, his heart lighter than it had been in a very long time. "I did notice, actually. And I..." He shook his head. "I have so many questions that honestly, I don't even know where to start."

"I doubt I can answer your questions," said Merletta ruefully. "It's all as much a mystery to me as it is to you."

"Start with telling me what happened that day," Heath said, a slight shudder passing over him. Merletta was still standing very close, and he reached a tentative hand toward her, then let it fall. "How did you survive? I thought for sure you were dying. I thought you were moments from drying out."

"I was," said Merletta wryly. "I did dry out. And I discovered that drying out doesn't have quite the effect I'd been led to believe."

Heath stared at her. "You mean...all you had to do to grow legs was—"

He broke off at Merletta's mischievous grin. "Watch this," she said, before turning and jogging, in a slightly uneven way, toward the waterline. Once she was up to her knees, she dove forward gracefully. For the briefest of moments she was fully submerged, then her head once again broke the surface, with a flash of purple and green shining in the shallows behind her. Heath stared in amazement at the golden tips of her fins protruding into the air. This was the Merletta he knew.

She flipped herself over, diving under the surface again and propelling herself into deeper water. Heath found himself moving forward without realizing he'd decided to, everything in him drawn toward her. But before he could splash into the water, she reappeared.

"Sorry," she said. "I've been above for hours, and I wanted to cool off. Now let me show you my new trick."

She'd just about beached herself by the end of her speech, and with a strange waddling motion, she used her hands to walk herself almost all the way out of the water. Then she flipped her tail up and to the side, so that it was fully on the sand. A strange ripple passed over her scales, and before Heath's eyes, her tail split in two and her fins shrank and solidified. One more blink, and he was looking at a very human girl, sitting on the sand with her legs curled around her, and a skirt of scales fitted around her hips.

His astonished gaze passed up to Merletta's face. "That's quite a trick," he said faintly.

"And it doesn't hurt anymore, thankfully," she said, her voice cheerful. "That first time I was as convinced as you were that I was dying. But I guess my body just wasn't used to the sensation. It is now, though. For a month after that day I stayed on the island, changing back and forth several times a day, and now the process is quite commonplace."

"Commonplace," Heath repeated. "Of course."

She laughed. "All right," she admitted. "It still blows me away every time." She pushed herself to her feet, taking a step toward Heath. Her eyes were shining. "When I dry out, I'm *human*, Heath. Like you."

He stared back at her, suddenly finding it hard to swallow. His conversation with his grandmother flashed vividly across his mind. He remembered the deep embarrassment, almost shame, he'd felt when she accused him of being in love with Merletta, or at the very least drawn to her.

But this...this changed everything.

He was still self-conscious, but for quite different reasons. He certainly no longer had any hope of convincing himself that he wasn't drawn to Merletta. He was drawn to her with a magnetism that was unnerving. He remembered the spark of connection that had passed between them the first time they'd met, and how he'd sensed something familiar in her, some reflection of his own restlessness. Some deeply buried part of him had known she was like him, he realized. Something in his core had recognized her as human, as his own kind.

He suddenly realized that Merletta was watching him in concern, probably because he was standing there staring at her like he'd lost his wits.

"What about you?" she asked, softening her tone to match his mood. "I was afraid you would die of your injuries. I didn't know whether a human could survive losing that much blood."

Heath swallowed. "My injuries healed. They just needed time." He couldn't quite keep the intensity out of his voice. "The guilt wasn't so easy to recover from."

"Guilt?" Merletta repeated, looking genuinely startled. "What would you be feeling guilty for?"

Heath stared at her. "For leaving you here to die, of course!" His eyes searched hers, begging her to believe him. "I tried to get Reka to turn back, I swear."

"Heath." Merletta's eyes were suddenly as intense as his. "You had no choice. You were on death's door yourself. Reka did the right thing by taking you back to your kingdom with all possible speed."

Heath's brows lowered. He couldn't agree with her, but he didn't want to argue about it.

"Besides," said Merletta, in a practical spirit, "if he'd helped me back into the water, Ileana would probably have finished me off. As it was, she thought I was dying too, and she left me be." She flashed Heath a smile. "And as you see, I didn't die."

"But what does it mean?" Heath asked, still unable to comprehend it. "How is it possible that drying out gets you legs?"

Merletta shook her head. "I don't know. But I can only assume that the history we've been taught isn't accurate. At the very least, there must be large chunks missing." She grimaced at him. "I know for a fact that what they're teaching us about humans isn't true. And from what I've experienced, everything we were told about dragons was false as well." She glanced up at the sky. "Where is Reka, by the way?"

Heath cleared his throat. "He's not here. I came by sea." He gestured back toward the boat, pulled up on the sand, and Merletta blinked at it, apparently noticing it for the first time.

Her eyes passed from the boat to Heath's face, their expression shrewd. "I think you have a great deal to tell me, as well."

Heath let out a long breath and ran a hand through his hair. "I do," he acknowledged.

He thought about his strange visions. Merletta was alive after all. Did that mean his grandmother was right, and he'd been somehow seeing her from afar, by use of his magic? He wondered how Merletta would feel about him having watched her, however unintentionally.

"Come on," said Merletta, taking his hand and pulling him over to sit on the sand near the boat. As usual, she seemed to feel no awkwardness about touching him, but Heath's hand tingled from the contact for minutes afterward.

The mermaid-turned-human shifted so that she was facing him, her legs under her and her eyes compelling. "Let's talk."

CHAPTER SIXTEEN

"What happened to the guards wasn't your fault," Heath said softly.

Merletta was still sitting with her legs curled under her, but now she was facing out to sea, her penetrating eyes fixed on the horizon. Their tortured expression tugged at Heath's heart as much as her confession about the guilt that had been eating at her since that day. She'd been just as anguished over the events as he'd been, but she had handled it much better. No descending into surliness, or risking her life with pointless pranks. He was both ashamed of himself, and more proud of her than he could say.

"It wasn't entirely my fault," Merletta admitted, after several moments of silence. "But if it wasn't for me, they would still be alive and well and with their families."

Heath shuffled closer to her. He hesitated for a moment, then reached out a hand, placing it over hers where it rested on the sand. Merletta didn't look at him, but he felt the slight stiffening in her body that told him she was as aware of the contact as he was. Then she arched her hand slightly, so their fingers were interlaced.

The indescribable rush that passed over him was so powerful he could barely gather his thoughts to respond. But the defeated look on Merletta's face reminded him of their conversation, and he gave her hand a squeeze.

"You can't blame yourself. You didn't do anything to hurt them." His voice turned dry. "It was more the other way around, as I recall."

Merletta's eyes flew to his, her expression apologetic. "You're right, they were the ones attacking you. I was angry with them myself at the time. Of course you'd still feel—"

"I'm not angry now," said Heath, shaking his head. "Not at them. They were just acting according to what they'd been taught. I wouldn't have chosen for them to pay such a price for their attack." He looked at Merletta seriously. "But you didn't make that choice, either."

Merletta groaned. "You make it sound simple, but I can't help feeling guilty." Her expressive features set in determined lines. "If I can just find out what really happened, at least that might bring their families some peace."

"Putting your life in danger to get a few answers won't bring them back," said Heath sharply. Alarm filled him at her familiar unyielding expression. "And if they really were killed to cover up the Center's deceptions about humans and land, then finding out what happened to them won't be a simple matter that gives a little closure. It will set your underwater world on fire."

Merletta blinked. "It will do what?"

Heath sighed. "I think you know what I mean."

"I do," Merletta said, serious once again. "But do you really think I should just leave it? Just accept the lies and make no effort to tell everyone the truth?"

Heath frowned, barely aware of it as his hand tightened over hers on the sand. "I suppose not," he said. "But I just wish someone other than you could be the one to uncover it."

Merletta gave a hollow laugh. "So do I."

Heath raised an eyebrow, looking her over. Something flickered inside him, some certainty that didn't come from his normal senses. His power at work, perhaps.

"No you don't," he said, unable to keep a hint of accusation from his voice. "You don't actually wish you could back off, and let someone else confront them. You're spoiling for a fight, aren't you?"

Merletta gave him a smile that was half grimace. "Maybe I am." She shrugged. "I hadn't thought about it in those terms. It's irrelevant, anyway. No one else knows all I know, and no one else is willing to fight back."

"I doubt that's true," Heath mused. "There must be others. You just don't have a safe way to find out who they are."

"Maybe," said Merletta, sounding doubtful. Her eyes were back on the western horizon. "I need to return to the water soon," she said softly.

Heath followed her gaze, his heart growing heavy at the sight of the sun sinking in the sky. His minutes with Merletta were slipping away far too quickly. They must have been talking for two hours, and they hadn't moved from their place on the sand.

He could still hardly believe Merletta was alive, let alone that he was sitting on the beach with her in human form, actually holding her hand. He wished he'd chosen a longer time than three hours when he asked his cousins to stall the captain. Of course, he had no idea whether they'd managed even that. But he felt he owed it to them to return in the time he'd set, if only so they were spared taking news of his disappearance back to his family.

"Are you expected back at the Center?" Heath asked, an edge

to the question. He'd already expressed his alarm at Merletta's decision to return to the Center and take her chances with whoever was behind all the lies. In total honesty, he was amazed she'd been back so long without anyone attacking her. He applauded her decision to get her bearings before making any moves, but he also found it a little hard to picture the passionate mermaid successfully keeping her head down.

"Not just yet," Merletta said, removing her hand from under his. "But I'm getting dry. I need to dip in, just for a minute."

"Getting dry?" Heath repeated curiously. "What do you mean? I thought you weren't in danger from drying out."

"I don't think I'm in danger," Merletta said. "But it's not pleasant. It seems I'm not a true human, even in this form. On some level I'm still a mermaid. I can't be away from the ocean too long without getting this irresistible desire to take in water. It starts in my throat, and it's a dry, scratchy feeling. It's especially strong when the sun is hot, or when I've been working hard on my walking."

Heath stared at her for a moment, then let out a laugh. "You mean you get thirsty?"

Merletta frowned. "What do you mean by thirsty? I don't know that word."

Heath shook his head in amazement. "Of course you don't," he marveled. "Why would you, living underwater?" He saw her bewilderment and laughed again. "Sorry, it's just so bizarre, to think of someone not knowing what thirst is. Humans need to drink as well as eat, Merletta. In fact, it's a more urgent need."

Merletta frowned thoughtfully. Heath was still amused by the absurdity of it, but he thought the earnest crinkle of her forehead was adorable.

"What do you mean you need to drink? I thought humans couldn't take in breath through water."

Heath shook his head. "Not breath. We don't get air from the water. We *drink* the water. It gives our bodies...I don't know. Moisture."

Now it was Merletta's turn to laugh. She cast her eyes over his figure, her features alight with humor. "You don't look to me like you have much moisture to you." She poked him in the ribs. "No, very solid."

Heath rolled his eyes, although he couldn't help grinning. "We don't become liquid. But our bodies need water, for lots of things." He shrugged. "I honestly have no idea how to explain it. But I think it will make sense if you experience it. Come on."

He stood, offering her his hand, which she took without hesitation. Once she was on her feet, he started toward the trees, keeping his pace slow so she could match it. He watched her progress critically. She'd clearly been working on the skill. She was steadier on her feet than he'd first supposed, now that she wasn't reeling in shock from his arrival.

"Where are we going?" Merletta asked curiously, as she navigated around a patch of rock in the sand.

"There's a fresh stream not far into the jungle," Heath said. "I've drunk from it myself. I'll show you."

"I'm not sure about this, Heath," Merletta said warily, once they were looking down at the trickling water. "Any time I've swallowed water while my head was above the surface and my throat was open, it's been horrible. It stings, and makes me feel like I'm suffocating."

Heath smiled. "But that was salt water, wasn't it? From the ocean? Humans can't drink salt water. It has to be fresh, like this stream. It's different, you'll see."

She still looked skeptical, but she copied him as he knelt beside the stream and showed her how to cup her hands. When Merletta managed to get the fresh water down her throat, her eyes opened in sudden surprise, and she rocked back on her heels.

"That's so much better," she breathed. Then, without warning, she pitched forward, sticking her whole torso into the stream and gulping down great mouthfuls of water. When she raised her head, flicking her now sodden braid over her shoulder, Heath was still staring at her.

"What?" she asked.

He choked back a laugh at her bemused expression. "Nothing." Of course she wouldn't have any hesitation about submerging any part of her body. Not only was water her natural environment, but she didn't have elaborate clothes to worry about getting wet.

"I can't believe all that time, I could've just drunk water instead of going back into the ocean," said Merletta, shaking her head. "It would've been much simpler." She glanced up at the jungle. "Of course, I had to go underwater to find food, anyway. I don't know the first thing about finding human food for myself."

"Neither do I, to be honest," said Heath ruefully, following her gaze. "If I do end up stranded here, I'll probably be starving within a day."

Merletta laughed. "I'll fend for you," she promised. "I'll go diving and bring you back some mussels or something."

"So you're rethinking your decision to return?" Heath asked suddenly, leaning forward. They were both still on their knees beside the stream. "You're planning to stay on Vazula?"

Merletta looked surprised by the sudden intensity of his tone. "Of course I'm not rethinking my decision. I've come too far to give up on discovering what's really happening."

"I don't like it," Heath said, unable to stop himself from making one last attempt to dissuade her. "We both know those guards didn't die from land sickness. You're gambling your life on the hope that if you don't openly defy them, the Center won't see you as enough of a threat. Surely it would be easy for them to make you disappear like the guards did."

A shudder went over Merletta. "I already told you, Heath. What happened to the guards is the main reason I can't just swim away now. They died because of me." Her eyes met his, their expression uncomfortably piercing. "Because of us. Because we met here, and created a link between our separate worlds. A link that someone clearly considers dangerous."

"Dangerous enough to kill for," Heath agreed grimly. "Merletta, sharing their fate won't achieve anything."

Merletta sighed, her expression pained. "I'm hoping it won't come to that," she said. "But I have to go back Heath, you know I do. I can't just let it go, pretend the lies are true, and the guards died from their own foolishness, or some human attack." She looked over at him quickly. "I'm not saying I'll abandon you, of course. If you need food, I'll gladly find it for you. But surely *you* aren't staying here?" She frowned. "You still haven't explained how you got here, if Reka isn't with you."

For a moment, Heath was tempted to tell her that he *was* staying, and needed her to stick around to fend for him, just to keep her from returning to her tenuous position in the underwater kingdom. But there were a lot of reasons why that was a stupid idea.

"I came on a ship," he said again. "It's a large vehicle made of wood, which floats on the water, and it can cover great—"

"I've heard of ships," Merletta cut him off. "We've been learning about them in classes. Apparently," she rolled her eyes, "humans are traditionally jealous of merpeople's mastery of the deep ocean, so they used to make these ships and ride across the surface of the water in poor imitation of us."

Heath snorted. "We're not jealous. Truth be told, most humans are too afraid of the deep ocean to want to venture far from land. And not without reason."

"To be fair, we're also taught that humans are afraid of water," Merletta said matter-of-factly. "Ibsen claims that if humans become fully submerged, they die, just as mermaids supposedly die when fully out of the water."

She cast a calculating look at Heath, and he laughed.

"You've seen me fully submerged lots of times, remember? It's not like drying out. I don't grow a tail."

"Shame," said Merletta, her lips twitching. "You'd make a great merman."

Heath shook his head with a smile, unable to picture it. He was fascinated by Merletta's world—how could he not be? But he couldn't say he'd ever felt any desire to have his lower body replaced with a scaly fish tail.

"So where is this ship?" Merletta asked, looking out to sea. "Surely you can't have come all the way from your kingdom in that?" She gestured at the rowboat.

"No, I only swapped to the boat once I reached the magical barrier around Vazula," Heath explained. "The ship couldn't pass through. It's hopefully waiting just out there, although not for much longer. Two of my cousins are on board, and I asked them to stall the captain for three hours if they could manage it."

"Your cousins are just past the barrier?" Merletta demanded.

Heath nodded. "I wish you could meet them." He hesitated for a moment, then rushed on, his voice coming out a little thick. "You could, you know. What's to stop you coming with us? You're human now—you could live in Valoria. You'd be safer than in the triple kingdoms."

Merletta stared at him, her lovely brown eyes wide and shocked. "Me? Live in your kingdom?" She swallowed visibly, and her voice wasn't quite natural when she added, "I doubt I'd be welcome. Aren't your people already suspicious of magic? How do you think they'd react to a mermaid in their midst?"

"Of course you'd be welcome," said Heath fiercely. He leaned forward and seized her hand, unable to help himself.

"No one would have to know you were a mermaid, and if anyone raised trouble, I'd protect you."

Merletta stared down at their linked hands for so long that Heath began to feel self-conscious. He let go, wishing he knew what she was thinking. It wasn't like her to have that type of reaction to the contact. She was usually disconcertingly casual about touch.

"Thank you, Heath," she said at last. "But I can't come with you."

Heath deflated slightly. He wasn't surprised, but he'd had to try. "When will I see you again?" he asked.

Merletta shrugged. "That's more up to you than to me, isn't it? I'll try to come back to Vazula on rest days, because I want to keep learning to use my legs. I'll only stay away if I'm being too closely watched for it to be safe." She gave him a hopeful look. "I'm sure I would learn much more with a teacher."

Heath forced a smile, although his stomach was still churning with unease at the thought of Merletta returning to the Center. "It may not be as easy for me to come as it used to be," he admitted. "I'm expected back in Bryford soon. I can't afford to take a several day voyage too often."

"Can't you come with Reka next time?"

"Maybe." Heath frowned, steeling himself as he muttered, "I'll just have to convince him."

He saw Merletta's puzzled look, and bit his lip. He hadn't told her the extent of his falling out with Reka, and he didn't want to get into it now.

"I'd better go, I suppose," he added hurriedly.

Merletta nodded. "I'll swim with you. I want to see this ship, and I think I'd better make sure it's still there before I leave. We can't have you finding yourself alone in the middle of the ocean, can we?"

Heath couldn't bring himself to match her bantering tone.

His heart was growing heavier with every passing moment. Impossibly, Merletta had been returned to him, as if from the dead, and now he had to leave her, knowing she wasn't safe, not knowing when or if he'd see her again.

"It's not me you need to worry about, Merletta," he said.

Her eyes softened as she took in his furrowed brow. "You say that now."

She reached out, casually tugging his shirt halfway up his chest to reveal the scar from where the spear had pierced his side. Her fingers were gentle but not at all hesitant as she ran them over the raised skin.

There was that unnerving—and exhilarating—unconcern about touch.

Heath found that he was holding his breath, nowhere near able to match her apparent indifference at the contact. Her touch was warm in her human form, but not enough so to explain the fire that raced out from her fingers into his every nerve. It was magic of a different kind, and it seemed impossible that she could really be oblivious to the effect of her touch, and the intensity of their connection.

But perhaps she wasn't oblivious. Merletta's hand lingered on the scar longer than necessary, her expression shifting, and her demeanor no longer so casual. As her hand hovered over his side, Heath was suddenly certain that she felt some flicker of his own protectiveness—she didn't want to let go, to let him out of her sight again. Not after last time.

"I was afraid you'd died, too, you know." Merletta's voice wasn't entirely steady as her eyes moved slowly up to his, holding him in thrall. "And I don't ever want to live with that feeling again."

What he saw in her eyes was anything but indifferent, and for a moment Heath struggled to find words. Merletta's fingers were still stretched over his skin, and he clamped his hand suddenly over hers, trapping it in place.

"I'm not in danger anymore, Merletta," he said earnestly. "But you are. And I would do anything to protect you."

She met his eyes, and for a brief moment, something potent crackled in the air between them. Heath's breath hitched in his throat, and he found himself unable to look away from those expressive brown eyes.

Abruptly, Merletta pulled her hand away, smiling ruefully.

"Well, you can't do anything to protect me. And you know it as well as I do."

Heath sighed, the moment broken. She was right, of course.

"That doesn't mean I don't appreciate the impulse, though," she said, her voice a little wistful. She turned away from him, and her tone became brisk. "Now, let's get this boat back in the water."

Reluctantly, Heath gathered his bow, trying to give his racing heart time to slow. He collected the oars, and together he and Merletta dragged the boat off the sand. He climbed into it, pausing to watch Merletta claim her spear and satchel, then dive into the water. As before, the change was instantaneous. A flash of silver, and her tail was back, golden fins brushing the surface of the water before she disappeared completely.

She resurfaced quickly, pushing a strand of wet hair from her eyes and giving him a curt nod. Heath pulled at the oars, but his progress was painfully slow compared to the mermaid gamboling around his craft. After a very few minutes, Merletta appeared alongside the boat, treading water with that powerful tail.

She latched on to the side with her elbows, pulling it dangerously low to the water. "It's not quite like having fins, is it? You're very slow."

Heath grunted. "Real sailors are much faster," he admitted. "I'm not very good at rowing."

Merletta shook her head, laughing openly at him. "Let me help you out."

She pulled herself along the side of the boat until she could reach the rope tied to the bow. She drew it out from the inside of the boat and looped it around one shoulder before splashing back into the water.

It was a bit of a sting to his pride, but Heath couldn't deny that with Merletta pulling and him rowing, they made much faster progress.

He knew the moment they reached the magical barrier, and he could tell that Merletta did too. The ripple of power had barely passed over him when she disappeared silently beneath the waves, leaving his rope trailing aimlessly through the water. He reeled it back in, searching the waves for her. But as soon as they'd passed through the barrier, the mild afternoon had become threatening. The clouds loomed above, and the swells rose to alarming heights. It was all he could do to keep control of his boat, and the water was far too choppy for human eyes to penetrate below the surface.

But are my eyes really human?

The question flashed across Heath's consciousness, and without thinking too hard about it, he sought Merletta in his mind. At once, he saw her, not just her face, but her whole form. She was twisting in the water, steering herself with her arms, unconcerned by the rough sea around her. She was peering upward, the familiar face looking curious in the weak light of an obscured afternoon sun.

Satisfied, Heath raised his own eyes, and jumped in his seat. The ship was much closer than he'd realized, emerging formidably from the unnatural gray of the afternoon. He pulled frantically at one oar, worried about his boat being splintered against it. He managed to turn, and the ship shifted direction slightly as it crested a wave, so that there was no collision. But Heath's little craft lurched dangerously in the ship's wake.

He shouted, but his voice was lost in the crash of waves. Fortunately, someone had been looking out for him, because a cry from on deck was followed by the thud of a rope landing across his boat. He seized it, his sharp eyes picking out the familiar forms of Brody and Bianca, leaning over the railing toward him.

Without bothering to turn his head, he searched again for Merletta. She was deep under the water now, swimming rapidly, her face set for home.

CHAPTER SEVENTEEN

"Are you sure you're all right, Merletta?"

The sound of her name pulled Merletta from her thoughts with a jolt. She looked up at Sage, noticing that her friend's expression was as exasperated as her voice had been.

"I'm sorry, I wasn't listening."

"I know," said Sage dryly. She raised an eyebrow. "You've been acting funny ever since I got back last night. Was everything all right when you visited your friend?"

Merletta stared blankly at Sage for several long seconds, until she remembered what she'd told Sage about her rest day plans. She felt a flash of guilt at her deception, but even though she hadn't been thinking about Tish, Sage's question did remind her of the uncomfortable visit.

"I don't know," she said slowly. "To be honest, it was a little...weird."

"What do you mean?"

Sage, always a good listener, put down her squid tentacles and gave Merletta her full attention. They were the first of the trainees at the breakfast table, so they had relative privacy.

Merletta could see other Center employees, Emil included, scattered across the dining hall, but none were in hearing range.

Unlike Sage, Merletta didn't meet her friend's eye. She gazed down at the cod on her plate, her throat tightening as she remembered Tish's reluctance.

"I think I came at a bad time," she said. "Tish wasn't really free to talk." She swallowed, adding in a rush, "But it was more than that. I don't think she wanted to see me."

"I'm sorry," said Sage, sympathetically. "Did you two have a falling out?"

"Not that I know of," said Merletta, exasperated. "And you'd think I would know, wouldn't you?"

Before Sage could answer, Andre swam up to the table, and they let the subject drop.

"Good rest day?" he asked brightly.

"Not bad," said Merletta, smiling to herself at the understatement. Her thoughts, now diverted from the strange encounter with Tish, flowed straight back to the topic that had kept her lying awake last night.

Heath was alive. Not only alive, but well, and still willing to brave the dangers of the ocean to continue their friendship. She didn't think she'd forget that moment as long as she lived, when she looked up and saw him standing by her spear, staring at her like he was seeing a ghost. Her heart had seemed to stop, then instantly start beating at double time to make up for it.

There were no words to describe the release she'd felt at seeing him. Not just because finding out that he was alive lifted one of the crushing weights of guilt she'd been carrying. Almost as exhilarating was the relief of finally being able to tell someone everything, without doubt about their trustworthiness, and without fear of the consequences to them. She'd always been able to speak freely to Heath, and she'd never needed his listening ear more.

And he'd invited her to come and live in his kingdom!

But it was better not to think about that. Too many conflicting emotions. It was a tantalizing offer, and she couldn't deny to herself that she'd been tempted. But quite apart from the fact that she couldn't abandon Sage, and Tish, and everyone, she could still see his eager face as he said it.

No one would have to know you were a mermaid.

She knew he meant well, but his words had sent a pang of grief through her heart. She was fooling herself to think that her impossible legs made her a human. She was still a mermaid— the sea would always call to her. She didn't think she could maintain the pretense of being human all the time, and she didn't even want to.

She shook the thought from her mind, trying to pay attention to Andre's chatter about his day off with his family. Reading between the lines, it sounded like he'd spent most of the day boasting to his parents about how well he was doing in combat class. Merletta and Sage exchanged indulgent smiles.

"I'll be seeing them again tomorrow," he added, his face suddenly dropping into more serious lines.

"Why?" Merletta asked curiously.

Andre lifted one shoulder slightly. "They're having a public memorial for the guards who died from the land sickness. I've told Father that I'll come. I'm hoping Instructor Wivell will give me special leave."

"I'm sure he will," Sage said gently.

Merletta couldn't find anything to say. Her stomach was churning with the usual horrible guilt. Heath had been kind to say it wasn't her fault, but she didn't set much store by the reassurance. It was like him to try to make her feel better, but he wasn't really one to talk. Hadn't he admitted that he'd been consumed with guilt over her drying out? And that hadn't been his fault.

She wondered if she should try to get leave to attend the memorial as well. She'd done nothing further toward her vow to find out what had happened to the guards, and the event might be a good opportunity to do some sifting. It would be illuminating to hear the official story of what had happened. Surely whoever was responsible for spreading the tale about land sickness was also responsible for the guards' deaths.

As it happened, neither Merletta nor Andre had any need to get special leave. In the first lesson of the day, Wivell announced in a somber tone that they were all to attend the memorial at dawn the following day.

They were therefore all up before the sun. It wasn't yet the normal breakfast hour, but a number of other Center dwellers were attending the memorial, too, so special breakfast arrangements had been made. Merletta filed behind the other trainees to collect her shell of boiled fish. It had presumably been cooked over a thermal vent nearby, because it tasted fresh. The trainees sat at their usual table in a subdued mood, eating quickly and not talking much.

"I don't think I've had this type of fish before," Merletta commented, trying to break the tension. "I don't even recognize it."

She saw Oliver's lip curl as he looked at her bowl, but she ignored him. She had long ago become used to the derision of the Hemssted trainee at any display of her ignorance.

Andre peered into her shell. "Looks like some kind of bream."

Merletta smiled her thanks, but he'd already bent over his food again, his crimson tail passing slowly back and forth through the water. He was surely thinking of his father's friend. The familiar churning started in her stomach and she said no more, putting aside her barely eaten fish.

The patrol had been made up of Skulssted guards, so the

memorial was held in the wealthiest of the cities. The trainees made their way into Skulssted in a block, accompanied by both Wivell and Ibsen. Agner, they were told, would be traveling with the guards.

They had almost reached the site of the memorial—a public square considerably larger than the one where Emil had teased Sage—when Andre pulled to a sudden stop, and sprang into a salute.

Following his gaze, Merletta saw a burly merman, looking to be about fifty, swimming up behind them. He wore the sash of a Skulssted guard, and was flanked by two younger guards.

He paused as he drew level with them, exchanging a quick word with Instructor Wivell.

"That's my father's superior," muttered Andre to Merletta and Sage. "The head guard of Skulssted."

Merletta regarded the merman before her with interest. This was the one who'd told Andre's father that August and the others were dead, but hadn't allowed them to see the bodies. She'd wondered how to get the chance to speak with him, and here he was before her.

The head guard's gaze passed to the trainees, and Merletta saw a hint of recognition as his eyes rested on Andre.

"A sad day," he said gravely.

"Yes, sir," Andre said, dipping his head respectfully.

"We appreciate you stopping classes to allow the trainees to attend," the guard said, looking back at Wivell.

"Of course," said Wivell. "We wish to pay our respects."

"We all do," Merletta interjected, and everyone's eyes snapped to her.

She could see Ibsen's anger, Wivell's indignation, and the varying levels of shock on all the trainees' faces. The head guard raised an eyebrow, but she pushed on. This might be the best chance she'd have to try to identify whether the head guard was part of the deceptions. It was no time to worry about whether she seemed too forward.

"I for one," she continued, "would like to pay my respects at the graves of the fallen guards as well. Where are they?"

"That won't be possible, Trainee," said the head guard gravely. "They were buried outside the barrier for safety reasons. We don't know enough about land sickness to understand whether there's danger of the infection spreading."

Merletta tried to keep her expression innocent as she searched his face. "But you had contact with them, didn't you? While they were ill?"

The older merman gave a humorless smile. "You are in no danger from the infection, Trainee. It's been months, and I am in perfect health."

"Were you worried, sir?" Merletta pressed. "That you might catch it? I heard they were violently ill."

The head guard's face was grimly expressionless. "I managed to avoid such close contact," he said curtly. "The medical team from the Center are the ones who showed the most bravery."

"From the Center?" Merletta repeated, startled.

The guard inclined his head toward Wivell again. "Of course. The Center medics are the best trained in the kingdoms, and in such a serious case, we called for them immediately. Unfortunately, there was nothing even they could do."

Merletta felt her forehead crease slightly. It was difficult to read the older merman. The secrecy around the guards' burial was suspicious, but it was also believable that he had been deceived himself, rather than perpetrating the deception. She wondered who the medics were. She opened her mouth to ask about them, but Wivell cut her off.

"This is inappropriate, Trainee," he said coldly. He didn't show the anger Ibsen had unleashed on her when she spoke out of turn during the containment patrol, but he was clearly offended by her behavior.

"It's all right, Instructor," said the head guard tolerantly. "It's natural for the trainees to be curious. We all want to learn from this tragedy."

"You are very gracious," said Wivell, inclining his head. He sent another cold look toward Merletta, but she didn't care. She'd discovered one more level of involvement in the deception.

"This way, trainees," said Ibsen. But as the others started swimming, he remained in place, reaching out a hand to grab Merletta's arm. She started at the touch, unable to remember him ever actually laying a hand on her before.

"I have warned you before," he growled. She watched him warily, sure he would say more, but after casting a quick look around, he released her. He contented himself with throwing Merletta a glare that promised consequences later, then swam after the rest of the group. Merletta floated for a moment, pulling in a gulp of water to settle her racing heart, then swam into the square herself.

When she emerged into the space, Merletta's mouth fell open in amazement. Large though the square might be, it wasn't nearly big enough to hold all the merpeople present. Spectators lined the square at the level of the ocean floor. But they were dwarfed in number by the guards, who floated above the square in varying, well-organized levels, tapering in toward the center the higher they got. Together, they formed a kind of sloped ceiling for the square, four sides reaching upward and meeting in a point at the top. It was an impressive formation.

Merletta continued to stare up at them as she swam behind Sage. She'd had no idea this many guards existed—she'd never seen so many weapons all in one place. For a moment she thought that every guard in the triple kingdoms had attended to honor their fallen companions, but a moment's reflection told her that couldn't be true. Some must still be conducting patrols, at the very least, and she doubted the Center had emptied itself of security. She marveled at the thought that the triple kingdoms held even more guards than this.

She was so overwhelmed by the sight that her vision actually spun. The formation seemed to play a trick on her eyes, because for a moment it seemed as though the lines of guards were moving, spiraling inward and making her dizzy. She blinked rapidly, and the vision cleared.

She looked back down until the world righted itself, then glanced upward again.

The four sides of the merperson ceiling were made of four quite separate blocks of guards. It was clear at a glance which ones came from the Center. She recognized the seaweed sashes they wore over their chests, but their expensive driftwood weapons would have set them apart anyway. Merletta frowned as her gaze passed over them, unmoving in their formations, with their weapons pointed upward.

"Why are the guards set up like that?" she muttered.

"Like what?" Sage asked, glancing back over her shoulder.

"In blocks." Merletta gestured at the four distinct groups of guards.

"Those are obviously the Center guards," Sage said, reaching the same conclusion Merletta had. "So I guess the others must be the units from the three cities."

Merletta frowned thoughtfully, and Sage raised an eyebrow.

"What's wrong?"

"I don't know," shrugged Merletta. "It's just, all lined up like that, they look like..."

"Like what?" Sage prompted.

But Merletta just shook her head. She had been going to say that they looked like armies facing off, but a memorial for a fallen patrol wasn't the place to make ominous comments about the triple kingdoms' guards.

"Is it usual for the units to be separated by city?" she asked. "I've never been to an event like this before."

"I have," said Andre from Sage's other side, his voice still subdued. "Although never one as big as this. And yes, that's how they always arrange themselves on formal occasions."

Merletta nodded, her eyes passing over the crowd now as they followed their instructors toward a ridge on one side of the square. The stone had been carved into ascending levels, forming a multi-layered seating area. She raised an eyebrow as she saw other merpeople drifting to seats on the four sides. She suddenly realized that each guard unit was hovering above one side of the square, with a distinct block of merpeople seated below them.

"Are the spectators divided by city as well?" she asked.

"That's right," nodded Andre. "One side per city, and one for the Center."

"Do they have to sit in their area, then?" Merletta asked.

Andre looked surprised by the question. "I suppose so," he said. "I mean, they get directed on arrival."

Merletta's forehead creased as she took in the seating area on the far side of the square from theirs. It wasn't entirely accurate to call it seating, since alone of the four sides, it was merely open water, without a stone ridge. Merpeople were floating upright, unable to sit. It wasn't a large space, given that a coral garden bordered that side of the square, and although there weren't many of them, the spectators were pressed quite close together. A quick glance up showed that the guards floating above that section weren't nearly as well organized, or as well equipped, as the other units. As she watched, one of the guards scratched his nose. Compared to the rigid and unmoving Center guards, they looked like a bit of a joke.

"I think I can guess which area is Tilssted's," she said dryly, her eyes returning to the merpeople floating below.

Following her gaze, Andre gave a shrug. "I suppose it's not as comfortable for them, since they don't have anywhere to sit. But from what I've seen, not many from Tilssted bother coming to these types of public events, so it makes sense that they get the smallest area." His normally cheerful face darkened. "I don't know why they don't show up. After all, the guards who died were patrolling the Tilssted boundary when they got drawn out so far past the barrier. They were chasing a thief who'd been stealing from a Tilssted farm, weren't they?"

"I doubt it's because they can't be bothered," said Merletta frowningly. "More likely they don't have the leisure to attend a memorial. Most Tilssted residents work hard from morning until night to provide for their families."

Andre considered her, an arrested look on his face. "I'd never thought about it like that before," he admitted. His gaze passed back to the few Tilssted attendees, his expression now thoughtful.

Merletta followed with her eyes, once again frowning. The forced segregation of the cities from each other, and from the Center, seemed like the opposite of what these types of public gatherings were supposed to achieve. She looked up behind her, spotting a silver-haired figure at the top of the Center's seated tiers who she was fairly sure was the Record Master, the most senior merman in the whole Center. She'd met him at the Founders' Day celebration the previous year. As on that occasion, he was flanked by two guards, who also looked familiar. Perhaps they were the same ones who'd been protecting him at the Founders' Day event.

As she looked, the Record Master glanced down her way, and something strange once again happened to her vision. His eyes, which she remembered from their previous meeting to have been storm-cloud gray, were suddenly yellow, blazing with the intensity of the sun. She stared in stupefaction as what seemed to be bubbles of boiling water poured out of them, reaching through the ocean toward her. She was frozen to her seat, unable to move, moments from being scorched, when—

"Merletta? Are you all right?"

Sage's voice cut across her thoughts, and she turned, blindly, her heart racing. Couldn't Sage see? They were about to burn!

But Sage's face showed nothing but a faint anxiety as she searched Merletta's features. Merletta turned frantically back toward the top tier, but there was no scalding stream, no danger. The Record Master was still there, but he wasn't looking toward her, and his eyes certainly weren't spewing anything.

Merletta swallowed, her heart still pounding unpleasantly fast. What had just happened?

"You're quite right," Sage said, still sounding anxious. "It's not fair that the Tilssted attendees have nowhere to sit."

Merletta stared blankly at her friend. She'd completely forgotten about their conversation, but now she once again fixed her eyes on the floating Tilssted residents.

"I should watch from there," she said, in a moment of sudden decision. She felt weighed down, oppressed by the living shadow of armed guards hovering over them and alarmed by the bizarre vision she'd just seen. An urgent desire swept through her to put some distance between herself and all things Center. "I'm from Tilssted, that's my section."

She rose from the seat she was occupying, on the lowest tier of the Center's seating, ready to swim across the square.

"Trainees are to sit in their allotted section." The terse voice from behind her made her turn, to see Ibsen glaring at her. "You are studying at the Center, are you not?"

Merletta held his gaze for a pregnant moment, her thoughts in such a whirl, she could barely remember her intention to keep her head down and not cause trouble. But gradually, as he glared at her, her breathing slowed, and sense reasserted itself. She'd already pushed Ibsen to his limit that morning. She subsided, sinking back into her seat. The faint look of triumph on Ibsen's face as he turned away made her clench her teeth. This playing along approach was as difficult to swallow as she'd known it would be.

Before she could stew over it too much, the memorial began, and all thoughts of Ibsen floated away. Merletta was still on edge, confused and already doubting whether she'd actually seen anything out of the ordinary. She couldn't quite sit still, her fins flicking compulsively beneath her. Nevertheless, her attention was fully caught by the sight of Agner swimming to the center of the square. She'd known he was a high-positioned guard, but she hadn't realized he was quite so senior.

Silence had fallen at his approach, and his voice carried clearly through the water. He solemnly welcomed the attendees, and reminded them all of the reason they had gathered.

"This is a tragic loss," he added, his voice grave. "But their sacrifice has achieved one thing, in reminding us of the dangers beyond our barrier, and the importance of being united in our defense of our home."

A shifting behind Merletta made her glance back. Ibsen wore a slightly exasperated look as he watched his colleague, and Merletta had the sense that Agner had drifted off script a little. But she couldn't see anything controversial in what he'd said. Well, except for the bit about the highly exaggerated dangers beyond their borders, but she doubted Ibsen would object to that, since he spent half their classes selling them the same cautionary tale.

Agner's speech was drawing to a close, and he turned, inviting up the head guard of Skulssted whom they had met earlier. The muscled merman threw out his chest before addressing the crowd, and his voice had a booming quality that Agner's had lacked.

"Our comrades did indeed sacrifice themselves for a worthy cause. In bringing back the news of the proximity of land, and of the threat of human aggression, they reminded us to be on our guard," he barked out.

It occurred to Merletta that Agner had actually made no mention of either humans or land. He certainly hadn't said anything about land sickness.

As if reading her thoughts, the Skulssted guard continued. "That, having survived a vicious attack, these guards succumbed to land sickness, is a tragedy that must cut at all our hearts. But it, too, is a reminder for us of the dangers outside our borders, and of the true nobility of our guards in taking risks for the rest of us to live in safety."

Merletta was frowning, feeling vaguely that it was highly suspicious that the guard had begun speaking about land sickness just as she thought it—could he somehow read her mind? —when the water was filled with a loud thumping. She jumped, her mind spinning crazily as she tried to understand what she was seeing.

Looking up, she saw that all the guards floating above them were banging their weapons against one another's in a coordinated, rhythmic salute. They didn't smile or cheer—their faces remained somber—but there was a fierce pride in their eyes as they stared straight ahead. She forgot the speaker's suspicious knowledge as her heart went out to them. Surely most of them had no idea of the lies they were perpetrating regarding humans and land, except perhaps the Center guards. And for all she knew, even they didn't know the truth of what had happened to that Skulssted patrol.

Her eyes fell on Ileana, and a flash of anger went through her. One guard, at least, knew how much of this was a sham.

There was no way Ileana believed those guards had died of land sickness. She must know they'd been conveniently gotten rid of. A swirling discomfort filled Merletta's stomach. Was it possible Ileana had helped kill them? It was a horrible thought. Her eyes narrowed as she noted that the other girl was floating halfway along the row of Center guards. She was surrounded by guards significantly older than her, whereas others her age were at the end of the line. Surely she was in too elevated a position for a brand new guard?

As Merletta stared at Ileana, the water around the guard seemed to shimmer, and Merletta's mouth fell open in a soundless scream of terror. Ileana's head! What was happening to Ileana's head? It was morphing into a shark's head, then back again. The older girl's long, fair hair was twisting in the water, taking the shape of so many writhing sea snakes. It was impossible—what magic was this that turned Ileana into a monster before Merletta's very eyes?

She looked around frantically, but the others were watching the head Skulssted guard with somber expressions. No one else seemed to have noticed Ileana's transformation. And when Merletta looked back up, Ileana looked normal once again, her attention also on the head guard.

Now shaking violently, Merletta followed Ileana's gaze, watching as the head Skulssted guard listed the names of the patrol members.

Through a sheen of panic, Merletta watched as family members came forward to receive tributes on behalf of the deceased guards.

"That's August's wife," Andre muttered, as the last one swam forward. She was a mermaid in early middle age, and she held her back straight as she accepted a large and beautiful conch shell, inclining her head graciously to the head guard before turning and swimming back to the Skulssted seating section.

The head guard turned to the crowd and began to speak again.

"Not just in their deaths, but in their illness, our companions have reminded us of the importance of vigilance," he said, in his barking voice.

The words seemed to bounce around Merletta's mind, like the cries of playful seal cubs. She shook her head. What a strange thing to think at such a serious moment.

"It wasn't easy to watch them succumb to the land sickness," the head guard went on, "but they did us a service in that we have now been reminded of a peril that we once knew, which had almost been lost to our history."

Merletta scowled. Lies, all lies. Land sickness wasn't part of their history. It was a myth. Wasn't it? She ran a hand across her forehead, shivering. Her skin felt like it was burning, as if she really had been scorched by heat from the Record Master's eyes.

But that was nonsense. What was she thinking? Land sickness. That's what the guard was saying. And it wasn't true. She'd been above water more than any other mermaid. She'd even been *on* land! She knew better than anyone that there was no such thing as land sickness.

"Delirium," the guard barked, "hallucinations. Suspicion of those nearest and dearest."

A strange ringing was sounding in Merletta's ears, and a horrible fear began to creep in at the edges of her consciousness. Hallucinations?

The speaker glanced toward the relatives of the deceased, floating at the front of the Skulssted section and clutching their conch shells. Merletta saw that August's widow had a fixed, expressionless look on her face. Merletta knew it well, because she'd worn it many times. It was the look of someone who was in pain, but determined not to show it to the world.

"She didn't get to say a proper goodbye," Andre muttered in

Merletta's ear, his emotion clearly close to the surface. "She wasn't even allowed to be at the burial, for fear of infection."

Something about that was highly suspicious, but Merletta was struggling to focus enough to figure out what.

"They *are* dead, aren't they?" she asked stupidly, forgetting to be discreet. It was only when she realized that Andre was staring at her in bemusement that she remembered he wasn't privy to her suspicions.

"Of course they are," he said, his voice strange. "Why would you even ask that? My father attended two of the burials himself, and saw their bodies lowered into the tombs."

"Oh," said Merletta, blinking rapidly to try to clear her head. "That seems conclusive, then." Sage shot her a warning look, and Merletta fell silent.

Andre was still looking a little scandalized, and Merletta had a feeling she'd put a fin wrong with her words. But she couldn't chase the thought down. There was a buzzing in her ears, like the sound made by the small flying creatures that liked to hover around the lagoon on Vazula. The heavy, scented air of the island was clearly affecting her mind, just like it had the guards'.

But no, that was absurd! She didn't have land sickness! It wasn't even real!

"It's not easy to remember them that way," the speaker was droning on. "But take comfort from this—to give their minds as well as their bodies to our protection is worthy of the highest honor we can give."

He sprang quite suddenly into a salute, and all the Skulssted guards copied him. Merletta reeled forward, the familiar guilty churning in her stomach rising rapidly until she was over-whelmed by it. She was filled with a mad desire to race into the center of the clearing, to confess to everyone that it was all her fault, that the guards hadn't died for honor, or duty, but for her illicit discoveries.

She had a vague feeling that she wasn't supposed to say any of that, but she couldn't remember why. She could hear Sage's voice, and Andre's. They sounded concerned, but the words were muffled. She tried to focus on their faces, and her eyes widened in further alarm. They were speaking, but it wasn't words pouring from their mouths—it was ink, thick, dark, swirling ink. Merletta blinked stupidly, her eyes passing up to the cold, disapproving face of Ibsen, watching angrily as she flopped out of her seat, making a scene.

"What's wrong with you?" The instructor's cold voice cut through the cloudiness surrounding her mind. He seemed to be speaking much too loudly. "Why are you behaving this way?"

His face was distorting strangely, lit with a luminous glow. His words reached visibly toward her like jellyfish tentacles, ready to wrap around her and sting her.

Merletta's mouth opened to say that she was losing her mind, that land sickness was claiming her. But a wordless warning rang out in her mind, and Heath's face flashed before her vision.

You're in danger. That's what he'd said.

She couldn't grasp the reason, but she was suddenly certain that she shouldn't tell Ibsen that her mind was slipping out of her own control.

"I'm ill," she gasped. "In my stomach."

She tried to clutch at her stomach in proof, but she couldn't seem to control her arms or her tail. Turning her head to the side, she became aware that she was somehow floating horizontally, the scene around her jumping erratically as her body convulsed. The speaker appeared to have stopped, the ceremony suddenly arrested.

"Someone help her!" A sharp voice cut suddenly across her abstraction. "That's *our* trainee!"

Merletta blinked stupidly across the square, and saw that

the small number of Tilssted attendees were all leaning forward from their section. Even the Tilssted guards were watching with concern, their already dubious formation losing shape even further.

"Aren't you going to do anything?" Merletta didn't recognize the speaker from the Tilssted section, but he seemed to be glaring at the Center attendees at large. "She's a trainee, isn't she? Don't you even take care of your trainees?"

Merletta wasn't sure if she needed to be taken care of. She'd told Ibsen she was ill, but she wasn't sure if her stomach was churning from nausea, or just from the guilt. That merman thought she was a hero, but he didn't know her part in the deaths of the guards. The guilt inside her began to roil so violently that she didn't think she could contain it.

Her consciousness was overcome by a sinking feeling, then all at once she became aware that her face was pressed against the bedrock. Clearly it wasn't just a feeling—she truly had been sinking down through the water, falling into the open central space. It didn't matter. Nothing mattered except the upheaval in her gut. She turned her head to the side and without warning emptied the contents of her stomach into the water.

She'd never been so ill in her life, and her whole body shook with the realization. She'd hidden it from Ibsen, but she couldn't deny it to herself. She'd thought she was onto the Center's lies, but all along they'd been right. Land sickness was real, and it had finally caught up with her. She should never have gone to Vazula on rest day.

She opened her mouth to say as much, but no words would come. The last thing she was aware of was Sage's terrified face leaning over her before she sank mercifully into uncon-sciousness.

CHAPTER EIGHTEEN

Heath stepped onto solid ground with a definite feeling of relief. It wasn't that he disliked ocean voyages. On the contrary, he'd come to quite enjoy the rocking of the ship, and thought he was getting the hang of what the sailors called sea legs. But ever since his unsanctioned expedition in the rowboat—not to mention the incident with the maelstrom that preceded it—he had well and truly fallen out of favor with the captain.

He was grateful that Brody and Bianca had managed to convince the captain to wait for him. Presumably the man hadn't wanted to face the potential consequences of returning to Valoria without the Duke of Bexley's younger son. One thing was certain, at least—chartering the ship to travel to Vazula a second time would not be an option.

The return journey had felt tedious and slow compared to the journey out. Bianca was too depleted to speed them all the way back, even if Brody and Heath had been willing to ask it of her, which they weren't. It wasn't as though there was any particular hurry from Heath's perspective—he still had a week left of his leave of absence. He was just eager to get off the ship and away from the captain's reproachful scowl.

Of course, the captain wasn't the only one who was a little put out with the young lord. And reaching shore only increased his cousins' opportunities to let him know it.

"All right," said Brody sternly, as they trudged through the small port town where they'd disembarked. "There's no crew listening in now, so are you going to finally tell us what you were up to?"

"Did you reach the island?" Bianca added eagerly, as Heath turned in the direction of the inn where they'd stabled their horses. "Did you find out if the person survived?"

"Yes," said Heath, a small smile lighting his lips. "I reached it all right. And she—the person survived."

Brody rolled his eyes at Heath's attempt to correct his slip. "If you think we didn't already realize this mystery person is a girl, you must think we're exceptionally thick."

Heath laughed. "All right, she's a girl," he said, his heart curiously light. "Happy?"

"You certainly seem to be," Bianca said, eyeing him.

Heath shrugged. "I thought she'd died because of me, and it was eating me up inside. I can't help but be relieved." He was also relieved that she really was a girl—a human girl—but there was no need to mention that.

"So where does she come from?" Brody pressed.

"From another kingdom," said Heath, evasively. "One we didn't even know was out there."

The twins exchanged a look, their expressions troubled.

"What?" Heath demanded.

They were silent for a moment, and then Brody spoke, surprising Heath by his uncharacteristically serious tone. "Don't you think we should be telling King Matlock if there's an unknown kingdom concealed only a few days' sail from our borders?"

"It's not like that," Heath said quickly. "It's hard to explain, but...they're isolated. Extremely isolated. And they won't trouble us. Believe me, they want nothing to do with us. They just want to be left alone."

The twins still looked unconvinced, and Heath felt a surge of alarm.

"I promised," he said earnestly. "I promised her I wouldn't reveal their existence. They truly want isolation. Please, can you trust me in this?"

Brody and Bianca nodded reluctantly, and Heath let out a breath. He could tell this wasn't the last he would hear of the matter, but he would take what he could get for now.

He spent a few more days at Bexley Manor, entertaining his cousins in the way they'd expected when they first joined him. He fully intended to try again to reach Vazula the following week, and spent the time gearing himself up to contact Rekavidur.

But when he rose on the morning of Merletta's next rest day, Heath felt a creeping sense of unease. Before attempting to call Reka, he thought he'd better see if he could use his extra sight to check whether Merletta was going to the island.

Unfortunately, he was still far from mastering the new skill. He sat on the edge of his bed, focusing his mind on the thought of Merletta. He could see nothing. He tried picturing the island instead, but he was almost certain that the image before his eyes was simply his memory of what Vazula looked like.

He sighed, rubbing the heels of his hands over his eyes. Then he leaned forward, resting his elbows on his knees as he again tried to picture Merletta. Unbidden, the memory of her hand splayed against the scar on his side leaped into his mind. His skin seemed to tingle from the remembered touch, and heat raced up his neck. He felt again the intoxicating new warmth of her skin, saw in memory the sand speckled across her cheeks, and the drops of water clinging to her dark eyelashes. With her usual lack of self-consciousness, she had stood so near that if he'd leaned his head down, their foreheads would have been touching.

He drew in a sharp breath as her face flashed before his eyes. This time it was no memory, it was an actual sight of her.

But it was so fleeting he couldn't glean much from it. It was murky again, like it had been when he'd seen her during his time in Kynton. He realized in amazement that the change was probably because she was underwater. She'd been on Vazula for a month after his accident. No wonder his visions of her had been clear instead of obscured back in those first weeks. His eyes, sharp as they might be, were not accustomed to looking through deep water.

But it wasn't just the murkiness of the image that was troubling. Merletta hadn't looked right, the general impression being one of illness or pain. Heath felt anxiety curl in his stomach. Had she been attacked after all? Had whoever was behind the Center's deceptions decided it was safer to get rid of her?

But she was alive, that much seemed certain. Surely if they'd decided to kill her off, they would be able to achieve it with ease. He screwed his eyes shut, trying to block out all distractions as he again focused on the thought of Merletta.

Nothing.

Heath groaned, flopping back across his bed. Why had it been so much easier on the ship?

He hesitated, uncertain of what to do. Should he still try to get to Vazula, in case Merletta was going? He didn't get the sense she was up to a long journey, but he had no idea if he was reading what he'd seen correctly.

He cleared his throat. "Reka?" His voice was soft, although of course that was irrelevant. "Reka, are you listening?"

He waited, straining his mind to see Reka the way he'd done on the hilltop outside Bryford. But his extra sight was still unco-operative.

"Reka," he persisted, "I don't know if you were watching me, if you already know everything that happened. I want to tell you about it in person. I want...I want to go there together. I want to fix this."

He hesitated, remembering the bitter words he'd thrown at the dragon only months ago. He'd said he would never forgive Reka, and the dragon wasn't likely to have forgotten that. But all at once Heath realized that his anger toward Reka hadn't just faded. It had disappeared. He wasn't sure if it was his grand-mother's cryptic hints, or the fact that Merletta was alive after all, or perhaps some combination of the two. But his resentment for Reka was gone, only the years of companionship remaining. The deep loneliness he'd been denying for weeks rushed in, and he finally admitted to himself how much he missed his friend. His grandmother was right. He'd be an utter fool to throw away a friendship so rare and powerful.

"I'm not giving up," he said stubbornly. "I'll travel to Wyvern Islands if I have to. I know for sure now that I can pass through a magic barrier without you. But it would be a lot easier if you came here, and saved me the trouble."

He waited hopefully, but his eyes saw nothing but the room before him. He went about his day, his heart growing heavier as no reptilian shape appeared in the sky.

Heath swallowed his disappointment, determined not to show his cousins anything but a cheerful face. He'd moped enough for a lifetime in the last few months. It was time to pull himself together and do something useful.

In pursuit of that goal, he announced to Brody and Bianca

that he was ready to leave for Bryford again whenever they were.

"I thought you weren't expected back until next week," Bianca said, surprised.

Heath shrugged. "I'm not, but I've done what I came home to do. It's time for me to focus on the role King Matlock has given me. Percival's loyalty ceremony is only a couple weeks away." He frowned. "I hope he hasn't been getting himself into trouble while I've been distracted."

Brody chuckled. "You do realize you're the younger brother, don't you? You're as bad as Percival was when you were injured."

"No he's not," said Bianca dryly. She gave Heath a reproachful look. "Percival was completely unmanageable when he thought your life was in danger."

Heath sighed. "That's probably the first time I've ever been the one needing looking after, so I'm not surprised he didn't know what to do with himself."

The three of them left early the next morning, reaching Bryford before noon. Heath rode through the city gates with mixed emotions. He was frustrated to be riding away from Vazula, but on the other hand, he was much more cheerful than he'd been last time he was in the capital. He was still deeply concerned about Merletta's safety, knowing that she was balanced on a knife's edge in her training program. But the discovery of her survival had pulled him from the spiral of grief and guilt that had been crippling him since he nearly died on the abandoned island. Merletta's ongoing danger notwithstanding, now that he was looking around with fresh eyes, he found he had much more attention to spare for the challenges facing his own kingdom.

He didn't follow his cousins to the castle, where they were staying, but rode on to his family's city residence. He had barely handed his horse over to a groom when he heard himself hailed.

"Heath!"

He turned to see his mother hurrying across the small court-yard, an expression of relief on her face.

"Mother," he greeted her, with a smile.

"You're here early," his mother said, her eyes raking over him. "I'm so pleased."

Heath was touched by the anxiety on her face, but before he could say anything, she hurried on.

"Your brother might listen to you. We've warned him, but he doesn't seem to understand how it might appear."

Heath turned toward the house with a wry smile. "Percival up to mischief, is he? I see why you missed me."

His mother blinked, and a look of consternation came over her face. "I didn't mean that, Heath. Of course I'm delighted to see you on your own account." She cast another look over him as he walked, her gaze appraising. "Do you feel well? Your leg really is fully healed?"

Heath paused at the residence's front door, which was being held open by a servant, and gestured for his mother to precede him inside. "It's all right, Mother," he said with good humor. "I'm fine." He sighed. "And I was worried about what Percival might be up to. It's one of the reasons I came back earlier than expected. Where is he?"

"Over at the royal training yard, apparently," she said, pausing in the small entrance hall to wait for him. "Or at least, that's what we were told. He didn't mention his plans to us."

"Even worse," muttered Heath to himself. Louder he said, "I'll head over at once, Mother. Just give me a minute to change. It was very dusty on the road."

"Of course you need some time to settle in." The Duke of Bexley's calm voice cut across their conversation, as Heath's father appeared in the doorway of his personal study. "Come in, Heath. I'm glad to see you returned to us safely and, I trust, well."

"Very well, Father," said Heath respectfully. He strode into his father's study, his mother close behind him.

"How was your journey?" the duke asked, as he closed the door behind them.

Heath hesitated, casting a glance at his father's face. The expression was serene, giving no indication that the question referred to anything other than the morning's ride into Bryford. Still, Heath wouldn't want to gamble on the chance that his father was unaware of his recent voyage. The Duke of Bexley often knew more than he let on.

"Uneventful, thank you," said Heath. "What's this Mother was telling me about Percival?"

His father gave a small sigh, his gaze flicking to his wife then back to his younger son. "Whatever you might think, Heath, we don't expect you to answer for Percival's actions. You've just had a long journey. Take some time to rest, and join us for luncheon."

"But, Norik—" the duchess began, but her husband cut her off.

"Give the poor boy time to catch his breath, Elsabeth." He frowned slightly at Heath. "I hope you know that your role as His Majesty's liaison to power-wielders doesn't make you responsible for restraining Percival from whatever he might choose to do."

"Of course I know that, Father," said Heath staunchly. "And I think *you* know that it's not my role as liaison but as brother that makes me determined to go straight to the royal training yard. At least," he amended, "after I change."

His father waved him from the room, but he still looked troubled. And Heath heard him murmur to his wife, with an uncharacteristic note of anxiety in his voice, "Perhaps he *is* too young for the responsibility of this liaison role."

Heath frowned as he hurried to his own room. He couldn't help feeling a little stung. He knew he'd been distracted, and a bit reckless, when he came back from Vazula last time. But had his behavior really been bad enough to make his father doubt his capacity for the role? And he wasn't being reckless now—he'd come back with the specific intention of shouldering his responsibility.

What would it take for him to prove that he could do this?

CHAPTER NINETEEN

Half an hour after his arrival, Heath—who had not only changed his clothes but had been forced by his parents to eat a few sandwiches—was hurrying back out the gate into the bustling city. It didn't take him long to reach the castle. He didn't go in, instead skirting around it until he reached the royal training yard.

He could tell before he arrived that something unusual was going on. The yard itself was a square, surrounded on all sides by a covered walkway with no walls, held up by supporting pillars. It wasn't unusual for guards to gather around the edges of the training yard to watch a much-anticipated bout, but this was something else entirely. The walkway was so crowded with onlookers that Heath couldn't even see into the training yard. And most of those watching clearly weren't guards.

Heath, his heart sinking, had barely begun to elbow his way through the crowd when a cheer rang out from those in front.

"That's me done up," groaned someone to his left, and Heath grimaced. The crowd placing wagers on the fight was just the element of tawdriness the situation needed.

He finally pushed through to the front, in time to see

Percival throwing a burly guard over his shoulder and slamming him to the dusty ground. Mingled cheers and groans went up from the spectators, and Heath's eyes, sweeping across the yard, noted four more prostrate guards.

Percival, who had been fighting unarmed, wiped his face on his sleeve. Then he held out a hand, grinning, and helped the nearest guard to his feet.

"Any other takers?" he asked cheerfully.

A particularly muscular guard stepped out from the crowd, but Heath had seen enough.

"Percival," he said grimly, emerging into the open space.

A whisper of amusement went through the crowd, a couple of voices audible above the rest.

"Uh oh, now you're in trouble, My Lord."

"His Majesty's messenger is here."

Heath ignored the jabs, his focus on his brother. Percival looked over at him, eyebrows raised in exaggerated surprise.

"Heath! You're back early." He shook his head, a grin on his face. "You know I hate to be a spoilsport, but I'm afraid the answer's no. It just wouldn't feel right to fight my little brother."

Heath wasn't impressed. He knew he shouldn't rise to the bait, but frustration welled up within him. He wished his father was right, that he wasn't responsible for Percival's conduct. But he left his brother alone for less than a fortnight, and he returned to this?

Heath clenched his teeth. It was beyond infuriating that he couldn't even afford the time it took to reassure himself that Merletta was alive without Percival threatening to uproot everything he'd been working toward.

"This isn't a joke, Percival," he said, his voice low and tense. "Do you realize how foolish this is?"

Percival shrugged an impatient shoulder, turning away and making a show of wiping his sweaty brow with a towel.

"Don't start lecturing. You're as bad as Father. If you want to talk about foolish, let's discuss a certain idiotic challenge on the bridge above the falls."

"I don't deny that was foolish," said Heath curtly. "But at least I was only endangering myself. This is bigger than you, Percival, you surely must realize that."

"You're making a fuss over nothing," Percival said, his voice not nearly as quiet as Heath's. "Steffan did this all the time in Kynton, you saw him yourself. I watched him fight six guards at once, and no one seemed bothered by that."

"Prince Steffan is a prince," said Heath, through his still-gritted teeth. "His father is the heir to the throne. And it's different in Kyona, you know it is."

"I know that, all right," said Percival, a hint of bitterness in his tone. He turned back around, meeting Heath's eyes boldly. "But I don't see how Steffan's position is so very different from mine. It's not like he's the future king—that's his brother."

"He's royal," said Heath. "He's the grandson of the king, and it wouldn't take much at all for him to find himself on the throne. He can afford to take licenses." He stopped, exasperated with himself for letting Percival draw him into an argument about an unimportant detail.

"And I'm the great-grandson of a king," said Percival, shrugging again. "We're royal too, or on the cusp of it."

"It wouldn't take so much for you to find yourself on a throne either, My Lord," called a clear voice.

Heath's eyes grew wide, and even Percival stilled at the unexpected words. Heath whipped his head around, searching the crowd for the speaker. Everyone had gone quiet, and there was no way to tell who had called out.

"Who said that?" he demanded. "Who's talking such nonsense?"

The onlookers were still hushed, many of them looking a

little nervous. But some of them, Heath noticed, were looking at Percival appraisingly. A horrible crawling sensation rose up Heath's body. He was sure the men were imagining what Percival would be like in the role of crown prince. Were they really so short-sighted as to be impressed by Percival's physical strength? Prince Lachlan's cool head and genuine dedication to his people was far more desirable in a ruler. Certainly, Percival was more charming, more personable than the reserved young prince. But surely these men must realize it was *because* he wasn't the crown prince that Percival could be so free with his manners.

"We're going home," said Heath curtly, turning back to his brother.

Their eyes locked, and he could see Percival's belligerence.

"I don't answer to you, little brother," said Percival, quite calmly.

Heath stood rooted to the spot, completely at a loss for how best to answer. He could see now how poorly he'd handled the situation. He should never have allowed things to come to a confrontation in front of all these witnesses. Could he really expect Percival to give in tamely when it would mean losing face with the whole royal guard?

Percival turned to his newest challenger, and Heath took a step back, finding that he was shaking slightly. How had things deteriorated so quickly? A few months ago, it had been Percival hovering protectively over Heath, and now this was where they found themselves? Clearly the effort of being responsible for his brother's sake had been taking a greater toll on Percival than Heath had realized. Or maybe Kyona had just turned his head. Either way, Heath felt a surge of guilt for his role in Percival's current state of mind. He should never have left the city to sail to Vazula.

But then, how could he regret doing it? Merletta's image

swam before his mind, and a surge of delighted amusement cut through the tension of the moment. She was so endearing, holding out her feet proudly, for Heath to admire. Utterly oblivious to the fact that in Heath's world, no respectable girl would walk around with bare feet, let alone invite a young man to observe them. Let alone have legs bare from the knees down, not to mention her shoulders...

Heath shook his head slightly, horrified to realize he'd been distracted thinking about Merletta's shoulders while Percival casually hacked away at the monarchy. This was why he couldn't afford to disappear off to Vazula again.

And yet, he couldn't bring himself even to pretend he wasn't going to try to get back there the first chance he got.

"Percival." His soft voice cut across the clamor as wagers were placed on the new match being formed. Percival turned his head, responding more to the quiet plea than he had to Heath's anger. "I'm trying to help."

Percival met his eyes in silence for a long moment. "Trying to help who, Heath?"

He turned back to his opponents, and Heath fell back a step, feeling like he'd been slapped.

He didn't linger to watch Percival continue to showcase his abilities. But neither could he bring himself to return to his home and admit to his parents that, if anything, he'd made things worse. It would just reinforce his father's concern that Heath was unfit for his responsibilities.

The crowd of onlookers parted for him as he left the training yard, many of them throwing him furtive glances. He didn't meet anyone's eye. He had no desire to know what the spectators thought of his confrontation with Percival. But he couldn't avoid noticing, with a sinking heart, that even more people were running toward the scene, eager to watch the spectacle.

Unable to think of anywhere else to go, Heath made his way

to the castle and sent a message with a servant, notifying Prince Lachlan of his return. He thought vaguely of seeking Brody and Bianca out again, but to his surprise, the servant came back in search of him immediately.

"His Highness will see you now, My Lord," the servant said, dipping his head. "If you'll follow me?"

Heath did so, and soon found himself in a handsome room he'd never entered before. Prince Lachlan was sitting behind a large mahogany desk, and a quick glance around convinced Heath that he was in the crown prince's personal study.

The prince gestured Heath to a seat opposite the desk, and the servant bowed himself out.

"Your Highness," said Heath respectfully, as soon as the door closed behind the servant. "I hope my message didn't get mixed up. I didn't intend to interrupt you, just to let you know I'd arrived."

"No, your message was clear," said the prince gravely. "But I wished to speak with you. I hope I don't inconvenience you."

"Of course not," said Heath quickly. "I'm at your disposal."

Prince Lachlan watched him enigmatically for a moment, one finger tapping on the smooth surface of his desk. Seated here, surrounded by neatly stacked parchments and framed by an intricately drawn map of Valoria on the wall directly behind him, the crown prince looked older, and less accessible.

"I trust your break was pleasant?" Prince Lachlan said at last.

"It was, thank you," Heath said, hoping that his wariness didn't show. "But I'm ready to work now. I have some ideas about the loyalty ceremony, and I—"

"Do you?" Prince Lachlan cut him off, eyebrow raised. "I would love to hear them."

"Well," said Heath, feeling a little rattled by the prince's manner, so different from their last meeting, "I was trying to think of ways to make it feel like a celebration as well as a ceremony. In Kyona, it wasn't unusual for the power-wielders of my generation to perform little displays of their abilities, for the entertainment of the populace. It was always with the permission of King Eamon, of course, and it was very popular. I wondered if King Matlock would consider coordinating such a showcase as part of the ceremony. It might make our magic seem a little more accessible to everyone else, and hopefully the power-wielders would feel valued if His Majesty invited them to demonstrate their skills."

Prince Lachlan stared at him for an uncomfortably long time, his expression inscrutable. "And what form would these displays take?" he asked at last. "Give me an example of the type of thing you pictured."

"Well, my family's talents are a little bit difficult to work into a ceremony like that," acknowledged Heath. "But my cousin Brody, for example, could manipulate flowers, perhaps cause a bed of our emblem to weave itself into a wreath to present to the king. Or Bianca could play music on a set of wind chimes, or Jasmine could—"

"Lord Heath," Prince Lachlan interrupted again. He stood up, striding to the window and putting his back to Heath as he looked out of it.

Heath blinked after him, wondering if he was supposed to follow.

"Have you spoken to your brother since your return?"

Heath's wariness tripled, and he took a moment to consider his answer. The last thing he intended to do was carry tales about Percival to the crown. But he also wasn't going to lie to Prince Lachlan and pretend he hadn't seen his brother.

"I spoke with him very briefly," he said. "We haven't had the chance to discuss the ceremony."

Prince Lachlan turned quite suddenly, his eyes searching Heath's face shrewdly.

"You are making a genuine suggestion then, about the ceremony?"

"Of course, Your Highness," said Heath, nonplussed. "What else would I be making?"

The prince let out a sigh, and crossed back to his desk, lowering himself into the chair almost wearily. "I very much want to believe that you're being honest with me, Lord Heath."

"I am," Heath insisted. "I don't understand what you mean."

Prince Lachlan sighed again. "Then I'll be honest with you, and acknowledge that your suggestion is a good one. Had you made it a week ago, I would have wholeheartedly endorsed it to my father."

"But now?" Heath asked, a sense of foreboding overtaking him.

"Now, I don't think it would be well received," said the prince dryly. He fixed Heath with another penetrating look. "I don't know if you're aware, but Lord Percival has, on his own initiative, organized...I suppose I must call it a competition, between any of his relatives who wish to take part. It has been publicly advertised, to take place a week before the loyalty ceremony. I believe the idea is for any participating power-wielders to display their magic in the most potent form they can devise, and for the spectators to decide on a winner, presumably demonstrated by the volume of their approval." His voice was decidedly dry by the end of this speech.

Heath gaped at Prince Lachlan. Could Percival really have been so foolish as to organize such an event without consulting the royals, such a short time before his loyalty ceremony? It wasn't as though he didn't know how sensitive the whole issue was. Heath had a sinking feeling that Percival didn't just know, but fully intended to play on that sensitivity in encouraging his cousins to make a public display of their talents.

"I wasn't aware," he said, trying to transform his expression into something devoid of emotion. He felt a surge of irritation with his brother. The display in the training yard had been bad enough. It had never occurred to Heath that it was just practice for something larger. No wonder Percival hadn't wanted to come with Heath and the twins. He'd clearly had plans of his own for the time they were gone.

"It's a shame," said the prince candidly. "If the idea had been brought to my father for inclusion in the ceremony, at his instigation, and with a focus on celebrating the beauty of our people's magic, rather than the overwhelming force of it…"

He trailed off, and Heath understood what he meant. After Percival's stunt, the king wasn't going to approve an idea that made it look like he was trying to belatedly—and less impressively—mimic Percival's competition. Percival had ruined what was probably Heath's best idea for the ceremony, one which could really have brought the two camps together.

"Do you think you can persuade him to change his mind?" Prince Lachlan asked abruptly. "It would be much simpler if it wasn't necessary for the crown to step in."

Heath felt a thrill of dread at the words *necessary for the crown to step in*. But he still hesitated before replying.

"To be honest, I doubt it. I have no authority over Percival, and I have less influence than you might imagine."

The prince ran a hand over his face. "I suspected as much. And actually I probably have more of an idea than you think." He gave Heath a weary smile. "I have a younger brother of my own, remember. There may have been a time when he was able to persuade me into not doing what I wanted to do, but if so, I can't immediately think of it."

Heath blinked, a little taken aback by the image presented. He'd always thought that the seventeen-year-old Prince Knox was the more likely to need talking out of a foolish idea, but of course he knew nothing of what Prince Lachlan might be like in private. Still, he reflected with a touch of bitterness, it was hard to imagine that Prince Lachlan had ever required anything like the constant reining in that made Heath feel like Percival was aging him before his time. Perhaps he should have allowed himself to spiral destructively for a little longer. His return to responsibility had clearly been Percival's signal to once again go his length.

Heath returned to his home with a heavy heart, and was therefore irritated to encounter Percival crossing the courtyard, whistling cheerfully, as though he had no care in the world.

"Back, are you?" said Heath bitingly. "Done making a fool of yourself?"

Percival paused, raising an eyebrow at Heath. "I don't think I'm the one who was made a fool of, little brother. What possessed you to come clucking into the training yard like a mother hen? Did you think I would meekly follow you home?"

"I thought you would listen to sense like a rational person, but that was my mistake," said Heath. "What's this nonsense about some competition between the power-wielders? Don't tell me you're still pining over the tournament? I thought you'd accepted that you can't compete in that anymore."

"Oh, the tournament," laughed Percival. "As if I care about that. Where's the achievement in beating an ordinary fighter?"

Heath stared at him. "You used to think a great deal of that achievement a couple of years ago."

Percival shrugged, turning away. "That was before I went to Kynton."

"You're being an idiot, Percival," Heath snapped. "There's a reason Grandmother invited me and not you to visit her in Kyona."

He regretted his words a moment later, as Percival whipped back around to face him. "Ah, so you admit it, do you? You were just as eager as she was to keep me from finding out what it's like for our cousins over there. What it *should* be like for us here!"

Heath's mouth dropped open. "What are you raving about?" he demanded. "You know I'd never been to Kynton before. I had no more idea what it was like over there than you had!"

Percival made a noise of disbelief. "You and Grandmother are always holed up, drinking your tea." He put an impressive amount of scorn into the last word. "I'm sure she told you all about it, and how I wasn't to be trusted with the knowledge."

"That's ridiculous," said Heath, forcing himself to speak calmly. "We never had any conversation like that, and if you'd stop being so self-absorbed, you'd know it. You think I have nothing better to do than sit around talking about you?"

Percival glared at him for a moment, then the anger suddenly melted from his face. "Oh, this is stupid, Heath. Why are we fighting about this? What do you care if I want a friendly competition? No one's making you take part."

"I care because unlike you, I'm trying to bridge the gap between the power-wielders and the rest of the kingdom," Heath protested. "Surely you must see this will make it worse. Prince Lachlan said—"

"Ran straight to your new best friend, did you?" Percival interrupted, the anger creeping back into his eyes. "I should have known you'd report it all to him. I know you promised to keep an eye on me before you went away."

It was Heath's turn to give an incredulous grunt. He had no idea who had reported to Percival about his earlier conversation with Prince Lachlan, but he supposed he shouldn't be surprised that his brother had placed a sinister interpretation on it.

"I never promised anything of the kind," he said, willing himself to be patient. "And I didn't say a word to him today about our run in at the training yard." He felt a surge of anger. "I can't believe you think I would!"

Percival looked him over silently. "Well, it's hard to know what to think, Heath. I thought you'd have my back."

"I do have your back," Heath insisted. "That's why I don't want to see you run into the kind of trouble you're headed toward, Perce."

"You're making a big deal out of nothing," said Percival dismissively.

"Nothing?" Heath protested. "You think it's nothing when a crowd starts saying it wouldn't take much for you to find your-self on the throne?"

"It was one person," said Percival impatiently.

"One person in front of an eager crowd," corrected Heath, his voice sharp.

"I mean, he wasn't exactly wrong," Percival muttered.

"Percival!" Heath gasped. "It would take the deaths of Prince Lachlan and Prince Knox to put you in the succession. You think that's nothing? That's *treason*."

"Let's not get carried away," said Percival placatingly. "No one's talking about killing anyone, not even the hecklers in the crowd. You were saying that Prince Steffan is vastly different from me, so he can afford to do what he likes. My point is just that he has one brother before him in the succession, and I have two cousins. It's really not so different."

Heath stared at his brother. The ominous feeling from Prince Lachlan's study was back, and it was more powerful than ever. Percival's words alarmed him, but it was the dismissiveness with which he spoke that was really frightening. It seemed to Heath that Percival was on a knife's edge, and far from walking with care, he wasn't even taking his situation seriously.

"Oh relax, Heath," said Percival impatiently, taking in his expression. "I'm not after the throne. I just want to be able to celebrate my magic, instead of being made to feel ashamed of it.

You'd understand if you had any. It's easy for you to think nothing of the crown's restrictions on the rest of us."

Heath clamped his lips shut over the retort he was longing to utter. Without a word, he turned and began to stride toward the house. The last thing he wanted to do right now was tell Percival of his burgeoning power. His brother didn't deserve that kind of trust.

Not to mention, Heath felt no desire to align himself with the power-wielders if this was their attitude.

CHAPTER TWENTY

Merletta

The first thing Merletta was aware of was the pained groan that reached her ears. The second was the realization that it had come from her own mouth.

She blinked groggily, but made no effort to push herself upright. Everything was too sore.

"Merletta? Can you hear me?"

The sound of Sage's familiar voice sent a current of calm over Merletta. If Sage was with her, she was probably safe. She hadn't even realized until that moment that her body had been tensed with fear, but once she identified it, her mind raced back, trying to find the source of her alarm.

With a gasp, her eyes flew properly open, her gaze latching wildly on to her friend's face as recollection returned. The memorial! Her hallucinations! She thought she'd been dying of land sickness, so how was she not only alive, but fully lucid again?

She frowned to herself, remembering her panicked thoughts. But of course she didn't have land sickness. The illness was a lie, formed to cover up even deeper deceptions. She'd lived *on* land for a month without anything addling her mind. How had she allowed herself to be fooled into believing it?

Unpleasant details began to emerge from her confusion, and she groaned again, covering her face with her hand and blotting out Sage's image.

"Merletta?" Her friend sounded anxious.

"I heaved up my guts in front of the entire triple kingdoms, didn't I?"

There was a moment of silence, and when Sage spoke again, she sounded like she was trying not to laugh. "Well, sort of, yes."

Merletta lowered her hand, grimacing. "What in the ocean happened?"

"I was hoping you could tell me that," said Sage frankly. "You went all rigid, and it seemed like you couldn't hear us talking to you. Then you sort of flopped out of your seat and...well, you remember that bit."

Merletta shuddered. She was remembering not only her humiliating moment of illness, but what had come before.

"I was delirious," she said. "I was hallucinating all kinds of strange things. I thought I had land sickness."

"What?" Sage's voice sounded panicked, and she glanced around.

Following her gaze, Merletta realized that she was in a hammock in an unfamiliar room, and she and Sage were mercifully alone. She really should have checked that before half-confessing that she'd spent time near land.

"Do you really think you might have it?" Sage pressed anxiously. "Does that mean it's not a lie after all?"

"Of course I don't have it," said Merletta, running a hand down her face and trying to banish the memories still dancing through her mind. "If it was real, I would have died from it a long time ago." She frowned thoughtfully. "But something affected my mind. No question about it. I saw...the strangest things."

"What could affect your mind like that?" Sage demanded.

Merletta shook her head helplessly. "I don't know. But it was just as they described, wasn't it? Hallucinations, panic, then illness."

"Are you saying," Sage sounded more frightened than ever, "are you saying that whatever happened to the guards really did happen to you?"

Merletta glanced around to make sure they were still alone, then met her friend's eyes seriously. "Except I didn't die, did I? I feel fine. Which supports the theory that the guards were killed, rather than dying of the ailment, whatever it is."

"If someone was going to kill the guards to silence them," Sage objected, "why not just do it? Why not attack them when they were next out on a patrol? What's the point of making them sick first?"

Merletta thought it over for a moment. "I suppose," she said slowly, "the point was to discredit whatever they'd reported by making everyone think they'd been hallucinating. And," she added, on a sudden thought, "to make everyone more afraid than ever about going near land."

"I suppose that makes sense," said Sage reluctantly. It was clear to Merletta that part of her friend still wanted to believe the whole thing was just a big misunderstanding.

"Of course it does," said Merletta, pushing herself to a sitting position at last. "The idea of losing your mind to an invisible and incurable sickness is enough to terrify anyone. It terrified *me* when I was delirious. I know better than anyone that land sickness isn't real, but even I started to believe I had it. I almost said it aloud. I was regretting going to the island on my rest day, and I nearly said that, too."

"You went to the island on your rest day?" Sage repeated, sounding horrified. "And you didn't tell me?"

But Merletta was barely listening. She felt her eyes go wide as the implication set in. "Whoever caused my delirium must have known it," she whispered. "They must have been trying to discredit me, maybe even to use the false illness to prove that I'd been near land. And it almost worked—I almost blurted it out. But I was so careful on rest day," she muttered to herself. "I was sure no one was following me."

"Merletta, I can't believe you didn't tell me you'd been—"

Sage broke off abruptly, and Merletta looked up to see the last merperson she expected float into the room.

"Emil," she said blankly.

His gaze flicked to Sage, then returned to Merletta, looking her over calmly. "You're awake. That's a good sign."

"I...yes," said Merletta lamely. "I feel fine now."

He nodded wisely, drifting over to float near Sage. "That's good to hear."

"What are you doing here?" Merletta asked blankly, looking between the two of them. "And come to think of it, where is here?"

"You're in the Center's infirmary," Sage explained quickly. "And Emil has been here a lot since you collapsed. One of us has been with you all the time. You've never been alone."

"What do you mean since I collapsed?" Merletta asked ominously.

"The memorial was two days ago," Emil said.

"I've been out for two days?" Merletta demanded.

"I believe you were given a sedative when you were brought in here," said Emil, still placid. "But as Sage said, one of us has been with you at all times since then."

Merletta stared between them. "Thank...you?" In her confusion, it came out like a question.

Sage gave a tight smile. "It was Emil who suggested we shouldn't leave you alone," she said. "He seemed to think you might be in danger."

Merletta looked at the young record holder in amazement. "What made you think that?" she asked, as innocently as she could manage.

Emil lowered himself onto an empty hammock beside Merletta's, his face even more serious than usual. "It struck me," he said evenly, "that you displayed symptoms similar to the ailment that gripped that unfortunate guard patrol. And they, as we all know, died shortly after falling ill."

Merletta stared at him. Was he acknowledging her theory? Did he know what had happened? Or was he just sharing her suspicion? Either way, she was completely stunned to hear him expressing such thoughts.

"Well, I haven't died," she said bluntly. "And it occurs to me that I may well have the two of you to thank for that."

"Perhaps," said Emil, looking thoughtfully at Sage. "Perhaps not."

Merletta waited, but it seemed he wasn't going to elaborate. After a prolonged silence, he said, still in his usual calm voice, "Am I right in guessing that prior to your collapse, you experienced some kind of hallucination?"

Merletta hesitated, looking over at Sage, who gave an encouraging nod. Clearly her friend trusted Emil, but then, Sage had always been very trusting.

"I did," she said carefully.

Emil showed some emotion at last, his features marred by a slight frown. "That is...troubling."

"Well, it wasn't land sickness, that much is certain," said Merletta firmly. "Do you have any idea what else could cause something like that?"

A frown was still etched across Emil's face. "I've been

researching that question for some time," he said slowly. "I have access to records you do not. And there are creatures whose venom can addle the mind. Have you been stung by anything recently?"

"I don't think so," Merletta said, surprised. She frowned in thought, and her voice became excited. "But Ibsen did grab my arm! It was after I spoke with the Skulssted head guard. Ibsen was furious with me for asking questions, maybe enough to try to get rid of me once and for all."

"I heard about that," said Emil dryly. "You weren't very discreet, were you? It wasn't exactly surprising that Instructor Ibsen reacted as he did. However, I doubt very much that he swims around carrying rare venom on him just in case a trainee enrages him."

"I wouldn't put it past him," muttered Merletta, but without much conviction. It would be so convenient if she could prove that Ibsen was behind the attacks on her. She knew him to be her enemy in terms of passing the program. It would be reassuring to discover that he was her only enemy, rather than there being another one who was targeting her life rather than her studies.

Merletta frowned up into Emil's calm face, framed by the long fair hair that floated gently with the current. "What's your part in this?" she asked bluntly. "Why are you helping me? Why have you been researching what could cause hallucinations?"

Emil's expression didn't change. "Just because not everyone is as flagrant as you are, doesn't mean you're the only one capable of questioning what you're told," he said.

"So you think the story about the guards doesn't add up?" Merletta pressed eagerly. She was sitting up very straight now. "You never said anything!"

Emil's gaze flicked to Sage, a crease once again appearing

between his brows. "Why would I say something to you? Did it occur to you that I was kinder *not* to share my suspicions?"

"You think I want to endanger my friends?" Merletta protested, stung. "I tried to keep it to myself until I had proof, but Sage is sharper than you give her credit for!"

"You do realize I'm floating right here, don't you?" Sage interjected, a bite in her voice. Merletta threw her an apologetic grimace.

"Of course we realize," said Emil calmly. "I'm not saying anything I don't wish you to hear, Sage. You already know my thoughts on the advisability of you setting yourself up as sole guard and confidant to Merletta, after all."

Sage flushed slightly, and Merletta found herself raising an eyebrow as she looked between them yet again. Clearly she'd missed some serious developments while she was unconscious.

"So who are you helping by keeping watch over me here?" she asked wryly. "Me, or Sage?"

"Both, I hope," said Emil. He frowned at her. "You're smart enough to know how dangerous your secrets are, Merletta. I hope you know what you're about, bringing Sage into them."

Merletta squirmed guiltily as his words hit a sore spot. She'd never been quite at ease about endangering Sage, but she didn't see that she had much choice. "What do you know of my secrets?" she asked evasively, over the top of Sage's irritated splutter.

"I have my guesses," said Emil placidly. "But I'm sure there's a great deal I don't know. I would be very interested to discover where you actually were over your break, for instance."

"Well, I'd tell you if I knew for certain I could trust you," Merletta said frankly.

"Merletta!" Sage admonished, but Emil shook his head.

"I don't take offense. She's right to be careful." He frowned, but he didn't look annoyed. Just thoughtful. "Did you find out anything useful?" he asked, changing tack abruptly. "When you interrogated the head guard before the memorial?"

Merletta shot him a startled look, but he seemed to be asking a genuine question rather than criticizing her.

"Not much," she acknowledged. "I think it's possible he believes the guards really died of land sickness. It seems like he handed them off to Center medics when they were ill."

Emil looked more thoughtful still, and Merletta went cold as a sudden realization hit her.

"The same medics who brought me here after I was ill, probably," she said hollowly.

"Possibly," Emil agreed, still deep in thought. "But if someone was trying to recreate what happened to the guards, they made a strategic error."

"They did?" Sage asked faintly.

"Of course," nodded Merletta. "Because I'm alive. And now all they've achieved is to give me more information on what happened to the guards."

"I'm not sure how experiencing the illness firsthand gives you more information on how it came about," interjected Sage dryly.

Emil clearly wasn't listening to her, his eyes on Merletta, but his gaze unfocused. "If you didn't get stung, then I wonder..." He trailed off, then rose from the hammock where he was sitting. "I'll research further."

Voices floated in to them from the next room, and Emil dropped his voice. "If I were you, I wouldn't linger here now you're awake. Get out, be seen, go about your life."

There was no time for more. A medic was drifting into the room, and with a curt nod, Emil moved toward the door in a leisurely fashion.

"Be seen?" Merletta asked Sage, bemused.

"I imagine he's referring to your admirers," Sage said quietly.

"After you passed out, there was a bit of a scene. You may have noticed that the Tilssted attendees had recognized you."

Merletta nodded. "*Our trainee*, they called me."

Sage nodded as well, smiling faintly. "Well, they got very worked up about you collapsing, and about what they clearly considered a lackluster response from the others in our stand."

Merletta raised an eyebrow. "That would have been worth seeing," she said, amused. Her smile dropped. "I'm sorry to have disrupted the memorial, though."

Sage shrugged. "You couldn't exactly help it."

The medic had reached them now, and Sage fell silent while the other mermaid checked Merletta over and asked her some basic questions. To Merletta's relief, she was released within minutes, and told to take it easy until she felt back to her full strength.

Merletta wasted no time in pushing herself out of her hammock. She shook her arms out and flicked her tail back and forth, finding that the movement helped reduce the stiffness.

"So what day is it?" she asked, as they swam out of the building. She felt disoriented by the discovery that she'd been unconscious for so long.

"It's the first training day for the week," Sage said. "They would have started a couple of hours ago, but I'm sure Agner will be understanding."

"Well, that's something," said Merletta cheerfully. "It's almost worth being violently ill to escape Ibsen's class and skip straight to training." Her smile slipped away as they swam, however, and she found herself chewing her lip anxiously.

"What's the matter?" Sage asked quietly. "Are you worried about how you caught the illness or whatever it was?"

"No," sighed Merletta. "Well, yes, of course I am. But I was thinking about the medics who treated me. I don't know how much they did, and I'm not going to be able to pay for it. To tell the truth, I have no idea what will happen when they charge me."

"Charge you?" Sage repeated in astonishment. "You don't have to pay for that. You're a trainee, the program covers it."

"Really?" Merletta was amazed. She'd never been looked at by a trained physician before. "Even for me?"

"Especially for you," laughed Sage. "They wouldn't be able to get away with less." She shook her head ruefully. "Your *admirers* would have stormed the gates otherwise. I was a bit distracted checking you were still alive, but I heard that some of them actually did try to follow us back here, to make sure you were all right."

Merletta said nothing, dazed by this information. Most of her life she'd had no one on her side, just her own determination, and the moral support provided by Tish's friendship. It was surreal to think of strangers being willing to vehemently fight her cause.

And speaking of unexpected allies...

"Was it really Emil who said I shouldn't be left alone?" she asked.

"It was," said Sage, shooting her a sideways glance. "He insisted on sharing the load himself. He obviously thinks highly of you."

"He doesn't seem to want me dead, anyway," said Merletta. "So that's something. And I'm starting to warm to him as well," she added fairly. "I must say, it's nice to have someone we can trust among the record holders." She threw Sage an apologetic glance. "He's right, you know, about it being dangerous for me to drag you into this. You're only a trainee, like me, and more vulnerable than someone like Emil."

"He's not right," Sage snapped, with unexpected heat. "I'm not as fragile as you both seem to think. I have just as much right as either of you to make my own choice about taking the risk."

Merletta stared at her friend, surprised. "I'm sorry, Sage," she said tentatively. "I didn't mean—"

"It's fine," said Sage with dignity. And without another word, she put on a spurt of speed that left Merletta blinking in her wake.

CHAPTER TWENTY-ONE

Merletta

Taking Emil's advice to heart, Merletta did her best to be visible after her return to classes. The other trainees had all greeted her with interest when she and Sage joined them at training the day she awoke. Andre was so pleased at her recovery, he even wrung her hand. She was a little touched by his response. She'd wondered if he would be offended that she had disrupted the memorial.

To her relief, she could see no sign that anyone suspected her of having suffered from the mythical land sickness. She was heartily glad she'd kept all her delusional thoughts to herself. From all most of them saw, she'd had a severe case of nausea, nothing more.

"You must have eaten something that disagreed with you," Andre said when she first returned, shaking his head sympathetically. "Now it's out, you should be fine."

Lorraine stifled a snigger at the mention of Merletta's embarrassing display, but Merletta ignored her, turning Andre's words over in her mind. He'd spoken innocently enough, but the guess certainly made her think. She'd completely forgotten that they'd been served their breakfast in individual portions the day of the memorial. Was it possible someone had slipped something into her food? Shame on her, if so. She should've been more careful, after Ileana and Jacobi tried to poison her with pufferfish the year before.

She barely had the opportunity to discuss her thoughts with Sage, however, let alone seek Emil out to tell him. Unfortunately, she had mastered the shorthand as quickly as Emil had predicted, so she no longer had classes with the junior record holder. And even Sage was difficult to get on her own. The instructors were all working the trainees harder than ever, and given that Merletta was trying to avoid secluded situations, opportunities for private conversation were pretty slim.

With regret, she accepted that it wasn't wise to return to Vazula the next rest day, both in terms of her physical strength after the illness, and her need to avoid attracting attention.

Beyond Andre's sympathy on her first day back, no one had mentioned her illness, and she certainly hadn't seen any sign of an attack. But she thought she'd still better be cautious, and she wasn't the only one of that opinion. In a rare moment of privacy in their barracks, Sage had dragged out of her the information that she'd seen Heath when she returned to Vazula the previous week. Swallowing her reaction to learning that her friend had once again cavorted with a human and then hidden it from her, Sage demanded that Merletta promise not to return the following rest day. Her position was too fragile, Sage insisted, and Merletta had to admit she had a point. Lorraine had swum into the room at that moment, so there was no time for more discussion. But Sage clearly considered Merletta bound by the promise, and when rest day came, Merletta made no attempt to give her friend the slip a second time. She just hoped that Heath wasn't on the island, waiting in vain for her, as she had for him so many times the year before.

In spite of her sensible decision, Merletta found herself

leaving the barrier sooner than expected, albeit under quite different circumstances.

"All right, Second Year," Agner addressed her briskly one training session, after giving the rest of the trainees their instructions. "Do you remember I told you that you would be doing training outside the training yard this year?"

Merletta nodded.

"And you said, if I recall correctly, that you have no objection to completing some of your training outside the barrier?"

Merletta raised her eyebrows. "I'm going outside the barrier today?"

"You are," Agner said. "A guard patrol will be accompanying a group of harvesters to a natural oyster farm not far to the south of the barrier. It's the perfect opportunity for you to begin your acclimatization training."

"My what?" Merletta demanded.

"It'll all be explained on the way," said Agner, with a dismissive wave of his hand. He nodded to a small group of Center guards on the far side of the yard. "They're expected at the oyster farm, they're just waiting for you." He glanced down at the spear in her hand. "Got your weapon, I see. Good. Off you go."

Merletta swam quickly over to join the group, which she was relieved to see did not contain Ileana. In fact, there was no one near her age. They were all at least fifteen years older than her, if she judged correctly.

"You're the trainee for the acclimatization exercise?" the oldest, a silver-haired mermaid, asked her curtly.

Merletta nodded.

"I'm Freja," said the mermaid, clearly the patrol's leader. She gave the order for the guards to move out, then fell into place beside Merletta.

"Got your weapon? Good, good. Need to be prepared for the

ocean beyond the barrier. You get all sorts out there." She squinted through the water at the tip of Merletta's spear. "Confident with it, are you?"

"Fairly," Merletta said respectfully.

Freja nodded. "Had a trainee several years back sent out for acclimatization training with a blunt pole." She made a noise of disdain in her throat. "Shouldn't allow them to progress to second year if they haven't even earned the right to their own spear yet, if you ask me. But then, no one would ask me. They do their own thing in the training program, and it's all a bit above my head."

Merletta looked at her sideways. "You didn't come to the guards through the program, then?"

The older mermaid barked out a laugh. "Hardly. I never had any interest in being a record holder. Dull job, from what I can see. I always knew I wanted to be a guard. I started out as a Skulssted guard, actually, then transferred across to the Center when they were recruiting."

"I didn't know that happened," said Merletta, interested. "One of the trainees has a father who's a Skulssted guard, and he's been telling me a bit about it, but before that I never really knew anything about how the guard training worked for the different cities."

"Ah yes, young Andre," said Freja, with a touch of fondness. "I know his father well. Everyone's given him a hard time for entering the program instead of training with the guards, but we're all proud of him, really." She cast a fiercely affectionate look back in the direction of the training yard. "*He* won't be moving to second year with a blunt pole, that's for certain. I'm surprised he hasn't been given a spear already."

Merletta chuckled. "I imagine it won't be long. Agner's working him to the bone, which means he likes him, and sees his potential."

Freja smiled tolerantly, and Merletta studied her surreptitiously. After swimming in silence for a while, she plucked up her courage for another question.

"If you know Andre's father, does that mean you knew the patrol leader who died?"

The other mermaid's face became grim. "August? I knew him all right. Worked with him for twenty years. He was a good merman."

"I'm sorry," said Merletta, subdued.

They had passed out of the Center by now, and were crossing the drop off. They swam silently over the dark ocean floor far below, heading south. Merletta felt a flicker of excitement. Tilssted was the northernmost of the cities. She'd never been outside the barrier to the south before.

They didn't pass through Skulssted this time, instead making for a low wall that ran along the southern edge of the drop off. It was a visual barrier only, of course. The patrol swam up over the marker, and found themselves in a wealthy neighborhood.

"Is this Skulssted, or Hemssted?" Merletta asked.

Freja grunted. "Hard to say. It's right on the boundary of the two. Depends which house you knock on as to what answer you'll get. Those who drifted this way from Skulssted say it's part of Skulssted, and those who...well, you get the idea."

The residents of the neighborhood were stirring, going about their morning's business as the patrol passed. Merletta was surprised by how much attention their group was getting, and even more surprised when she realized that the whispers and gestures seemed to be focused on her.

One of the other guards had clearly also noticed. He looked back curiously at Merletta, and sudden recognition lit his eyes.

"You're the Tilssted trainee, aren't you?"

"Uh, yes," said Merletta, taken aback. "That's right. I'm Merletta."

The guard grinned. "I'm Felix."

Freja looked Merletta over appraisingly. "I thought you looked familiar. I saw you collapse at the memorial. Glad to see you've recovered."

Merletta winced. "Not my finest moment."

Felix chuckled. "It's one way to make yourself memorable, I suppose."

He cast another glance at the interested onlookers, and Merletta followed his gaze. She'd found it strange enough to attract the attention of strangers when the trainees had been in Tilssted. It was even more unnerving to realize that she'd become recognizable even in this unfamiliar neighborhood.

Soon enough, they reached the oyster farms that sat at the southernmost tip of the triple kingdoms, nestled between Skulssted and Hemssted, although here also there was no clear boundary between the two cities.

Merletta gazed in amazement at the farms. They were both like and unlike the kelp farms she was used to. For one thing, they were very clean. And for another, there were well-dressed merpeople floating around the edges, obviously there to buy pearls wholesale.

But the strands reaching upward were in some ways reminiscent of the kelp towers, except that these were covered in clusters of oysters rather than waving fronds. And the workers hurrying up and down the rows could have been laborers from the kelp farms.

Merletta scowled slightly. Of course. She should have realized that the wealthy residents of Skulssted and Hemssted wouldn't want farm jobs, not even in an oyster farm. These workers were probably from Tilssted, like her.

They didn't linger in the farms. The patrol collected a group of a dozen merpeople, each with a sagging empty satchel slung over a shoulder. Then they continued down one of the long rows, between pillars of oysters that disappeared upward out of sight. She knew the moment they crossed the barrier, because the familiar ripple passed over her.

No one else showed any reaction to the barrier, so she didn't realize she'd erred until Freja gave her a sidelong glance.

"Not easily rattled, I see. Most trainees find it unnerving, passing through the barrier for the first time."

Merletta grimaced internally at her slip. She should have remembered that, unlike everyone else in the group, she was believed to have spent her entire life inside the boundaries of the triple kingdoms.

"I was prepared for it," she said, which was of course true. "I read about it in the records room at the Center." This was also perfectly true. "It wasn't quite like the records described, though. They made it sound like it would be painful."

Freja frowned. "Really? I wouldn't say it's ever felt painful. Uncomfortable at first, perhaps, but that's probably only because it's unfamiliar, and therefore unsettling."

Merletta said nothing. She didn't think she'd ever found it even slightly uncomfortable, even as a child. But since so much of the Center's job seemed to be to convince everyone to stay inside the barrier, it wasn't difficult to imagine why the public records would describe the experience as unpleasant.

"How far is this natural oyster farm?" Merletta asked.

"A fair distance," Freja said. "About half an hour's swim. It's not harvested often, and we always try to take trainees with us if there are second years. It's in a particularly good position for acclimatization training."

"Instructor Agner never explained what that—" Merletta began, and the older mermaid cut her off with a nod.

"Ah yes. Well, as you know, the triple kingdoms are built on a large, mostly flat section of the ocean floor. Although there is some variation within the cities, no dwellings are built very high above the base level. The work towers, and the farms, extend quite far up, but it wouldn't be safe to actually live so close to the surface."

Again, Merletta held her peace.

"But as a guard, you will need to be capable of not only passing through, but maintaining your skill level at the deepest and shallowest points of our territory. And that territory extends beyond the borders of the triple kingdoms. We regularly patrol outside the barrier, and take groups for activities such as this."

Freja gestured at the harvesters, who were glancing around them nervously, as if expecting the ocean to suddenly erupt with dangers now that they had left the barrier.

"The thing is," she continued, "our bodies are used to a certain depth. We aren't conditioned for the shallows up above. Going too high often leads to light-headedness. And we also aren't used to the true depths. The pressure down there can do funny things to both body and mind. It is possible to develop that conditioning, though. That's where acclimatization training comes in. You'll stand a better chance in your test if you have some experience with heights and depths."

"So why is the spot we're going particularly good for the training?" Merletta asked.

"You'll see," said Freja, with the hint of a smile.

And when they reached the wild oysters, Merletta did see. The oysters were perched on a rocky shelf some distance above where the group had been swimming. Above them, the water was clear and unobstructed all the way to the surface high above. Below, the rocky ocean floor gave way to one of the steepest drop offs Merletta had ever seen. The bottom wasn't visible, the vertical shelf disappearing into blackness.

The harvesters headed straight up to the oysters to begin

their work. Merletta followed, watching in awe as one of the mermaids extracted a stunning pearl.

"This one's a beauty," the harvester commented, holding it up. The others clustered around to have a look, nodding.

"It's not very round," Merletta pointed out.

The mermaid chuckled as she stowed it safely in her satchel. "That just gives it extra value. It's how you can tell it's natural, not from a farm."

"Trainee."

The call brought Merletta's attention back to Freja, and she hurried to rejoin the patrol. The older mermaid sent the other guards to sentry positions around the harvesters, then turned to Merletta.

"We'll start with the height training, I think. Proceed up toward the surface until you begin to feel discomfort, then come back down. I want to test your natural limits to establish a base line."

"What if I don't feel uncomfortable at all?" Merletta asked.

Freja raised an eyebrow, but she looked more amused than disapproving. "Confident, aren't you?"

Merletta shrugged. "Just asking."

"Then you can go all the way up. Don't actually break the surface, though, or I'll be in trouble with the program for endangering a trainee."

Merletta nodded, then turned upward. It was strange to be swimming for the surface with an audience of official Center guards rather than in secrecy. They were deep under the water line, and it took her a couple of minutes to swim up to where the shafts of sunlight were piercing the water. She reached up a hand, a suffocating feeling coming over her at being so close to the air but not allowed to enter it. But she knew she was already taking a risk in so openly displaying her comfort in the uppermost layer of water. She wasn't about to disobey her instructions as well.

She swam back down, trying to pay attention to how the depth affected her body. She was so used to going up and down from the surface that she didn't generally notice it. But now that she was focused on it, she noted the sensation of building pressure in her head. It wasn't pleasant.

She reached the oysters again to find Freja staring at her. "Did you go all the way up on your first try? I told you to turn around when it became uncomfortable, and take it by degrees."

Merletta shrugged. "I didn't find it uncomfortable. If anything, it was more uncomfortable descending again."

Freja narrowed her eyes thoughtfully, and Merletta's heart picked up speed. Perhaps she shouldn't have been so honest. But the older mermaid sounded more surprised than suspicious.

"Well, I don't know when I've seen a stronger natural aptitude. We won't waste much time on height training, then. Let's see how you fare in the depths." She jerked her head toward Felix, and he swam over. Merletta noted that he was the youngest of the group except for her, probably not much older than thirty.

"I'll come with you," he said kindly. "Swimming into a drop off is pretty unnerving the first time, plus there could be some dangerous creatures in there."

Merletta nodded gratefully, not at all sorry to have company when venturing into the dark hole. She was determined not to show any fear, however, and she swam forward without waiting for him to go first.

"Turn back when your head begins to ache," Freja called after them. "Unless you're impervious to depth as well as height, of course."

But Merletta very soon realized that she was anything but

impervious to depth. She hadn't gone far at all when the pressure became uncomfortable, and she had barely entered the dark part of the drop off when the discomfort turned to pain. She pulled up.

"We'll go back up for a break," Felix said, his voice reassuring. "You did well for a first time."

Merletta didn't tell him that she'd explored drop offs before now. She'd never liked going deep, but she hadn't previously attempted it so soon after ascending to the surface. Clearly her body didn't like the change in pressure any more than the next mermaid's.

Determined to improve, she went down again, and again, shivering with the increased cold, and fighting against the suffocating feeling of the darkness closing around her. The harvesters worked for several hours, by the end of which time she'd barely managed to reduce the discomfort at all. Freja assured her this was normal, but Merletta still felt a little discouraged.

Any time she needed a break from the repeated descent, she was set to sparring with the other guards at varying heights. She was pleased to find no noticeable difference in her strength or endurance, even when she fought Felix a mere two feet below the surface. On instructions from Freja, she collected increasingly large rocks from the shelf just below the oysters and carried them almost to the water line above. Her arms ached after half a dozen such exercises, but she was able to complete the task without serious strain.

Freja was clearly impressed, but Merletta just wished she could perform similarly when it came to descending into the drop off. Not only did her skin crawl in the blackness with the feeling of being watched by many invisible eyes, but her strength seemed to flee. The pressure weighed so heavily on her that, despite many attempts, she couldn't successfully carry a boulder down and back up again. Her arms, straining with tension, always dropped it before she could begin the ascent, and it sank into the darkness below. There was no sound of it hitting the ocean floor. Merletta wondered, with a shiver, just how deep the drop off went. She was fervently grateful that Freja had prohibited her from taking her spear down with her. She would almost certainly have lost it.

Felix, more experienced in acclimatization exercises, was allowed to carry his weapon. On one of their descents, it became clear that he was under instructions to defend the unarmed trainee if necessary. They had stopped for a rest, surrounded by darkness and out of sight of the rest of the group above, when a flash of movement near Merletta's shoulder caused her to turn quickly.

Felix sprang into action, thrusting forward with his spear almost before Merletta had recognized the creature in front of her. Merletta gave a cry, reaching out to grab the wooden handle of the weapon as it shot past her. Clutching it, she yanked it back.

It grazed the guard's side, and he let out a grunt of pain.

"I'm so sorry!" Merletta gasped, horrorstruck. "I didn't mean to hurt you."

"It's nothing," said Felix, examining the skin carefully. "No blood."

They both relaxed visibly. The last thing they wanted was to attract sharks to the group. Merletta's eyes darted behind the guard, watching the startled ray gliding rapidly away, its fins rippling gracefully in the water.

"What were you thinking, though?" Felix demanded. "Don't you know how dangerous it is to grab a spear mid-lunge like that?"

"I'm sorry," she said again. "I know you were just trying to defend me. But I was closer, so I could see that it was only a ray. I didn't want it to get speared because of me."

"Only a ray?" the guard demanded. "Rays are incredibly dangerous. That stinger could kill you if it got you in the wrong place."

"Well, it could," said Merletta slowly. "But it wouldn't, would it? Not unless provoked. They're gentle creatures, generally speaking." She realized that the guard was staring at her in utter bemusement, and she hastened to add, "From what I've read, anyway."

"I have no idea where you read that," he said emphatically. "Because what I was taught in my guard training is that they're deadly. Just like most of the animals out here past our boundaries. Why do you think they're among the creatures that can't get through the barrier on their own?"

Merletta frowned. She hadn't, of course, read any such thing. No doubt any records held by the Center regarding rays would align with what Felix had been taught. She was speaking from her own experience of the creatures. She knew they could be dangerous—as her companion said, that was why the magical barrier kept them out. But that didn't mean that they were always dangerous, and it certainly didn't mean they needed to be speared on sight.

Worried that she was already giving herself away too much, she remained silent. But the deception continued to wear on her. Felix seemed well-intentioned and reasonable. She would so much like to tell him what she knew, educate him about how to navigate the open ocean without the constant fear he'd been drilled in.

Her head was aching furiously by that time, and instead of descending further as intended, she was forced to admit that she needed to rise. Still, undaunted by her continued failures, she didn't stop her forays into the drop off until Freja insisted on it. And that was only after Merletta had grown so faint on her deepest descent yet that Felix had to half drag her back up to where the harvesters were working.

When they returned to the triple kingdoms Merletta was exhausted, but filled with an obsessive determination to master this new skill.

"When will you return to that spot?" she asked Freja eagerly, as they swam back through the oyster farm.

The older mermaid chuckled. "Eager, aren't you? I'm impressed. You've got the greatest natural aptitude I've seen yet. Most trainees would rest on that, but I see you combine it with a drive to improve. That's an unstoppable combination."

"So you'll take me back?" Merletta pressed.

Freja chuckled again. "We won't be going back there for six months, most likely. But you can practice in the drop off surrounding the Center."

Merletta deflated. "That's not nearly as deep."

"No, but it's a good place to start," said the guard calmly.

Merletta gave an absent nod, her thoughts far away. She knew of a number of deeper drop offs than the Center's one, they just weren't within the triple kingdoms. She'd have to make a detour the next time she left the barrier clandestinely.

The group had just re-entered the Center when a pair of young mermen caught Merletta's eye. She glanced over at them, floating together outside the recruit-master's office. It wasn't hard to see why her eyes had picked them out. With expressions hovering somewhere between trepidation and awe, they looked very out of place.

She had almost passed them when one of them caught sight of her, and he nudged the other excitedly.

"That's her!" he whispered.

The other merman's head whipped around, and the two of them raised their hands in clumsy salutes. Merletta just blinked at them, totally unsure how to respond. The guards didn't stop, and she continued along in their midst, still feeling bemused.

"I wonder who they were," she said, half to herself.

"Applicants for the program, I imagine," said a guard right behind her. "That was the recruit-master's office."

"He won't be happy," said another guard, and the first one grunted.

"Why not?" Merletta asked.

Felix, swimming alongside her, raised an eyebrow. "You haven't heard what a foul temper he's been in? All these new applicants are making extra work for him, without any actual returns."

"New applicants?"

Freja gave her a searching look. "It's strange that you're not aware of it, since you're the cause," she said bluntly. "I don't think we used to get many applicants from Tilssted, but since you got into the program, it's a different story."

"I heard there were ten applicants from Tilssted in the last month alone," piped up the other guard. "Obviously—" He shot a self-conscious look at Merletta and corrected himself. "Uh, that is, as it happens, none of them have actually passed the entry test. So most of the recruit-master's staff think it's a waste of time. I have a friend who works in that office, and she was complaining about it to me the other day."

Merletta said nothing. The sudden increase in applicants from Tilssted was news to her. She recalled being told, when she applied more than a year ago, that they hadn't had a single applicant from her city for years, not even an unsuccessful one. She was stunned to learn that her acceptance into the program had such far-reaching impact.

But turning it over in her mind as she swam, she realized it shouldn't have been a surprise. She remembered perfectly how much opposition she'd faced, even within Tilssted, to her ambition to become a record holder. No one had ever given her the smallest encouragement to think it was a viable path for her to pursue. It was only natural that her success had proven to others in Tilssted that a different future was possible.

"Well, this is where we leave you," said Freja, as they drew close to the trainees' barracks.

Still lost in her thoughts, Merletta simply nodded, but Freja's next words drew her out of her abstraction.

"I'll be frank with you, Merletta. You've impressed me today. I'm aware from Agner that you intend to continue past second year and become a record holder. But I would love the chance to try to change your mind. You'd be a real asset to the guards, in my opinion. You'll have lots more training with the guards over the coming months, as you prepare for your test, and I'd love to take a hand in it. If you don't object, I'll ask Agner to assign you to my patrol again."

"Of course I don't object," said Merletta, stunned. "I would be honored."

Freja gave a curt nod of acknowledgment. "Good. We'll keep working on your depth training, but we'll also need to step up your combat. From what I saw today, you show promise, but you have a bit of water to cover. You'll improve more quickly sparring with my guards than with the other trainees. It's only a couple of months until your practice test, so we don't want to waste any time."

"Practice test?" Merletta asked, hoping her apprehension didn't show in her voice. She hadn't been told anything about a test in only a couple of months.

"It's standard to do a practice test to gauge your progress," Freja said. She gave another nod. "I'll be seeing you again soon, then, Merletta."

Still a little dazed, Merletta thanked her. Felix gave her a friendly smile as he followed the rest of the patrol toward the guards' complex.

Merletta watched them go, her thoughts swirling unexpectedly. She'd never seriously considered it before, but perhaps the life of a guard wouldn't be so bad.

CHAPTER TWENTY-TWO

Heath kept his face expressionless as he watched Percival approach the throne. The frustration that had been growing over the last two weeks was so all-consuming he couldn't even feel relief that the day of the ceremony had finally arrived. For the first time since accepting his role, he had actually thought he could contribute something helpful to the relationship between the crown and the power-wielders. But thanks to Percival's pig-headedness, his suggestions had been worse than useless. Prince Lachlan still seemed to believe in his goodwill, but Heath had the distinct impression that the king now regarded him with suspicion. Certainly none of his ideas had been incorporated into the ceremony. Instead of a celebration of magic, it was a somber and unembellished formality.

His brother didn't meet his eye as he passed Heath on the long walk down the throne room. Percival was at least as angry with Heath as Heath was with him. He'd barely spoken to Heath since King Matlock had formally prohibited the proposed competition between the power-wielders. In the rant that Percival had unleashed on Heath before imposing his frosty silence, he made it clear that he blamed Heath for this turn of events. Heath didn't know how Percival reached that conclusion, but he was no stranger to Percival's volatile moods. He figured his brother would cool down with time.

Apparently, two weeks wasn't enough time.

In spite of his own irritation, Heath felt a pang as he looked at his brother's determinedly stiff back. He'd listened to more impassioned tirades from Percival than he could count. But until now, he'd always been just a sympathetic ear. Or an exasperated ear, depending on how unreasonable Percival was being. Either way, this was the first time he'd actually been the focus of Percival's anger on any matter of true substance.

He didn't like it at all. Reka was still ignoring him, and now Percival wouldn't talk to him. And to make matters worse, the tension in the lead up to this loyalty ceremony had required his constant presence and his full attention. He'd had no chance to even think about returning to Vazula. And he was too distracted by his duties to practice using his extra sight. He'd barely had a glimpse of Merletta since returning to Bryford.

Heath's sister, Laura, shifted beside him, and he glanced over at her. Her eyes were fixed on Percival, who had reached the front of the room and was standing to one side of the throne, his face visible in profile.

King Matlock had stood, and was giving his young cousin once removed a welcome that was not entirely convincing. Laura risked a murmur, her eyes still on their brother.

"Isn't he worried the wind might change?"

Heath gave a grunt of wry humor. She was right that Percival's grim expression was difficult to look at. He was supposed to be demonstrating to the kingdom his intention to serve the king with his magic, and instead he could barely look his sovereign in the eye. Percival had never been good at hiding what he was feeling.

Heath and Laura were in the front row, seated in a block with the other power-wielders of their generation. Glancing along the line of them, Heath saw that everyone looked tense and serious. Whether they were concerned about Percival's behavior, as he was, or troubled by the king's response to recent tension, he couldn't tell. His eyes fell on Brody and Bianca, standing together nearby. He couldn't help thinking gloomily of the light-hearted demonstration he'd described to Prince Lachlan. Needless to say, none of the power-wielders had been asked to entertain the gathered onlookers with their abilities.

"Do you, Lord Percival, heir of the Duke of Bexley, swear your allegiance to Valoria?"

King Matlock had come to the point a little more quickly than Heath had expected, and he whipped his eyes back to the front of the throne room. Percival was kneeling in front of the king, and for a heart-stopping moment, silence reigned. Heath could almost feel the tension flowing off Prince Lachlan, who stood behind his father, along with the queen and Prince Knox, dressed in full ceremonial garb of Valorian purple and silver. Heath had a frantic moment of alarm as he remembered promising the crown prince that he wouldn't allow him to unknowingly walk into a disaster. But then Percival spoke, his voice carrying clearly throughout the silent room.

"I swear my allegiance to the crown. It is my honor to use the power with which I have been gifted in service of our great kingdom of Valoria. On my head be it if I ever break these vows."

Heath's breath caught in his throat, and his eyes flew to the man standing over his brother. King Matlock's expression didn't change, but Heath was sure he could see anger. Perhaps it was his unnatural sight, because the rest of the audience seemed to notice nothing amiss. On the contrary, their tension drained away as soon as Percival spoke.

Prince Lachlan hesitated only a moment before stepping forward and taking his cue.

"For Valoria!" he called solemnly.

"For Valoria," the crowd echoed. The king's elite knights were ranged along either wall, and they all thumped their fists to their chests in unison, over the embroidered emblem of Valoria on their livery.

It was an impressive sight, but all Heath could think of was Princess Kiana of Kyona, and the respect and affection in her eyes as she'd turned to her grandfather the king after creating her water sculpture. *In your service, and for your honor*, she'd said, and it had been plain that she'd meant it from the bottom of her heart.

The king gave another short speech, his face and voice still showing no sign of the anger Heath was certain he could see beneath. Then he turned and exited through an antechamber, leaving the audience free to make their way out of the throne room, the spectacle over.

"What is it?" Laura muttered from beside Heath. On her other side, her husband was chatting cheerfully with one of Heath's cousins, but Laura's gaze was serious as it rested on Heath's face. "Why am I being suffocated by the tension rolling out from you?"

Heath let out a long breath. Of course Laura wouldn't miss his distress. Part of her power was the ability to sense emotion.

"He didn't say it how he was supposed to," Heath told her, just as quietly. "He was supposed to swear his allegiance to King Matlock by name, not to 'the crown'. And he was supposed to swear to use his power in service to His Majesty as well as to Valoria."

Heath's brow lowered as he looked at his brother, who had risen from his knees before striding over to speak with Brody.

"Subtle but significant differences," said Laura dryly, and Heath nodded.

"Exactly."

"No one else seems tense, though," Laura observed, her face screwed slightly in concentration as she scanned the people closest to them, presumably using her power to read everyone's emotions.

"Hopefully no one else noticed," said Heath. "The wording of the loyalty oath has been a matter of substantial discussion behind closed doors, but most people would have no idea of the final wording." He scowled. "Prince Lachlan knows it very well, though, and King Matlock most definitely noticed."

"Are you sure?" Laura pressed. "He didn't look angry to me. I'll admit I wasn't specifically looking for it, but I also didn't feel any great surge of emotion from him."

Heath shook his head. "He's a king. He must be an absolute master at controlling his emotions. Trust me, he was angry." Heath didn't voice it aloud, but a bitter voice in his head told him that he would face the consequences of the king's anger as surely as Percival would.

He turned, and was surprised to find his sister's eyes fixed not on Percival, but on him.

"I'm worried about you, Heath."

"About me?" Heath protested. "I'm not the one you need to worry about."

She shook her head slowly. "I can worry about both my brothers at once, can't I? However well you might hide them outwardly, you're *not* good at controlling your emotions on the inside, Heath. No offense, but when it comes to emotion, you're a tangled mess. And that's not normal for you."

"Yes, well, things have been...complicated," said Heath noncommittally.

She subjected him to another shrewd look, but all she said

was, "I'm glad Edmund and I came to Bryford for the ceremony, anyway." A shadow of discomfort passed across her face, and she pressed a hand to her mouth for a moment.

"Are *you* all right?" Heath asked, his irritation with Percival momentarily forgotten. "You don't seem well."

"I'm fine," said Laura dismissively.

Heath stared hard at her, trying to pin down the vague sense that was growing within him, of something more.

"You're hiding something."

Laura rolled her eyes. "That's very dramatic."

"No," Heath clarified. "I mean you're literally hiding something *inside* you."

Laura stilled, her eyes widening as she studied Heath. "How...how did you know?"

"How did I know what?" Heath started, then suddenly it fell into place. It was his turn to widen his eyes, and he gaped at her. "Laura, are you...are you going to have a—"

"Yes, I am," said Laura, trying to look stern but not quite managing to keep a smile off her face. "But no one is supposed to know yet, so keep your mouth shut."

Heath's mouth was indeed hanging open, and he closed it promptly. "That's wonderful, Laura," he said sincerely. "I'm happy for you."

"Thank you," she said, but her gaze was still calculating. "I'm more interested in knowing how you figured it out." She suddenly looked excited. "Maybe it's magic! Maybe you have Father's ability, and can identify deception."

"I don't have Father's ability," said Heath firmly. But even as he said it, a connection formed in his mind, as though he was gaining a new layer of understanding regarding the origins of his own still unformed power. Now he thought about it, his ability to see things others couldn't did have something of the flavor of his father's power to see when something was being hidden.

"Hm," was all Laura said, and she still looked very thoughtful as she turned away to accept her husband's offered arm.

Heath walked behind them out of the throne room, struggling to comprehend her news. He would be an uncle soon. It cheered him to know that in the midst of all the stress and tension, something as fresh and happy as a new birth was coming to the family.

A moment later, he realized that Laura's child represented the first of a new generation of power-wielders. Who knew what shape magic would take in the fourth generation? Would it weaken, or become more potent? Would it be a form that the rest of the kingdom found more or less threatening?

And, he thought grimly, how big a mess would his own generation leave for the next group of power-wielders to inherit?

The ceremony, while not exactly a festive occasion, was still followed by the obligatory spread of food. People milled through the castle's large ballroom, not currently set up for dancing, discussing the cooler weather when the dull topic of the ceremony failed to occupy more than two minutes' conversation.

Heath had no opportunity for private speech with Percival, which he told himself was for the best. He couldn't say the things he wanted to in a ballroom, and it was probably better that he speak with his brother when the first flush of irritation had passed. He was both frustrated and uneasy to see that Percival didn't mingle much. He seemed to be surrounded at all times by a block of their cousins. In fact, when he glanced around the room, Heath realized that virtually all the power-wielders were clumped together in small groups, both avoiding and being avoided by the rest of the luncheon's attendees.

The exceptions were all in their parents' generation. Heath's parents, for example, were conversing with Princess Anne, the king's sister, with their usual unruffled grace. But Heath wasn't deceived. Underneath, they were almost as tense as he was. Knowing them as he did, he didn't even need extra sight to identify it.

Heath twice stopped himself from joining his cousins, irritated by their self-imposed segregation, and determined not to contribute to it. But when he made to walk over to Prince Lachlan instead, he found himself reluctant to do that either. He had no idea what he would say to the crown prince about Percival's disregard of the vow they had all agreed on after much debate. He couldn't read Prince Lachlan well enough to know if he was angry at Heath, but he certainly hadn't made any attempt to approach him.

Caught between two camps, Heath felt annoyed with both, but not so much that he wanted to see them destroy each other. It was maddening to watch them pull further apart, in spite of his efforts to bring them together. Efforts which, all things considered, had been pretty feeble. But what could he do? If he approached either group now, the other would cease to see him as an ally.

He sighed. What wouldn't he give to have a friend here, a true friend who was outside of the conflict, and was genuinely there for his sake? His thoughts flew to Merletta, but it was a foolish thing to wish for. She was as far away from his world as she could be.

But Merletta wasn't his only friend. She certainly hadn't been his first. All at once, an ache for his estranged friend rushed over him. Without thinking about it, Heath placed his goblet on a nearby table and slipped out into the corridor. He hurried for a door not far from the ballroom, leading into a public garden. A lonely hilltop would be preferable, but it wasn't necessary, and he didn't have the time.

Once he was alone next to a bed of late-blooming roses, he closed his eyes and drew a deep breath, allowing the perfumed air to soothe his agitation.

"Reka," he said, without opening his eyes. "Please talk to me. I'm alone here, and I need a friend."

At once, the dragon appeared before his sight, and he was surprised to see that Reka was underwater. The dragon cocked a head to the side, clearly listening to Heath's plea. Rekavidur propelled himself upward, breaking the surface of the water and floating on top of it like a duck on a pond. In the background, Heath thought he could see the rocky slopes of Wyvern Islands protruding from the ocean.

He focused his attention back on the dragon, and realized there was something in Reka's mouth. It gave a sudden, ferocious wriggle, and Heath recognized it as a live salmon. Reka flicked his jaw in a strange, complicated movement, and the salmon slid, whole and still wriggling, straight down his throat with a gulp that Heath could actually hear through the magic connection.

"That was...disgusting," he said aloud, unable to help himself.

Reka stilled, an arrested expression on his face. "What does that mean?" he asked quietly. The question was clearly about Heath rather than directed at him, but Heath's heart still lifted at the sound of the familiar, gravelly voice.

"It means I can see you," he said matter-of-factly. "I can hear you, too, it seems. There's a lot I haven't told you. I'd apologize, except you haven't really given me the option of telling you anything, have you?"

Reka had frozen at Heath's words, and he remained unmoving for so long that he seemed like a statue, albeit one that was bobbing impossibly on the choppy surface of the ocean.

"I could really use your help figuring some of it out, incidentally," Heath said. "And I think you have some things you need to tell me."

At that, the mask descended again on Rekavidur's face, and he closed his jaws with a snap.

"Come on, you stubborn reptile," pleaded Heath. "This is me we're talking about. Surely whatever it is, you can tell me."

It was hard to be sure, but he thought that Reka wavered. Unfortunately, before he could press his advantage, a voice cut across his long-distance conversation.

"Lord Heath? What are you doing out here? Who are you talking to?"

Heath spun around, his heart sinking at the sight of Lord Niel, the king's Chief Counselor. The man was as interfering as they came, and his was one of the loudest voices pushing for restrictions to be placed on power-wielders.

"No one," said Heath quickly. "I was just clearing my head."

And with a regretful glance back at the privacy of the rose garden, he followed Lord Niel back inside.

It wasn't until the evening, when he returned to his own home, that Heath came face to face with Percival without any witnesses.

"What was that?" he demanded, without preamble.

"You meant to say, 'congratulations on your rite of passage,' I assume," Percival said dryly.

"No, I didn't," snapped Heath. "Why didn't you say it properly? Prince Lachlan is going to think that I agreed to change it."

"I don't know what you're talking about," said Percival airily. "After so many different versions were thrown around, it was hard to remember the exact wording. But *I* thought I said it perfectly."

"You know you didn't, Perce," said Heath, his voice suddenly serious instead of angry. "What are you playing at? What do you hope to achieve by being defiant?"

"I'm not trying to achieve anything," said Percival mulishly. "I'm just not going to make a vow I'm not willing to keep."

Heath frowned at his brother. "You need to get it into your head that your actions have consequences that affect more people than just you, Percival."

"I can't believe you're going to side against your own people," said Percival darkly. "I thought better of you, Heath. You saw what that ceremony was like. It was a show of force, the crown demonstrating to us that we can be contained, silenced, *crushed* if necessary."

"Stop talking like we're at war!" Heath protested, frustrated. "This isn't about taking sides!"

But Percival cut him off angrily. "That's exactly what this is about! And it's time you decided which side you're on, Heath."

And with that, he turned on his heel and strode away, back out of the courtyard and into the gathering gloom.

CHAPTER TWENTY-THREE

Merletta

"Are you ready?" Freja's expression was calm, but Merletta could hear the tension in the older mermaid's voice. Her self-appointed mentor wanted Merletta to succeed in her test almost as much as Merletta wanted it herself.

"I'm ready," said Merletta, gripping her spear tightly as she fixed her eyes on the open ocean beyond the barrier. "It's only a practice test, after all."

Freja frowned. "You should take it as seriously as if it was your real test," she said reprovingly.

"She's just trying to give herself confidence," said Felix to Freja, as he swam up alongside Merletta with his spear in hand. "I don't think any of us could accuse her of not taking her training seriously enough."

"That's true," said Freja, her expression relaxing as she gave Merletta a nod. "You're the hardest working trainee I've taught in a long time. You'll do fine."

Merletta ducked her head in acknowledgment of the praise, hoping the gesture hid her burning cheeks. In spite of Agner's encouragement, she still wasn't used to so much approval. But

Freja had been fantastic to work with over the last several weeks, and the members of her patrol had been accommodating about adopting a trainee into their midst two days a week. Merletta spent most of her training days with Freja's squad now, and her combat had improved enormously as a result.

"She's right," said Felix kindly, as he led Merletta away from the rest of the squad, and toward the barrier. They weren't near the oyster farm this time. They were northeast of the Center, in the neighborhood where Hemssted and Tilssted met. "You'll do great."

"That depends on how much of the test involves depth work," said Merletta ruefully.

She wished her depth acclimatization had improved as much as her combat, but unfortunately it wasn't so. It didn't help that she'd been reduced to training in the shallow drop offs to be found within the Center, unless Freja's squad happened to be leaving the triple kingdoms. She hadn't risked crossing the barrier alone since her mysterious illness.

And, even more frustratingly, she hadn't made much progress on finding out the cause of that illness. She didn't see much of Emil in an ordinary week. Sage saw more of him, especially on rest days, when they both tended to visit their families in Skulssted. At Merletta's request, she'd told Emil about Merletta's speculation regarding the food, in case it helped in whatever research he was undertaking. But Sage had been so stiff when Merletta asked her to take the message, that she refrained from asking her friend to carry updates back and forth. The other mermaid was still a little cold whenever the topic of Emil's assistance came up. It seemed she hadn't entirely forgiven the two of them for agreeing that she would be safer out of it, although Merletta couldn't confirm that guess, since Sage changed the topic if Merletta tried to bring it up.

But enough of that. It was time to clear Sage's uncharacteristically cool behavior from her mind. Merletta needed her full focus to be on the day's challenge. Looking behind her, she realized with surprise that the edge of the triple kingdoms was no longer visible.

"How far are we going?" she asked. She realized for the first time just how tense Felix was, his spear half raised as he swam, and his eyes darting constantly to all sides.

"Pretty far," said Felix, casting her a look. "Didn't Agner warn you about that? The area immediately outside the barrier is patrolled by regular guard squads, and they're not allowed to know what we do in our Center guard training. We go far enough out that no patrols will happen upon us."

"Oh," said Merletta, trying to sound casually interested rather than nervous.

Felix gave a knowing smile, and she reflected ruefully that he probably thought she was worried about being exposed to the dangers of the open ocean. Better to let him think that than the truth, which was that she didn't like being so far from her trusted friends and the security of crowds. Felix, for example, was likable and helpful, but how well did she really know him? He was a Center guard, after all.

"Where is Agner, anyway?" Merletta asked. "I kind of thought he'd be there to see me off, seeing as this is his test, and I'm the only trainee taking it."

Felix's smile widened. "He's around."

"Why does that sound ominous?" Merletta asked darkly, and Felix gave a small chuckle.

"Here we are," he said at last, drawing to a stop at what seemed to be a random patch of ocean.

There was a rocky shelf below them, with a couple of sea turtles swimming lazily across its surface. On one side, the rocks disappeared into a forest of tall seaweed, and on the other the stone gave way to sand. The area was unfamiliar to Merletta, and she could see nothing remarkable about it.

"Your task is to find the hidden treasure and bring it back to this spot," said Felix solemnly. "And to escape injury if possible. You have three hours." He permitted himself a small smile. "Good luck."

And without another word, he turned and swam back toward the Center, disappearing rapidly into the gloom. Merletta stared after him, her mouth slightly open. She knew that the rules prohibited her being given any advance warning of what the test involved, but she'd expected a little more instruction than that at the actual time.

After a moment, Merletta pulled herself together, turning her gaze back toward the empty water. She needed to be alert. For lack of a better plan, she swam slowly forward in the same direction she and Felix had been heading. Her eyes scanned the seabed below, and the waters above, looking for anything unusual. What would qualify as hidden treasure? Should she go looking for wild pearls? She angled herself downward, swimming to where the rocky ledge rose up in ridges, providing her with some cover.

After several minutes of uneventful progress, she reflected that the practice test was, so far, much less daunting than she'd expected. Then it occurred to her, as she weaved her way in and out of the natural sculptures, that most trainees would probably be terrified already. The test wasn't designed for someone like her, who'd spent many hours in solitary exploration of the open ocean.

At least she was unobserved out here, she thought happily, as she did a barrel roll in the water for the sheer joy of it.

The thought had only just crossed her mind when something slammed into her from the side. Gasping, she twisted rapidly, bringing her spear out in front of her. But whatever it was had disappeared. The only sign that she wasn't alone in the water was the rippling of the long fronds of seaweed below her and to the right. She hovered for a moment, her heart beating frantically, and her side aching where she'd been struck. What creature had that been? Was she supposed to follow it, subdue it somehow?

Deciding not to risk it, she hurried on, her senses much more alert now. She floated upward, not as far as the surface, but far enough to give her a broader view of the ocean floor below. She had been foolish not to realize that if she had cover amongst the rocky crags, so did other creatures.

As she continued east, the feeling of being watched grew on her. Her scales seemed to ripple in the cold water, and her eyes couldn't search the gloom rapidly enough. Any number of things could be stalking her out here, of course. But based on her experience, a predator such as a shark would have attacked by now. She suspected that she was dealing with merpeople.

With that in mind, as she drew alongside a tangle of multi-colored coral, she turned her head pointedly the other way.

Sensing the movement immediately, she whipped both her head and her weapon back around. This time she was quick enough to block the blow aimed at her torso. The figure facing her was masked, but it was definitely a merman, and his spear proclaimed him as a Center guard. He was lashing out with the butt of his weapon, and Merletta parried with her own. With their spear shafts still locked together, Merletta brought her tail around and slammed it hard into the guard's hip. He made no sound, and his mask prevented her from seeing any expression on his face. But he fell back slightly, and Merletta raised her weapon in a defensive position.

She glanced around her, half-expecting to see herself surrounded. But she appeared to have only one opponent. As he floated, still silent and motionless, a ripple of fear went over

Merletta. *Was* this part of the test, as she'd first assumed? Or was he sent to kill her? It had occurred to her before now that her practice test would be a convenient opportunity to get rid of her and make it look like an accident.

She was still debating the question when the merman suddenly struck out again. He was still using the butt of his spear, which reassured Merletta that he probably wasn't there to murder her. She deflected his blow, then went on the offensive. After two sturdy hits to his midriff, she had the satisfaction of seeing him retreat. He turned quite abruptly and swam back west, toward the triple kingdoms. Merletta floated for a moment, catching her breath. She had the sense the guard could have fought on easily enough. Presumably he was the easiest of the obstacles she was to face, and these challenges would increase as she proceeded.

She continued east for a short while, but saw and heard nothing of interest. Pulling up, she thought about the two attacks. Both had come from the same direction. If she was right that they would intensify as she got closer to her goal, perhaps that meant whatever she was seeking was back that way, under their protection.

She turned around, hurrying back to the point where the masked guard had attacked her, and bravely swimming straight into the mass of coral. She ducked and weaved her way around the many prongs stretching stiffly out from the ocean floor. Before long, she emerged out the other side, and found herself swimming across a large expanse of sand. The water was noticeably warmer, although she wasn't particularly close to the surface. Movement caught her eye, and peering down, she saw a thin trail of little crabs scuttling across the sand.

After a quick scout of the immediate area, Merletta dove down for a closer look. Surprisingly, the water didn't get colder as she descended. If anything, it was warmer. The crabs were headed for a patch of rocky ground that formed the end of the sand. Her approach sent them scampering more quickly, and they soon disappeared into the rocks. The space was too small for Merletta to follow, and she was forced to swim up and over the rocks. The clump into which the crabs had scuttled quickly rose into a jagged maze of ridges. Before Merletta could do more than reflect that it was another ideal hiding place for attackers, no fewer than three figures rose out of the rocks.

With barely a moment to think, Merletta acted on instinct, and dove down between the razor-sharp edges, only just evading the swipe of the closest masked guard. She could see a relatively open area not far away, and she hurried into it, positioning herself with her back against a vertical rocky shelf. She knew it was risky to place herself where she couldn't easily escape, but she didn't think she stood much chance of fighting off three opponents in open water, where they could so easily surround her.

The guards followed her, and it soon proved that she'd chosen her battleground well. They couldn't sneak up on her, and hampered by the jagged rocks around them, they couldn't come at her all at once. The first one, a mermaid who was again masked, rushed forward. Merletta struck out with her spear, managing to prevent the guard from getting close enough to properly grapple with her. Merletta was using the blunt end of her spear, in imitation of her attackers. But as she whipped her weapon around, the sharp tip caught the tail of one of the others, who had been surging forward in an attempt to get under her guard.

The merman drew back, and a thin trickle of red spread into the water from his injured tail. He gave a small grunt of annoyance, and pressed harder than ever against Merletta. Even with the advantage of facing them one at a time, and the fact that they were obviously not aiming to kill, Merletta was soon struggling to hold her own. She kept hoping that they'd retreat once she reached a certain unknown milestone, like her first opponent had done. But so far, they showed every sign of persisting until she capitulated. But she couldn't give in. She was sure she was close to her goal—why else had the defense escalated so dramatically?

The outcome of the clash was still undecided when a sudden chill swept over Merletta, in spite of the warm water. She clearly wasn't the only one who felt the undefined rush of dread. There was a lull as all the fighters stilled, looking around for whatever danger had triggered the instinctive response.

There it was, emerging from the gloom, its sleek body swaying from side to side as it swam. It had their scent in its nose and death in its eyes.

CHAPTER TWENTY-FOUR

Merletta

The shark was among the largest Merletta had seen, and clearly bold to approach such a group. The injured guard gasped, clapping a hand to his tail. The wound had been slight, and the bleeding had already stopped. But obviously not quickly enough.

Merletta's heart was racing frantically, and her hands shook as they gripped her weapon. She'd been struggling to hold off the guards as it was. She couldn't defend herself against them and a shark.

But to her relief, none of the others seemed to have any further thought of attacking her. They turned toward the shark, their eyes widening as they took in its size. Merletta swam forward to join the line of defense. The shark was almost upon them, and Merletta wondered optimistically if it would back off without the need for a fight. Surely a united group of four merpeople wasn't the easy prey it would be looking for.

But even as the thought flashed through her mind, the other three seemed to reach a silent decision. As abruptly as a school of minnows after a rock had been dropped through its center, the guards scattered. Merletta wasn't sure if they were abandoning her to her fate, or if they'd assumed she would flee too. If so, she'd missed the cue. The shark, with only one target in its sights, put on a burst of speed as it made straight for her.

Merletta had no time to plan. She just reacted with the instinct born of many hours wandering the ocean alone. She whipped up her spear, and at the last possible moment, rolled powerfully to the side. As the shark, not having changed direction quickly enough, shot past her, she lashed out with her spear and struck it between the eyes with all her strength. It faltered, and Merletta drove home her advantage. Bringing the spear back around, she struck again, this time straight on the gills.

The shark writhed in pain. Merletta knew such attacks wouldn't kill it, but she was hampered by the need to use the blunt end of her spear. The last thing she wanted to do was to spill the creature's blood and attract more of its brethren.

As Merletta gripped her spear, readying herself for another assault, a movement made her flick her head momentarily to the side. She was surprised to see two of the guards hovering nearby, their posture communicating surprise although their faces were still covered.

The shark had evidently seen them, too. After a moment's hesitation, it seemed to decide that this prey was too risky. With a flick of its powerful tail, it fled, disappearing back into the gloom.

For a long moment, Merletta and the guards just floated, staring at each other with heaving chests. Then the guards exchanged a look, raising their spears uncertainly as if unsure whether they were supposed to start attacking her again.

A strange keening noise that Merletta had never heard before cut through the water. Alarmed, she looked around for its source. She couldn't see anything, but the guards withdrew in one synchronized movement, disappearing behind the rocky crags within moments.

Merletta pulled in a shuddering mouthful of water. She could only assume she'd performed sufficiently to be left alone for a time, but she didn't feel much relief. She was too shaken by the appearance of the shark, and she was afraid that it might come back, or that others might have been attracted by the blood she'd accidentally spilled.

Still, floating there immobile wouldn't get her closer to finishing her task. Wincing at the soreness brought on by the movement, she started to swim back over the rocky patch, looking for any sign of where the crabs had gone. The water grew warmer with each stroke, until suddenly, the rocks fell away and Merletta found herself looking down into a deep, round hole, much deeper than any point in the Center. It wasn't as deep as the drop off where Freja had begun Merletta's acclimatization training—Merletta could dimly see the bottom. But it was still plenty deep enough to fill her with dread.

Her heart sinking, she saw a number of small crabs scuttling down its sides, as if chasing the warmth that seemed to emanate from the drop off. She had a strong feeling this was where she needed to go. She'd been afraid of this—her depth work was her weakest point.

"At least it's not cold," she muttered to herself as she moved cautiously forward into the drop off.

She squinted in an attempt to see the bottom, but visibility was getting worse as she descended. It wasn't just because of the lack of light, either. The water was so warm now it was uncomfortable, and one side of the chasm was obscured by a cloudy substance that made it seem like someone was constantly stirring up the sand of the ocean floor. As Merletta went still deeper, her head beginning to ache, and her mind becoming foggy, she realized that the cloudiness didn't originate from the bottom of the drop off. It was issuing from a hole in the far rock wall. Merletta couldn't have approached the hole even if she'd wanted to. The water was now so hot her instincts were screaming at her to ascend, to get out before she was boiled.

Suddenly it hit her. It was a thermal vent! She'd never seen one before, although since moving to the Center, she'd eaten plenty of food prepared in one.

As she marveled at the clouds billowing from the vent, she felt her back hit something solid and sharp. Without even realizing it, she'd backed away from the source of the heat, all the way to the other wall of the drop off. She was about to push off when something closed around her arm and pulled, hard.

She let out a yelp and turned, spear point out. Even amidst the fear arising from being grabbed from behind, she couldn't help but respect whatever guard was acclimatized enough to lurk down here waiting for her all that time. But her yelp turned into a scream when she saw what actually had her.

It wasn't a hand that had grabbed her arm, but a thick, purple tentacle. The octopus was the largest she'd ever seen, its head the size of her torso, and it was clearly intent on yanking her back into its hole.

Merletta lashed out blindly at it, whacking it with more force than finesse. The creature let go of her arm, but another tentacle immediately seized her fins. For a moment, panic clouded Merletta's mind, then the same strange keening noise reached her ears. She realized what it must mean—it was surely a signal used by the guards. They would save her! But—her thoughts suddenly clicked into place—if they intervened, she would surely fail.

"No!" she shouted, still raining down blows on the octopus. "Don't rescue me—I can do it!"

She didn't wait for a response. Abandoning her attack on the octopus, Merletta put the butt of her spear against the wall and pushed out with all her might, sending herself lurching back toward the vent. She swam furiously, struggling against the octopus's pull, until the water was scorching her face. The creature had clung on doggedly until then, but just as the heat became unbearable, it let go, retreating back toward its hole.

With a powerful upward stroke of her arms, Merletta sent herself shooting down, below the point of the vent and away from the octopus's home. In spite of the warmth still surrounding her, shivers were running down her body. She could feel her scales rippling uncontrollably, and she knew her eyes were wide with horror. The pressure was beating at her skull, and her mind felt thick. Everything in her screamed to ascend, to get out of the drop off. But she could see the floor not far below her, and she forced herself to go on. She was so close.

Her eyes were locked on the bottom below as she moved downward, and for a moment she thought she was hallucinating again. The very sand seemed to be moving. Then she realized that the surface was swarming with crabs of varied sizes. Merletta had never been afraid of crabs, but there was no denying they were unnerving, gathered together like that. Her eyes moved along the floor, widening as she realized that what she'd taken for a large rock at the center of the space was actually an enormous crab. She'd never seen one half as big—it could snap off her arm with one of those pincers.

But more interesting even than its size, was its bed. It seemed to be resting on a motley collection of objects piled into a mound. Merletta could see pearls—not just individual ones, but ropes that had clearly once belonged to a mermaid—turtle shells, lumps of a shiny substance the color of the sun, even what looked like a rotting driftwood spear. As she watched, a medium-sized crab scuttled down the near wall of the drop off, a single, lopsided pearl clutched in its pincers. Merletta nodded to herself. This was surely the treasure she was supposed to retrieve.

She drew up, suppressing a groan at the idea of fighting yet another terrifying sea creature. Honestly, this test was making the official position on the dangers of the open ocean seem accurate. But a second look made her expel a long and relieved stream of water. The crab looked to be asleep, and she fully intended to keep it that way.

Her eyes scanned the mound, wondering what she was supposed to bring back. Felix hadn't said—he'd just told her to bring back treasure. Perhaps she could just choose whatever object she wanted. She moved slowly downward, her eyes on a rope of pearls that was lying abandoned, far across the sand from the giant crustacean.

But even as her hand reached for it, she hesitated. Maybe it mattered what she selected. What if her choice was part of the test? A model guard wouldn't be dazzled by jewelry. She glanced back over the pile, and her gaze fell on a small dagger which looked like it was made from a sharpened paua shell. Surely that was both treasure, and worthy of a guard.

Moving carefully, she inched through the water toward it, her eyes flicking between her prize and the sleeping crustacean. Some of its smaller fellows scuttled angrily, clicking their pincers at her in a menacing fashion. She ignored them. Her hand closed over the dagger just as a small crab, half the size of her palm, charged toward her and snapped its pincer around her fingers.

Merletta bit her lip to keep from crying out, but she made no move to dislodge her miniature attacker. She was worried that any violent movement would wake the patriarch. Her treasure in her hand, she pushed herself upward as silently and gently as she could. Only once she was just below the vent—and therefore the den of the octopus—did she give a powerful flick of the tail, shooting up toward the top of the drop off. Once the billowing clouds began to thin, she pried the crab off her hand, dropping it immediately. It sank back into the cloudy darkness, still furiously clicking its disapproval.

With a gasp of relief, Merletta emerged back into the open water, her paua knife clutched in her hand. She'd done it! She'd retrieved the treasure, and she was alive!

"Well, well," said a familiar voice to her right.

She turned quickly to see Agner grinning at her, half concealed in a forest of tall seaweed.

"Instructor!" she cried jubilantly. She held up her prize. "I've found myself some treasure."

Agner was still smiling, but he didn't emerge fully. "I'm not really supposed to talk to you until the task is over," he said, with a wink. "But if I was allowed to, I'd tell you I'm impressed."

With that, he sank back into the seaweed. Merletta blinked at the fronds, trying to make sense of his words. The task wasn't over? There was still more? Her heart sank.

But then she recalled Felix's words.

Your task is to find the hidden treasure and bring it back to this spot.

She hadn't brought her treasure back to the starting point. That was all she still had to do. That wasn't so bad.

She set off swimming at once, retracing her strokes back over the rocks, across the sand, and through the coral. But she was only halfway back to the spot where she and Felix had parted when yet another masked guard emerged from the gloom, weapon raised.

Merletta felt irritated more than anything as she brought her own weapon up. She'd fought them off, she'd done the task. Did they really need to attack her on the way back, too?

But this attack wasn't like the others. The guard didn't attempt to land her any heavy blows, just shoved at her with the shaft of her spear. It took Merletta several moments to realize that the guard wasn't fighting her so much as forcing her back, off course from her route. And it was another moment before Merletta realized, with a horrible jolt in her stomach, that she recognized that dull green tail.

"Ileana," she hissed. "What are you doing here?"

But she realized even as she said it that she knew what Ileana was doing there. She was a Center guard. Merletta should have realized the former trainee might be involved in administering her test.

A strange mixture of anger and anxiety flooded through Merletta. Her gut told her that Ileana meant her real harm, and she should fight her off with whatever force was necessary. But if Ileana was just performing her assigned role in the practice test, Merletta might get into a spot of trouble if she speared her.

All the time these thoughts were chasing themselves through Merletta's head, Ileana continued to force her backward, further from the meeting point with Felix.

"What...are you...playing at?" Merletta grunted, trying to dart around the other mermaid.

Ileana said nothing, just moved with snakelike speed to prevent Merletta from getting past her. Without a word, she resumed her advance.

Merletta was just beginning to think she should abandon caution and let her anger win, when Ileana pulled back abruptly. Before Merletta could react, Ileana had struck out with her spear, thrusting the blunt end straight into Merletta's forehead.

Merletta went hurtling backward through the water, her vision spinning as pain erupted from the point of contact. She barely managed to hold on to her weapon, but she clutched it like her life depended on it, sure Ileana would follow up her advantage.

But no attack came. Instead, Merletta felt a horribly familiar brush along her arm, and caught a glow of white in her peripheral vision. She turned convulsively, and gave a cry of horror. She was surrounded on every side, floating in frozen terror in the midst of an entirely different type of cloud from the one she'd seen in the drop off.

The bloom of jellyfish was the biggest she'd ever seen. Or possibly she'd just never seen one up this close. She'd always avoided them. Another jellyfish brushed along her tail, and she let out an involuntary whimper.

They're just jellyfish, she told herself. *You've dealt with worse.*

But she couldn't seem to make herself believe it. She'd been afraid of the creatures since childhood, with an unreasoning fear. Her mind was clear enough to curse her own idiocy in mentioning that fear in her first ever lesson at the Center. This wasn't the first time the information had been used against her. But knowing that it was a calculated attack by Ileana didn't make it any easier to control the panic rising within her.

Just stay still. Let them swim around you, and wait until the bloom passes.

She was fully encased in the bloom now, shaking from head to fin, rapidly losing control of herself. A third jellyfish slid along her shoulder, and she could hold on no longer. Letting out a gurgling gasp, she flailed wildly, trying to get it off her. Immediately, its tentacles lashed her arm, and a sharp stinging sensation went through her. She thrashed more frantically still, blundering around in her attempt to get out of the bloom. Soon she was enmeshed in tentacles, pain shooting across every inch of exposed skin.

And still the bloom continued. It seemed endless. She swam blindly, trying to find the edge of it, trying to fight the throbbing in her head, and the much more dangerous panic that had gripped every one of her senses. Through the wispy white bodies she could see dark rock, and she made for it, hoping it indicated the edge of the bloom.

She reached the rock, and almost without realizing it, she darted into an opening, away from the jellyfish. For a long minute, she huddled in the dark, shaking all over. She tried to assess the sharp pain lancing across her body, but she was still so panicked, it was hard to think straight. Was she dying? How strong was the venom of these particular jellyfish? How many times had she been stung?

A minute flowed past, and she found that she was still alive, although in a substantial amount of pain. Her mind was spinning in a way that was unpleasantly reminiscent of her hallucinations. She could still see the pearly glow of the jellyfish moving past her hiding place, and she drew further back into what turned out to be a decent-sized cave.

Her eyes were adjusting to the darkness now, and she glanced around her nervously. It would be about right to find that she'd fled the jellyfish only to land herself in the den of some predator.

But she could see no sign of sea monsters in the large space. She frowned, momentarily forgetting about her pain as she swam deeper. What *was* she seeing? It wasn't just an empty cave, that much was clear. A large clump of seaweed stretched across one corner, weighed down by rocks. It almost looked like...a bed. And on the other side of the cave were fish bones, and empty mussel shells. Merletta's eyes, catching up to the darkness at last, were drawn back to the rocky wall above the seaweed. She swam forward slowly and ran her fingers along the scores. Someone had scratched a tally into the rock, as if counting out the days.

Merletta fell back, a strange feeling creeping over her. Someone had been living here—a merperson. No other creature would leave marks like that. It didn't look like they were here still, but it couldn't have been too long since they left.

Who could it be? She was well outside the barrier now. No one lived out here, no one ever had.

Merletta's gaze fell on her own empty hand, and she realized with a start that she no longer held her paua knife. All at once, her task came rushing back to her, and she abandoned the mysteries of the cave and swam back to the entrance. To her relief, the last few straggling jellyfish were just drifting past, leaving blissfully clear water behind them.

Once again acutely aware of the stinging still spreading across her whole body, Merletta retraced her strokes. Her paua knife was there, lying abandoned on the sand below. She dove down and retrieved it, her arms still shaking.

Now that the jellyfish were gone, and her panic had ebbed away, she felt the additional sting of humiliation set in. With nothing else to do, she followed the bloom—at a safe distance— until she rejoined her original route. She couldn't shake the unpleasant feeling that she was being watched, and she kept glancing around her, expecting Ileana to burst out of the coral and start attacking her again.

But she saw no sign of anyone until she reached the place where Felix had said goodbye to her. Not only Felix, but Freja, Agner, and almost a dozen other guards were waiting for her. None of them wore masks now, and Ileana was among them. Merletta sent a look of pure venom toward her, but Ileana just raised a disdainful eyebrow.

"Merletta, there you are!" Agner boomed. "I can't imagine what took you so..." He trailed off, his own eyebrows almost disappearing into his hairline as he looked her over. "What in the depths happened to you? You were unscathed when you emerged from the drop off."

Merletta glanced down at herself. Angry red welts were

beginning to appear on her skin, and she realized she was shaking harder than ever.

"Jellyfish bloom," she said through teeth that were gritted in an unsuccessful attempt to stop them chattering.

"That's unlucky," said Agner mildly. "Performing the test so perfectly, then falling afoul of a bloom of jellyfish on your way back, once it's all done."

"Very unlucky," Merletta forced out, sending another glare at Ileana. The guard looked utterly unconcerned.

Freja swam forward and cast a shrewd eye over Merletta's arm. "I imagine it stings something brutal, with so many welts."

Merletta nodded.

"Not dangerous though, these ones," said Freja reassuringly. "Just unpleasant."

Merletta's stomach unclenched in relief, and she cast a quick look at Ileana. The other mermaid's face was inscrutable. It was impossible to tell whether she'd just meant to humiliate Merletta, or whether she'd thought these jellyfish were as dangerous as the deadly one she'd once smuggled into Merletta's hammock.

"Well, I was going to give you a perfect score," said Agner, a trifle wistfully. "But the instructions were to escape injury if possible. Dangerous or not, I really think we have to count those welts as injuries."

Merletta said nothing.

"Not to worry, though," said Agner, smiling slightly at her mutinous expression. "It's only a practice test, remember. Your score doesn't really affect anything."

Merletta nodded. She knew he was right, but she still felt angry. It wasn't just the pain. It was the fact that Ileana had made her victory feel like defeat. And from all appearances, it had been out of pure spite.

But as she followed the group back toward the safety of the

triple kingdoms, Merletta found her mind not on her test, or even on Ileana's behavior. Her thoughts drifted instead back to the cave, and the mystery of its departed inhabitant.

There was only one conclusion to draw. She wasn't the only one who had spent unsanctioned time outside the barrier. She squared her shoulders as the ripple of power went over her, indicating that she had re-entered her approved borders.

If someone else was doing it, surely she could once again venture beyond the barrier.

CHAPTER TWENTY-FIVE

Heath walked away from Prince Lachlan's study with slow, heavy steps. He felt like he'd aged several years in the two months since Percival's loyalty ceremony.

He scowled as his thoughts flew to the formal dinner the night before. Prince Lachlan claimed that the seating arrangements, placing the younger generation of power-wielders all in one group far from the royal family, weren't a targeted snub. But Heath wasn't convinced. The trouble was, he had no counter for the prince's waspish comment that the power-wielders wouldn't choose any differently even if they were given the option. Unfortunately, it was all too true that, in Heath's generation at least, the power-wielding and non-power-wielding factions of the court were separating themselves more and more consistently. Every social event, every formal ceremony, seemed to show less crossover between the two groups.

Heath let out a sigh. He was sick of all of it. Sick of Prince Lachlan's caution, sick of Percival's resentment, sick of Bryford. He wanted to be at his coastal home or, better yet, on Vazula. But he still hadn't been back there.

It wasn't that he'd forgotten about Merletta's request for his help in learning to use her legs. Every week, he attempted to discern her movements through use of his extra sight. It was possible he'd missed something, but he didn't think she'd returned to Vazula. And since he had no way to get there rapidly, it seemed foolish to attempt another sea voyage when she probably wouldn't even be there.

His thoughts brought him back, as they usually did, to Reka. He needed to convince the dragon to forgive him, at least to *talk* to him again. He'd had the impression that Reka was surprised and intrigued by what Heath had said to him last time. But Heath had been struggling to get his extra sight to work, and he'd had no real conversation with the dragon since then. Reka, of course, would think nothing of the passage of a couple of months. He was probably still mulling their conversation over, deciding what, if anything, to say in response.

Dragons were never in a hurry.

"Heath."

Heath turned in surprise at the greeting, a true smile crossing his face at the sight of his grandmother.

"You look troubled," she commented, as she took his offered arm. "Is something amiss?"

"Not really," said Heath lightly. "Nothing new, anyway."

His grandmother regarded him thoughtfully, saying nothing until a passing servant had rounded the corner out of sight. "You certainly don't seem as disheartened as you were when you visited us in the summer. I gather that you took my advice, but you never told me how your voyage went."

Heath's steps faltered, his mouth falling slightly open.

"You're not the only grandchild who likes to take tea with me," the elderly princess said with a smile. "And really, it's a bit much to expect anyone to keep such a thrilling tale secret."

"Bianca," said Heath grimly.

But after a moment's consideration, he realized he wasn't

annoyed with his cousin. He'd expected a great deal of the twins, asking them to keep the whole expedition silent. And Bianca knew as well as he did how safe a confidant their grandmother was.

"Yes, Bianca," the princess acknowledged. A slight frown creased her already wrinkled forehead. "I'm not sure you quite know what you started there, but never mind that."

Heath opened his mouth to ask what she meant, but before he could do so, his grandmother, with surprising strength, whisked him out an open door and into one of the castle's internal courtyards. Obeying the pressure of her hand on his arm, he found himself helping her to sink onto a stone seat underneath an arbor. Winter was upon them, and the air was biting. But the gardeners had done their work well, and enough of the foliage was evergreen for them to still feel like they were in a garden.

"Did you reach your island?" his grandmother asked eagerly, before he was properly seated. "In the rowboat?"

Heath hesitated for only a moment before answering. "I did."

"And?" His grandmother was unusually impatient. "Merletta?"

Again a strange thrill went over Heath at hearing Merletta's name on someone else's lips. It so often felt like she lived only in his mind. This time he hesitated longer, but it would truly be a relief to tell someone.

"She's alive," he said, unable to help the grin that spread across his face. "And more than that."

His grandmother actually clapped her hands. "I'm so pleased! She didn't dry out, then?"

"Actually…" Heath took a breath, and turned to face her properly. "She did. And it turns out she'd been taught a lie when they said that drying out was fatal. Its effect is something altogether different."

He was silent for a moment, but his grandmother didn't press him again. She clearly knew he would continue when he was ready.

"She has legs," he blurted out at last. "She becomes...well, human, when she's fully out of the water."

His grandmother started so dramatically, the bench wobbled.

"Human?" Her mouth had fallen open. "But that's impossible!"

"That's what I thought," said Heath, still smiling. "Until I saw it with my own eyes. She showed me the transformation back and forth. I've never seen such magic. I don't think even you have."

"I don't doubt you," his companion said quickly. "It's clearly possible. What I meant was that it's not possible for my guess about the cause of Merletta's existence to be correct. Not if she can change into a human." She frowned to herself. "Surely not even a dragon's magic could do that."

"What do you mean?" Heath pressed. "What was your guess about the cause?"

His grandmother shook her head slowly. "Ask Rekavidur," she said. "If I'm wrong, I don't want to plant the idea, even in your mind. For all they claim that humans are the hasty ones, I've known dragons to attack first and ask questions later. If they knew what I suspect..." She trailed off, then shook her head decisively. "It's best for me to say no more."

"That's very frustrating, you know, Grandmother," Heath scolded.

She chuckled. "I know it is, but you'll have to forgive the eccentricities of old age." She bent a sharp eye upon him. "What did Rekavidur make of the discovery?"

"I haven't told him," shrugged Heath. "I've tried, but he still won't come when I ask him to."

"Hm." She frowned. "I think you should tell him, whatever it takes. If he takes the same view of it as I do, it might allay his concerns."

Heath was silent for a moment. "What am I supposed to do? I can't just stroll over to his colony on Wyvern Islands, can I?"

His grandmother smiled. "Try harder to get him to listen, I suppose. Dragons are supposed to be invincible, but it's not true of all of them, you know."

"What do you mean?" Heath asked, startled. "There's a way for humans to kill dragons?"

"Who said anything about killing?" protested the princess, half laughing. "All my life, people have thought my friendship with Elddreki shows that I'm something special, because dragons are usually aloof, and uninterested in humans. But the truth is, it's not me who's special. It's Elddreki. He was never like the other dragons. His fondness for humans began long before my lifetime. And from what I've observed of Rekavidur, he's inherited that trait from his father."

"What are you saying?" asked Heath, mystified.

His grandmother got to her feet. "I'm saying that Rekavidur isn't invulnerable. He has a weakness." She smiled. "You."

And she ambled back into the castle, leaving Heath alone with his thoughts.

Despite his grandmother's confidence, Heath found it difficult to nerve himself to try again with Reka. He felt foolish, speaking to the air so many times in a row, and he was a little disgruntled with his friend for continuing to ignore him.

In the end, his extra sight was what gave him the necessary

motivation. He had been continuing in his attempt to "see" Merletta from afar, with mixed results. Sometimes he caught glimpses of what seemed to be her underwater life, but more often he saw nothing at all.

She was never far from his thoughts, however, and he was always aware of when her rest days fell. One such morning, he happened to rise much earlier than normal. Winter had truly set in now—the Winter Solstice Festival was only a week away —and it had been a particularly cold and stormy night. Heath could rarely remember being so eager for the sun to rise. As he made his way down the freezing corridor, hoping to weasel some hot tea from the kitchens, even though breakfast wasn't to be served for another couple hours, he was arrested by the sound of hushed conversation.

Frowning, he followed the sound. He knew those voices. Sure enough, he rounded a corner to see Bianca disappearing out of sight in the opposite direction, accompanied by Jasmine, another of his cousins. Heath hesitated for a moment, then followed them. To his surprise, they didn't go toward the warmth of their chambers, but headed out into the snow by way of one of the castle's back entrances.

He slipped out after them, wishing he'd bundled himself up more warmly. He felt half-ashamed of spying on his own cousins, but his curiosity was well and truly roused. Hurrying through the sleepy streets, the two girls soon reached the city's southern wall, which was closest to the castle. Heath watched in growing suspicion as the guard on duty nodded to them, holding the gate courteously open.

After waiting a couple of minutes, Heath followed, trying to look confident. The guard started in surprise at sight of him, then broke into a smile.

"If it's not too bold, I'm glad to see you joining in, Lord Heath," he said gruffly. "Do you good."

Up close, Heath recognized the man as a friend of Percival's. His heart sank, but he said nothing, just giving the guard a tight smile.

Once he was outside the gate, he had no difficulty following his cousins' footsteps. The snow hadn't been cleared out here, like it had in the city, and they'd cut themselves a fresh path through the drifts. He picked up his pace, and could soon see them up ahead. Jasmine seemed to be using her power—an ability to move things without touching them, albeit not a very strong one, as she could only move small things a short distance—to clear the snow from in front of their feet.

They were climbing a hill now, and in a few minutes, they descended the other side, into what Heath knew to be a pleasant meadow in warmer weather. He paused at the top of the slope, letting out a low growl of irritation.

Gathered in the snow were five of his cousins, plus his brother. Although he couldn't hear their conversation from his vantage point, he could see them perfectly, and the purpose of the little family reunion was clear. On her arrival, Bianca had sent a wind rushing around the edges of the group, buffeting the others inward and making them laugh. Brody greeted his sister by causing wildflowers to grow up impossibly through the snow, then scooping them into a bouquet and presenting it to her with an exaggerated flourish.

Jasmine seemed to be giggling, which was evidently all the encouragement Brody needed. An intense look of concentration came over his face, then he waggled his eyebrows ridiculously, and wildflowers sprung up from the snow all over the meadow. Jasmine lifted a foot, and one wriggled up through the turf right where her shoe had been. She didn't bend down, but with a twirl of her fingers, she lifted the flower into the air and inserted it into her hair, before giving it a satisfied pat.

Percival, of course, wasn't to be outdone. On the pretext of digging up a flower, he had unearthed an enormous boulder, which he lifted above his head, his muscles straining. He sent it skidding across the snow, creating a path of destruction through Brody's newly grown garden.

It was as the girls squealed in protest that Max, another cousin, suddenly spotted Heath on top of the hill. He sprinted to Percival's side, moving more quickly than any human should be able to. As he muttered something, all activity ceased. Six familiar pairs of eyes looked up at Heath, with expressions ranging from guilty to defiant.

Drawing a breath, Heath strode down into the clearing. A powerful rush of frustration was rising in him, but he did his best to master it. Losing his temper would achieve nothing.

"Seems I missed my invite to the cousin gathering," he said lightly.

Bianca winced slightly at the words, and an apologetic look flashed across Brody's face. Heath locked eyes with his brother, and was unsurprised to see that Percival, on the other hand, showed no sign of discomfort.

"What are you doing here?" he grunted.

"I followed Bianca and Jasmine," said Heath evenly.

Percival shot a scowl at the girls. "I thought we agreed that those in the castle were going to be careful when leaving."

"So you were *conspiring* to keep me out of it, were you?" Heath let his anger color his voice, hoping it concealed the terrible hurt clawing at him. This was his family. These were supposed to be his people.

"Of course we were," snapped Percival. "We couldn't have you running to your master to tell tales on us, could we?"

"That's out of line, Percival," said Brody sharply.

"We never agreed to anything like that," Bianca added, frowning at Percival before turning back to Heath. "I'm sorry you were left out, Heath. But we thought it might put you in a position of...intolerable conflict, if you knew what we were up to."

Heath glared at her, although inside he had to admit she was right. He half wished he'd never followed them, and had remained in blissful ignorance.

"And what are you up to?" he snapped.

"Nothing dangerous, or...or defiant," said Jasmine anxiously. "We just want to practice our power. And it's...well," she looked apologetic, "fun, to be honest. Experimenting with our magic like this, together."

A slight frown creased Heath's forehead as he looked at his cousin. Her guilty demeanor brought home how truly wrong their situation was. Why should she be apologizing for enjoying her magic?

"You know how this will look," he said quietly, addressing himself to Bianca. "Particularly now, while everyone is so sensitive to magic."

"Everyone is always sensitive to magic," she said seriously. "If we're going to hone our craft, learn how best to control and apply it, we have to be able to use it. And with all of us here for the Winter Solstice Festival, it's a rare opportunity to try our powers in combination." She met his eye unblinkingly. "It was our experiences on our visit to, uh, Bexley Manor that gave me the idea. I realized how little I'd really experimented with my power before."

Heath frowned at her, at a loss for how to respond. Clearly this was what his grandmother had meant by him not knowing what he'd started when he asked for Bianca's help on his voyage. So the elderly princess must know about these meetings as well. And even she hadn't told him.

The trouble was, Bianca was right. He glanced around the frozen meadow, dotted with the bright colors of Brody's flowers. Bianca had used wind to push a snow drift up to an unlikely height, and before she'd spotted him, Jasmine had begun sculpting it, even while laughing at the others' antics. At present it was a shapeless mass, topped with the half-molded head of a dragon.

It was impressive. Beautiful, even. And it was exactly where Heath would like to be. But he couldn't shake the image of Prince Lachlan's earnest face, as the prince said that successfully integrating power-wielders was essential to Valoria's future. And here they all were, hiding away to practice their magic.

"It's not like what we're doing is illegal," Brody said defensively.

Heath gave him a look. "You're going to pretend you're not trying to hide this?"

"You should be glad we're hiding it," Percival cut in angrily. "I thought it was your rule that we're not supposed to be openly defying the crown."

Heath sighed, exasperated. He didn't even grace his brother's words with a response, instead turning again to Bianca. "This is exactly the sort of thing that will make the court afraid of us. They'll think the power-wielders are conspiring in secret, figuring out how to combine powers to take control or something."

"Maybe it's not so bad for them to feel afraid," muttered Percival.

Heath shot him a warning look, as Max said, "They'll only think that if they find out about what we're doing."

For a moment Heath blinked in confusion at his young cousin's hopeful, anxious face. Then Max's meaning hit him, and he felt another stab of hurt pass through him.

"I'm not going to report this to anyone! I can't believe you think I would."

"That's a relief," said Max brightly, apparently oblivious to Heath's tone. He turned back to the clearing. "What do you want to try? What if Bianca sends one of these flowers up as high as she can, and then you can try to hit it with...oh, you didn't bring your bow and arrow. Well, I'm sure we can think of something!"

Heath was barely listening to his cousin's chatter, overwhelmed by the conflicting emotions within him.

"You look cold, Heath," said a kind voice. Leonora, Jasmine's younger sister, stepped up to him. "Let me help." She placed a hand on his shoulder and wrinkled her nose in concentration. Immediately, the air around Heath heated up significantly, enough that the snow melted a little under his boots.

"You've gotten so much stronger!" he said, amazed.

She nodded, smiling shyly. "I've been practicing. I can control temperature pretty reliably now. I can make it hotter *or* colder, although still only a small area."

Heath stared at her, the struggle continuing inside him. Five hopeful faces were turned to him—Percival's still looked a bit mulish—and he wavered. It would be such a relief to forget caution, forget duty, to tell them all the truth of his developing powers, and let them help him push the boundaries of his magic. But a voice of caution in his mind told him that he was walking along a precipice, and if he threw himself down one edge, there would be no recovering the peak. He was exhausted by balancing on the line, but he wasn't confident he wanted to fall into either gully.

Before he could say a word, before he'd decided *what* to say, his vision flickered. He gasped, and suddenly he saw Merletta's face, as clearly as he saw his cousins in front of him. Her expression was satisfied, and she was swimming with determination. Heath caught a flash of coral as she darted past it. She wasn't in her underwater city. She must be heading for Vazula.

For a moment Heath just blinked stupidly. He hadn't even been consciously trying to see Merletta, but the image had been so clear. He had to get to Vazula—he couldn't bear to think of her going there to see him, and finding the place deserted. But he couldn't get there in time, not without Reka's help.

As soon as he thought the dragon's name, another image flashed before his mind.

"Rekavidur," he gasped, once again thrown by the clarity of his sight.

The dragon was sitting at the very pinnacle of a rocky slope, presumably on Wyvern Islands somewhere. Heath could almost feel the thinness of the air through their connection. But as soon as Heath spoke the dragon's name, Rekavidur turned his head sharply to the side. Heath was sure he was looking south-west, toward Heath's location.

"Rekavidur," Heath breathed again, his grandmother's words in his mind. "I need you." He made no attempt to reason with his friend, to persuade or reassure. He just let his emotion sound in the three simple words.

For a moment Heath stared into the dragon's eyes, and almost caught his breath at the familiarity of their expression. They may be of different species, but the two friends were fighting the same internal battle. He could read the anguish of divided loyalty on Reka's face.

Then, with an abruptness that made Heath jump, many miles away, Rekavidur dropped from the pinnacle like a stone, snapping out his wings and catching the wind as he fell. Within moments he had reached the impossible speed of dragons, and his features were nothing but a blur. Still, the image didn't fade. Heath had to forcefully wrest his mind away from the dragon's surroundings, to return to the snowy meadow where his cousins were all staring at him, mouths wide.

"What was that?" Brody demanded. "What just happened?"

"Reka's coming," Heath said, the words tumbling out joyfully. "He's coming here!" They all stared blankly at him.

"Don't you realize how amazing this is?" Heath pushed on. "I haven't seen him—I mean, properly seen him—in months!"

Bianca blinked. "I'm...I'm happy for you," she said carefully. "But how do you know he's coming?"

It was Heath's turn to stare. In his excitement, he'd forgotten that his growing abilities were a secret.

"Never mind that," he said quickly, his mind returning to the situation before him. His family dilemma could wait. He was going to see Merletta, no matter what it took to convince Reka. But one thing he wanted to settle before the confrontation was over. He turned to his brother.

"Did you keep this secret from me because you knew I'd disapprove? Or did you really think I would report you?"

Percival's expression was unreadable. "I don't know what to think anymore, Heath," he said, more calmly. "It's hard to tell where your loyalty is."

Heath didn't know how to answer him. He'd always considered himself unshakably loyal to Valoria, but he was also loyal to his family. Once, the two allegiances had aligned comfortably. Now, he felt anchorless, unsure where to tie his rope.

But no response was required of him. He and Percival were still staring at each other when a rushing sound filled the meadow. Heath stared up into the sky, his heart leaping at the familiar sight of a dark shape descending, wings outstretched. Reka must have flown with unbelievable speed—perhaps as quickly as he'd done the time he carried a half-dead Heath back from Vazula.

The dragon landed lightly in the snow. He barely disturbed the white powder, but the snow sizzled and melted around his taloned feet. His scales flashed yellow in the cold morning light, and his eyes were fixed on Heath.

"I've missed you, Dragonfriend," he said quietly, his gravelly voice breaking the silence that had descended on the clearing.

"And I've missed you," said Heath, reaching out and laying his hand on Rekavidur's side. The dragon's scaly hide felt warm under his fingers. "I'm sorry for what I said, after I woke from my injuries."

"Your words were harsh," Reka said frankly. "But I did not stay away because I was offended."

"Why did you stay away?" Heath asked.

Reka glanced around the group. "It is not a matter I am willing to discuss with you," he said with his usual candor. "Certainly not with your family."

Heath followed his gaze. He'd almost forgotten that his cousins were there.

"There is a noticeable concentration of magic in this place," Rekavidur said with interest. It seemed they were done discussing the matter of their estrangement. "What are you all doing here?"

Bianca cleared her throat, looking dazzled. Power-wielders or not, it was highly unusual for most of the family to see a dragon this close up, let alone converse with it.

"Greetings, Mighty Beast," she said, her voice a little breathless. "We are practicing our magic, trying to develop our abilities. We are honored by your presence among us."

Rekavidur inclined his head in a manner more regal than King Matlock receiving homage from his subjects. Heath barely refrained from rolling his eyes.

"It is a good idea. Your power must be worked, kneaded, or it will not reach its full potential." He turned his reptilian head back toward Heath. "Heath should follow your example."

Percival threw Heath a triumphant look, and Heath actually did roll his eyes this time. Reka, young and inexperienced among his own colony, was clearly loving the opportunity to grace the overawed humans before him with his sage words. But

Heath had more important things on his mind than the dragon's vanity.

"Reka, can we speak in private?" he pressed.

The dragon regarded him with a curious eye. "You do not wish to speak your mind in front of your own family?"

"Honesty isn't much of a family trait at the moment," said Heath bitterly. He regretted the petty words as soon as they were uttered, and not just because of the winces of his cousins. Reka's head swiveled between Heath and the others, and Heath could tell the dragon's curiosity was now well and truly woken.

"What does that mean?"

"Nothing," said Heath quickly.

"It is absurd to suggest that it meant nothing," Rekavidur said calmly. "There was a definite meaning behind it, and I wish to know what it was. I am happy to wait."

He gave Heath a steady look, and Heath deflated. His friend knew how to manipulate Heath's weak point. Reka must have sensed the urgency in Heath's request, and unlike Heath, Rekavidur was in no hurry whatsoever.

To his surprise, Bianca came to his rescue.

"He was talking about our secrecy in meeting here without telling him," she said, sounding half-ashamed, half-defiant. "We didn't mean any disrespect to him, but we thought it better if our activities didn't become widely known."

Heath scowled at her, still stung by the suggestion that he couldn't have been trusted to keep their secret.

"What do you mean, young power-wielder?" Reka asked, frowning. "I haven't been paying as close attention as I ought, perhaps, but surely things have not reached such a pass? Surely the use of your magic is not outlawed by your king?"

"Not yet," muttered Percival.

Heath glared at him. "Of course it isn't," he told the dragon quickly. "Can we go now?"

"No." Rekavidur's eyes were still fixed on Heath's brother.

Percival seemed to feel it, because he looked up, and his tone became defensive. "Well, it's true that we can't use our magic freely in the city." He frowned at his brother. "If anyone's outlawed what we're doing, it's Heath."

"That," said Rekavidur, in a voice that made everyone go still, "is untrue." His orb-like eyes rested sternly on Percival. "Even if I couldn't sense the dishonesty in your words, human, I would know it was untrue. Heath may struggle to embrace his own magic, but he has never had any fear or distrust of anyone else's."

The clearing was silent for a long moment, but Reka seemed oblivious to the effect of his words. He turned calmly back to Heath. "You wished to speak to me privately?"

Heath nodded. He felt an odd mix of elation at the dragon's defense of him, and cowardice at his own inability to meet his brother's eye. Without another word, Reka seized Heath's shoulders in his front talons and took to the air with a rush of wind that sent the unprepared onlookers tumbling backward into the snow.

The sensation was familiar, but it had been some time, and Heath's stomach dropped unpleasantly. The flight was mercifully short, however. Reka set him down on a nearby hilltop, landing gracefully beside him.

"What is it you wish to say to me in private, Heath?"

Heath paused, still catching his breath. He expected the dragon to make one of his usual lofty remarks about humans and their tendency to deceive and hide things from one another, but Reka remained silent.

"Reka, how closely are you watching me?" he asked. "Did you know I went back to Vazula by sea?"

Reka started visibly, an unusual display. "I did not."

Heath nodded. "I thought I might have heard about it if you

did. Well, I convinced a captain to take me on his ship. Although I had to go by rowboat to actually cross the magical barrier."

"Why would you do that?" Rekavidur pressed. "Surely it was painful for you to witness what must have awaited you."

"But it wasn't!" Heath said, excitement warring with nervousness as to how the dragon would respond to the mention of their mermaid acquaintance. "Reka, Merletta is alive."

Again the dragon's reaction was visible, although this time he stilled. "Alive? How can that be? She regained the water without our assistance, then?"

Heath shook his head. "She didn't. She—" He broke off as something obvious occurred to him. "How did you not know that, though? Couldn't you have used your farsight to see what became of her?"

Reka shook his head. "Farsight doesn't work that way. We can't see anything and everything." He tilted his head to the side, considering. "Except for the most powerful of dragons, perhaps. The rest of us have to choose what to target our sight upon, and then develop that ability. I can always see my own home when I am away from it, for instance. And I can see you because I have invested in you, in our friendship. You are within my sight. But that is not the case for everyone. It is not the case for Merletta."

Heath thought dryly that he didn't need Reka to tell him that Merletta wasn't important to him. But he didn't say it, not wanting to break the new peace. Reka's comments about farsight were fascinating, and Heath would love to question him more. But it would have to wait. Again, Merletta's form flashed before his mind. She was at the island now, above water, and her image was no longer murky and obscured. He could see her in vivid detail. The drops of water on her dark eyelashes glistened in the sunshine, and the white sand of Vazula glinted behind her.

"What was that?"

Heath pulled his thoughts back to the dragon in front of him. "What was what?"

"What did you just do that drew so powerfully on your magic?" Reka pressed. "I could feel it, more strongly than I've ever felt from you before."

"It's a lot to explain," said Heath quickly. "And I want to tell you all of it, but not right now."

"Very well," Reka agreed comfortably.

Heath had to bite back a laugh. He couldn't think of a single human who would give that reaction. It was nice to know that sometimes the maddeningly unhurried pace of dragons could work to his advantage.

"Where was I?" Heath asked vaguely.

"When you interrupted yourself, you were explaining to me how it was that Merletta was not dead," Rekavidur reminded him patiently. "Or at least, so I understood."

"I was," nodded Heath, his excitement growing. "Reka, she dried out, just like I thought. But it didn't kill her! Once she was fully out of the water, her body transformed. Her tail disappeared, and she became human!"

Reka once again stilled completely, his expression impossible to read.

"Human?" he repeated slowly. "She lost, in effect, that part of her that was fish? Instead of becoming completely sea creature, she became completely land creature? Completely human?"

Heath nodded eagerly. "That's right." He watched in silence as—unless he was much mistaken—some kind of internal explosion went off in Reka's mind. It was encouraging to see the dragon's response tallying with his grandmother's prediction. For a moment he debated telling Reka what his grandmother had said, but he decided against it. She'd seemed to think her speculation was dangerous, and Heath had no way of knowing how much the information might reveal to Rekavidur.

"That is...unexpected," said Reka at last.

"For me too," said Heath mildly. "And even more so for Merletta, I think." He looked cautiously up at the dragon. "So, does that knowledge make you more or less inclined to return to Vazula? To see her again?"

Reka had been looking into the distance with unfocused eyes, but he now bent his gaze upon Heath.

"More," he said decisively. "Definitely more."

Heath bounced on his toes, barely able to contain his excitement. "Can we go right now? She's there, on Vazula, at this minute."

"How do you know that?" Reka asked, his eyes searching Heath's.

"Part of the story I'm going to tell you later," Heath said, trying to keep the impatience from his voice.

Reka nodded slowly, abstractedly. "In that case," he said at last, "let us go."

CHAPTER TWENTY-SIX

Merletta

Merletta wriggled her toes in the sand, letting out a long, relieved breath of pure air. It had been far too long. She shouldn't have let herself be frightened out of returning to Vazula for so many weeks. If there were hermits living in underwater caves well beyond the barrier, surely she could brave the patrols for one day.

She stepped across the sand, encouraged to find that she no longer needed to walk carefully. Her body remembered the movement, and she felt entirely steady on her feet. After a minute, she broke into a run, trying to mimic the way she'd seen Heath move. She didn't feel graceful, but she covered the ground quickly, and she didn't fall. The next thing she wanted to learn was how to jump, like Heath did when grabbing at a coconut just above his head. But all attempts had ended in her flat on her back in the sand. She needed someone to coach her.

She sighed at the thought of Heath. Of course she'd indulged the foolish hope that he'd be there to greet her, but she hadn't really thought it likely. She had no way to communicate with him, to tell him that this was the rest day where she was leaving the triple kingdoms at last.

She strolled over to the place where they'd been reunited last time they were here. She remembered the light in Heath's eyes as he'd seen her. His relief at her survival had been palpable, as had his amazement at her new form, but it had been more than that. She would have expected him to be astonished and fascinated by her legs. But she hadn't been prepared for the sheer delight she'd seen in his eyes. His every feature had radiated excitement, and—did she dare to think it?—longing. As if his mind was filled with more than just their present reunion. As if he, like Merletta, was realizing the implications of her ability to live above water. Implications for their future.

But she was getting carried away with the tide. Heath had never spoken about a future between them, any more than she had. Still, it was hard to forget the way he'd stilled when she'd touched his scar. At the time, in her elation at seeing him again, she'd momentarily forgotten that he was sensitive about clothing. She'd gotten the impression the year before that it was a human trait to be self-conscious about others seeing or touching your skin. She'd always found it humorous.

Until her fingers had explored the jagged skin on his side, a souvenir of Ileana's spear, and he'd stilled like a shrimp hypnotized by a cuttlefish. All at once she'd become hyper-aware of the warmth of his skin, and of his closeness—almost near enough for their breath to mingle—and she'd suddenly understood. Laying her hand against Heath's skin felt intimate in a way no friendly brush of cold scales with Sage in passing, or collision of equally cool limbs in combat training, ever could. Suddenly Heath's caution about personal space had seemed not comical but wise. And yet she'd been unable to bring herself to pull back, intoxicated by the sensation of warmth and attachment.

He'd felt something as well, she was sure of it. When he'd

laid his hand over hers, and told her he wanted to protect her, his sincerity had been undeniable.

He even invited you to live in Valoria with him, reminded a hopeful voice in her mind. But she shook off the thought. Heath had been afraid for her life if she returned to the triple kingdoms, and not without reason. His offer had been another instance of his desire to keep her alive. She'd established that he didn't want to see her die. That wasn't the same thing as wanting a future with her.

She tried to push Heath from her mind. The opportunity of a day on the island was rare now. She would soon be submerged in preparation for her final test, and probably unable to afford the time to come. She shouldn't waste the day mooning over the absent Heath.

She turned her eyes to the crumbling ruins visible from the beach. A thought had been growing in her mind ever since she'd seen the underwater cave with its signs of habitation. The idea that there were merpeople surviving outside the triple kingdoms had caused a vague hope to grow within her, probably as foolish as her wistful imaginings about Heath.

Her parents were supposedly dead, and they certainly weren't in the triple kingdoms anywhere. Was it possible they'd survived outside it? She'd been told they died by drying out, the ultimate dishonor for merkind. But now she knew better about what drying out really meant. The story of her parents' deaths might be just another malicious lie from the charity home's head, designed to shame Merletta. But was it even the tiniest bit possible that her parents really had dried out? That they, like her, had discovered their hidden legs, and moved onto land?

Vazula was, as far as Merletta knew, the only land within easy reach of the triple kingdoms. So it wasn't too much of a stretch to think that her parents might have come to the island if they'd gained their human forms. She didn't think they were living there now. She'd spent a whole month on the island, not to mention her weekly visits the year before. It wasn't large, and she was confident it was abandoned. But perhaps they'd been there once. Perhaps they'd somehow found their way somewhere else, to Heath's kingdom, for example.

It was a slim hope, but Merletta couldn't help indulging it. The idea of having living family was too enticing not to pursue. She remembered Heath's stories about his own parents, his brother and sister, his power-wielding cousins, and his more distant—and magic-less—royal cousins. She sympathized with the difficult position he found himself in, given the rising tension created by his family's magic. But privately, she'd often thought that she would give anything to have a complicated, conflict-filled family, instead of being a nameless orphan.

Most of the time when practicing her walking and running, she stayed on the familiar track between the beach and the lagoon. But this time, she turned her steps toward the ruins instead, making her way into the jungle. After a very short time, she returned to the beach, finding the place where she'd stashed Heath's boots months ago. They were distinctly the worse for their time out in the weather, but they would still offer some protection against the debris of the jungle floor.

During her month on the island, she'd sheltered overnight in the ruins near the lagoon, and she could only guess that someone else trying to live on Vazula would also make use of the crumbling buildings. The first several that she searched showed no sign of being inhabited by anything but jungle creatures for many years. She told herself she was being foolish—even if her parents had been here, it had been sixteen years since their supposed deaths. Most likely no sign of their presence would remain.

But still, she continued on, penetrating into the heart of what had clearly once been a small city. A central square had been mostly reclaimed by the jungle, so that the location of the buildings was only identifiable by the concentration of creepers growing over them. Trees had forced their way through the ancient paving stones, and it took Merletta some time to realize that the middle of the space had once been adorned by some kind of stone sculpture.

She gazed up at it curiously, reminded of the sculpture in the middle of the market square in Hemssted. This one didn't look like it had been carved out of an existing rock column, however. Although mossy and crumbling with age, its shape was discernible. The base formed a large basin of sorts, with a pillar rising up from the middle and branching out at varying levels. A tree had grown almost sideways along one edge of it, so that the circle wasn't complete. But she could get the idea.

"I wonder what your function was," she said absently to the sculpture.

She made her way across the square, stepping over bracken as she went. A tall building rose up on one side, looking important even in decay. Merletta entered it cautiously, not trusting the deteriorating walls. She couldn't tell what the building had been for, not anymore. She braved the stairs and prowled through three different stories without finding anything of interest. Not that she really knew what she was looking for.

She returned to the lowest floor and sat on a moss-covered stone bench to rest. Immediately, there was a loud crack, and she leaped back up with a shout. The stone top of the bench had broken in two. At her movement, a large chunk of it fell to the ground, revealing to her amazed eyes a clever compartment inside the bench.

"Seat and storage," she muttered. "Efficient."

She leaned down to look inside the opening, and her heart leaped at the sight of several scrolls of paper, like the one Heath had once found on Vazula. She lifted one out with trembling hands, her eyes wide with excitement.

It crumbled a little as she unrolled it, but the words were still legible. She ran her eyes down it. It seemed to be a household record of some kind, listing such items as "linen" and "silverware". Not terribly exciting content, but Merletta's heart still raced at the thought of how ancient this record must be.

The next scroll was more interesting. She unrolled it carefully, scrunching her face in concentration as she tried to read the writing, which had faded drastically with time.

"Dragons," she breathed. She could definitely make out the word. She bent her head closer.

"Since the dragons departed," she read slowly, piecing the faded words together, "conflict has increased. Almost a quarter of," here a few words were illegible, "have departed for..." Again, she couldn't make out the next line. "There is very little communication between us," she read out.

She'd just lowered her head back to the page when a distant rushing sound made her snap her head up. She stilled, listening. She knew that sound. All she could hear now was the normal noises of the jungle, but she had to find out for sure.

Rolling up the scroll, she hastened out of the building, back through the square and into the jungle. She moved more quickly than was wise, and fell more than once. But she was always back on her feet quickly. She was only about halfway back to the beach, in a section of relatively sparse jungle, when she heard the rushing sound again. She looked up, and her heart leaped into her throat at the sight of a reptilian shape descending toward the trees.

Or perhaps it was the much smaller figure clutched in its talons that made her heart react that way.

Although the space between the trees didn't seem large enough, Reka folded himself in with apparent ease, and the next thing Merletta knew, she was blinking at the two companions as they landed gently on the jungle floor.

"Heath," she breathed. "You're here."

"I am," he said, and something fluttered in her stomach at his grin. It was a little like the nausea that had preceded her collapse during the memorial. "And this time I've brought Reka," Heath added.

"Yes, I see that," said Merletta, with the ghost of a chuckle. Her gaze moved up to the dragon. "Greetings, Rekavidur. I'm glad to see you again."

Most unusually, the dragon didn't respond. Merletta had learned in her time with the pair of friends that dragons generally placed high importance on formalities such as greetings. So she was taken aback when Reka ignored her words, addressing himself instead to Heath.

"I think you mean that I brought you."

His disgruntled tone sounded a little forced, like he was too pointedly ignoring Merletta. Disconcerted, she turned to Heath. She saw in her peripheral vision that as soon as she wasn't looking at Rekavidur, the dragon studied her surreptitiously. Unless she was mistaken, his gaze was fixed on her legs.

"What are you doing out here in the jungle?" Heath asked, either not noticing or choosing to ignore the dragon's strange behavior.

"I was exploring," said Merletta, too embarrassed to admit to her childish hope about her parents. "And I found something. Look."

She handed Heath the scroll she'd found. Knowing how he loved old records, she expected him to pore over it immediately. But his eyes remained fixed on her as he took it, and that smile was still lingering around his mouth. Inexplicably, she found herself blushing.

"I've missed you," said Heath quietly. "It feels like a long time since I was here last."

"It is a long time," she said, raising a hand to brush hair out of her face. She felt strangely self-conscious under Heath's scrutiny, in a way she couldn't remember ever feeling before.

Heath's gaze traveled from her face across to her arm, and a frown marred his pleasant features. "What happened to your arm?" His eyes raced over her, and his frown deepened. "And the rest of you!"

Merletta glanced down in surprise. She'd forgotten about the welts from the jellyfish stings. They'd long since ceased to hurt, and they'd mostly faded. But they were still visible to a careful observer.

"Jellyfish," she said, trying to sound careless, but unable to restrain a shudder. "Ileana managed to force me into the middle of an entire bloom of them during my practice test. I'm just lucky these ones weren't dangerous."

Heath's eyes flashed in anger. "I can't believe Ileana is still on the loose after what she's done to you. She should be locked up."

Merletta snorted, although secretly she was pleased by Heath's defense of her. "Don't get your hopes up. More likely she'll be given an award." She frowned thoughtfully. "Although I think the jellyfish stunt might not have been sanctioned."

Ileana had looked surly every time Merletta had seen her since the incident, and she'd noticed that the mermaid was training with others her age now, instead of with the higher ranking guards she'd floated among at the memorial.

"How did the practice test go?" Heath asked curiously.

"Really well," said Merletta brightly. "I got this!" She pulled out her paua shell knife, and displayed it proudly to Heath. "It's my prize."

Still beaming, she told him about the practice test. Heath's eyes widened as she described the various perils she'd faced, but he refrained from expressing his horror with what seemed to be a painful effort. Merletta smiled to herself, appreciating his forbearance, but not minding his protectiveness at all. For a moment she indulged the absurd thought of what it would be like if Heath could come underwater with her, have her back in dangerous situations. But even if that was possible, it would be foolish. Heath would be as out of his depth in her world as she would be in his. She would be the one watching his back.

The whole time she'd been speaking, Rekavidur had watched her unblinkingly, still crouched between the trees. When she'd finished recounting her adventures to Heath, she took a deep breath, telling herself it was ridiculous to be nervous. This was Rekavidur, whom she knew. There was no logic behind the instinct of danger that made her want to flee from him, that reminded her of her fear when she'd first set eyes on him. She turned to face the dragon, smiling in a way that wasn't quite natural.

"Rekavidur, I know you were interested in what happened to the dragon inhabitants of this island," she said. She inclined her head toward the parchment now in Heath's hand. "They're mentioned in that record. I don't know if it's a letter like the one Heath found, or some other kind of account. But it definitely talks about dragons."

Throughout this speech, Rekavidur continued to watch her in an expressionless way that she found unnerving. But once she was finished, he unbent slightly, showing a faint sign of interest.

"Does it indeed?" He lowered his head toward the parchment, but Heath didn't unroll it.

"Let's get out of the jungle," he said, swatting some kind of tiny flying creature from his face. "There'll be more space on the beach, then you can have a proper look at it."

"Very well," said Reka with dignity. With his usual abrupt-ness, he shot up into the air, somehow dodging the trees.

Heath turned to Merletta with a grin. "Well, that's him out of the way."

"What do you mean?" asked Merletta blankly.

Heath hesitated. "He's been acting strangely," he said, seeming uncomfortable. "I don't fully know why, but he…well, he wasn't sure about returning. I just think we'll talk more freely without him hanging around."

Merletta didn't know what to say. She felt heat rising up her cheeks again at the thought that Heath wanted to be alone with her. It was very inconvenient, this sudden self-consciousness around him. It had all come from her ridiculous daydreams earlier about the fact that they could now inhabit the same world, if they chose.

"How are you, actually?" Heath asked quietly, as they made their slow way through the jungle. "I mean, you're alive, so that's a start."

Merletta chuckled. "I'm more than alive." She glanced over at him. "But I can't deny things have been eventful."

Heath gave a sigh that was half-groan. "Tell me," he said grimly.

So she told him all about the memorial, and her illness. She told him her suspicions regarding the guards' deaths. When she couldn't take his look of anxiety any longer, she changed tack, telling him of Emil's decision to help her, and the way Freja's patrol had adopted her into their midst so generously.

"If it wasn't for Ileana, I would think the guards are the best of us," she mused. "It might not be a bad life, you know."

Heath disregarded her comment about the guards. "Well, I'm glad that this Emil is helping you from inside the record holders," he said, although for some reason, he didn't look especially glad. "But I'm more interested in your new fame in Tilssted. And in the other cities, by the sound of it."

Merletta raised an eyebrow, bemused. "Surprising, isn't it? But why are you so interested in that?" She'd told Heath that detail as an amusing anecdote, nothing more.

"They even followed you back to the Center," Heath mused, "making sure you were being looked after." He met her eyes, his expression serious. "They may well have been the ones to save your life, you know, not Emil and Sage."

"Why would you think that?" Merletta asked in astonishment.

They had made it back to the beach by now, and were sitting in the sand. Rekavidur was stretched out some distance away, studying the parchment Merletta had found. Merletta shifted so she was fully facing Heath, who was looking thoughtfully out to sea.

"You're too visible," he said grimly. He turned to look at her again. "It's exactly the problem King Matlock is having with Percival right now. Percival's done some things that really should have earned some kind of consequence, like meddling with the wording of his vow at the loyalty ceremony."

"His what at the what?" Merletta asked, perplexed.

"Oh, I forgot you don't know about that," said Heath, quickly filling her in on the incident.

Merletta frowned. "That sounds like he's heading for trouble for sure," she agreed. "But what does that have to do with—"

"The point is that the king can't easily reprimand him," Heath cut her off. "Because everyone is watching too closely. And although the members of the court are more suspicious of Percival—of all of us—than ever, the rest of the kingdom loves him. They think he's some kind of hero, and they wouldn't take kindly to him being punished, especially for something that would seem unimportant to them. They wouldn't understand the implications of Percival's subtle defiance. The king would make himself unpopular, and the last thing he wants to do is to create a rift between the crown and the power-wielders that would push the common people to choose a side. In fact," he added dryly, "the entire purpose of giving me the role I have was to avoid such a rift."

Heath fell silent for a moment. Then, to Merletta's surprise, he gave a sudden laugh. "The irony isn't lost on me," he muttered.

"It's lost on me," Merletta commented, a little disgruntled.

Heath turned to her, his easy smile disarming her instantly. "Sorry. It's just that I spend most of my time trying to convince Percival not to be so open with his defiance, and his anger over the crown's attitude toward magic. And here I am, giving you the exact opposite advice."

Merletta frowned. "You're advising me to be openly defiant? I thought you agreed last time that I should keep my head down."

Heath shook his head. "I'm not encouraging you to rock the boat regarding the Center's lies," he said quickly.

Merletta stared at him. "Rock the boat? What in the ocean does that mean?"

Heath laughed again. "Poor choice of words. I'm not saying I think you should be obvious about what you know. Just that you should make the most of your popularity. Make yourself, and your movements, so well known that it would be noticed if you disappeared."

Merletta frowned, starting to grasp his meaning. "I think it would already be noticed," she said, realizing it for the first time. It was still hard to see herself as a figurehead. "I see what you mean, about how that might have saved my life. I suppose it's not such a simple thing to kill me off anymore. Not if whoever does it wants to avoid drawing attention to me."

Heath nodded. "Precisely. You've made enough of a splash that—"

"I've what?" demanded Merletta, half laughing.

Heath gave a comical groan. "I forget what different worlds we come from. Water is clearly on my mind."

Merletta smiled at his expression. She sometimes forgot it too, impossible as that seemed. But as she looked out toward the horizon, the smile slipped from her face.

"If I *was* killed off," she said quietly, "I would have achieved nothing. Whoever is behind the lies would have won, because I haven't uncovered their deceptions at all. I'm starting to think they're already winning. Fear of attack has kept me quiet all this time." She turned, willing Heath to meet her eyes. "The reason your brother is dangerous to the crown is that he's outspoken. Everyone knows his attitude, and his abilities. If something happened to him as a result of that attitude, it wouldn't just make his admirers angry. It would make them more determined to support his cause, wouldn't it?"

Heath nodded slowly, warily, as if suspicious that she was leading him into a trap.

"Well, I haven't done anything to make others take up my cause. They've noticed me because I'm from Tilssted, so it's unusual for me to be in the Center. But if I disappeared, no one would rise up and challenge the Center on their lies. No one would know about them. I need to start sharing what I know."

Heath looked troubled, but he didn't actually contradict her, which surely meant he knew she was right.

"I need to do it carefully, of course," Merletta assured him, unable to resist the mute appeal in his eyes. She still hadn't gotten over the thrill of having someone care so much for her safety. "I just need to start encouraging others to question what we've been told. To see the things that don't add up." She felt her face set in grim lines. "And I know just where to start."

"Just promise me you really will be careful," Heath said, his voice pained. "I happen to like you being alive."

"So do I," grinned Merletta. She looked back at the horizon, suddenly unable to meet his eye. "And I'm glad you're here. It's the first time I've been back since we met here last, and I thought it was too much to hope that you'd be here as well."

"Actually..." Heath sounded uncomfortable, and Merletta looked at him curiously. "Actually, I only came because I knew you were here. I...well, I saw you."

"Saw me?" Merletta repeated blankly. "What do you mean?"

His voice half-apologetic, half-eager, Heath told her what had been happening with his sight. Merletta felt her mouth fall open as he spoke, her mind racing with the various implications.

"That's incredible," she said, when he fell silent. "That's an unbelievable power, Heath. I can't believe you didn't tell me that straight away!"

Heath still looked hesitant. "You don't mind?" he said. "You're not offended that I was watching you?"

"Of course not," said Merletta. "It sounds like you couldn't really control it, and in any event, it could be so useful. We don't have any other way to communicate, after all."

She saw the relief on Heath's face, and she smiled. It was like him to be sensitive to her feelings, but she wasn't troubled in the least. She'd already gathered that privacy was much more important in Heath's culture than in hers. It sounded like he even had his own room in his family's home. Between the charity home and the trainees' barracks, Merletta hadn't slept in a room by herself in her entire life.

Besides, she liked the idea that Heath was following her progress from his world. It made her feel as though they were connected somehow, even when apart.

"Shame there's no way to make the communication go both

ways," she mused. "Wouldn't that be useful!"

"I can't even get it to reliably work one way," Heath said ruefully. "But I'll keep working on it."

She felt his eyes on her, and raised her eyebrows inquiringly. "What is it?"

That same warm smile was back on his face, the one she didn't remember seeing before he'd returned to find her alive, and with legs.

"It's just nice," he said, "talking to you. I don't have to worry what is and isn't safe to say, or whether telling you about my power will have unintended consequences. I feel like I can never speak freely anymore. You have no idea what a relief it is."

"Actually, I have a very good idea," smiled Merletta. "There aren't many I can trust in my world, and I'm afraid to endanger my friends. But you're not at the mercy of my world." She looked up to find his eyes boring into hers. "And I trust you completely," she finished, her voice quiet.

Heath was silent for a moment. Then he reached for her hand. She thought he would place his over the top of hers on the sand, like he had last time. But instead he curled his fingers over hers, so that her hand was clasped inside his. Then he raised the pair and placed her palm flat against his chest. She could feel his heartbeat—did humans' hearts usually beat so quickly? But then, hers was racing as well.

"I swear I'll never betray that trust," Heath said quietly.

Merletta stared into his eyes as her heart beat even faster, its frantic pace almost painful now. Perhaps it was trying to make up for the fact that she seemed to have forgotten how to breathe.

Heath held her gaze, and when she didn't look away, didn't remove her hand from his chest, something shifted in his eyes. She thought he leaned toward her slightly, but it was hard to be sure. She still hadn't drawn breath, and she was almost as dizzy as she had been when she started to hallucinate.

Suddenly, a powerful rush of wind swept over them, flinging sand into Merletta's eyes and causing her to throw her arms up over her face. The moment broken, she blinked up at the sight of Rekavidur, towering above them with his wings outstretched.

"Time to return to Valoria, Heath," he said, and his voice was grim.

Merletta expected Heath to protest, to complain in his usual lighthearted way about the dragon's lack of tact. But the scowl he sent at his friend held anger rather than exasperation. She didn't get the sense that Rekavidur's intervention came as a surprise.

"I should return, too," she said quickly, pushing herself to her feet. She sent Heath a smile, a little more shy than usual. "I'll return when I can. Keep an eye out, won't you?"

"Of course I will," he said quietly.

For a moment he hovered, looking like he was considering saying or doing something more. Then he stepped away from her and allowed Rekavidur to seize his shoulders. The dragon offered Merletta no farewell. Within moments they were high in the air, a rapidly disappearing speck in the blue sky.

Merletta wrapped her arms around her shoulders, her emotions tugging at her. She felt elated, almost giddy, at the thought of Heath's touch. It was rare for him to initiate contact at all, let alone such an intimate gesture. Perhaps it went with his more private culture, but he'd always seemed very shy about touching her at all.

But her excitement was marred by unease as she thought over Rekavidur's strange behavior. She was sure it wasn't a coincidence that the dragon had intervened just as Heath had been leaning toward her. Something had definitely changed since the year before. Merletta didn't understand the reasons, but the conclusion was clear.

The dragon no longer approved of her. And Heath knew it.

CHAPTER TWENTY-SEVEN

Merletta

"You should enter the combat competition, Merletta. You'd be great at it!"

Merletta shook her head, smiling at the eagerness in Sage's voice. "I get pummeled enough in training, thanks. I don't want to spend my Founders' Day getting beaten up by fully trained guards for fun."

"You wouldn't be," said Andre reassuringly.

Merletta threw him an incredulous glance. It was flattering that Andre's admiration for her didn't seem to have abated as the year progressed, but surely even he didn't actually think she could win a combat competition open to every guard in the triple kingdoms.

Andre grinned, as if reading her mind. "I meant that you wouldn't be fighting fully trained guards," he explained. "Not that you wouldn't get pummeled. You still might."

Merletta chuckled. There was the candor she'd come to like in the younger trainee.

"There are two divisions to the competition," he explained. "The qualified guards fight in one, everyone else in the other.

Center trainees in third year or above have to go in the top category, since they've technically qualified to be guards."

"Which is why I will most certainly not be entering," Sage cut in.

Andre chuckled. "Sage is right that you'd be good though, Merletta. As a second year trainee, you're among the most trained of the fighters who are allowed in the bottom category."

Merletta narrowed her eyes at him. "As are you."

Andre's grin grew. "I've already signed up."

Merletta rolled her eyes at him and shook her head indulgently. "Forget it, Andre. I'm not fighting you for fun on a holiday."

Andre shrugged, his expression still cheerful. "Your loss."

"Well, if not combat, what about one of the races?" Sage pressed. "Or I think there's a competition that involves height and depth performance. You'd be great at that after all your acclimatization training!"

Merletta just shook her head absently.

"Come on, Merletta," said Sage, exasperated. "What's the point of coming to Founders' Day if you don't take part in *any* of the festival games?"

"I just like watching," Merletta shrugged.

Her eyes were indeed on the relay race being swum before her. Felix had just completed his lap of the course, and was floating at the finish line, partway across the Center's drop off, where the events were held. He caught her eye, and she returned his wave with a smile.

"Really?" The snide voice from behind made all three trainees turn. Unnoticed, Oliver had drifted up behind them, and he was giving Merletta his usual disdainful look. "I thought you'd want to be front and center, make the most of your newfound fame."

Merletta scowled at him. When she'd started in the

program, Oliver had mainly been content to ignore her. But now that he'd passed his third year test, and had earned his place as the program's only current fourth year, he seemed to have gained confidence in his superiority.

"I'm amazed you haven't found a way to draw attention to yourself yet," Oliver went on. "Or are you still waiting for the ideal moment, when you can have the most witnesses as you regurgitate your lunch and faint dramatically?"

"That's out of line, Oliver." Andre's snapped retort took Merletta aback. The first year trainee was usually so respectful of all his peers, especially those older than him.

Oliver raised an eyebrow, cold fury radiating from him. Clearly he had also been stunned by the outburst from someone below him in the Center's hierarchy.

"Watch yourself, Skulssted," he hissed. Without another word, he swam away, his deep blue tail flicking angrily as he went.

Merletta and Sage exchanged startled glances as Andre glared after Oliver.

"You know," the younger trainee growled, "I think some of the others saw the whole memorial as a bit of a joke. I bet it would be different if it had been a Hemssted guard patrol instead of a Skulssted one."

"I don't think he meant to disrespect the memorial," Merletta said mildly. "Just me."

Andre just shrugged a shoulder, and Merletta subsided into her own thoughts. Oliver's words had been meant as pointless malice, she was sure. But they had actually reminded her of a task left undone. She had determined, when last on Vazula, to start encouraging others to ask questions of the Center. And she hadn't yet done it. In fact, she'd more or less continued to keep her head down, too focused on helping Sage study for her imminent third year test, and on training hard for her own test, which would be held only a couple months later. She felt a tiny spurt of guilt at the memory of Heath's plea—he would no doubt wish her to do something like what Oliver sarcastically accused her of plotting. She shook off the thought, holding in a snort at the absurdity of feeling guilty for not making a childish scene. Surely that can't have been what Heath meant.

But one thing she *had* determined to do, and today might be a good opportunity for it, with so many of the triple kingdoms' residents gathered. For the rest of the afternoon, she scanned the crowds. She knew it wasn't the case for everyone, but in her case, the excellent memory that had won her a place in the program extended to faces. She knew she'd recognize the mermaid she sought if she saw her.

But by the time the festival games were packed away, she'd circled the entire drop off, and seen no sign of her quarry.

"Andre," she asked, as the Center dwellers and other invitees began to drift toward the complex, ready to partake in the Center's exclusive Founders' Day feast, "I don't see August's widow here. The one who received the conch shell at the memorial."

Andre's face fell slightly. "I don't think she comes to things like this anymore. She's still pretty devastated, you know. Keeps to herself mainly, from what my father says."

Merletta thought this over, frowning. "I don't feel right about feasting while she's grieving all alone," she said. "Do you think you could tell me where she lives? I passed out at the memorial before I got the chance to pay my respects."

Andre looked startled, and Sage shot Merletta a sharp look.

"You want to visit her?" the first year asked. "Now?"

Merletta nodded. "Do you think that's too disrespectful?"

"Noooo," said Andre, drawing out the word. "Not disrespectful, but...won't it make you late for the feast?"

"I don't care about the feast," said Merletta, with perfect

truth. The more she thought about her idea, the better it seemed to be. She could speak with the bereaved mermaid without fear of being overheard. Everyone important, from the Record Master down to the lowliest Center guard not currently on duty, would be at the Founders' Day feast.

"Well, I don't mind showing you where she lives," said Andre, still seeming surprised by the request.

"Can't you just tell me?" Merletta asked. "I don't mean to pull you away from the feast."

Andre shook his head. "You don't know the neighborhood. I doubt I could give clear enough directions for you to find the right house. Plus," he added frankly, "she knows me. I want to be the one to knock on the door, to make sure she's willing to receive visitors."

"That's fair," admitted Merletta. After all, the feast hadn't actually started yet. If they swam quickly, Andre could show her the way and be back before it was truly underway.

"I'm coming too," said Sage.

The look she cast at Merletta said plainly that she was coming to keep an eye on her friend rather than give her condolences to the widow. Merletta grimaced at the other mermaid, but didn't protest.

They turned, changing direction so that instead of entering the Center, they swam back across the drop off, toward Skulssted. They had almost reached the Center's receiving hall when another figure glided up alongside Sage.

"Going for a swim to clear the head? Mind if I join?"

Merletta raised an eyebrow at Emil, not sure whether to be pleased or exasperated at the close tabs he seemed to be keeping on her. Sage's expression showed an equally mixed response.

Andre, however, expressed only enthusiasm. "Of course we don't mind!" he said. For a moment, he seemed to forget the somber nature of their mission in his excitement at the company of the junior record holder.

"Where are we going?" Emil asked, easily keeping pace with Sage.

"Merletta and Sage want to pay their respects to one of the widows from the recent guard patrol," said Andre. "August was a family friend, so I know his wife."

"Is that so?" Emil's eyes were on Merletta, their expression challenging.

She gave a defiant half-shrug. She knew they were working together now, but opportunities to speak to Emil privately were so impossible to come by, he couldn't really blame her for not clearing her plans with him first.

"It's likely to be a...confronting conversation," she said meaningfully. "You may not want to be part of it."

Emil's eyes flicked between her and Sage. "I'm coming," he said firmly.

They had entered Skulssted by now, and Andre directed them toward his own neighborhood. The streets were busy, full of merrymakers heading to their own, smaller, Founders' Day dinners. The three trainees and the junior record holder slid between the throngs, attracting no especial attention.

Before long, Andre pulled up in front of a large, well-carved home. "This is it," he said, gesturing.

"Thanks Andre," said Merletta. "I'm guessing the feast is just starting, so once you introduce us—"

"Oh, I'm not going back," Andre interrupted her. "I'll stay. I'd like to speak with her as well."

Merletta hesitated. She hadn't counted on Andre witnessing what she wanted to say to August's widow. Her eyes were drawn irresistibly to Emil, and she could see from his furrowed brow that he had grasped her intention enough to understand her dilemma. He gave a tiny shake of his head, but Merletta wasn't so sure. Emil didn't know Andre, but she and Sage had spent months with him. She had more reason to trust him than the stranger she was about to approach. Still, he should be warned, as far as was possible.

"Andre," she said slowly. "I want to talk to her about...about something that might be dangerous. It would be safer for you not to hear it."

She knew long before she finished speaking that she'd been out of her mind to think her warning would make him *less* determined to join them. His face was alight with curiosity, and he puffed his chest out in an apparently unconscious gesture as he responded.

"I'm not afraid to take risks. And you can trust me."

His words sent a strange shiver over Merletta, drawing her thoughts irresistibly back to her last conversation with Heath, and their interrupted moment. But she shook the thought off.

"If you're sure," she said quietly.

Andre swam forward boldly, and knocked on the door. Merletta immediately recognized the woman who answered as the widow from the memorial. The older mermaid looked surprised but not unhappy to receive a visit from Andre. Merletta and the others had hung back, so they couldn't hear her words. But they saw Andre gesture toward them, and the mermaid, looking more surprised than ever, nodded and moved to let them all inside.

Although Merletta felt awkward as she swam through the doorway, she couldn't help looking around in fascination. She'd never been in a home like this before. The charity home had been every inch the institution, and although the trainees' barracks were more pleasant, they certainly weren't a family home. This place was nicely set up, everything neat and the furniture in good condition. The decorations were fresh, and clearly replaced regularly. But there was a hushed feeling that was hard to articulate, an emptiness to the house that had nothing to do with its material contents.

Andre performed introductions, and the middle-aged mermaid greeted them all politely.

"Glad to meet some of Andre's friends," she said in a stately way, as she gestured them to seats. "Are you all in the program, then?"

"Emil has graduated," said Andre quickly. "He's a record holder."

"Congratulations," she said, her eyes resting shrewdly on the pale-haired young merman.

Emil inclined his head in acknowledgment. Merletta could tell he was tense, and she wondered if he regretted inserting himself into a situation he hadn't planned and couldn't control. She was still unsure why he'd done it.

"So what brings you here, Andre?" their hostess asked.

"Merletta asked me to," said Andre frankly. "She wanted to pay her respects. She didn't get the chance at the memorial."

The widow's eyes passed to Merletta, her expression thoughtful. "I recognize you, of course," she said. "Your unfortunate collapse was memorable. I hope you're well now?"

"Perfectly well," said Merletta. "I don't wish to waste your time, ma'am. I'm glad you remember what happened to me at the memorial, because it makes my errand easier to explain." She drew in a deep pull of water. "I wasn't entirely honest with Andre." She threw him a glance, and saw that he was watching her intently. "The truth is, I didn't just come to express my sympathy. I came to tell you what I know, and what I've suspected for some time. I think you have a right to know, but I also want to make sure I'm not the only one who knows that we haven't been told the truth about the guards' deaths."

The widow was frozen now, watching Merletta unblinkingly.

Merletta paused, trying to master her nerves. "The truth is, it's my fault your husband died."

She saw Emil and Andre start, and she felt Sage's eyes on her. But she didn't look at any of them.

"I'm more sorry than I can say," she went on, her voice cracking slightly in spite of her best efforts. "I didn't mean for it to happen. But I showed him, and the others, something they weren't supposed to see. Something *I* was never supposed to see. And I believe they were killed for it."

For a long moment, there was silence. "If that's so," the widow said at last, "then why weren't you also killed?"

Merletta blinked, surprised by the older mermaid's calm response. "I don't entirely know," she said frankly. "They initially thought I was dead, I believe. I was afraid to come back to the triple kingdoms, for fear I'd be killed when they saw I was still alive. But too many others saw me once I was back here, and I've become, well..." she thought of Heath's words, "visible since then. I think maybe it's risky to kill me off."

Again, their hostess was silent for a moment. Merletta had expected her to be horrified, or angry, or perhaps disbelieving. She hadn't anticipated a calm, thoughtful response.

"I think you need to explain what happened," the older mermaid said finally.

So Merletta told her, haltingly, what had really happened on that day. She told her about how she'd already known of the land, and how she had met the human there. She tried to keep her anger at bay as she spoke of the total falseness of calling Heath aggressive. She knew she'd be more convincing if she could keep her emotions out of it. She described the attack on him, and her own injuries.

"So you stayed there, near the land, for a whole month?" the widow asked sharply.

Merletta nodded. For a moment she teetered on the edge of

revealing to them all that she'd actually been *on* land. But she wasn't at all sure their hostess believed even what she'd already said. If she started talking about sprouting legs, the mermaid would probably think she'd gone mad, and would disregard her whole story.

"But..." Andre's eyes were wide. "How are you alive? How did you escape the land sickness?"

"Very easily," said Merletta dryly. She met the widow's eyes. "There's a reason none of us had heard of land sickness before. It's a lie, conveniently created to explain the deaths of your husband's patrol."

The mermaid jerked perceptibly, but it was Emil who spoke, his voice calm.

"I had heard of it. In my studies."

The older mermaid's eyes flew to his, her expression searching. "So you believe it's real, do you?"

Emil paused for so long Merletta thought he wouldn't answer. Then he said, slowly but clearly, "No, I do not."

He said no more. His words hung in the water, and Merletta could see the change in Andre's demeanor as he grasped what the junior record holder was saying. Her heart ached for the young trainee, experiencing for the first time the disillusionment that they'd all faced in their studies. The realization that the program lied, even to its own trainees, was hard to swallow at first.

"If your suspicions are correct," the older mermaid said quietly, addressing herself to Merletta, "then my husband's death was not your fault. You were a victim of the same corruption that claimed his life. But what I still don't understand is how he actually died. Land sickness may not be real, but something certainly affected his mind, and his body."

"I don't doubt it, since I've experienced it myself," said Merletta grimly. "When I collapsed at the memorial, I wasn't just ill in my stomach. My mind turned on me. I saw..." She shook her head at the unpleasant memories. "I saw all kinds of strange things. But I retained enough suspicion not to tell anyone what I was experiencing, not to give any outward sign that could allow someone to claim I was suffering from land sickness. And after I passed out, Sage and Emil stayed with me the whole time. If someone intended to do me a mischief, they had no opportunity."

"You believe someone meant to claim you had also died of land sickness?" their hostess asked sharply. "Does someone else know, then, about the month you spent near the land?"

Merletta shrugged helplessly. "I don't know for certain. But..." she hesitated, "I'd been to the land again two days before the ceremony. I think someone knew, or perhaps guessed, where I'd been. I think they hoped I would betray myself if I believed I had land sickness. Which makes me think they didn't know just how much time I've spent near land, and how well I know that land sickness can't be real."

There was another lull as everyone pondered her words.

"I'm afraid I don't know what caused the hallucinations I had," Merletta added. "But I don't doubt for a moment that it's the same thing that caused your husband's."

"Actually," Emil cut in, "I have more information on that." He looked at Merletta. "I haven't had a chance to tell you. But Sage passed on your thoughts about the food you ate for breakfast. It took me a long time to find any mention of it, and as a junior record holder, I definitely wasn't supposed to be reading the relevant record. But there is a type of bream that can cause hallucinations. It's to do with what the fish eats, apparently."

Merletta gasped. "I ate bream that morning. Remember, Andre? I didn't recognize the fish, and you said you thought it was bream."

Andre gaped back at her.

"So the fish is poisonous?" the widow pressed. "Did you survive because you threw it back up?" She frowned. "August threw up as well, though."

"It's not poisonous," said Emil. "I very much fear that the illness was just an excuse. The guards died in…some other way."

Again there was silence, as everyone grappled with the fact that the fallen patrol, publicly honored for their sacrifice in protecting the barrier, had most likely met a violent end within the triple kingdoms themselves.

"Thank you." The older mermaid's quiet voice broke the stillness. "Thank you for telling me the truth. I understand the risk you take in doing so, and I won't do anything to expose you to danger if I can help it."

"Thank you," Merletta echoed her.

The widow's face hardened. "But I don't intend to just let this go."

"Neither do I," Merletta assured her. "That's why I'm here."

The older mermaid nodded. "I've thought from the first that my husband's death was suspicious. I have even wondered," her voice took on a wistful quality, "if it's possible that he isn't really dead."

"But," Sage protested, her eyes flying to Andre's, "I thought you said your father attended the burial himself."

"Not August's burial." Andre's voice was little more than a whisper. "He attended two burials, but he was told that August's case was so much worse that they didn't want to take chances with the infection." His eyes flew to Merletta's, stricken. "It sounds so obviously suspicious now. I can't believe I didn't even question it. It never occurred to me that they would lie."

"Of course not," said Merletta kindly. "Don't blame yourself for trusting them. Like most of the triple kingdoms, you've been trained from earliest memory to think that the Center knows best, and can be trusted with all our knowledge."

"I attended those two burials myself," interjected their hostess. "I'm afraid there can be no doubt that those guards are dead, poor souls. But that still leaves August and two others."

Merletta stilled as a sudden thought occurred to her. The hermit in the cave! If there was the slimmest chance that some of the guards were still alive...

But before she'd decided whether to say anything and possibly raise false hopes, there was a knock at the door, and all five of them jumped. For a moment they all just stared at each other, then August's wife rose into the water and swam to her door with quiet dignity.

Merletta could feel her own shock mirrored in the rest of the trainees when Agner was revealed on the threshold. Emil's expression didn't change, but she saw his hand clench into a fist on his lap. Andre, on the other hand, looked visibly guilty. Merletta forced her own features to remain impassive. She wasn't ashamed of what she was doing, and the whole point of her actions was to start spreading her knowledge. Granted, she hadn't intended for it to come to the attention of any of her instructors so quickly, but at least it was Agner, not Wivell or Ibsen.

The instructor's gaze passed over the whole group, but definitely lingered longest on Merletta. He looked irritated.

"Founders' Day is a strange time to be paying social visits," he said mildly.

Merletta met him look for look. "I was concerned when I saw that one of the guards' widows wasn't at our celebrations. I wanted to pay my respects—you'll remember I didn't quite get to do so at the memorial—and Andre kindly agreed to introduce me."

"Well," said Agner, after a moment's silence. "It's not a good look for the program to have three of our five trainees absent from the feast, to be honest. I think it's time you all returned with me."

They rose without protest, taking their leave of their hostess, whose expression was hard to read. Merletta was uncomfortably aware of Agner scanning all their faces, taking careful note of who was part of their little group. Sage and Emil had already been in it with her, and by their own choice. But Andre had been plunged into their conspiracy without really understanding what he was getting into. Merletta could see how overwhelmed he was—he had the same expression Sage had worn when Merletta first told her about Heath.

No one spoke as they passed through Skulssted. Plenty of onlookers glanced curiously at the group, and Merletta knew their expedition had little hope of remaining secret. But she wasn't trying to keep it all secret, she reminded herself. She was trying to be visible.

They had almost crossed the drop off when Agner tapped Merletta's arm, and she pulled up, bracing herself.

"I like you, Merletta," he said tightly. "I think you could be an asset to our program, whether with the guards or the record holders. But not if you insist on making foolish decisions."

Merletta remained silent, searching his features by the dim light of the plankton lanterns lining the nearby edge of the drop off. It was impossible to tell how much he knew, and what he was really trying to say. She appreciated his concern, but she had no intention of apologizing.

Seeing that she wasn't going to speak, Agner pulled away and followed the rest of the group. By the time Merletta caught up, they'd reached the feast. She floated up between Sage and Emil, dropping her voice to a mutter.

"I'm sorry I didn't warn you," she said. "I've been meaning to speak to her, but I didn't plan for it to be today. I just saw that she wasn't at the festival, and I thought it was a good opportunity, because I expected everyone of importance to be safely here. I should have realized that with all of us gone, we'd be missed."

"It's not your fault," said Sage, with her usual kindness. "I wonder who missed us. Do you think it was just Agner who noticed?"

Emil cut in grimly before Merletta could answer. "Not everyone of importance is here," he said.

"What do you mean?" Sage asked, when he didn't elaborate.

"Look around," said Emil, and the two mermaids did so.

"What?" Merletta asked impatiently, when he still failed to explain himself.

"I don't see the Record Master anywhere," Emil said. "He wouldn't normally miss the Founders' Day feast, would he?"

Sage looked aghast. "Surely you don't think *he* went looking for us, too? Before we met him last Founders' Day, he didn't even know we existed."

"Everyone knows Merletta exists," said Emil shortly. In his usual frustrating fashion, he didn't elaborate.

Merletta exchanged a glance with Sage, trying to silence the voice of foreboding inside her. She'd made her choice, and there was no point second guessing it now. For better or worse, she'd started the process of spreading the truth. And like blood disseminating through water, its progress couldn't be measured, let alone contained.

CHAPTER TWENTY-EIGHT

"Come on, Heath."

Percival's exasperated voice sounded in Heath's ear, although his brother barely moved his lips. It was a skill they'd both perfected over the course of many dull formal events. "You can't ignore me when you're forced to stand next to me all morning."

Heath was sorely tempted to mutter *watch me*, but that wouldn't really be ignoring Percival.

"We're in the middle of a ceremony," he hissed instead.

The sound of his voice, quiet as it was, caused his mother to look around suspiciously at her sons. She saw two attentive faces directed at the king as he gave his speech.

"Exactly," murmured Percival, in triumph, once the duchess had looked back around. "So you can't dodge me. You've been avoiding me since Reka showed up last week and interrupted our—"

"Secret society?" Heath interjected bitingly.

Percival couldn't actually make the gesture given their visible position at the front of the castle courtyard, but Heath could hear the eye roll in his voice. "You make it sound so dramatic."

Heath didn't reply. He kept his eyes on King Matlock, who was still addressing the assembled crowd. Percival was right that Heath had been avoiding him all week, and he wasn't happy about being forced to stand alongside him at the Winter Solstice Festival. He could muster no enthusiasm for the event, not even given that Reka was to attend again, to light the Flame of Friendship for the second year in a row.

"We are honored," King Matlock was saying, "to mark the passing of another year of peace with our allies."

Heath turned his eyes upward, along with the rest of the onlookers, who clearly also recognized the cue for the dragons to arrive. And sure enough, with a rush of wind that sent swirls of snow dancing around the courtyard, half a dozen dark shapes suddenly dominated the sky, blocking the already dim winter light.

Heath's eyes latched on to Reka, landing at the back of the group. The young dragon scanned the crowd until he found Heath, and dipped his head in greeting. Heath smiled back at him, his heart lifting slightly. He might be utterly failing in his role as liaison between the crown and the power-wielders, and he might be feeling more distant from his own family than he could ever remember being before, but at least he and Reka were friends again. That was something.

Heath's eyes passed to the other dragons, all of whom were significantly bigger than Reka due to their age. As the youngest, Rekavidur was also the one with the brightest hide. His yellow scales, edged with purple, looked cheerful against the snow. Reka's father, Elddreki, was greeting Heath's grandmother, and Heath felt himself tense slightly. At the previous year's ceremony, the dragon had given greater deference to the power-wielding princess than to King Matlock, and the court had noticed. It didn't matter how subtle the gesture had been, not with how sensitive everyone was to the issue, even a year ago. Now, it was much worse. He hoped Elddreki would turn his attention quickly to the king.

He was destined to be disappointed. The medium-sized dragon, his blue, purple, and green scales glinting in the morning sun, shifted to the side without even speaking to King Matlock. The usual awed hush had fallen on the onlookers when the dragons descended, but now a muttering went around the gathered crowd. Another dragon, a large one with burgundy scales, moved forward to take Elddreki's place.

"Greetings, King of Men," he said to King Matlock.

Neither his tone nor his expression gave any hint of awareness that Elddreki had just breached etiquette. And yet Heath knew that dragons were acutely conscious of, and—somewhat bizarrely—very attached to formalities, even human ones. An ominous feeling began to sweep over him. He could see the unnatural stillness of his father, standing just in front of him, and he could feel his brother's nervous energy. Percival was rocking slightly on the balls of his feet.

"Greetings, Mighty Beasts." The king gave the traditional greeting. His face also showed no sign of the slight he had received. "You are welcome here."

The burgundy dragon inclined his head slightly. Heath, his eyes riveted to the creature, let out an audible gasp that made Percival start beside him. The gesture had looked respectful, but all at once Heath had been filled with the certainty that the dragon was angry. Very angry. And angry dragons were never a good thing.

"I do not detect dishonesty in your bearing, King of Men," the dragon said. "So I will thank you for your words. But I am surprised to hear them. We did not expect to find ourselves welcome here."

The muttering in the crowd increased, so that it sounded like an uneasy wind was sweeping fitfully around the courtyard. King Matlock's expression didn't change, but his face was suddenly almost as pale as the snow.

"I am distressed to learn of your expectations," he said, and his voice was impressively even. "You have always been welcome here, and I cannot imagine what would have caused you to think that had changed."

The dragon waited politely for the king to finish before he spoke.

"You do not need to imagine," he said. "I will tell you." His voice was calm, but still, Heath could sense the anger below the surface. And it wasn't just the speaker, he realized. An unfamiliar fire was burning inside every dragon present. They were offended, and Heath could tell King Matlock understood just how dangerous that was.

"We are creatures of magic," the dragon continued, his breath coming out so warm that it melted the snow in front of his taloned feet, despite his head being level with the battlements around the castle. "We have long understood that humans fear magic. We have tolerated your fear in the belief that it stems from reverence for a force you cannot match or understand, and that it will lead to wise caution. But when that fear becomes aggressive, our tolerance wanes."

There was a moment of nervous silence before King Matlock spoke.

"I am grateful for your explanation," he said carefully. "But I am afraid that I still do not understand."

The burgundy dragon gave a huff of impatience, but it was Elddreki who spoke.

"The existence of power-wielding humans in your living generations is a gift that is unprecedented in the history of this land. We know, for our memory is long. You have treated this gift with such suspicion that your power-wielders must meet in secret to exercise their magic, as if it was shameful."

The burgundy dragon was snaking his head back and forth in agreement. "This offends us," he intoned solemnly.

An invisible hand seemed to clench around Heath's throat, and horror washed over him. His gaze was locked on Reka, who was listening placidly to his more senior fellow's words. What had the dragon done?

Reluctantly, Heath felt his eyes drawn to the royals. King Matlock looked stupefied. Heath could almost see his struggle not to glance toward the power-wielders. But Prince Lachlan was looking. With a jolt, Heath saw that the prince's eyes were fixed on him. They were narrowed in an expression that looked inscrutable, but as with the dragons, Heath could see his true emotion as if it was written on his forehead.

Betrayal.

"I don't know what you're referring to," King Matlock said at last.

Elddreki cocked his head to one side, considering the king. "You are telling the truth," he mused, sounding intrigued. "You were truly not aware, then, that your power-wielding relatives are practicing their magic clandestinely for fear of reprisals if they use it openly." He glanced back at Rekavidur, who still looked entirely unruffled. "My own offspring has witnessed it."

King Matlock's eyes passed to Reka, and inevitably on to Heath. How could he fail to draw the connection? Everyone knew of Heath and Reka's friendship. The dragon had even declared Heath to be a dragonfriend at the previous year's Winter Solstice Festival.

The king didn't reply to Elddreki's words. He was still looking in Heath's direction, his gaze now encompassing the power-wielders at large. A hardness had descended on his face that made the ominous feeling within Heath triple in intensity.

The whole situation was a nightmare. The world seemed to spin for a moment, and Heath felt himself wobble on his feet. A firm hand steadied his elbow, and Percival's voice sounded once again in his ear.

"They're taking our side! You did this, Heath, didn't you? I *knew* you couldn't really be against us!"

"I didn't do this!" Heath hissed, his lips feeling strangely numb. "Don't you realize what a disaster this is, Percival? Do you really think anyone, including the power-wielders, will gain if there's war with the dragons?"

"Silence."

The Duke of Bexley's voice was harder, more urgent, than Heath had ever heard it. He closed his mouth at once, still trying to master his alarm. He had never dreamed, when he called Reka to come to that frozen meadow, that something like this would happen. He hadn't expected Reka to carry the tale back to the other dragons, but even so, he wouldn't have guessed that they would be interested in such petty human problems.

But as his eyes passed again over the assembled dragons, and he saw with his inexplicable sight that strange fire of offense burning inside each, he thought he understood. Percival was wrong. The dragons weren't taking the side of the power-wielders. They didn't care about human politics. With a few exceptions, such as Rekavidur and his father, they didn't generally care about humans at all.

But the magic of the power-wielders came from dragons, and the dragons clearly still felt some sense of ownership over it. They still saw it as an extension of their own power. In their eyes, the behavior of the Valorian crown toward the magic in its population was a slight not on the power-wielders, but on the dragons.

"We still desire peace," the burgundy dragon said in his deep voice. "Dragons have never been apt to seek out conflict." At a nod from him, Rekavidur snapped open his wings and took to the sky. He dropped down again quickly, hovering above the stone basin and its faint, flickering fire.

Opening his jaws wide, he breathed his purple-tinged orange flame over the basin, reigniting the Flame of Friendship for another year. Unlike the previous year, the display was not greeted with any exclamations, or applause. Everyone watched in tense silence.

"However," the burgundy dragon continued, as if his speech had not been interrupted by Reka's actions, "we offer you a warning. We watch from Wyvern Islands. If our magic is not welcome here, we will not return next year."

With another incline of his giant, reptilian head, the burgundy dragon crouched against the flagstones, then shot into the sky. The others followed within moments. A stunned silence gripped the courtyard for maybe five seconds. Then pandemonium broke loose.

Heath could sense many eyes on him, and a clawing sensation began to rise up his body. Ignoring Percival's excited whispers, he pushed out of the block of power-wielders, hurrying blindly through the crowd. He had no idea of his destination, just that he needed to get away from the courtyard.

"Reka," he muttered, as he maneuvered through the onlookers, aware that the royal family were watching him. A glance back at his family showed him that Bianca looked stricken, and Jasmine terrified. Percival, of course, was still jubilant.

Fool, Heath grunted to himself. Of course Percival couldn't hear him. He checked his pace for a moment. But someone else could.

"Rekavidur," he murmured, hoping that no one in the crowd was listening too closely. "Rekavidur, I need to talk to you."

The dragon's face flashed immediately before his eyes, the blur of his surroundings showing Heath that Reka was still in the air, flying home to Wyvern Islands. The dragon cocked his head to the side, inviting Heath to go on.

But Heath didn't immediately speak. A group of three men had caught his eye as he continued to fight his way across the square. They seemed immune to the panic spreading around them, just watching the chaos with sharp, emotionless eyes. There was something about them that was familiar, although their faces didn't spark any memory inside him.

He took half a step toward them, barely aware of what he was doing. The man standing in the middle seemed drawn to the movement, because his gray eyes snapped suddenly to Heath. The intensity of his expression made Heath falter to a stop, halfway across the courtyard. The other two men looked as well, their eyes narrowing as they took in the strange standoff. Their faces were so expressionless, it made Heath shiver. One was weedy, and so pale both in hair and in skin that he looked faded, almost sickly. The other was thickset, the muscles of his arms bulging out of his tunic.

But it was the one in the middle who captured Heath's full attention. Two things were exploding across Heath's mind, so that he hardly knew which to latch on to. The first was that a faint power surrounded these men. It was familiar—tantalizingly so. But Heath knew every power-wielder in Valoria personally. He didn't remember seeing these men in Kyona, but he had really only spent time with his own generation. The silver-haired man now holding Heath in his gaze was at least as old as his parents. Heath frowned as he tried to figure out whether all the men had power, or just the one in the middle. It was difficult to tell. But it was entirely possible that the man was a Kyonan power-wielder whom Heath hadn't met in Kynton.

Except, he had met the man, sort of. The other thing making Heath reel yet again in this day of unpleasant shocks was that he recognized the silver-haired man. When Heath had last seen him, he hadn't been silver-haired, of course. He'd been younger, because Heath had only been five. Heath had seen him in the marketplace, and had recognized his power without knowing that was what he was doing. He'd pointed at the man and declared shrilly that he was different until his mortified mother had him removed from the public place. She'd said she didn't think the man was Kyonan, but she must have been wrong.

Heath had no idea what to make of the man's reappearance. Who was he? Why was a Kyonan power-wielder—a royal, presumably—attending the Winter Solstice Festival incognito? All the time these thoughts raced through his head, Heath stood transfixed, his gaze still locked with the other man's. For a moment, he had the most absurd impression that the man recognized him as well, that he was also reliving that encounter when Heath had been five.

But that was impossible. The man had already been an adult back then, so it wasn't such a stretch for Heath to recognize him after fourteen years. Heath, on the other hand, had changed dramatically in that time.

Heath?

The voice, ringing in Heath's own thoughts, reminded him that his connection to Reka was still open.

What do you wish to speak to me about?

The disastrous events of the ceremony rushed back, and Heath hesitated. He did want to speak with Reka, but he also wanted to know who the power-wielder was. While he vacillated, the silver-haired man turned, giving a barely-perceptible flick of his head. His two companions followed him swiftly, and the three were soon lost in the crowd.

"Rekavidur," Heath said grimly, closing his eyes so as to better lean into his other sight. "What did you do?"

You will need to be more specific, Reka said calmly.

"Why did you tell the other dragons about my cousins

meeting in secret?" Heath said impatiently. "Now they're offended, and I'm going to be in all kinds of trouble!"

"Heath? Who are you talking to?" Percival's bemused voice was right in Heath's ear, and Heath jumped, his eyes flying open. "I guess you did report us after all, huh?"

But Percival didn't sound annoyed. On the contrary, he looked nothing short of gleeful.

"*I* didn't report anything," said Heath irritably. "Reka did that, and I'm not thanking him for it."

"Well I am," grinned Percival. "It's nice to know your pet dragon is good for something."

A gravelly growl in Heath's mind made him realize that Reka was still listening. Heath winced. He knew how the dragon would feel about being called Heath's pet.

Your brother is becoming bothersome, Reka said, his growl still audible through their connection. *I think I ought to begin keeping an eye on him as well as you. I will need to hone my craft. I am not invested in him at present.*

Heath barely held in a groan. Nothing good could come from Reka following Percival's actions from afar. They already had enough offended dragons on their hands.

"We can talk later," Heath muttered, the words directed at Reka.

"Uh, all right," said Percival. He had clearly assumed Heath was speaking to him, and he sounded bemused.

"I'm afraid you will have to talk later," interjected a crisp voice.

Heath turned, wincing once again at the sight of the crown prince.

"Because right now," Prince Lachlan continued coldly, "you and *I* need to talk, My Lord."

CHAPTER TWENTY-NINE

Merletta

"So, how does it feel to be a fourth year?"

Sage tried to roll her eyes at Merletta's question, but she didn't quite manage to hide her grin. "Much the same as being a third year."

"I don't believe you," said Merletta flatly, and Sage grinned again.

"All right, it's pretty great. Even if I fail next year, I can still be an educator." She shot Andre a look. "No offense, but I didn't really want to become a guard."

Andre chuckled as he scooped cod into his mouth. "No offense taken. You lack the killer instinct for a guard, anyway."

Merletta and Sage exchanged amused looks. It wasn't that he was wrong, of course. But it was entertaining to hear Andre, whose heart was as soft as a sea sponge, talking about "killer instinct".

"Morning."

At the familiar voice, Merletta shifted along, making room for Emil. He sank into a seat between her and Sage, helping himself to some of the food laid out for the trainees. He nodded to each of them, but made no comment on Sage's return for her first day of fourth year classes. It wasn't like him to forget, so Merletta could only assume he'd already spoken to her, sometime between Sage's arrival the afternoon before, and when Merletta and Sage went to bed.

Interesting. Sage hadn't mentioned speaking with him yesterday.

Merletta's eyes rested thoughtfully on Emil's profile. She remembered telling him frankly that she wasn't sure she could trust him, when she'd woken in the infirmary after her hallucinations. That felt like a lifetime ago. She tried to recall when he'd started sitting at the trainees' table to eat, instead of with the other record holders. It was difficult to pinpoint, because the change had been gradual. The process had begun after their visit to August's wife during the Founders' Day celebrations. But back then, he used to just drift over to say hello after he'd eaten, hovering behind their seats while he chatted with them. Occasionally he'd join for another squid tentacle or two.

Now he was there every meal. And the four of them had spent the last few rest days together as well, leaving the Center to spend pleasant afternoons wandering through the markets of Skulssted with Sage while she was still on break. In fact, Emil was now such a fixture that Andre had stopped being starstruck. He gave the older merman a natural smile as he moved along to accommodate Merletta's shift in position.

Merletta saw Oliver send a suspicious look at the four of them, but Emil met his eyes so unflinchingly that the trainee turned away without comment.

"Strange that there's no one in third year now," mused Andre.

"There will be soon enough," said Sage, as she nudged Merletta.

Merletta shook her head. "I've just eaten, Sage. Don't talk about my test—you'll make me feel sick."

"We've all seen more than enough of that," muttered Lorraine, and Oliver gave a nasty grunt of laughter.

Again, Emil just looked at them. He said nothing, but his expression made them both subside. Something swelled inside Merletta as she watched Emil return calmly to his food. Having him on her side was worth more than pearls, and not just because he had the influence and access of a record holder. She'd had Tish at the charity home, and in her first year at the Center, she'd had Sage. And, in her stolen other life on Vazula, she had Heath. But she'd never had a group of friends like this before, a team who had each other's backs.

She sometimes felt a twinge of unease at the inclusion of Andre—so young and enthusiastic—in their group. He'd wanted to be on good terms with them since he'd started in the program, but she still wasn't sure he understood the cost at which the friendship had come. She'd tried, haltingly, to say something to that effect after their visit to August's wife. She'd almost wondered whether he'd take the offered out eagerly, perhaps even be angry with her for throwing him into something so dangerous. But he'd surprised her with his fierceness in declaring that he wanted the truth as much as she did. August, he reminded her, had been a friend of his family's.

She knew she should let him make his own decisions, but she still worried sometimes. Not that there was anything she could do about it. To anyone who might be paying the kind of close attention Merletta was worried about, Andre's presence on their excursion to pay respects to the widow had already marked him as part of their group.

Her thoughts were cut off as the two Hemssted trainees rose into the water. The dining hall was beginning to empty.

"We'd better get to class," Sage said.

As always, Merletta half expected Emil to drift along to class with them, like he had the year before. But of course he didn't, instead nodding his usual calm goodbye and floating across the room toward the far exit, where the other record holders were disappearing.

Merletta entered Ibsen's class without enthusiasm. She remembered dully a time when she'd thought it would be exciting to learn the history of the triple kingdoms as a trainee at the Center. She had an unpleasant feeling that the true history of the triple kingdoms probably would be exciting, and for all the wrong reasons. But as she was increasingly confident that what she was being taught was a heavily censored version, it was hard to take Ibsen's classes too seriously.

She could be training for her guard test right now. She knew from what Felix had told her the week before that Freja's patrol was once again going beyond the barrier today, to oversee a group of hunters. Now that would have been interesting!

"Rise."

Ibsen's curt voice pulled Merletta from her thoughts, and she realized the other trainees were all pushing off their seats, up into the water. She copied them, wondering what they were doing. She hadn't been listening to a word.

"All year levels will participate in this task," Ibsen said, his eyes narrowing slightly as they rested on Merletta. She was fairly sure he knew she hadn't been listening. "You are to work in groups—according to your city of origin. Each group will give its presentation after lunch. You may access the public records in order to form your arguments."

Merletta wanted to roll her eyes. It was childish, really. She'd been in the program for almost two years. Was Ibsen really still looking for opportunities to embarrass her for being from Tilssted?

There was very little movement in response to the instructor's words, given that everyone already sat according to city.

Oliver and Lorraine bent their heads together as they sank back into their seats, and Andre turned to Sage.

"You can join us, Merletta," Sage invited.

Merletta saw Ibsen open his mouth to protest, but she forestalled him. "Thanks, but no thanks," she said cheerfully to Sage. She gestured flippantly down her body. "This is the Tilssted team."

Of course, it would help if she knew what she was supposed to be doing, but she wasn't about to let Ibsen think he was getting to her. Fortunately, the trainees all drifted out of the room to take advantage of the public records. As soon as Ibsen was out of sight, Merletta put on a burst of speed and caught up to Sage and Andre.

"So what are we doing?"

Andre grinned, and Sage rolled her eyes. But before either could answer, a young mermaid wearing the bracelet of a Center messenger swam up to them.

"You're Trainee Merletta, right?" she asked, and Merletta nodded. "There's someone waiting to see you in the receiving hall."

Merletta could feel her own wariness reflected in the suddenly tense posture of her companions. Who would be asking to see her alone, away from her friends?

"Who is it?" she asked cautiously.

"She said her name is Letitia," the mermaid answered.

Merletta's stiffness fell away at once. Tish was there? In the receiving hall to the Center of Culture?

"I'll come now," she said.

With a quick wave, she left the others and swam rapidly after the messenger. They had almost crossed the drop off before her companion spoke.

"I'm from Tilssted, you know."

"You are?" Merletta looked at her in amazement, and the other mermaid smiled.

"My family lives quite close to the border with Skulssted. We're better off than most in Tilssted. Still, my parents were really proud when I got this messenger job. We didn't know if they'd give it to someone from Tilssted." She hesitated, and her pale face flushed with color. "I'm not proud to admit it, but when I first started working here, I used to hide the fact that I came from Tilssted. I didn't tell anyone if I could help it. I was ashamed."

Merletta was silent, wondering why the other mermaid was telling her this.

"Not anymore, though," the messenger said, her back straightening. "I tell everyone. I'm proud to be from Tilssted."

Merletta stared at her. "What changed?"

The messenger gave an incredulous laugh. "Surely you know the answer to that! You're what changed. Everyone was impressed that someone from Tilssted could get a job as a *messenger* in the Center. But you got into the program! You're one of them, and you're proving from the inside that our problem has always been opportunity, not capability."

"I...don't know what to say," Merletta said, a ripple that was half pride, half discomfort passing over her. "Thank you, I suppose."

The other mermaid laughed again. "Actually, thank *you* is what I'm trying to say."

They had reached the edge of the drop off, and there was no time for more. The messenger peeled away once they entered the building, and Merletta swam into the lobby alone. Tish was floating there, her arms wrapped around her frame in obvious discomfort.

"Tish!" Merletta cried, and Tish brightened.

She swam forward to meet her friend, but Merletta thought Tish returned her embrace only half-heartedly.

"What's going on?" Merletta asked, when Tish didn't speak. "Are you all right?"

"Yes, I'm fine," said Tish. "I'm sorry to interrupt you here. You're probably supposed to be in class."

"Don't apologize," said Merletta firmly. "I'm always glad to see you."

Tish's face flushed, and Merletta realized too late that her friend may have misunderstood her words as a reproach for the last time they'd met.

"Can...can we talk for a minute?" Tish glanced toward the middle-aged mermaid sitting behind a desk nearby.

"Of course," said Merletta. She glanced around. "How about you come through into the drop off?"

"Trainees can only invite friends and family into the Center with prior permission," the older mermaid interjected, her voice bored.

Merletta scowled at her, then turned back to Tish. "Oh all right, let's go out into Skulssted. There's a public coral garden not far away."

When the two mermaids were seated in as private a corner of the garden as Merletta could find, she turned expectantly to Tish.

"What's really happening, Tish? Has someone hurt you? Threatened you?"

Tish stared at her. "Why..." She swallowed. "Why would you ask that?"

"Tish, what aren't you telling me?" Merletta asked in an ominous voice.

Her friend sighed. "Nothing terrible has happened, Mer. I came to apologize, first and foremost." Her eyes were on her hands, twisting in her lap. "You haven't been back to visit me since that day when I was working with the others, and..." She trailed off.

Merletta waited, but it seemed Tish had nothing more to say. "To tell the truth, I wasn't entirely sure I was welcome," she said. "But I don't bear you any ill will, Tish. I just want to understand."

Tish looked miserable, and she still wouldn't meet Merletta's eye. "I'm sorry," she said. "It was cowardly of me not to tell everyone we were friends, or to invite you to join us." She looked up at last. "But you know me, Mer. I've always been better than you at keeping my head down. It's how I survive. And I wasn't sure I wanted people to know I grew up with the famous Tilssted trainee. I was worried that they would want me to introduce them, or to use our friendship to ask you to do things for us, things I know you wouldn't have the influence to achieve." Her face darkened. "And I was absolutely right."

Merletta felt guilt swirl in her own stomach. "I'm sorry, Tish," she said gently. "I didn't even think of that, but I should have. I guess I'm protected from unreasonable expectations, living here in the Center. It didn't occur to me that people might want things from you if they knew of our friendship." She grimaced at her friend. "I'm still not sure how to respond to being known by strangers. It's unnerving, if I'm honest."

"I can imagine," said Tish emphatically. "I'm sure I'd hate it." She looked up, her expression strangely shy considering they'd been friends all their lives. "I am proud of you, though. I hope you know that. I'm proud of all you've achieved. I just don't think I'm brave enough to be in the thick of it, like you are. To tell the truth, I felt that way even before...well, from the beginning."

"Before what?" Merletta cut in sharply. "You could never keep things from me, Tish, so don't even try. What's happened?"

Tish squirmed, her fins curling underneath her in a way

Merletta knew meant she was deeply uncomfortable. "It's nothing."

"It's not nothing," contradicted Merletta curtly. "Tell me, Tish."

Tish pushed out a long stream of water. "I had a visit, a couple weeks before your birthday. I guess you were on your break, after your first year test. Two Center guards came and asked me about you. They didn't exactly make threats, but…I don't know, Merletta. Something was so off about them. I felt afraid from the moment they arrived."

Cold dread was clutching at Merletta's insides. She'd been worried about something like this, which was why she hadn't told Tish all she knew. And yet her gentle friend had been in danger anyway.

"What did they say? Did they hurt you?"

"Of course not," said Tish quickly. "I told you, they didn't even make threats. They asked about you, and whether you were staying with me during your break."

Merletta swallowed, not daring to ask Tish what her reply had been.

"I wasn't sure what to say," said Tish pleadingly. "Obviously I knew you hadn't been staying with me, but I wasn't sure you wanted them to know that. So I gave a kind of non-answer. I said that I wasn't able to accommodate guests in my actual building, but there was accommodation nearby."

"That was very clever," said Merletta, impressed. "Did they swallow it, do you think?"

"I don't know," admitted Tish. She was hugging herself again. "They were impossible to read. They asked me a few more questions about you, then they left."

Merletta frowned, thinking it over. "And you said they were Center guards?"

Tish nodded, then paused. "Well, I assumed they were Center guards. They didn't actually say."

"What did they look like?"

Tish frowned in thought. "I don't know, Mer, it was months ago now. One of them was tall and thin, the other very muscled. They seemed a little mismatched to me somehow."

Merletta nodded, locking the words away and resolving to search the guards during her next training day. She wasn't hopeful. The description didn't give her much to work with.

"I'm sorry I put you in that position, Tish," she said earnestly. "I never wanted to make you feel unsafe."

"I know you didn't," said Tish. "And I'm sorry I haven't been more loyal. But the truth is," she twisted her hands again, "I think I'm better out of it, whatever it is you're caught up in. I mean, look at us." She gestured between them, her eyes passing over Merletta's ever-present spear and resting on the arm that held it. "We don't belong in the same world anymore."

Following her friend's gaze, Merletta realized how different she must look to Tish from the friend of her childhood. And it wasn't just the weapon, or the armband that marked her as a trainee. Her very muscles showed the strength that she'd gained through relentless training. And Tish was the same pale, timid mermaid Merletta had grown up with.

Merletta's heart sank. She wasn't sure what was worse, the realization that Tish was probably right, or the flavor of goodbye to her friend's words.

"I understand," she said, as evenly as she could.

"I still want to see you," Tish said quickly, her eyes searching Merletta's face with their familiar kindness. "You're my oldest friend, Mer. You always will be."

Merletta nodded, her throat too thick to form words.

"I should go," Tish said, after an awkward moment. "I only have a half day off today, and I need to get back to Tilssted."

Merletta did her best to smile as she embraced her friend, and waved goodbye. But as soon as Tish was out of sight, she sank back onto her bench, feeling small and forlorn. It was as though her last link to her old life had just been severed, leaving her drifting aimlessly. Ibsen's task was forgotten as she faced the unpleasant reality. She'd started down a path that endangered not only herself, but everyone close to her. And she could no more turn back from it than Tish could become a record holder.

CHAPTER THIRTY

"I'm telling you as a courtesy, Lord Heath." Prince Lachlan's voice was even, but his face was implacable. "I wasn't asking your opinion."

"I thought the whole point of our partnership was to share such opinions," Heath argued, frustration rising in him. "I thought you wanted to find a solution to the tension that—"

"This is a solution," said the prince tonelessly.

"With respect, Your Highness," snapped Heath, "it's not a good one."

Prince Lachlan raised an eyebrow. "Do I take it, then, that you do *not* wish to tell the power-wielders yourself?"

"Of course I don't!" Heath protested. "They'll think it was my idea, or that I agree with it, at the very least."

"Duty," said the prince coldly, "often requires us to undertake tasks which are unpleasant. It is your role to facilitate communication between the crown and the power-wielders. Just as it is supposed to be your role to communicate to me any threats magic may pose to the well-being of our kingdom."

"The gathering I saw didn't pose any threat to anyone,"

insisted Heath. "Honestly, the dragons' claim blew the whole thing completely out of proportion. The restrictions you propose would create a much bigger danger. Firstly, how *can* you even impose a rule against power-wielders gathering? We're all family—of course we'll want to spend time together. There's nothing sinister in that. And if you go and tell the power-wielders that they're not allowed to use their magic without direct supervision, you'll risk creating exactly the kind of mutiny you're trying to avoid. Surely you can see that it's not wise to—"

"It's not a proposal," Prince Lachlan interrupted. "The decision has been made. If you decline to inform the power-wielders of the new restrictions, then the Chief Counselor will do so formally."

Heath drew a long breath, trying to calm his tone. He could imagine how well it would be received when the king sent the pompous Lord Niel to deliver the news.

"Your Highness," Heath tried again. "You're not unreasonable. And you're not prone to overreaction. Surely together we can find a better solution than this."

The prince turned to look out his window, so that his back was to Heath. "There's no point saying any more, Lord Heath," he said blandly. "It's out of your hands." There was a pause, then he added in little more than a whisper, "It's out of my hands, too."

Heath was silent as he processed this. He couldn't be sure that the prince agreed with him, but even if that were the case, Prince Lachlan wouldn't—couldn't—say so. And he evidently felt he couldn't do anything to change his father's mind.

"King Matlock is decided, then?" Heath asked at last.

The prince spun back around to face him, irritation coloring his face. "What did you expect, Lord Heath? The decision hasn't been made rashly. You may have forgotten, but two months ago, our king was insulted and humiliated by the dragons, in front of his own people. It is not magic that rules in this kingdom. It is the crown. His Majesty deserves the absolute loyalty of every one of his subjects, including those with power. He's not a tyrant. He doesn't demand anything outrageous. They don't have to agree with every opinion he expresses. But carrying tales to the dragons—"

"No one carried tales," Heath interjected quickly. "It was the purest chance that Reka happened to find out about that gathering."

"There is nothing to be gained by going over the events in question yet again," said Prince Lachlan, with forced patience. "We must try to find the best path going forward."

"I wish I could see it," said Heath, unable to keep the bitterness out of his voice. "But I'm struggling to find any path from here that brings us all together."

With a stiff bow, he let himself out of the prince's study and strode from the castle. The snow had melted, but the air was still bitingly cold. Heath's steps were agitated as he made his way toward home. He was fuming so much, he could hardly see where he was walking. As Heath dwelt on the disastrous conversation, the crown prince's face flashed before his eyes, no longer expressionless like he'd been in his study, but looking weary, defeated, too old for his twenty years.

All at once Heath's own shoulders slumped with the same sense of defeat. He had failed utterly in his task. The tensions between the power-wielders and the rest of the court were higher now than they had been when Heath had taken on the role of liaison, nearly a year ago. He hadn't just failed to make it better, he'd made it much worse, by unintentionally passing news of the conflict to the dragons, through Reka.

When he reached his family's residence, his anger had

settled, but he was no less distressed. The sight of Percival, his sword over his shoulder as he strode, whistling, across the courtyard, did nothing to improve his mood.

"There you are, Heath," said Percival cheerfully. He'd been maddeningly friendly since the Winter Solstice Festival, utterly undeterred by Heath's continued coldness. Apparently Heath's unplanned and unwilling efforts for the power-wielders' cause had restored him to Percival's good graces. "I heard you got called to the castle. Don't tell me they're still sulking over the dragons telling them off during the lighting of the flame."

"No," snapped Heath. "They're done sulking. They're ready to start acting."

Percival stilled, a slight frown marring his features. "What does that mean?"

"It means," said Heath, completely forgetting his insistence that he had no desire to tell his family the news, "that as of tomorrow, there will be a ban on more than three power-wielders gathering privately together."

"What?" Percival demanded. "You can't be serious. That would mean we couldn't even spend an afternoon with Brody and Bianca!"

"I'm perfectly serious," said Heath, still speaking in the same biting voice. "And there's more. Power-wielders are only to use their magic under supervision by the crown, or certain approved members of the court."

"WHAT?!" Percival's shout was loud enough to make a passing servant jump. "No. That can't be allowed to happen."

Heath gave a mirthless laugh. "It has happened."

"Well, you have to stop it," said Percival, angrily. "You're the liaison, you're supposed to speak up to the crown on our behalf. You'll just have to go to the prince, and—"

"Where do you think I've just been?" demanded Heath, his own voice raised. "So *now* you want to work with the crown?

Now you want me to use my influence to resolve things diplomatically?"

"Is there a reason my sons are brawling in public?" The Duke of Bexley's calm voice made both brothers jump guiltily, although their argument was hardly a brawl, and their own courtyard couldn't really be called public. Clearly their father had been drawn by the sound of their shouts.

"Father, surely you won't just let this happen?" Percival demanded, turning to the duke.

"Let what happen?" their father asked, still speaking calmly.

Forcing his own voice into more even tones, Heath explained the king's decision.

"It's outrageous," blustered Percival.

But Heath's anger had melted away again in the face of the alarm he read in his father's eyes. Only the sense of weary defeat remained.

"Just face it, Percival," he said bitterly. "We've made a mess of the whole thing. You messed up when you started secret gatherings, I messed up by calling Reka to come see it, Reka messed up by passing it on to the rest of the dragons. We've made everything ten times worse than it already was."

"*We* messed up?" Percival repeated, outraged. "How can you say that, Heath? How can you *possibly* be taking their side now, after this? Can't you see now that they're the problem, not us? They're so afraid of our power, they'd rather watch the kingdom dwindle and weaken compared to Kyona than embrace what we have!"

"Percival," said the duke, an edge of warning to his steady voice.

But Percival seemed to have worked himself into too much of a state to heed his father's words. "It's an abuse of power by the crown!" he raged.

"Hold your tongue," the duke said, his voice as near a snap

as Heath had ever heard it. Heath was acutely aware of the servants watching them, mouths open, all around the courtyard. Clearly their argument had drawn more attention than just their father's.

For a moment the duke just stood there, his eyes passing calculatingly between his sons, Heath sagging in defeat, Percival's eyes blazing with suppressed fury. Then he seemed to reach a decision.

"We're going home," he said curtly. "Back to Bexley Manor. The snow has melted now, it will be an easy journey. We all need a break."

"But—" Heath and Percival began in unison. Their father cut them off with a gesture.

"We'll leave first thing tomorrow."

His tone made it clear there was no room for argument, and without another word he strode back into the house.

Heath threw a rock off the edge of the cliff, past his dangling legs. It crashed off the cliff face on the way down, and eventually splashed into the water far below.

He wasn't sure what his father had been hoping to achieve by forcing the family back to Bexley Manor, but from Heath's perspective, the last two weeks had been no better than those which came before. It was usually multiple times a day that he fled to his old haunt by the sea, just to escape the dour atmosphere in the manor. He hadn't even seen his brother that day, and that was fine with him.

Percival was still furious over the restrictions, and his approval of Heath had evaporated the moment Heath dared to place the tiniest bit of blame for the fiasco on Percival's own shoulders. A visit from Brody and Bianca—the legality of which was still uncertain—had done nothing to lighten the mood. They were angry too, and Heath couldn't blame them. They'd been more reasonable than Percival, enough to acknowledge that their secret gatherings had been unwise. But they argued that the response was disproportionate. Heath made no attempt to disagree. It was undeniably true.

He just couldn't understand it. King Matlock, as Prince Lachlan had said, wasn't a tyrant. He wasn't usually unreasonable in his demands. It was understandable that he'd been chagrined at the dragons' words during the festival. But why had he allowed himself to be goaded into abandoning all the careful diplomacy he'd invested into the debate over magic? Who was in his ear so successfully?

"Heath?"

Heath turned quickly. He hadn't even heard his father approach. Leaning back, he made to rise, but the duke held up a hand to stop him.

"Don't jump up, for goodness' sake. You'll overbalance."

To Heath's surprise, his father lowered himself alongside Heath, so that his own legs dangled into open space.

"It's always terrified your mother that you come out here, and sit so close to the edge. I always told her not to worry about you, that you were responsible enough to be trusted on the cliffs." He gave his younger son a genuine smile. "So thank you for never falling off and getting yourself killed, or I would have been made to look quite a fool."

Heath chuckled. "My pleasure."

The duke looked out to sea, and for a minute there was silence.

"I thought you had gotten yourself killed, you know. Last summer."

Heath squirmed uncomfortably. The last thing he needed right now was to be interrogated about his secrets. They'd done this dance so many times, back when Reka had first brought him home. He had thought—had hoped—that they were past it.

"I'm sorry, Heath," said the duke heavily.

Shocked, Heath swiveled so violently to face his father that he actually wobbled on the rocks. Those words were the last he'd expected.

"What could you possibly have to be sorry for, Father?" he protested.

"I'm your father," the duke said simply. "And I haven't protected you as I should have."

"Father, my injuries weren't your fault," said Heath, still stunned. "You couldn't have prevented—"

"I'm not talking about your injuries," said his father calmly. "I'm talking about your role as King Matlock's liaison. I'm talking about your overdeveloped sense of responsibility." He looked over at Heath's confused face and let out a long sigh. "You know that this mess isn't your fault, don't you, Heath?"

Heath looked away, shrugging uncomfortably. "I know I'm not the only one at fault," he said. His thoughts were on Percival's mulish attitude, and there was a touch of bitterness to his words. "But I haven't helped." He looked up at his father. "I keep thinking it over, trying to figure out how I could have prevented things getting to this pass."

"Maybe you couldn't have prevented it," said the duke. "Or any of the rest of us. Maybe this was inevitable, sooner or later."

"I wanted to believe we could work together," said Heath.

"Of course we can work together," said his father firmly. "The story isn't over yet. But maybe things needed to reach a crisis before we'd all take each other seriously."

"Maybe," said Heath, without conviction. "I wish I'd never

called Reka that day, though. If he hadn't seen Percival and the others practicing their magic..." He trailed off with a sigh.

"Then things would have reached a head another way, most likely." The duke pushed himself carefully to his feet, clapping his son on the shoulder as he went. "Don't fall off the edge, Heath."

Heath gave a half-hearted smile as his father retreated back to the manor. He felt even worse than before, knowing his father was blaming himself for Heath's troubles. He still didn't really understand what his father had meant about not protecting him.

He was staring out to sea, thinking of nothing in particular, when a familiar rushing sound made him look up in surprise. For a moment, a dark shape blotted out the sun, then Reka landed lightly beside him.

"Greetings, Heath," said the dragon placidly. "Did you call me?"

Heath blinked at him in confusion. "No." He thought for a moment. "I was talking about you, though. To my father."

"Ah, I see," said the dragon, nodding wisely. "That would be it."

Heath frowned shrewdly at his friend. Reka had never responded to a reference like that before.

"You were just bored, weren't you?" he accused.

"Dragons do not get bored," said Reka loftily.

Heath rolled his eyes, his lips twitching. "No need to use your superior dragon voice, Reka. I don't blame you for looking for an excuse to get out of your home. In fact, it makes two of us."

"Is that so?" Reka asked brightly. With an unnerving abruptness, he launched himself off the cliff face. He wheeled down and out in a large semicircle, then ended on Heath's other side, where he reached out his taloned front feet and perched precariously at an angle, right on the edge of the rock.

"Want to explore?"

Heath couldn't help laughing. Reka was like a frisky puppy. "What's got you in a good mood?" he asked.

Reka did the strange rippling shrug favored by dragons. "I like having you back at the coast. The air is too heavy in that city of yours. There's so much tension, it's uncomfortable to focus my farsight on you when you're there."

"How unpleasant that must be for you," said Heath dryly.

"It is," Reka acknowledged, with a regal nod of his vast head. "So where do you want to go?"

"Anywhere other than here," said Heath, a bit petulantly. But even as he said the words, he knew they weren't true. He knew exactly where he wanted to go. Or rather, whom he wanted to see. But it was unlikely that Merletta would be on the island. He hadn't been able to see her from afar in weeks, and even then, she'd shown no sign of going to Vazula.

But as her name flashed through his mind, he saw her, with perfect clarity. She was above water, her whole form visible to him. She was exploring the island's ruins, looking for what, he had no idea.

"Let's go to Vazula," he said, forgetting he was on the edge of a cliff, and jumping to his feet a little too quickly for safety.

Reka let out a long sigh that smelled faintly of smoke. "We used to go other places as well, you know. Back before you met the mermaid."

"Come on, Reka," Heath pleaded. "I haven't seen her in an age."

That made the dragon give a gravelly chuckle, his expression once again superior. "An age? How inaccurately you humans speak of time."

"Stop pretending that you're ancient," said Heath impatiently. "You're only a few decades older than me. Now, are we going or not?"

Reka's sigh actually caused smoke to swirl around them this time. "Very well."

With the usual lack of warning, he seized Heath's shoulders and launched into the air.

CHAPTER THIRTY-ONE

Merletta

Merletta slapped her palm down onto the table, trapping the record she was studying beneath it. What was she doing? It was too early in the morning for study. And she wasn't sitting her educator test in a week. She was taking her guard test. If she was going to spend her rest day working, it should be in the training yard.

She rose into the water.

"I'm sorry, Andre," she said to the young merman bent low over a record at the desk beside her. "I know I said I'd study with you, but I just can't think clearly this early in the morning."

Andre just grunted. His test wasn't until three weeks after hers, but he was already in full fever mode.

Abandoning the public records room, Merletta swam toward the training yard. Sage had actually invited her to spend the rest day with her family in Skulssted. Merletta still wasn't sure she'd made the right decision in turning her down. She'd been too embarrassed to admit it, but the thought of meeting Sage's parents, of being in her actual home, terrified Merletta. And she'd been telling the truth when she told Sage she needed to prepare for her test.

Reaching the training yard, she glanced around. As it was rest day, there was no formal training going on, but several pairs of guards sparred with each other on the far side of the square. She swam between two stone pillars, into a large supply room that opened off the training square. She would do some target practice with the slings. There was no saying what might come up in her test.

She had ducked down, rummaging through a supply chest, when she heard a familiar voice drifting in from the doorway to the main yard. Before she could straighten, ready to greet Freja, she caught her own name, and froze, still half-buried in the chest.

"I'll make sure we do something this week that will interest Merletta. It's our last chance before her test, and I'm not sure I've done a good job of following my orders."

"Of course you have." Agner's voice was as jovial as ever. "She likes you, I can tell."

Merletta could barely draw breath. What orders were they talking about? It was Freja's last chance to do what?

"I'm still a little confused, sir," Freja went on. "Where exactly do these orders regarding Merletta come from?"

"Not for us to worry about the chain of command," said Agner, still cheerful. "Guards follow orders, that's all we need to worry about."

Merletta didn't catch Freja's murmured reply. The two guards must be drifting away from the doorway. For a long moment, Merletta stayed frozen, still bent over the supplies. Her heart was racing, and her stomach was churning almost as badly as it had at the memorial. Freja, whom she'd liked so much, had thought so honest, was following orders regarding her? From a mysterious source she didn't know herself?

What were those orders? Merletta thought back over the words she'd overheard. Was she overreacting to place some sinister meaning on the conversation? Had it actually been innocent? It was the uncertainty that was so wearing, so destructive to her peace. Whom could she trust? Who was truly on her side?

She'd lost all interest in training in the yard. Without conscious thought, she found herself swimming out of the building. But she wasn't going to Skulssted to visit Sage. She wasn't going to Tilssted, where Tish no longer wanted to receive her. She was going further than that. Back to the only place she felt truly safe.

Merletta sighed, hugging her knees to her chest as she wriggled her toes into the wet sand. What had she expected? That Heath would once again appear, as if by magic, on the one day she made it to Vazula?

Yes, she acknowledged to herself. That was exactly what she'd hoped. And although she knew it was foolish, she couldn't help feeling disappointed. She pulled her braid forward over her shoulder and ran her fingers through the dark, wet strands, disentangling them. Shaking her head out, she let her hair flow free, like it had before she became a conforming trainee. It felt good.

In spite of the hours that had passed, the overheard conversation between Agner and Freja was still weighing heavily on her mind. So was the uncomfortable visit from Tish. So was her looming test, and the danger to Andre, and the grief of August's widow, for which she still felt responsible.

She let out a long sigh, closing her eyes and tilting her head toward the sky, so that heavy raindrops splattered on her face. It would have been such a relief to tell Heath all of this, to know he was on her side without question. She unlocked her arms, stretching her legs out straight in the sand and relishing the moisture between her fingers. She knew she should return to the triple kingdoms, stop taking risks, and continue training for her test. But she lingered, not quite ready to let go of her sanctuary.

Then, suddenly, she heard it. The familiar rushing sound. Before her mind had even grasped it, her heart had leaped into her throat, from force of habit. She jumped to her feet, staring up at the shape descending from the sky, barely daring to believe it. So late in the day, she'd thought there was no chance of him coming. Did this mean he'd seen her from afar, with that incredible magic of his? The thought made her heart race even faster. He was thinking of her, then, even though it had been months since they'd seen each other.

Within moments, Rekavidur alighted on the sand, releasing his grip on his human cargo. Heath stepped forward, his familiar smile lighting his face at sight of Merletta.

"You are here!" he said delightedly. "I thought I saw you, and I was right."

"Looks like it," said Merletta cheerfully, her spirits already lighter than they had been in weeks. She looked up at Rekavidur, looming up behind Heath. The rain was pattering against his scales with an almost musical sound.

The dragon inclined his head to her in a half-hearted greeting, then took to the sky, off to do whatever he did when on the island. She had the uncomfortable feeling that his main motivation was to get further away from her, but she didn't waste much time on the thought. Not when Heath was here at last.

"You're late," she scolded. "It's well into the afternoon."

Heath grinned. "My apologies." After the barest hint of hesitation, he grabbed her hand, pulling her toward the jungle. "Come on, let's get out of the rain."

"Why?" Merletta asked, confused, although she allowed him to tug her along without resistance.

Heath just laughed. "You might not mind getting wet, but most humans try to avoid it."

"Really?" Merletta was fascinated. "But why? I thought getting wet didn't hurt humans."

"It doesn't hurt," said Heath. "But it's not exactly pleasant, either."

"Humans seem very fragile," Merletta observed.

Heath didn't reply for a moment, and his grip on her hand tightened. "Mine certainly seem to be," he muttered.

"What do you mean?" asked Merletta. "What's wrong?"

"Never mind that," said Heath lightly. "I want to know what's happening with you."

They'd reached the jungle by now, and Merletta sank onto a fallen log that was moderately protected from the rain by the foliage above.

"There's a lot happening," she said frankly. "My test is in a week. Sage passed hers. And so did Lorraine, although that's nothing to get excited about. At least she's still away on break, so that's something."

"Are you nervous about your test?" Heath asked. He had let go of her hand when they sat, and Merletta wondered why. She wished she dared to take hold of it again, but she didn't, for reasons she couldn't fully articulate.

"Of course I am!" she said. "If I fail, it will be bad enough. But apparently trainees have actually died during the second year test."

"What?" Heath demanded, all traces of his smile disappearing. "People have died?"

Merletta shrugged. "Remembering what the practice test was like, it's not so hard to believe."

"I don't like that at all," said Heath, predictably. "Surely the instructors have a responsibility to protect you."

Merletta snorted, throwing him a meaningful look.

"Oh yeah," sighed Heath. "I forgot for a moment." His frown grew. "It seems like too good an opportunity, Merletta. If someone wants to get rid of you forever, the test is the perfect time to make it seem like an accident. Especially if trainees really have died in the past."

Merletta let out a sigh of her own. "The thought has occurred to me," she admitted. "And I've taken steps to make sure that if I do die, the things I've found out won't be completely lost."

She told him about her visit to the widow, and the group of sorts that had formed between her, Sage, Emil, and Andre.

"I know you told me to keep my head down," she said, half-apologetically. "But you were also the one who told me to be visible. And she had a right to know."

Heath shook his head. "I wasn't going to scold you, Merletta. You shouldn't take my advice, anyway. It turns out I make things worse, not better."

"Heath, what's going on?" Merletta demanded, alarmed by the uncharacteristic bitterness in his voice.

"Oh, everything's falling apart," he said simply. "The king has banned us from using our magic without supervision, and everyone's angry with me. The court, the power-wielders. My brother."

"Your brother's an idiot," said Merletta, earning a half-hearted smile. "Why is everyone angry with you? Don't try to tell me you're to blame, because I won't believe a word."

Heath smiled again. "I won't try, then." He hurried on before she could speak. "But we were talking about your test. I don't like to hear that you've made plans in case you don't survive it. Where's that fighting spirit that intimidates me so much?"

Merletta punched him lightly on the shoulder. "Take that back! I don't intimidate you." She hesitated, feeling suddenly self-conscious. "Do I?"

There was a strange edge to Heath's smile now, and his eyes took on the dreamy quality that she knew well.

"You do, actually," he said, reaching forward to flick an unruly strand of hair behind her shoulder. "But not because of your fighting spirit."

Merletta could find no response. The air was suddenly thick between them, full of something unspoken but tangible. Heath's hand lingered a few seconds longer than necessary over the bare skin of Merletta's shoulder, then fell back to his side.

"You could still change your mind, you know," he said, his voice hardly above a whisper. "You could come back with me. You don't have to face this test, risk your life to win a place among people who are trying to kill you."

Merletta shook her head, still held in thrall by the intensity of the moment. "Trying to find a place in your world would be an even more terrifying test, I think," she murmured.

"But you wouldn't be alone." Heath's voice was suddenly intense, and before she knew what he was doing, he'd slid along the log so that their legs were touching, and clutched her hand in his again. "You'd have me to help you, to keep you safe."

Abruptly, he let go, which was probably a good thing, as Merletta seemed to have forgotten to breathe while he was touching her. Heath pushed himself to his feet, turning his back on her.

"What am I talking about?" he said bitterly, and she had to strain to hear his words. "I can't protect you. I can't even keep my own family from turning on each other."

Merletta stood, moving silently until she was right behind him. "Heath," she said softly, placing a hand on his back. His muscles twitched beneath her touch, and he stiffened, but he didn't turn. "You're not responsible for their choices. And you can't be responsible for mine. Whatever comes of them."

He turned, again moving so quickly that Merletta was startled. Her hand, whipped from his back, hovered strangely in the air for a moment before Heath seized it, trapping it against his chest instead. His other hand was somehow on her neck, although she didn't remember him putting it there.

"You say that like you think you're going to die," he said, his voice rougher than she'd ever heard it. His eyes searched hers for a silent moment, their expression pleading. "Please don't die, Merletta," he whispered.

"Well, I'm obviously going to try not to," she said, in an attempt at lightness that failed dismally.

The intensity in Heath's eyes didn't lessen at all, and Merletta found she didn't want it to. She could sense the tension building inside him, and she suddenly realized she wanted it to reach breaking point. She needed to know what would happen when it did. She needed to know desperately.

She took a step toward him, so that they were almost touching. Heath's whole body stiffened, and his eyes flicked rapidly between hers, searching, asking, although what, she wasn't entirely sure. She shifted even further forward, and his eyes dropped to her lips. She found she wasn't interested in more words.

Apparently, Heath couldn't read her thoughts, because he spoke, his voice a strangled whisper. "I feel like I'm being torn into pieces, Merletta. There's only so long I can be pulled in opposite directions before I break."

"Stop letting yourself be pulled then," she said, her voice soft.

"I don't know how to do that," Heath said helplessly.

"Heath, you're trying to keep everyone else happy. When was the last time you asked yourself what you want?"

Heath didn't immediately answer, but his eyes once again dropped to her lips, and his hand tightened on her neck. Merletta read it in his eyes a moment before he moved. She closed her eyes as he leaned toward her, her heart somehow racing and soaring at the same time. If she was honest, she'd wondered before now whether humans kissed, like merpeople did. Wondered, and hoped. It seemed she had her answer.

But just as she felt Heath's lips brush hers—something in her stomach exploding as they did—a gravelly roar drowned out the rain, causing both of them to jump apart.

"Heath!"

Heath turned to the dragon who had appeared between the trees. Even through her confusion and disappointment, Merletta felt surprise at the anger on Heath's face.

"This is none of your business, Reka!"

"Heath," Rekavidur repeated, disregarding his words. "It's your brother."

"My—what?" Heath sputtered, thrown by the dragon's words. "Percival? What about him?"

"He's in danger," said Rekavidur.

Heath frowned, looking skeptical, although Merletta had no idea why he would doubt the dragon's words. "How do you know?"

"I told you that I would start keeping an eye on him," said Reka, with a touch of impatience. "I have been doing so. He is at present riding for Bryford, and I see a group of armed men moving toward him from the capital. My focus is on Percival. There is no reason for me to see those others, who are still a few hours from him, unless they are connected to his course. I deduce that they mean to attack him."

"What?" Heath paled, and Merletta gripped his arm.

"Go to him, Heath."

"But…" Heath turned back to her, and she could read her own frustration at their interrupted moment in his eyes. But she knew they couldn't recapture it, and he must realize it, too.

"Go," she repeated, actually chivvying him toward the dragon. "Your brother needs you." She stepped back, leaving the space clear for the dragon to take off.

"But your test," said Heath, turning back to her and looking anguished. "You're in danger too, Merletta, and I—"

"And you can't do anything to help me," she said calmly. "You know you can't."

"But I don't know when I'll see you again," Heath persisted. The unspoken words, *or if I'll see you again*, hovered in the air between them.

Merletta didn't respond, unable to deny it. "Just tell me you'll be watching for me on the other side," she said instead, with the hint of a smile. "So you know when to come and meet me, and hear all about it."

Heath held her gaze for one silent, heavy moment. Then he crossed back to her in three swift strides, muttering as he came, "Just in case."

The next thing she knew, he'd swept her into his arms, and his lips were pressed onto hers. She felt herself mold into him, as though they were made for this moment. Without realizing she was doing it, she twined her arms behind his back, as if to keep him there forever.

But a moment later, Heath had pulled away, releasing her and stepping back beside the dragon, who wore an openly disapproving expression. Merletta felt dazed as she raised a hand to her lips, her eyes locking with Heath's across the distance. He looked a little dazed himself. She knew, somehow, that the kiss hadn't been the heart-melting one that Rekavidur had interrupted. But it was still enough to make her new legs feel as wobbly as jellyfish.

"Don't die," Heath said, the words an order.

Merletta gave a shaky laugh, but there was no time to respond. Rekavidur had seized Heath's shoulders, and a moment later, the two companions took to the sky.

CHAPTER THIRTY-TWO

Heath's thoughts were swirling so frantically as Reka carried him across the water that he could hardly get his bearings.

Percival was in danger.

He'd kissed Merletta.

Merletta was half expecting to die in her test.

And he'd kissed her.

He didn't know when—or if—he'd see her again.

She'd kissed him back, though.

But Percival was in trouble.

Heath opened his mouth to shout to Reka, but closed it again. He wasn't sure if he wanted to tell the dragon to turn back, or to get to Valoria faster. Had he really kissed Merletta? Had she really put her arms around him, pulling him closer as her lips moved against his?

Why had he pulled away so quickly? Would a delay of a few minutes really have made a difference to Percival? A cold rush went over him. He hoped not. He remembered his last conversation with his brother, the night before. They'd snapped at each other, and gone to bed without even trying to make it up. If that was the last conversation he ever had with his brother, he'd never forgive himself.

What was Percival doing? He needed to see. At once, without Heath really trying, his unpredictable extra sight flared to life. He could see his brother's face, a hint of defiance mixing with his exhilaration as he pushed his horse hard. Reka was right, Percival was riding for the capital. But Heath had no idea why. And his sight was clearly not as developed as Reka's, because try as he might, he could see no sign of the armed men the dragon had mentioned.

"Can you still see those men?" he shouted above the wind.

"Yes," Reka replied instantly. Clearly he was also keeping an eye on the situation. "They are closer to him now."

"Will we make it?" Heath asked in alarm.

This time, the dragon didn't answer straight away. "It will be close," he said at last, and Heath's terror mounted. He didn't urge Reka to go faster. He knew the dragon understood, and was doing all he could.

By the time the coast of Valoria approached, far below them, Heath was in a state of such anxiety he could barely breathe. The dragon didn't pause as they soared over Bexley Manor, continuing northwest instead, toward Bryford. They didn't actually reach the capital, however. Reka had descended when they neared land, and was now flying low enough to elicit shouts of fear and excitement from humans below them as they crossed the country. They were moving too quickly for anyone to recognize the burden in the dragon's talons, most likely.

Straining his eyes, Heath saw Percival before he heard the dragon's grunt of warning. His breath caught in his throat at the sight of what looked like a dozen tiny figures, clearly locked in a deadly struggle in the middle of the main highway. Percival seemed to be giving a good account of himself, but even he couldn't fight off so many alone. As Heath watched, his brother went down, borne to the ground by the weight of the combined attack. Heath reached for his back, but his bow wasn't there. He'd left for Vazula in too much of a hurry to grab it earlier in the day.

But of course he didn't need it. Reka touched down beside the highway, letting out a gravelly roar as he did so. All of the men, Percival included, looked up in shock, and the fighting halted. Heath ran toward his brother, but before he even reached Percival, the men—who were masked—had all fled. They had horses nearby, and within moments they were all mounted and thundering away.

Percival struggled to his feet, his eyes wide and shocked. Heath swallowed at the sight of him. He'd never seen his brother bruised and bleeding like this. No one had ever been able to land him so many blows.

"Percival!" he cried, hurrying forward and reaching out a hand. It hovered in the air as he searched for an uninjured part of his brother's body to grasp. "Are you all right?"

"I'll live," muttered Percival, wiping a trickle of blood from his mouth with his elbow. "I guess ten is over my limit."

He turned to Rekavidur. "Thank you," he said. "For coming to my rescue."

Heath noticed with dry humor that Percival said nothing to him. He supposed it was easier to face needing rescue by a dragon than by your little brother. And there was no denying that it was Reka's presence that had sent the attackers running.

Reka did his rippling dragon shrug. "I didn't do it for your sake, so you needn't thank me," he said, with a brutal lack of human tact. "I don't really like you, Brother of Heath. But you are important to Heath, and he is important to me, so I intervened. And," he added, his eyes on the horses now barely in sight, "it is fun to watch them flee like little rabbits, after all."

Percival just blinked, clearly at a loss for how to respond to this speech. Heath found himself fighting the mad urge to laugh. He rubbed his hands vigorously over his face in an attempt to clear his head.

"What happened, Perce?" he asked urgently. "Who were those men?"

"That's the right question," said Percival furiously. "They were masked, like bandits, but they did a poor job of disguising themselves."

Heath frowned, an ominous feeling rising in him at Percival's tone. "What do you mean?"

"I mean," growled Percival, "that I saw the peasant cloaks on more than one of them slip, and underneath they were wearing the uniform of the royal guard." He actually spat on the ground at the words.

"What?" Heath protested, aghast. "That can't be true. No one in the royal guard would ever—"

"Wouldn't they?" said Percival, with a hollow laugh. "Isn't that the ideal situation from King Matlock's perspective? Have me killed off by bandits on the road, such a tragedy, never mind that his biggest problem has been solved."

Heath stared at his brother, unable to believe it. "Percival, you must be mistaken." He frowned after the departed attackers, trying to piece together the information his senses had taken in during those panicked moments when Reka first landed.

"Do you know why I was riding to Bryford?" Percival challenged.

"No," frowned Heath. "I was wondering—"

"I received a summons," said Percival angrily. "From the king's Chief Counselor."

"Lord Niel?"

Percival nodded. "Exactly. It was a trap, Heath, don't you see? I should've listened to Father."

"Now I know you're not in your right mind," said Heath

emphatically. "I'm sure I've never heard those words come out of your mouth before."

Percival gave a perfunctory smile, but there was no real humor in it. "He told me not to come. He didn't like the letter. He wasn't sure what, but he could sense something off about it. He can sense deception, Heath, don't you understand? He could tell it was a trick."

Heath ran a hand through his hair, trying to make sense of it all. "What did I feel?" he muttered to himself.

"What's that?" Percival said impatiently. "What did you say?"

Heath met his eyes, troubled. "I felt something, from those men. Something I recognized."

"What do you mean you felt something?" Percival snapped, clearly irritated by Heath's distraction. Heath couldn't blame him for being agitated. He'd taken quite a beating, for the first time in his life.

Heath shook his head, frustrated by his limited memory. It had all been so brief. He closed his eyes and tried to visualize the men. He hadn't seen their faces—he hadn't *seen* anything he recognized. But he'd felt something familiar. Something indefinable. Something intangible.

"I think they had power," he whispered, not daring yet to meet Percival's gaze. "I think they had magic."

The silence was so painful he couldn't take it any longer. He opened his eyes hesitantly, and saw Percival staring at him like he'd lost his mind.

"What are you talking about?" Percival demanded. "They didn't have magic! Heath, they were *royal guards*."

"I don't think they were, though," said Heath. "Did you recognize any of them?"

"That doesn't mean anything," said Percival, still impatient. "You think I know every member of the royal guard? My magic is stronger than yours, remember? I didn't sense any power."

"Your magic is substantially weaker than Heath's," interjected Rekavidur, but neither brother paid him any heed.

"Are you sure?" Heath asked Percival. "It was familiar, that much I know. It wasn't any signature you recognize?"

"Of course not!" Percival snapped. "Every power-wielder in Valoria is related to us, Heath. Do you really think any of them would attack me?"

Heath shook his head slowly. "No, I don't. But maybe someone from Kyona? Someone we didn't meet when we were there?"

"This is ridiculous. You're no use to me," Percival said angrily, apparently already forgetting that Heath and Reka had appeared out of nowhere and saved his life.

He stomped over to the side of the road, where his horse was grazing. Apparently he'd been dragged from the saddle by his attackers. A few travelers passed them, throwing curious looks at the visibly roughed up young lord.

"Where are you going?" Heath demanded, hurrying after his brother.

"To the capital," said Percival grimly. "If I go home, Father will try to convince me to hush this up. You know how obsessed he is with not ruffling any royal feathers."

"Percival," said Heath warningly. "What are you going to do?"

"I'm going to tell people what happened!" Percival yelled.

"We don't know what happened!" Heath said, shouting himself now. "You *think* you saw a royal guard uniform, but—"

"And you *think* you felt magic," retorted Percival angrily. He'd swung himself into the saddle now, and he gestured down at himself. "Look at me, Heath! They were trying to kill me, and if I didn't have extra strength, or if you two hadn't showed up when you did, they would have succeeded! And everyone would have thought it was a bandit attack."

"But you can't just ride into the capital and accuse Lord Niel without proof," Heath argued.

"Lord Niel?" There was a hysterical edge to Percival's voice. "We both know Lord Niel doesn't have the authority to order the royal guard to do anything. Only one person can do that."

Heath stilled. "What are you saying, Percival?"

"You know what I'm saying," Percival replied curtly, turning his horse's head toward Bryford. "King Matlock wants me dead, he just doesn't want anyone to know he was involved."

"Percival!" Heath's horrified reproach had no effect. Percival was already moving, urging his horse into a trot. Heath turned to Reka, his eyes wide. "He's going to get himself killed. Or start a war or something. Do you realize what will happen if he bursts into the castle and accuses the king of trying to have him murdered?"

Reka's scales clinked metallically as he did his rippling shrug. "I do not know, but if I'm honest, I am quite curious to see what will happen."

"This isn't a game," Heath said sharply. "This is worse than everything else. I don't see how we could come back from this." He stared after his brother in rising panic. "Reka, will you take me to Bryford? Please?"

Reka let out a gusty sigh, but he evidently wasn't agitated this time, because there was no hint of smoke on his breath. "All right. Even though I would have quite liked to see what would happen if you didn't intervene."

The dragon lifted Heath into the air, and they flew, more slowly than they ever had before. They caught up to Percival in moments. Percival glanced up as Reka's shadow passed over him, and the anger that flashed across his face told Heath there was no point trying to convince his brother to stop. All he could do was follow Percival to Bryford.

When the horse and rider passed through the city gates,

Reka flew over the wall, setting Heath down on the flagstones of the castle courtyard. By the time Percival appeared, the dragon had already attracted the attention of what felt like every resident of the capital.

"Maybe you'd better go, Reka," Heath muttered. "I'm not sure your presence is going to help."

"Very well," said Reka amicably. "I will watch from a distance, if you prefer."

And without another word, he took to the sky. Heath hurried forward to intercept Percival, who was striding toward the castle steps.

"This is a bad idea, Perce," he started, but Percival just put on extra speed as he ran into the building.

"Lord Percival," said a servant, hurrying up to him. "What's—"

"Are Lord Brody and Lady Bianca in the castle?" Percival demanded.

"I believe so," the servant said nervously.

"Ask them to join me," said Percival, with the air of royalty. The castle steward had appeared by this point, obviously sensing a commotion in his territory.

"Is anything amiss, My Lord?" he asked with dignity, his eyes traveling over Percival's extensive injuries.

"I wish to seek an audience with the king," Percival said, his anger barely contained.

"There is a process for such things, My Lord," the steward began, but before he could continue, Prince Lachlan came hurrying into view, his expression strained.

"Lord Percival, Lord Heath," he said, drawing up in surprise at the sight of the two brothers, one visibly battered. "Is all well? I was told there was a dragon in the courtyard."

"That was just Rekavidur," said Heath quickly. "He's gone now, and he meant no harm, Your Highness."

"Which is more than I can say of your father," muttered Percival.

Heath drew in an involuntary hiss of air through his teeth, and Prince Lachlan turned with terrible calm toward Percival.

"What did you say, Lord Percival?"

The look on his face sent a chill down Heath's spine, but Percival seemed to have lost what little control he had.

"I was attacked," Percival said, his voice far too loud in the public entryway. "Attacked on my ride here by royal guards poorly disguised as bandits. I saw their uniforms! And I was only coming because I received a summons from the king's Chief Counselor!"

Prince Lachlan stood frozen, shock breaking through his usual impenetrable mask. Slowly, inevitably, the shock gave way to growing anger.

"What exactly are you implying?"

"It's not enough to muzzle us, is it?" Percival raged. "You have to actually remove us before you can feel secure!"

"Percival," pleaded Heath. "Please stop. This isn't the way to go about it."

"How dare you?" growled Prince Lachlan, disregarding Heath. He took a step toward Percival, but then froze as a firm voice rang across the space.

"Is there a problem, My Lords?"

Everyone whipped around. King Matlock was standing on the other side of the entrance hall, framed by a giant tapestry in Valorian purple and silver. Heath swallowed. The king's expression was outwardly calm, but he knew inexplicably that fury was bubbling below the surface.

No one answered the king, even Percival apparently sobered by the sovereign's commanding presence, at least temporarily.

"Let us discuss the matter more privately," said King Matlock, and it was not a request. Miserably, Heath followed the king into a small audience chamber, Percival at his side. Prince Lachlan came as well, along with four of the king's personal guards.

"What is the meaning of this ruckus, My Lords?" the king asked coldly, as soon as the door was closed behind them.

With an icy fury to match the king's, Percival told his tale again.

King Matlock raised an eyebrow, not even pretending to show solicitude for the attack on a member of his court.

"No member of my royal guard would participate in such conduct, Lord Percival. And I have not sent any guards on an errand along the eastern highway. You should take great care before making such wild accusations. I will not tolerate rabble-rousing."

"I know what I saw," said Percival stubbornly.

"And what of you, Lord Heath?" the king asked, submerged danger in his tone. "Did you see any indication that the men were royal guards?"

"No, Your Majesty," Heath said, trying to keep his voice calm.

"Heath!" Percival roared.

"Well, I didn't," Heath reminded him. He turned back to the king. "I was with Rekavidur, Your Majesty, so the men fled as soon as we arrived. I didn't get a good look at any of them."

"So you have nothing to add to your brother's report?"

Under the king's raised eyebrow, Heath hesitated. He could feel Percival's eyes on him, and sense his brother's rising tension. But Percival should have more faith in him. He would never make a half-hearted accusation against unnamed magic users without proof. Especially when tensions were so high.

"No, Your Majesty," he said quietly.

Something flashed in the king's eyes, and Heath took an involuntary step back.

"You're not concealing anything from me, are you, Lord Heath?" he asked coldly. "It wouldn't be the first time, would it?"

"Your Majesty?" Heath asked, startled.

"Or have I been misinformed?" King Matlock continued. "Have you *not* been keeping a potential threat secret from your king?"

Heath simply stared, his mouth hanging open like a fool. He couldn't marshal a single word. How did the king know about the merpeople, and why did he think they were a threat? Had Brody or Bianca said something? But Heath couldn't believe either of them would tattle on him to the crown, especially now, when they were all so angry with the royals. Or was Heath reading something into the king's words? Was he referring to something else entirely?

"You have nothing to say, Lord Heath?" King Matlock pressed. Heath could feel Percival's blankly astonished stare and Prince Lachlan's expectant gaze drilling into him.

"Only that you *have* been misinformed, Your Majesty," he said, as firmly as he could.

The king's eyes seemed to darken, but he said nothing. "I suggest you both return to your home," he said after an uncomfortable silence, his eyes passing between the brothers. "I will overlook your use of magic today, Lord Percival, given that you apparently used it in defense of your life. But going forward, I expect you to comply with the regulations."

Percival swelled angrily, but King Matlock gave him no further opportunity to speak.

"Think carefully before taking any rash action to which I will be forced to respond."

The words were clearly aimed at Percival, but his eyes lingered on Heath. There was no doubt Heath would hear more of whatever tale the king had been told regarding Merletta's people.

The two of them strode out of the castle, Heath stunned, and Percival still fuming.

"What was that about, Heath?" he demanded, the moment they were clear of the building.

Heath just shook his head, at a loss for how to explain it to Percival without breaking his promise.

"You came down pretty hard on our harmless gathering," said Percival bitingly, "but it seems you're keeping secrets of your own."

Heath made a helpless gesture, but Percival's attention had already turned away from him.

"If he thinks I'm going to just let the attack go, he's lost his mind."

"Careful," muttered Heath, glancing uneasily at the curious onlookers in the courtyard.

"No," snapped Percival. "I'm done being careful." And without a backward glance, he strode toward the stables.

Heath followed, an empty, hollow feeling in his stomach. He'd saved Percival's life, and for that he was grateful, even if his brother wasn't. But it didn't mean Percival wasn't in danger.

And now it seemed Merletta was under threat as well.

CHAPTER THIRTY-THREE

Merletta

Merletta stared at the open water before her, focusing on the reassuring weight of her spear slung across her back.

"You can do this, Merletta. Have confidence in yourself."

Merletta could feel that her answering smile was a little stiff, but she didn't have room in her head for pretense right now. A couple of weeks ago she would have been bolstered by Freja's praise. But since the overheard conversation in the training yard, she wasn't sure what to think. And this wasn't the moment to try to figure it out. She focused instead on the encouraging words with which her friends had sent her off, and on Heath's stern command: don't die.

That was the plan.

Unbidden, her thoughts flew to what had come before the command, but she shook off the pleasant memory. She'd spent way too much of her last week of preparation dwelling on that kiss—the gentleness of Heath's lips, even while his embrace was delightfully possessive.

But she was doing it again. No matter how incredible that

moment had been, she needed to be a warrior right now, not a lovesick dreamer.

"You know your task?" Freja asked, drawing her back to the moment.

Merletta nodded. "Follow the trail, leave my mark, retrieve the stolen item, add my name, and return to the Center in one piece before the sun sets," she recited.

"That's right," said Freja approvingly.

Merletta glanced behind her, back to the southeast. "We're a long way from the triple kingdoms," she said, unable to help herself.

Freja just nodded, her expression solemn. She probably thought Merletta was nervous to be so far from the protection of the barrier. And if Merletta was honest, she was, a little. But she was also thinking of Heath's kingdom of land-dwellers. They lived to the west. Just how far toward Heath's home had Merletta come? And what had happened to Heath's brother? Had he made it in time?

But she couldn't afford to get distracted. She looked back at Freja, expecting to be told it was time to begin. But the older mermaid hesitated.

"You were supervised during your practice test," she said quietly. "I think you know that. You fought guards as part of the exercise, and they were never far away."

Merletta nodded cautiously.

"This isn't a practice," Freja went on. "The focus isn't combat in a controlled environment. It's survival in the open ocean, and that takes strength of mind as much as strength of body. You're on your own this time. Be careful."

Merletta thought she read real concern in the guard's eyes, and she nodded again. She hadn't needed the reminder, but she still appreciated it, not least because it encouraged her to hope that she'd been right about Freja in the first place.

Freja gave her a meaningful nod, and Merletta swam forward. A quick glance behind showed her that the older mermaid had turned, and was swimming swiftly back in the direction they'd come.

Merletta swung back around, looking for the beginning of the so-called trail. She hadn't been surprised by the vagueness of the instructions this time, after her experience in the practice test. But she was nervous about her ability to pick up a trail. The only reliable trail Merletta knew of was to follow blood through water, and she hoped fervently that she wouldn't be in that situation today. She moved slowly northwest, not wanting to miss whatever subtle sign might be there.

Floating near the ocean floor, the light was dim. It was no barrier for her sharp eyes, and she scanned the sandy bed and clumps of rock carefully. Something caught her eye and, frowning, she dove down to examine it. A large rock protruded from the sand on a slant. It was big enough for her whole body to lie across. Its surface was flat and smooth, except for a series of deep grooves that didn't look quite natural. It was as though something enormous had slashed its claws repeatedly over the rock's surface.

The thought sent a shiver down Merletta's spine, and for a moment she wondered if she should put some distance between herself and the spot. But another look around showed her that it was the only thing in the area that looked remotely like a trail. Squaring her shoulders, she followed the direction of the scores, which were pointing roughly northwest.

Her decision to follow her instinct was rewarded when, a short way along, she came across a similar rock, this one also marked with many scratches. Merletta paused again, peeling off and relocating a sea star so she could examine the grooves. Now she looked more closely, they didn't look like claw marks. They didn't have a predictable pattern that suggested a set of claws had made them. It was more like one sharp instrument had scored the rock over and over. She continued in the direction they seemed to point, and found more, this time on a vertical shelf that wasn't flat at all. She wouldn't even have noticed the grooves along it if she hadn't known now what to look for.

As she squinted at them, she realized the lines weren't identical. Some looked sharp and deep, others more gentle, as though they'd been eroded by the water over time. Merletta thought back over her instructions.

Follow the trail. She seemed to be on the right track for that. But what was next? *Leave my mark.*

She ran a finger along the grooves on the vertical shelf, and all at once she understood. She pulled her spear off her back and laid its tip in the scratch. Yes, this was surely what had made the indents. And her next instruction now made sense.

With a sense of elation, both at solving the riddle and at joining the tradition of those who had come before, she laid her spear tip against the rock and slashed as hard as she could. It took her a few attempts to make a score deep enough to satisfy her. She drew back, beaming at her work. Her own mark was indistinguishable from the others, of course. But it was satisfying, exhilarating even, to know that not only was she following all the trainees who'd preceded her, but she was doing her part to help guide those who would come after. When Andre took his second year test, he would be following her trail.

Now that she understood, Merletta followed the trail with more confidence. She noted that the number of scratches increased as she went, and she felt smug at the realization that she had figured out what she was supposed to do earlier than many.

The landscape varied as she went, and she noticed she was moving steadily deeper. It wasn't enough to make her uncomfortable, but she could feel the pressure in her head. The trainees' trail continued to lead her northwest, weaving through natural coral gardens, among rock sculptures, and over expanses of flat sand. Once, she was forced to swim through a forest of tall, waving seaweed. It was too large to go around, and she couldn't tell in which direction the trail would come out. She hated the feeling of the weeds brushing against her skin as she swam blindly in the darkness. It reminded her of the soft touch of a jellyfish. The eerie feeling wasn't helped by the appearance of a territorial eel whose body was longer than hers. At least she'd already found and added her mark to the rock sculpture in the middle of the forest.

The markings told her she needed to turn further westward, so she didn't resist when the eel chased her out of the weeds in that general direction. She shuddered as she emerged into open water again, relieved the creature showed no sign of following her. So far, the real test had involved significantly fewer dangerous sea creatures than the practice test. She didn't even feel afraid. Freja's words, about her being on her own, had made her heart lighter rather than heavier. The Center might talk of the dangerous animals to be found outside the barrier, but as far as Merletta was concerned, merpeople were by far the biggest threat to be found in the ocean.

Merletta kept her eyes open for any sign of her next challenge—*retrieve the stolen item*—but she didn't really expect to see anything while the trail was still going. Presumably it led to whatever she was supposed to retrieve.

The ocean floor was slanting ever downward, and Merletta's head was beginning to ache. She was grateful for all the acclimatization training she'd done, sure she would be struggling without it. Even so, the pressure was starting to wear on her. Taking note of a distinctive patch of luminescent coral that sat next to the latest mark on the trail, she decided to give herself a break. She swam straight upward, breathing more freely as the water became shallower. She kept going, further and further, until she could see the sky above her.

When her head finally broke the surface, she was surprised to see how brightly the sun was shining. She must have been deep for the water to remain so dark, even on such a sunny day. Closing her eyes, she turned her face to the warmth. It was sheer delight, to let the sun kiss her cold skin, to be out in the middle of the ocean, far from the triple kingdoms, far from anything she knew, basking in the fresh air and endless sky.

She felt the ripple of movement in the water, and thrust her head back under, suddenly wary. But she didn't need to be. A cry of delight broke from her at the sight of a small pod of dolphins coming toward her. Like Merletta, they apparently wanted to enjoy the sunshine. They broke the surface all around her, and she hastened back up to join them.

The dolphins didn't seem troubled by her presence, some of them buffeting her in a friendly way as she wove in and out between their sleek gray bodies. Copying them, she propelled herself upward with enough force to get her whole body momentarily out of the water. She laughed to herself at the image of changing to human form, then instantly back again when she landed with an enormous splash. But of course, she didn't really emerge for long enough to change form.

It was bliss, joining the dance of these beautiful creatures, letting her senses drink in the vast expanse of ocean both above and below her. She felt a stab of pity for the poor merpeople back in the triple kingdoms, kept prisoner behind their barrier by the fear they had been taught from infancy.

After a few minutes, she decided—regretfully—that she'd given herself enough of a break. It had been worth five minutes of her allotted time to alleviate the pressure headache, but the middle of her test was no time to get carried away. Before she could act on the thought, however, she felt the shift in the mood of her companions. She didn't need the dolphins' response as warning, though. Her instincts alerted her to the danger as surely as theirs did. She dropped further below the water line, pulling her spear from her back and gripping it tightly as she looked around her.

The sight of several large black and white shapes hurtling toward the pod sent Merletta's heart leaping into her throat. She knew what they were, of course, but she'd never seen one up this close.

She barely had time to hope that the name *killer whale* was another of the Center's tactics for promoting fear, when the whales sped at the pod. The nearest one closed in on a dolphin and opened its mouth wide. A single row of smooth white teeth was revealed, looking somehow small in its giant mouth.

The dolphins scattered, Merletta along with them. Undeterred by its failure to catch its initial target, the first whale set its sights on Merletta. Perhaps it was wondering what type of fish she might be. It had probably never seen a merperson before, she realized. An instance of how she'd undervalued the barrier.

But there was no time to think of such things. The whale was fast. Even swimming more quickly than she'd ever done before—her sides aching, and her spear clutched desperately in one hand—Merletta couldn't outpace it. With little chance of killing the whale, and no interest in trying, she knew her life depended on being quick enough to escape. None of the dolphins were in sight anymore, all having fled, pursued by the other whales. She was alone with the giant predator. She could feel the vibrations of the whale's movements through the water, and she had almost despaired of escaping when she spied a rocky crag below.

Diving down with an agility that was probably her only advantage over the whale, she hurtled toward a slim fissure in the rocks. She turned her spear so that it was point down and wouldn't catch on the edges, and dove blindly into the gap.

She felt the rock scratch against her shoulders and winced, hoping it wasn't enough to draw blood. A whale and a shark would be too much. As soon as she felt her fins follow her into the gap, she pulled up. Fortunately the space widened after the initial opening, and she was able to spin around. She poked her spear upward through the fissure, and waited, breathing hard. The whale had dived down with her, but it couldn't follow her into the rock. It swam back and forth in agitation, flashes of black and white filling her vision. Merletta had no idea about the hunting habits of whales. Would it wait for her to come out, or lose interest and go in search of easier prey? Would its fellows come to aid it?

It showed no immediate sign of giving up. Minutes slid by, and still Merletta was trapped, her heart racing and her hands shaking on the handle of her spear. All at once, out of the corner of her eye, she saw a luminous white glow, coming toward her with a horribly familiar flowing motion.

The jellyfish, probably disturbed by her violent entrance into the chasm, floated toward her, moving in uneven billows that had a rhythm of their own. Merletta felt her body freeze, but she couldn't afford to panic. The whale was still above, and while the sight of the jellyfish woke an illogical terror inside her, she could see at a glance that it wasn't a dangerous one. She would have to stay where she was.

The jellyfish was almost on her, and she squeezed her eyes shut, focusing all her effort on holding in a scream. The space was confined, and she was certain she wouldn't escape untouched. Sure enough, a moment later, she felt the soft brush of the jellyfish, followed instantly by the agonizing pain of its sting. It was significantly larger than the ones in the bloom Ileana had pushed her into, and therefore its sting was considerably more painful. Merletta thrust the end of her braid into her mouth and bit down hard on it to stop herself crying out. She didn't want to excite the whale.

When she couldn't take the blindness anymore, she forced her eyes open. The jellyfish was moving away from her, and she could no longer see black and white flashing above her. She waited, shaking violently from shock more than actual hurt. She had an angry red welt on her arm, but already the first pain of the sting was starting to recede. She poked her head cautiously out of the hole, and saw no sign of the whale. Pulling her head back in, she forced herself to count to two hundred, then checked again. The water was empty. Moving slowly, she emerged from her hiding place. Her arm was stinging, but she felt a curious sense of triumph. She had grappled with one of her deepest fears, and prevailed.

The elation of that thought soon faded as she realized just how unfamiliar her surroundings were. She swam up high, hoping to get her bearings, but she could see nothing she recognized in any direction. How could she have been so foolish as to follow that pod of dolphins in the middle of her test? Fighting panic, she picked a new landmark below her and began a methodical search, moving outward and back, outward and back, hoping desperately to see the luminescent coral she'd noted earlier.

It took her an hour to find it, and when she did, she shed actual tears of relief. So much for a strategic sacrifice of five minutes for a break from the pressure. She had begun to think she was lost in the middle of the ocean, with little hope of finding her way home, and no hope of passing her test.

Her lesson learned, she stuck close to the trail and moved quickly between each marker. She could only hope she was nearing her goal. Several minutes later, she saw with a rush of apprehension that a huge chasm opened up not far ahead. She couldn't help hoping the trail would lead her in a different direction, but she was unsurprised to see the latest mark pointing directly over the yawning edge.

"I hate depth work," she muttered to no one in particular.

But there was no time to hesitate, not since she'd wasted it frolicking with dolphins. Steeling herself, she dove down into the darkness. Her eyes adjusted quickly, as they always did, and she was able to find the next marker without too much trouble. Unfortunately, it led her even deeper.

As she descended into the drop off, she noticed fewer scores on the rocks. Clearly some of the former trainees had been anxious to get out of this dark hole, and hadn't paused to add to every marker. She didn't blame them, although she conscientiously scored each one with her spear. This chasm wasn't a round hole, but a long deep trench on the ocean floor, along which the trail led her.

Her eyes played tricks on her in the dark, and the memory of the huge octopus from her practice test was unpleasantly vivid in her mind. She kept imagining that she saw tentacles reaching for her from crevices in the dark rocks.

Then suddenly, she realized what she was seeing was no trick of the mind. She recoiled at the sight of a long, thick tentacle emerging from a gap up ahead. It was orange on the top, and glowed a ghostly white on the underside. Merletta floated, frozen in horror, as more tentacles followed. She lost track after six, her eyes riveted instead on the bulbous eyes and long, tubular head that seemed to squelch out of an impossibly small hole in the trench wall.

The creature drew itself up, one eye fixed unblinkingly on Merletta. It was huge, five times as big as she was, and its body blocked the entire trench. Merletta's spear trembled from the shaking of her hands, and she felt the certainty of death cutting its path toward her through the water, moving as swiftly and sleekly as a shark.

Then her eyes spotted something behind the creature's softly swaying tentacles. A marker on the rock behind, this one showing a sharp turn rather than just a straight line. It had the fewest scores of any yet, but the sight still bolstered Merletta. Trainees who had come before had made it past the squid, many of them. Sage must have, and Emil. She followed the line of the marker with her eyes and saw it was pointing directly into a round, dark hole in the rock. The hole was smaller than the one the squid had emerged from, and it was on the opposite side of the trench.

Fighting every instinct that told her to flee toward light and warmth, Merletta dove suddenly downward. She swam with all her might, aware that the squid was moving after her, but not daring to check how close it was. She surged toward the black opening, hoping desperately that she'd understood the marker correctly, that the gap was too small for the squid to follow, that she'd make it in time.

She felt the end of a tentacle slide along her scales as she shot into the hole. It was pitch black in there, and the tunnel was so narrow that having entered with her arms at her sides, she couldn't shift to extend them in front of her. She had to rely on her tail to propel her into the blackness. Her spear was laid flat against the underside of her arm, her hand twisted awkwardly to hold it at the right angle. She had no choice but to keep moving forward, and the tunnel felt endless. If the squid hadn't been hard on her fins at the time, she thought venturing into the tunnel would have been the greatest test of all for her bravery. As it was, she hadn't even hesitated.

The blackness seemed to press against her eyes, and her head was aching worse than ever from the depth. But still she kept moving forward, trusting in the trainees who'd gone before her, who'd emerged in one piece out the other side.

With foreboding, she heard a strange sound from up ahead of her, a churning, boiling kind of sound that grew louder as she moved forward. Then, all at once, the tunnel ended, and she popped out into open space.

But it wasn't calm water, like she'd been swimming in before she entered the trench. The water here was violent, thrashing with an intensity that reminded her of the waves pounding the shore of the island the day Heath had almost died, the day she'd discovered her legs. As soon as she left the tunnel, the unpredictable current seized her and flung her against the rock wall from which the tunnel emerged. It was all she could do to hold on to her spear as her head cracked against the shelf.

The current pulled her out again, and sent her tumbling head over fins through the water, whisking her far from her point of entry. She could see no new markings. In fact, she couldn't imagine how she was possibly to find markings in such a maelstrom of currents.

Maelstrom! The word brought sudden clarity to the swirling chaos, and she stopped fighting the water's pull. When she allowed it to tug her along, resistless, she realized she was indeed moving in a spiral. She tucked her arms into her sides and used her tail to steer, trying to keep herself moving with the current, not flung outward by it. When she rushed past the hole she'd come out of, she realized she'd done an entire circuit.

It was hard to think with the churning water thrashing at every inch of her, but Merletta felt a growing certainty that this whirlpool was the destination she'd been heading for. Whatever the "stolen item" she was supposed to retrieve, it must be here. She glanced up and saw a place, a little way above her, where a huge tower of rock jutted across her vision, obviously stretching up from the ocean floor. She let herself be carried around for another circuit, wincing as she knocked against smaller rock towers that stood out at various angles. She was sure she was bleeding now, but it didn't matter. She couldn't imagine any predators following her into this chaos.

When the whizzing water brought her back to the same place, she pushed up with her tail and seized the rock tower. Clinging on like a barnacle, she crawled along its underside, trying to make progress toward the center of the whirlpool.

To her amazement, in a short time, her head broke out into open space. Her throat opened immediately, and she gasped in air as if she'd been holding her breath like Heath did, instead of breathing water. Then, still clinging to the rock, she shook water from her eyes and peered around her. Below her, she could see the center of the maelstrom continuing all the way to the ocean floor, where a small patch of sandy rock was visible, exposed to the air. Above, the eye of the whirlpool grew ever wider, opening into a vast blue sky. The rock she was clinging to extended right into the open space, forming a ledge that she might be able to sit on, out of the water. With a supreme effort, she began to inch sideways up and around the edge of the nearly horizontal shelf. Her head was in air and the rest of her still in the water, although she was parallel to the ocean floor.

Arms burning from the strain, she managed it at last. For a moment she lay flat, face down on the rocky ledge with her spear trapped flat beneath her and her arms wrapped around the rock. Then she looked up.

At the end of the ledge, which hung into open space, was a rock. It was clearly treated by merperson hands, smoothed on one side into a large flat sign, and shaped around the edges to make it sit steadily on the shelf. It wasn't far—by crawling forward, Merletta could reach it without more than her torso extending from the water.

She could make out names chiseled into the sign, and she

remembered the fourth part of her instructions. *Add my name.* The name at the bottom of the half-filled space made her heart leap in excitement.

Sage.

Above it she saw Oliver's name, and Ileana's, and Emil's. Pulling Heath's knife from her satchel, she propped herself on her elbows and added her own name, the metal carving it more deeply than whatever her predecessors had used. She drew back, delighted with her success, and let her hands fall back to the stone. She frowned as they landed on something. She'd missed it in her excitement at finding the stone sign, but something was lying across the rocky shelf in front of it.

Three spears, not as expensive as her own, but still clearly the property of guards. She frowned at them. Was this, then, the stolen item she was supposed to retrieve? But it was three items, not one.

She looked back up at the stone sign, hoping for a clue, and her eyes were drawn to two words she hadn't noticed before, carved above the list of trainees.

Watchword: Vazula

Merletta stared at the words, her mouth hanging open. What did it mean? How was there a reference to Vazula, *her* Vazula, here of all places? What did it have to do with the guard test? Her hands closed unconsciously over the spear shafts as she gaped at the message, and she felt another hand close around her fins too late.

Turning, she saw through the churning wall of water the dim shape of two mermen, each seizing one of her fins. She tried to thrash out at them, but their grip was too strong. Before she knew what was happening, one had launched himself half out of the water, landing heavily on top of her and pinning her to the rock shelf. Before she could get her hands free, he forced something over her head, and everything went dark.

CHAPTER THIRTY-FOUR

Merletta

Merletta groaned, trying to master her wits. Her memory seemed to be a patchy jumble of darkness, churning water, and futile struggle. Where was she, and why was she relieved to feel the gentle familiar sway of the current around her?

The maelstrom! Her eyes flew open, and she tried to push herself upright from wherever she was lying. But hands seized her immediately, holding her down, as a firm voice said, "Easy."

Merletta blinked up into a face she'd seen before, although it took her a moment to place the dark-haired merman.

"I recognize you," she said slowly. Her eyes were drawn to his silvery-blue tail, swishing calmly back and forth in the water. She frowned as a memory of raging waves and rain-drenched shore jumped to mind. Suddenly the pieces fit together, and she gasped, trying once again to rise.

"You're August! You *are* alive! I hoped so, but I was afraid it was just wishful thinking."

The merman was so surprised, he loosened his grip, allowing her to sit up this time.

"You know my name?" he asked. "I recognize you, of course,

but I didn't know if you'd remember me. I certainly didn't think you'd know my name."

"The whole triple kingdoms knows your name," said Merletta. "You're a hero who died selflessly in the cause of protecting our boundaries." Her voice turned dry. "Congratulations."

August's brow darkened, and for a moment he said nothing. Making the most of the opportunity, Merletta looked around her, trying to make sense of her surroundings.

There was little sense to make. She was lying on a slanted floor of what seemed to be wood. It was like a human building, something she might see on Vazula. Except it was underwater. The walls were crumbling and rotting, as one would expect of wood submerged at the bottom of the ocean. Why would anyone build such a dwelling down here?

"How did I get here?" Merletta demanded. "The last thing I remember, I was in the middle of the maelstrom. I saw three spears, and then someone grabbed me from behind."

"That was us," said August. Following his gaze, Merletta started at the sight of two other mermen floating nearby. She hadn't even noticed them. "We saw the preparations being made, and we figured out there was a trainee test approaching. I was fairly sure it would be you. I saw you doing your practice test, when you found the cave I was living in at the time. Since then, we've been paying more attention to guard patrols out here. When we realized your test would be happening at the maelstrom, we decided to intervene."

"But why?" Merletta protested. "I need to pass that test." She looked upward frantically, trying to catch a glimpse of the light far above. "How long have I been here?"

"No time at all," said August calmly. "We didn't intend to knock you out, but unfortunately you got a bit battered in the struggle. A maelstrom isn't the easiest place to kidnap someone."

"I'm very impressed and all," said Merletta in exasperation, "but *why* have you kidnapped me?"

"Why do you think?" snapped one of the other guards. "We want answers. We followed you out past the barrier, to stop you from getting yourself killed, and next thing we know, we're facing land, and humans, and myths."

"And we find ourselves hunted by our own people," August added grimly. "Fleeing for our lives from Center guards."

"Is that what happened?" Merletta demanded. "Center guards tried to kill you?"

"Well, we don't know for certain they were Center guards," said August reasonably. "They were masked, and none of us recognized them. But that's our best guess."

"Are they still hunting you?" Merletta asked sharply.

The guard shrugged. "We can't be sure. We think they believe us to be dead. They took us outside the city to finish us off. We were all still delirious when we left the triple kingdoms, but I began to sober up before we'd gone far."

"August was brilliant," said the third guard gruffly. "He was the one who thought of pretending to still be hallucinating, and told us to do the same when we started to come out of it. Without that, we'd have been dead for sure."

"As it was, we were hard pressed to fight them off," said August. "We were all bleeding when we fled, and the sharks didn't take long to find us." His expression hardened, and Merletta felt a wave of sympathetic horror at the thought. "I suspect they were pretty confident we weren't going to make it. But we're tougher than they thought."

"So I can see," said Merletta, impressed.

"There were two others in our patrol, though," August

pressed. "They weren't with us when we were taken from the triple kingdoms. Do you know what happened to them?"

Merletta lowered her head. "I'm afraid they're dead," she said softly. "Your wife told me herself that she saw their bodies lowered into their tombs."

"You've seen my wife?" August demanded. "Is she all right?"

Merletta nodded. "I think so. She seemed...a little empty, somehow. But she's not hurt, or in danger." She squirmed inwardly. *At least, she wasn't until I told her my secrets and brought her into danger.*

August hid his face in his hands for a moment, drawing in deep pulls of water. "She's alive," he muttered to himself. "It's more than I dared count on." He raised his head again, determination in his eyes. "Since you're clearly a Center trainee, rather than the random thief we were led to believe, perhaps you can explain all this mess to us. What did we stumble on at that place? With the human?"

Merletta's voice was grim. "Something big enough to kill for, apparently. The short version is that everything we've been taught is a lie. Humans are real—but I guess you know that part—and they're as intelligent as we are. The open ocean also isn't nearly as dangerous as we've been told. I mean, there are dangerous creatures out here, that can pick you off if you wander around on your own, like the test has forced me to do."

She paused. "Now I think about it, both the practice test and the real test have led me to the lairs of especially dangerous creatures." It was true. She'd never been attacked by an octopus, or grappled with a giant squid, in her illicit wanderings. "I suppose part of the point of the test is to reinforce the lie we've been fed."

Shaking her head, she returned to the topic at hand. "Anyway, I guess you've figured out what the ocean is really like, if you've been living out here all this time. It certainly has its dangers, but it's not so hostile that it would be impossible for a group of armed and prepared merpeople to successfully live out here. The Center is definitely behind the deception, although I don't know how far it goes. I don't fully understand the reasons someone wants to keep us inside the barrier."

Merletta frowned. "What else? Land is close by, and it's not dangerous, either. And..."

She hesitated. She still hadn't told anyone in the triple kingdoms the most astounding secret of all, the truth about drying out. Should she trust these guards with it?

"Look," she said abruptly. "I'm sorry you were dragged into it. That was never my intention, and I can't tell you how glad I am that at least some of you survived. But if I'm going to change the way things are, I need to be inside the Center. And for that, I need to pass this test. I need to retrieve the stolen item, which I think is those spears." She frowned, her gaze passing between the guards, all of whom were now armed. "Wait a minute. Three spears for three guards. Did you put them there?"

August nodded. "Like I said, we decided to intervene. We'd ascertained that the center of the maelstrom was your target, and we planned to grab you when you reached it. We went there first, and left our own clues."

"Well, that's very clever and all," said Merletta, a little impatiently, "but it won't help me pass the test."

"You were never going to pass the test," said August brutally.

Merletta couldn't help being a little stung. "I thought I was doing well."

August shook his head. "I'm not commenting on your ability. You've already said it—whoever's scales we've all scratched the wrong way is willing to kill for their secrets. Two guards were waiting for you just beyond the maelstrom. You wouldn't have made it back to the triple kingdoms."

Merletta stared at the merman, her mouth slightly open. He

was speaking in such a matter-of-fact voice that it was hard to comprehend he was referring to her planned murder.

"How do you know they weren't there to escort me back?" she challenged.

One of the other guards snorted, but August didn't laugh. "They were masked," he explained calmly.

"Maybe they were part of the test," Merletta tried weakly. "In my practice test, I had to fight a series of masked guards to..." But she trailed off, remembering Freja's words. This test wasn't focused on combat. She was supposed to be alone out here.

"They weren't part of the test," said August flatly.

Merletta frowned at him. "You keep saying 'were'. What happened to them?"

He shrugged. "They'll live, though it's more than they deserve. We incapacitated them, and we did it without them seeing us, thankfully. So I don't think they'll come looking once they wake."

One of the other guards drifted up behind August, nodding. "It helped that we had the advantage of surprise this time."

"This time?" Merletta repeated.

August's voice had lost its matter-of-factness now. He looked grim in the low light of the strangely slanted wooden room.

"We've met them before. They may have been masked, but I recognized their tails. They're the ones who tried to kill us the first time. Center guards, we think."

Merletta's mouth was hanging fully open now. The mermen who had been responsible for secretly killing the compromised guards had been waiting, masked, for her to emerge from her test? August was right—there was only one conclusion to draw.

"You saved my life," she said fervently. "Thank you."

August nodded in acknowledgment.

"But where are they now?" Merletta pressed. "We can find

out who they are! Did you unmask them after you knocked them out?"

"We did," said August heavily. "But their faces meant nothing to us. One was skinny, with pale hair and a silvery tail, the other was stockier, with a deep blue tail."

Merletta frowned. "Very nondescript tail colors," she muttered. "Not likely to stand out."

August nodded again. "Whoever they are, they must be under orders."

"Take me to them," said Merletta, with sudden resolution. "Maybe I'll recognize them."

"It could be dangerous," said August warningly, but Merletta waved him off.

"My life is at risk anyway, I think we've established that. With four of us to two of them, surely we'll be all right."

She saw the three guards exchange looks, but she didn't give them the opportunity to say that as a trainee, she didn't count for the purpose. She rose into the water and turned toward the door, but August's voice called her back.

"Wait, don't you want your item? The one we replaced with the spears?"

"Oh, yes!" Merletta turned back. She'd momentarily forgotten about the object of the test.

"This is what was on the shelf when we got there." August pulled out a rolled-up writing leaf and held it out to her.

She took it, frowning. It was tied with a thin length of weed, and she pulled it open. For a moment she just stared at the page, unable to make sense of what she was seeing. It was a list of names, each with notations that made no sense to her. They were common names, ones she'd come across in Tilssted plenty of times, but there was nothing particular tying them together. Her eyes continued to scan the page, and her heart gave a great leap of fear at the sight of her own name. Running her gaze back over the whole list, she suddenly realized it was familiar after all.

"It's the page from the orphan records," she whispered. "My page. The one which was damaged."

Her mind raced back to the time, in her first year, when she'd found her entry in the Center's orphan records. She'd been shocked to see that, contrary to what she'd been told, she hadn't been abandoned at the charity home by unknown parents. Her entry had listed parents, but the record had been damaged, so that their names were no longer legible. This, surely, was an exact copy of that page. The other names and annotations meant nothing to her, except that now she was looking for it, she recognized that the common names all belonged to orphans from the home, of similar age to her.

Trembling, hardly knowing whether she wanted to see it, she followed the line next to her own name. Her date of birth was there, and two names which she'd never seen, never so much as heard.

Elminia and Elric, Hemssted.

Merletta stared at the names, drinking them in. Were those really the names of her parents? Elminia...that sounded unusual. Perhaps unusual enough to enable Merletta to track her down.

And her parents came from Hemssted? The room seemed to rock wildly around her. It was so central to her identity that she was the Tilssted trainee, and she didn't actually come from there? She didn't even like Hemssted! All the Hemssted trainees she'd met had been unpleasant, at the very least. Of course, she had no way to know if this record was accurate. Someone had written it out—if she'd learned anything, it was that this fact gave no guarantee of the record's truth. But still...what was the point in giving her a false record, when no record was necessary at all?

She looked up, her eyes wide and her mind racing. "Why would they put this in the maze?" she croaked.

A stolen item indeed! Truer words had never been spoken. As a nameless orphan, her history had been stolen from her as surely as the Center stole history from the whole triple kingdoms.

"I don't know what it is, or what any of that means," said August, and his unemotional voice steadied her. "But we know that their usual approach is to find a way to weaken their targets before they attack. I suspect that they hoped the test itself might finish you off, and if it didn't, they wanted to make sure you'd be weakened as much as possible when you emerged." He looked her up and down with a shrewd glance. "And no offense, but you don't exactly project strength at this moment."

Merletta looked down at herself, still clutching the record, floating in shock, immobile except for the violent trembling that was rocking her from head to fin.

"You're right," she acknowledged, swallowing. "I would have been rattled, and not at my most vigilant."

August nodded, satisfied. "Well, if you still want to see where we left the guards, we'd better go. I wouldn't be surprised if they'd already woken."

Pulling herself together, Merletta retied the record and stowed it in her satchel. She tried to project steadiness as she followed August and the others from the room, but on the inside, her mind more nearly resembled the maelstrom she'd just survived. When they emerged into open water, Merletta glanced back, and let out an involuntary cry.

"It's...it's a ship!" she gasped.

August looked back, studying their temporary haven with the impassive expression that seemed habitual for him.

"Yes," he said. "A human ship, like the legends."

"But it's underwater," Merletta protested, studying the

rotting wooden structure. It was lying at an odd angle, half-propped against a large rocky shelf that protruded from the ocean floor. The tall spire of wood that she'd seen rising from Heath's ship was broken on this one, more than half of it dangling down, barely connected to the rest.

"I suspect it fell afoul of the maelstrom," said August calmly.

And following his gaze, Merletta realized that she could see the water growing wild in the distance. Now they were out of the ship, she could even hear the churning.

"Of course," she muttered.

"We found all kinds of interesting things in there," said one of the other guards. He was considerably younger than the venerable August, probably in his late twenties. "Look at this." He pulled something out of a crude kelp satchel, and Merletta squinted at the round, flat golden disc.

"I saw something like that in my practice test!" she cried. "In the giant crab's treasure hoard."

The guard nodded. "It turns out that if you get far enough from the barrier, human treasures can be found scattered all over the ocean."

Merletta's eyes drifted back to the sunken ship, wishing that she had time to explore more. "It's a great hideout."

"We've only been here a short time," said August. "While we were watching preparations for your test. We can't afford to stay in one place for too long. We'll be moving on now that we've intercepted you."

"Shame," said Merletta. She looked at the younger guard, who was looking gloomy as he stashed his treasure back in his satchel. An idea began to form in her mind, but she said nothing, not sure yet whether it was wise.

It wasn't far to where the three guards had left Merletta's attackers and, as August had predicted, they were already gone.

"Do you think they've returned to the Center?" Merletta asked nervously. "Or are they searching for me?"

"I don't know," said August, looking sober. "But maybe we'd better see you back closer to the barrier, to be safe."

"But if you're seen—" Merletta started.

August cut her off with a gesture. "I'm not just being altruistic. None of us can enter the triple kingdoms with any hope of surviving. But you can. I want you to tell my wife that I'm alive. And you can't do that unless you're alive."

"Of course," said Merletta quickly. "Of course I'll tell her."

"And we want to help you," cut in the younger guard. "If you're really trying to change things, we want to be part of it. Whoever is keeping the world out here a secret was willing to dispose of us to maintain the deception, remember. If we don't do anything, it will just happen over and over, anytime someone asks too many questions, or sees too much."

Merletta nodded, her expression troubled. The fierce determination in his eyes filled her with guilt. She felt she should tell him the truth, that she had little influence, and no real plan. But she couldn't find the words.

August squinted upward, checking the light. "The sun will be setting in a few hours."

Merletta started. "I have to be back before sunset if I'm to pass the test."

"The test isn't my concern," said August grimly. "The open ocean really is dangerous at night." He started to move through the water. "Come on."

CHAPTER THIRTY-FIVE

Merletta

Merletta had to hurry to keep up with the three guards as they swam southeast. She was impressed by their stealth. Watching them, she saw that they were masters of concealment. Whether they'd always been that way, or had become so in their months of exile, she didn't know.

To her relief, they encountered no vengeful guards on their trip back. She wondered if her would-be murderers had returned to the Center already, or were still out near the maelstrom, searching for any sign of her. What did they think had happened to them? She hoped they wouldn't realize that the guards from almost a year ago were still alive.

The thought decided her. August and the others had saved her life, and she couldn't leave them to the mercies of an unsettled life in the open ocean when she knew of a safe haven nearby.

"This is as close as we dare go," said August, drawing up behind an enormous boulder. "The barrier is less than half an hour's swim away. You should be fine here. We're almost within the territory of the regular patrols."

Merletta nodded. "Thank you," she said fervently. "Thank you for saving my life, and for telling me all you have. I'll get the message to all your families." She drew in a big pull of water. "I can help you in another way, I think. There's a safe place you can go, where you won't have to move constantly."

"Where?" the younger guard demanded.

Merletta restrained a grimace. She didn't think they were going to like it.

"The island," she said. "The land, where you saw Heath, the human. He's not there now," she hurried on, at the sight of their expressions. "No one is there. But I hid there for a whole month after the incident last year." She hesitated. "There's more, but I don't think you'll believe me if I tell you. I'll have to show you. Do you think you can find the island?"

"Of course," said August dryly. "We know where it is. We've been carefully avoiding those waters for months."

Merletta nodded. "You have nothing to fear from the land," she assured him. "Go there, and I'll meet you as soon as I can. I'll be on break from tomorrow, for a whole month."

August hesitated, searching her face. She saw the moment he decided to trust her, and he gave a curt nod. Merletta didn't wait for more. She needed to hurry if she wanted to make it back before sunset.

She was on edge as she swam the last short distance to the barrier, but she didn't need to be. Nothing sinister emerged from the growing gloom, and she reached the northwestern edge of the kelp farms without incident. A pair of guards were waiting for her. She stiffened slightly, then saw that they were Tilssted guards, judging by their crude weapons and excited faces. Her people.

But were they her people? She suddenly remembered the scroll tucked into her satchel, and she experienced again that sense of being untethered, without foundation. She shook it off.

"Trainee Merletta?" asked one of the guards eagerly. "Returning from your test?"

Merletta nodded, and the guards both gave little cheers.

"We were told to watch out for you," said the other guard. "We were worried you wouldn't make it back by sunset. Congratulations!"

"Thanks," said Merletta, permitting herself a little grin. "But I can't stop. I have to make it back to the Center by sunset in order to pass."

The guard nodded enthusiastically. "We'll escort you, make sure you don't hit any trouble."

Merletta nodded her thanks, more grateful for their protective presence than they could imagine. She felt herself relax. The last opportunity for someone to attack her unwitnessed was gone. She'd made it. She couldn't help but chuckle to herself at the readiness with which the guards abandoned their posts to come with her. There was a reason she'd always had so much success sneaking out past the barrier when the guards on duty were Tilssted ones, bless them.

The guards swam all the way through Skulssted with her, sending her off with grins when they reached the entrance to the Center. Merletta swam eagerly across the drop off, her heart lifting. She'd done it. No one could take that away from her.

A lone figure floated ahead, halfway across the drop off, and Merletta recognized her at once. Freja. She slowed slightly, remembering the strange overheard conversation at the training yard.

"Merletta!" Freja cried, her delight evident. "You made it! Not much time to spare, but you did it." She beamed. "Did you retrieve the stolen item?"

Merletta nodded, fishing the record from her satchel and handing it over. "I think this is it."

Freja took it, looking interested. Merletta got the sense the older guard hadn't known what item Merletta was to locate. She'd never been a Center trainee, after all.

"Congratulations, Trainee!" Agner had appeared from nowhere, also beaming at Merletta. "You did it. I'm not surprised, of course." He looked down at the record in Freja's hand. "Was that your stolen item? What does it say?"

"I didn't read it," Merletta shrugged. "I didn't think it was a real record. I assumed it was just a prop, for the purposes of the test."

Agner held her gaze for a long moment. It was hard to tell whether he believed her lie, but he didn't comment. She wondered if it was really true that he hadn't known what item was in the center of the maelstrom. But he was the head instructor for second year. If he wasn't the one to set up her test, who was?

"Come on," he said. "I'm to take you to Instructor Wivell as soon as you return." They swam through the streets of the Center, and to Merletta's surprise, Agner and Freja both entered Wivell's office with her.

"Well, Wivell, we have a new graduate of second year!"

Instructor Wivell lowered the leaf he was reading, looking neither pleased nor disappointed.

"Do we?" he said. "Congratulations, Trainee." He raised an eyebrow at Agner. "The stolen item?"

Freja handed it over, and Wivell placed it, still unopened, on his desk. Was Merletta imagining that both instructors watched surreptitiously for her reaction to losing the record? It wasn't hard to keep her face impassive. She didn't need the written record to remember the information she'd read there.

"Well, Merletta," said Instructor Wivell, fixing her with a clear look. It was unusual for him to really look at her like that, and Merletta straightened her back. "You have earned yourself a place among the guards, should you choose to claim it."

"Thank you, sir," said Merletta. "But I wish to continue to third year."

Wivell was silent for a moment before replying. "I understand," he said calmly. "I know it has been your ambition for a long time to become a record holder. And it is indeed a noble calling. However, as Instructor Agner, and your mentor," he nodded to Freja, "will tell you, the role of a guard is noble as well."

"I know it is, sir," said Merletta quickly. "My decision is not intended as any disrespect to the guards. But I want to be a record holder."

The words rang with her certainty. She'd wondered, over the last few months, if the life of a guard really would suit her. But the overheard conversation in the training yard had shown that she wasn't truly a good fit for the role. She would never be able to accept orders without asking questions...without knowing the intent behind them, or even who'd issued them. And that was exactly what a good guard was expected to do.

Plus, the encounter with August and the others had reminded her of all the reasons she wanted to be inside the Center, right at its heart. Guards, while important, could never reach that level of access. This was no longer about her childhood ambition. It was about striking at the rot that was at the very core of their triple kingdoms.

Again, Wivell took a moment to respond. "Merletta, you have proven yourself capable these last two years," he said. "More, I will confess, than I ever expected. I also understand from Instructor Agner," he inclined his head to Agner, who nodded earnestly, "that you are extremely capable and determined in your training with him. I say without reservation that you would be an asset to the Center guards."

Merletta was silent, stunned. She'd never received the tiniest modicum of praise from the chief instructor before. His tone was actually respectful, and he was looking her in the eye, like an equal. Could she really be accepted if she took a guard position?

Her eyes passed over Agner, still nodding encouragingly, and Freja, who looked flatteringly hopeful. It was certainly a far cry from her interview with Ibsen at the end of first year, when he had tried, with poorly concealed disdain, to persuade her to take a position as a scribe. He hadn't been able to hide his anger when she refused.

But that memory made everything fall into place. It wasn't coincidence that both Agner and Freja were present for this meeting. Ibsen's aggressive approach hadn't yielded the desired result, that of stopping Merletta from progressing into the heart of the Center without using force. Now Wivell was trying a gentler approach, one based on praise rather than fear.

But it was no less a manipulation, and the object was the same. They didn't want her probing any further into their secrets, and she knew now that they had very good reason for it. And so did she have very good reason to continue.

"Thank you, sir," she said respectfully. She looked at Agner and Freja as well. "And thank you for your support. I truly appreciate it. But my decision isn't taken lightly. I wish to progress to third year."

Agner looked disappointed, but not really surprised. Freja looked genuinely crestfallen, and Merletta couldn't help but be softened. Wivell's face showed no emotion at all. The respectful look was gone, but he showed no scorn. He was once again impassive.

"Then you are dismissed," he said. "You will be expected to start third year classes in a month." He looked at her for a moment. "Will you once again spend your break in Tilssted?"

Trying to mimic him, Merletta kept her own face impassive. "I haven't quite decided yet, Instructor," she said. "I've been invited to spend some time in Skulssted with friends. I'm not sure what I mean to do." It was all perfectly true. Sage had invited Merletta to spend some time with her family during her break, but Merletta wasn't at all sure she wanted to accept, not when Sage would only be there on rest days.

Wivell's face still gave nothing away as he nodded her dismissal.

Agner clapped her on the shoulder as they swam from the room. "Ah well, you can't blame us for trying. We may get you yet, if you fail your test next year."

"No need to sound so hopeful," said Merletta, half laughing.

He gave her a wink and swam away, toward the dining hall. Merletta turned to Freja, who was still floating beside her, looking a little dejected.

"Are you sure, Merletta?" she asked. "I had requested you to join our squad if you chose to become a guard."

Merletta regarded her in silence. "Why do you want me to be a guard, Freja? What's your motivation?"

The normally stoic older mermaid flushed slightly, and Merletta knew she'd hit some point of discomfort. It was an encouraging sign, actually.

"My motivation is that I like you, and I see your potential, and I want you in my team," she said evenly. "You would make a great guard, Merletta, there's no doubt about it. But..." She hesitated. "But I'll be honest with you, I also received orders regarding you. Since you started training with our squad, I was instructed to do my utmost to convince you that the life of a guard would suit you. And I had no hesitation following those orders," she added, with a touch of defensiveness. "It's perfectly true that it would suit you, in my opinion."

Merletta nodded slowly, relief seeping through her. That was a level of deception she could handle. It wasn't even deception, really. Freja was under no obligation to communicate such innocuous orders to the trainee under her care.

Knowing from what she'd overheard that Freja wasn't sure herself, Merletta didn't bother asking whom the orders had come from. It didn't matter, anyway. There were plenty of merpeople who didn't want Merletta to progress through the program. Discovering which one had set guards to influence her wouldn't really tell her anything she didn't know. For all she knew the idea might have originated with Agner. He had his own reasons for wanting to persuade Merletta, and at least they were based on recognition of her abilities rather than a desire to prevent exposure.

At least, she was fairly certain.

"I appreciate your support," Merletta said, smiling at Freja. "I hope I can still train with your squad sometimes. Third and fourth year studies involve plenty of guard training, you know. And you did convince me that I'd probably like being a guard. It's just...not the path I've chosen."

Freja nodded, looking resigned. "I figured as much," she sighed. "But I thought it was worth trying to convince you." Her smile broadened. "But I shouldn't be bringing the mood down. You passed your test, Merletta. You're halfway through the program!"

"So I am," said Merletta, amazed at the thought. "I need to find my friends," she added, turning in the direction of the dining hall, where Sage, Emil, and Andre would presumably be eating their dinner. "They'll all be waiting to hear what happened."

"Of course," nodded Freja.

She drifted away toward the guards' barracks, and Merletta

hurried through the darkening streets. She hadn't gone far when the sensation of being followed became undeniable. Turning swiftly, she caught a flash of dull green.

"Come out, Ileana," she sighed.

The other mermaid obeyed, looking sulky.

"It's been so long since we had one of our little chats," said Merletta lightly. "But I can't say I've missed them."

"I have nothing to say to you," spat Ileana.

"The fact that you're lurking in my shadow suggests otherwise," Merletta pointed out. Her eyes narrowed. "What do you want, Ileana? Wondering how I survived? It must be a shock, to see me return from the dead a second time."

"I don't know what you're talking about," said Ileana, still sounding grumpy.

Merletta raised an eyebrow. "Why didn't they send you to finish me off this round, Ileana? It's surely a bit of an affront to you, to know they picked other guards to carry out my murder this time. Don't tell me you've fallen from favor."

Ileana flushed darkly. "You don't know what you're talking about," she said, her voice stiff.

Merletta regarded the other mermaid thoughtfully. She'd clearly hit a nerve. It seemed Ileana really had fallen from favor. And, unless she was a better actor than Merletta had seen evidence of before, she really didn't know what Merletta meant about the attack on her. Apparently, she wasn't part of whatever group had decided to use Merletta's test as an opportunity to get rid of her permanently.

"Why aren't you training with the more senior guards anymore?" Merletta asked quietly. "What did you do to lose the special treatment you were enjoying when I came back from my break?" She was thinking aloud, not really expecting a response. "Were they angry you didn't finish me off back then, after all?

But no, because you were still more elevated than you should have been at the memorial, months later."

Ileana ignored Merletta's words, her expression stony. "I'm surprised you survived the test," she said rudely. "You must have gotten lucky, and had an unusually clear swim."

"I had a fun little dance with the giant squid, if that's what you mean," said Merletta calmly. "Not to mention a run in with a pod of killer whales. The maelstrom itself is no paddle in the park, either. And did you have two armed guards waiting to murder you when you finished? I don't know if I'd call it an easy swim."

Ileana was staring at her by the end of this speech. Merletta found it strangely freeing to tell Ileana about the planned attack, when she usually had to be so careful what she said.

"I see you ran into one of your dear friends," said Ileana, recovering herself. Her eyes rested maliciously on the welt on Merletta's arm, from the jellyfish in the fissure she'd dived into when fleeing the whale.

Merletta looked up into Ileana's face, and saw bitterness beneath the taunt.

"That's it, isn't it?" she said, as comprehension dawned. "That's why you've been pushed out. Your little stunt with the jellyfish bloom wasn't a sanctioned attack. It was just you, acting out of malice. And you got in trouble for it."

"You don't know what you're talking about," Ileana said again, but her burning face and angry eyes gave her away.

Merletta thought back over her practice test, how much more heavily supervised it was, how many merpeople had known exactly where she was. It would have been much harder in the practice test to make her disappear without raising suspicion than in the actual test. No wonder the ones targeting her hadn't authorized Ileana to use that as an opportunity.

"You think you're invincible, don't you?" said Ileana angrily.

"So you've made it to third year, congratulations." Sarcasm oozed from her voice. "Don't think that means you're inside. Don't think that means you can't be touched, can't be exploited then thrown aside."

Merletta stared at the other mermaid. Ileana's words were bitter, certainly, but there was something more in her tone.

"Are you trying to threaten me, or warn me?" Merletta asked, perplexed. "Because if you think I'd ever trust you enough to accept your help—"

"I don't want to help you!" spat Ileana. "You've cost me everything I've worked so hard for." She hesitated. "Just don't think you can relax now."

Without another word, she turned and swam away, leaving Merletta staring blankly after her. Whatever Ileana said, that had sounded more like a warning than a taunt. But if there was one thing she was certain of, it was that Ileana hated her, and would love to see her fail.

Shaking off the bewildering encounter, Merletta swam into the dining hall. Sage, Emil, and Andre were sitting together at the trainees' table, and they all rose into the water at the sight of her. Merletta smiled at their expressions: Sage's open anxiety, Andre's eagerness, Emil's casual inquiry.

"I did it," she said, her face breaking into a grin. "I passed."

They erupted into cheers which brought disapproving looks from some of the dining hall's occupants. Merletta noticed, though, that at least as many were watching on with indulgent expressions. Ignoring Oliver's slightly sour expression, and Lorraine's usual unresponsiveness, Merletta hurried to join her friends.

Even in the midst of such a triumphant moment, her thoughts swam far away, to the world above the surface. She couldn't help wishing she could share her news with Heath like she was sharing it with the others. She imagined his look of delight and relief when she told him she'd not only survived, but passed the test. He'd surely break into that smile that always warmed her as much as the sun on her skin. Maybe he'd even take her in his arms, and—

Andre clapped her on the back in a congratulatory way, drawing her back to the present. Knowing she couldn't speak to Heath right now, she tried to put him from her mind. All she could do was hope he was watching from afar with his incredible extra sight, breathing more easily in the knowledge that she'd emerged from the test in one piece.

"I have a lot to tell you," she muttered to Sage, Emil, and Andre, when the fuss had died down. "And it's big. But it will have to wait until later." They looked intrigued, but they all knew better than to press her for details in the dining hall.

There was one thing Merletta couldn't resist asking Sage straight away, however. When they had returned to their food, a few minutes later, she bent her head close to her friend's and whispered, "You know that rocky ledge thing, at the middle of the maelstrom?"

"Merletta!" Sage hissed reprovingly. "We're not supposed to talk about the contents of the test. It's part of the rules!"

Merletta rolled her eyes. "We talk about a lot of things we're not supposed to talk about, Sage."

Sage apparently had no response to this.

"I know you've been there, because I saw where you carved your name," Merletta whispered impatiently. "Why didn't you tell me about the watchword?"

Sage looked at her like she was out of her mind. "It's a watchword, Merletta," she whispered. "The whole point of it is to be secret unless you've made it to that level and seen it. You need it in third year. There are some records you can't look at unless you can give the watchword, that kind of thing."

Merletta was silent for a moment, processing this. "But

surely it was worth making an exception," she argued, her voice still low. "You're a better actor than I realized, Sage. I can't remember you ever so much as flinching when I talked about Vazula—"

Sage shushed her so violently that Emil glanced over at them, his eyebrow raised in simultaneous disapproval and warning.

"You can't go bandying the watchword about like that," Sage said, whispering so quietly Merletta had to lean in to hear her. "You'll be in awful trouble. I don't know when I'm supposed to have flinched, since I've never heard you say it before now."

Merletta frowned, thinking it over. She'd just assumed, because she and Heath referred to the island as Vazula when together. But now she thought about it, she may not have mentioned the name in Sage's presence. She'd had no reason to think it would mean anything to her friend. She'd probably always just called it the island.

"Sage, Vaz—that word," she corrected herself hastily as Sage glowered at her, "is the name of the island where I met Heath."

Sage was so astonished, she actually dropped her mussel. It drifted back down into her bowl. "It can't be," Sage whispered. "How would you even know?"

"It was in a record, back in Heath's kingdom," said Merletta. "It's what sent him looking. And he found an old letter on the island, too, which used the name."

Sage was silent, still looking stunned.

"There's no way the two civilizations independently came up with the word," Merletta murmured. "You know what this means, don't you? It means Vazula is part of our history."

Sage said nothing, but Merletta didn't need her friend's confirmation to know she was right. Her thoughts flew to the island itself where, at this very moment, the three guards might be lurking in the shallows, finding shelter nearby to wait for her to come as promised.

Vazula was part of the merpeople's past. And if Merletta had anything to say about it, one way or another, it was going to be part of their future, too.

CHAPTER THIRTY-SIX

The week following the attack on Percival was one of the most anxious of Heath's life. As worried as he was about the further conflict that had been unleashed in Valoria, he was equally worried about Merletta's upcoming test.

He knew when it was, and he spent that entire day perched on the edge of his cliff, gazing southeast across the ocean and trying with all his might to watch her across the distance. Sometimes he got glimpses, but they were never clear, never definite. For some frustrating reason, he was much less able to see her from Bexley Manor than he'd been able to see Percival from Vazula. It was maddening.

At one point he could have sworn he saw her being thrown about by thrashing, churning waters that surely had no place in the deep ocean, far from any crashing waves. The sight reminded him horribly of the maelstrom, and his blood ran cold at the thought of Merletta anywhere near that violent phenomenon.

The uncertainty was torture, but the day after the test, he saw a vision of her that he was almost certain was real. She was talking animatedly to another mermaid, one with skin a similar shade to Merletta's, but with lighter brown hair, and a shimmering pinkish tail. He let out a breath, relief coursing through him. She'd survived then, and she seemed to be in one piece. For now, that would have to be enough. Asking Merletta for the details—perhaps even continuing the interrupted moment they'd shared—would have to wait.

Heath was still brooding on thoughts of Merletta the next day, once again sitting by the ocean, trying to avoid the tension simmering inside his family home. The duke had received a missive from King Matlock, following close on his sons' return from Bryford. To Heath's surprise—and relief—it made no mention of what the king had said to Heath. It related solely to Percival's public accusation. It was diplomatically worded, but the meaning was clear. Percival was a breath away from public sanction.

The duke had been angry, to say the least. Heath was sure that his father's sharp words were motivated as much by fear for his oldest son as frustration with Percival's poorly thought-out challenge to the king. But Percival didn't see it that way. He was enraged that his family's sympathy over the brutal attack was tempered with reproaches for his own conduct. In his view, his response to the king had been entirely justified, and Heath didn't really blame him. By the time he'd ridden all the way to Bexley Manor, Percival had been a mess. He should never have attempted such a ride without being first treated for his injuries, but he was too furious with the king, and too stubborn, to stay in the capital a moment longer.

In the last few days, he'd been mostly shut up in his room. He was supposedly recovering from his injuries, but Heath wasn't convinced. The little Heath had seen of his brother showed that Percival's superhuman strength was enabling him to heal from his injuries with unusual speed. Heath was certain Percival was doing more plotting than healing, and he dreaded the outcome. He felt like he was crouching under a poorly constructed shelter, waiting for a massive storm to break, one he knew was coming.

But at the same time, part of him didn't want to know. Part of him wanted to wash his hands of the whole miserable business. He was sick of the politics, sick of making everything worse, sick of Percival's attitude. Sick of his own expectations on himself.

An unnatural rush of wind caused Heath to look up, surprised but pleased by the sight of his friend's form suddenly filling the sky.

"Reka," he said, as the dragon landed. "I didn't expect to see you."

"I was watching you," said Rekavidur. "I could see that you had become disheartened, as you humans so easily do. I thought perhaps my presence might cheer you."

The words were spoken in his usual lofty tone, but as he said them, the dragon laid himself down so that his taloned front feet dangled over the edge of the cliff right next to Heath's legs. He rested his vast head upon them, turned slightly so that the tip of his snout touched Heath's leg. The dragon's breath heated Heath's skin uncomfortably, even through his clothes. Recognizing the gesture as a rare show of affection from the dragon, Heath felt a surge of gratitude.

"Thanks, Reka," he said quietly. "You were right, on both counts."

The dragon nodded sagely. "I thought so."

"We really made a mess of things, didn't we?" said Heath bitterly.

"We?" repeated Reka, raising his head and fixing reproachful eyes on Heath. "I don't believe either you or I have had any hand in the mess your kingdom finds itself in."

Heath stared at him incredulously. "We've had a huge hand in it! If the king hadn't found out about that gathering you saw...

well, I wish you'd never seen it, to be honest. *And,*" he added with some heat, "I wish you'd had the sense not to repeat it to the rest of the dragons, when it had nothing to do with any of you!"

Fortunately for their friendship, Rekavidur apparently wasn't in a mood to be offended. "I don't place even the smallest store in a human's idea of what constitutes sense," he said without rancor. "If you wish to benefit from the sense of a dragon, I hold to it that neither of us is to blame. You did not orchestrate that meeting. Your power-wielding relatives made their own decision. And the information I passed on was entirely correct. The rest of my colony made their choice as to how to respond, and that is not my responsibility. No more is it your responsibility how your king chose to respond to what was said at the Winter Solstice Festival."

Heath felt a surge of irritation rise up in him at the dragon's refusal to take responsibility. But after staring into Reka's calm face for a furious moment, he deflated, letting it go. He didn't have many friends at the moment. He didn't want to alienate Reka, too. Plus, it occurred to him that the dragon's words were strikingly similar to Merletta's comment, that he wasn't responsible for his family's choices, and he couldn't be responsible for hers.

"I'm sick to death of it all, Reka," he said frankly. "I don't want to be here."

"Where do you want to be?" Reka asked. His head was back on his taloned front feet, but he tilted it curiously in Heath's direction.

Heath didn't have to think hard about his answer. "I want to be on Vazula," he said, "with Merletta." He shot the dragon a defiant look. "But I suppose you won't approve of that."

Reka let out a long, smoky sigh. "It troubles me," he acknowledged, "but I understand it."

Heath stared at him. "You do?"

"Of course," said the dragon, nodding placidly. "You are different when you are on the island. Free, unburdened." He threw a sidelong look at Heath. "Although I hesitate to acknowledge it, you are at your happiest when with the mermaid." He paused, tilting his head to the side. "Even when you are not engaging in that somewhat revolting combining of mouths humans do, she brings out a side of you that seems like it's been desperate to be free, waiting for you to return to your island."

Heath said nothing, stunned—and a little embarrassed—by this candid outburst.

"But it is complicated," the dragon sighed. "And, as I said, troubling."

"Why?" Heath pressed. "Are you ever going to tell me what your problem with Merletta is?"

"Perhaps," said Reka, maddeningly unconcerned. "But not today. Nor tomorrow, I imagine."

Heath rolled his eyes, his tone turning slightly sulky. "Well, it doesn't matter if I want to be there. I don't think she's there right now."

He closed his eyes, focusing hard on Merletta. At once, her image popped into his mind, crystal clear. Or at least, as clear as it ever was when she was deep underwater.

"No, she's not," he said. He frowned. "I wonder why she's so easy to see now. I tried just a few minutes ago, and I couldn't even catch a glimpse of her."

He sighed, returning to the topic at hand. "Even if she was there, I can't just leave, not when things are such a mess." He flicked a small rock off the edge, sending it careening into the water below. "I feel like I'm constantly torn in two, Reka," he admitted. "I want to be with Merletta, but I owe it to my family to be in Valoria. And I'm useless in both places. I can't protect Merletta, and I can't hold the two camps together here." He grunted in frustration. "Even when I decide Valoria is where my loyalty lies, I'm still torn in two. And it's only going to get worse as the crown and the power-wielders move further from each other. Divided loyalties are a terrible thing."

"Indeed they are," said the dragon, with even more than his usual solemnity. Heath had the definite impression that Reka spoke from personal experience. "I think I know, by the way, why you were able to see the mermaid clearly just now."

"Why?" Heath demanded, turning to him.

"Because I am here," said Reka simply. "The presence of additional magic—powerful magic, in fact—helps yours. I believe that your magic is strong enough that you don't need external help. But reaching your full potential will take time, and a little more faith in your power than you currently have, I think."

Heath thought it over. It made sense. He thought of times when his sight had been clearest, such as on Vazula, within the magical ring surrounding the island, or in Reka's company. It had even flared to life at the clandestine gathering with multiple other power-wielders present.

"If you want my opinion," said Reka comfortably, "I think you should follow your inclination to forget the sorry affairs of your kingdom, and spend your time and attention with me. You are torn between Valoria and Vazula—perhaps you should chart a new path, away from either. Come to Wyvern Islands with me. I can help you train your magic, become one of us."

"One of you?" Heath repeated, startled by the suggestion. "What do you mean?"

Rekavidur smiled in an excess of humor. "Well, you have farsight—an astonishing development in a non-dragon—and you can tell when humans are deceiving you, or hiding something."

"No I can't," said Heath. "Not reliably, at least."

"We are speaking now of dragon powers," said Reka loftily. "I am the more knowledgeable, so do not contradict me. As I say, you have dragon-like powers. Who better to train you than dragons?"

Heath laughed in spite of his surprise. "I can't just become a dragon, Reka."

"Why not?" Reka asked flippantly. "If Merletta can be a mermaid and a human, why can't you be a human and a dragon?"

Heath was silent, noting that Reka had at least used Merletta's name instead of calling her *the mermaid*. It seemed like progress.

"All right," he said at last. "I'm convinced."

Reka lifted his head, looking like a dog who'd been offered a bone. "You wish to train with me?"

"I do," said Heath, his own excitement starting to rise. "Teach me to be a dragon, Reka."

The story continues in *A Kingdom Threatened*—Book Three of *The Vazula Chronicles*.

NOTE FROM THE AUTHOR

Thank you for reading *A Kingdom Discovered*. I hope you enjoyed this next venture into the world of Vazula! I would be so grateful if you would consider leaving a review on Amazon—it would really make a difference!

If you want to find out what happens next for Merletta, Heath, and Reka, check out *A Kingdom Threatened*, the next installment of the series. More adventure, fantasy, mystery, and romance await.

Join up to my mailing list at deborah-gracewhite.com to be kept up to date on new releases, specials, and giveaways, such as bonus chapters. You'll receive some great freebies, too, including *An Expectation of Magic*, a novella which serves as a prequel to *The Vazula Chronicles*, telling the tale of Heath's parents.

You'll also receive *Dragon's Sight*, an 8,000 word prequel to *The Kyona Chronicles* (a series set before *The Vazula Chronicles*, in the same world), told from the perspective of the dragon Elddreki (Rekavidur's father).

Again, thanks for entering the world of *The Vazula Chronicles*! I hope to see you back again.

The Vazula Chronicles: YA Fantasy

The Kingdom Tales: Fairy Tale Retellings

The Singer Tales: Fairy Tale Retellings
(releasing throughout 2023)

ACKNOWLEDGMENTS

Thanks so much to my team. Ray, my incredible husband and alpha listener, first thanks to you.

My betas are the best: Andrew, Adrian, Mel W, Steph, Tamara, Berri, Mum, and Dad. Extra thanks to Dad for developmental editing.

Thanks to my new proofreader, Shae, for doing such an awesome job in picking up my errors!

Karri, thanks for nailing this cover as always, and Becca, for the gorgeous map.

To you, the reader, thank you for giving me the privilege of being an author.

And most importantly, to God, who sees the full picture when we see only our tiny patch.

ABOUT THE AUTHOR

I've been a reader since I can remember, growing up on a wide range of books, from classic literature to light-hearted romps. The love of reading has traveled with me unchanged across multiple continents, and carried me from my own childhood all the way to having children of my own.

But if reading is like looking through a window into a magical and beautiful world, beginning to write my own stories was like discovering that I could open that window and climb right out into fantasyland.

I cannot believe how privileged I am to actually be living that childhood dream and publishing my own novels. I do so from my hometown of Adelaide, Australia, where I live with my husband and our three little ones.

I've never outgrown my love of young adult stories, so the genre of young adult fantasy was always going to be my niche. Feel free to email me at deborah@deborahgracewhite.com and introduce yourself! Or subscribe to my mailing list at deborah gracewhite.com for free giveaways, sales, and updates.

www.ingramcontent.com/pod-product-compliance
Lightning Source LLC
Chambersburg PA
CBHW060725190726
48285CB00001B/74